Trading Dreams
at Midnight

Also by
Diane McKinney-Whetstone

FICTION

Tumbling

Tempest Rising

Blues Dancing

Leaving Cecil Street

Trading Dreams at Midnight

A Novel

Diane McKinney-Whetstone

HARPER

An Imprint of HarperCollins*Publishers*
www.harpercollins.com

Mac

HarperCollins books may be purchased for educational, business, or sales
promotional use. For information, please write: Special Markets Department,
HarperCollins Publishers, 10 East 53rd Street, New York, NY 10022.

FIRST EDITION

Library of Congress Cataloging-in-Publication Data is available upon request.

ISBN-13: 978-0-68-816386-0

08 09 10 11 12   WBC/RRD   10 9 8 7 6 5 4 3 2 1

For the sisters

Trading Dreams
at Midnight

Chapter 1

T HAD BEEN twenty years since Freeda spun in and out of home the way that fabric did when it was unwound from those huge bolts all up and down along Fourth Street in South Philadelphia. A hot pink raw silk Freeda was when she was a happy girl, spreading herself out into a mesmerizing display with her thunderstorm hair and butter brown lips until her sadness hit and she'd scrunch herself up into a tight bland button and then poof, she was gone. That's how Neena was known to describe Freeda's comings and goings. Neena, Freeda's oldest daughter.

Freeda would leave Neena and her other child, Tish, with her mother, Nan, blowing kisses as she backed out the door promising to return in an hour that stretched into days and months. Nan, a small brick of a woman who didn't play, threatened to turn Freeda in to child protective services and dared her to try to see the girls again. Though Freeda always saw them again. She would return ebullient, twirling like a spinning top, newly hired as an administrative assistant to some small-business owner who'd found her irresistible. She'd move the girls to a rented house and paint the walls pink because she said she needed the pink to stay happy. Neena, begging Freeda just to stay, for good this time, the happiness will come Mommy if you just stay.

But Freeda never could stay. Certainly couldn't stay twenty years ago that February night back in 1984 when a gray winter had passed out over Philadelphia like a fat drunk, thick and immovable. She was trying to stay until at least the winter sobered up enough to grunt and move over some and make way for a stream of yellow. She thought that if she could just stay until the spring she could stay for good. Especially in the house that she owned finally that her man-friend Wendell, an almost-divorced real estate/insurance broker had bought for her, paid cash in full at a sheriff's sale. A charming row house on a big street where they could tell the time of day by hearing what the traffic did; where in the summer the porch had a plump-cushioned glider and red four o'clocks filled the garden and bloomed on schedule and prettied up a summer night; in the winter Freeda baked coconut layer cakes from scratch and she and the girls passed afternoons at the living room window counting the colors in the prisms the mammoth icicles made, Freeda singing "Let It Be" as the warmth from the radiator pulsed against their corduroys sending a sweet steamy smell through the room.

But by then Freeda was already trying to hold back the dark mood looming. When the girls were asleep and the whoosh of traffic outside was done, she'd sometimes lose herself for hours over the kitchen table cramming her mouth with Argo starch. She'd hold the starch in her mouth, then mash it into a paste until it inched down her throat thick like mud, or lima bean puree. Then the essence of the starch would drift to her brain in surges and she'd feel giddy, then drunk, then intensely focused, and then her sadness would back off enough for her to live like a halfway sane person lived: slicing mushrooms for Salisbury steak; ironing white cotton blouses for the girls to usher in when Nan corralled them to church; giggling with Wendell when he spent the night on the living room couch.

Always too soon though, the starch quit on her, and the space inside her head would become the Academy of Music featuring *Porgy & Bess* and Sportin' Life would commence to singing "It Ain't Necessarily So." And in between his declarations of seeing and believing, he told Freeda what to do. "Leave, Freeda, leave" was his usual sing-songy command. She always complied; the only way to shut down his voice was for her to comply. Not that middle of the night, though, in 1984. She couldn't believe what he told her to do then. Told her to get the extra pillow from the top of the dining room closet and start with Neena because Neena would be easier than Tish; Tish would kick and scream; Tish would fight back. But Neena adored her so, trusted her, it would be lovely how gently fifteen-year-old Neena would succumb.

Her whole body shook by the time she reached the black air of the dining room and opened the closet door. Neena herself had organized the closet so that the boots were lined in size order on the floor, the coats from light to heavy hanging on the thick steel pole, hats and scarves on the top shelf, and in the very back the extra bed pillow that Wendell used when he slept on the living room couch. She scattered the hats and scarves to get to the pillow, held the pillow between her hands and kneaded it to judge its thickness. She pressed the pillow to her as if it were her firstborn about to go down for a nap the way she'd pressed Neena to her when she was a baby, a tender desperation to the press as if to say if you die in your sleep know you were truly loved. Then she shouted, "No! I won't," as she threw the pillow across the dining room; the crystal pieces dangling from the chandelier made small crying sounds as the pillow whizzed by. She snatched a coat from the closet then. Put the coat over the starch-dusted paisley robe and covered her ears with her hands and ran through the living room on out the front door.

Neena had been perplexed by the line of spilled starch that tracked from the kitchen table to the dining room closet on through the living room until it seemed to disintegrate into the braided welcome mat on the vestibule floor. She took it as a sign that Freeda would be directly back but on the third day she woke to her mother still gone.

The absence was like a trough of cold air hanging over Freeda's bed; Neena and eleven-year-old Tish had been sleeping in Freeda's bed as if their combined scents rising off of their mother's bed might pull her back home. The air was really cold because the heater had grunted and then died the day before so Neena woke worrying about how to get them heat. They'd not yet told Nan that Freeda had disappeared again. Neena determined that they could make a go of it without Nan, convinced that's what Freeda wanted. Why else had she left them here and not with Nan the way she usually did.

Then Tish woke the way she'd fallen asleep, crying, insisting that she wanted to go back and live with Nan, she wanted Nan to take care of them again. Neena countering again the same way she had the night before, "We're not babies anymore, Tish, we don't need Nan to come flying in on her broom and carting us back to Kansas." Kansas is how Neena referred to Nan's middle-of-the-block row house on Delancey Street. She tried not to notice the puffs of smoke forming along the edges of her words as she pushed her point with Tish, the smoke mocking her point so she got completely out of the bed. To remain there, warm though it was under the covers, meant that she would be listening to Tish sob in wallows that went all the way to her bones.

She went down into the kitchen trying to shrug off the chill bumps racing along her arms, stopped at the closet in the dining room to grab her pile-lined pigskin jacket, then into the kitchen to turn on the stove and the oven so at least the kitchen would be warm. As far as Neena was concerned Freeda had left good provisions: cabinets filled with canned soups and beans and tomato paste; Raisin Bran and Shredded Wheat; eggs and cheeses in the fridge; dried fruits; nuts. A vinyl purse in the top of her closet with several twenty-dollar bills, a knotted handkerchief in her underwear drawer with five crumpled tens. Freeda even had oil delivered the day before she left.

Neena lit under the pot of water for their oatmeal, then went back upstairs and tossed the pigskin jacket on top of Tish as she instructed Tish to forget about a bath before school today. They'd wash up over the kitchen sink. "The kitchen will be nice and warm, Tish," she said to the lump Tish made under the covers. She closed her ears to Tish's whimpering, then went to look through the yellow pages for someone who could fix an old-fashioned oil heater.

She avoided the display ads. If they had a display ad, she thought, they were probably white. She decided on a repair man named Jones. She used her breathy voice as she told him that she and her daughter were freezing, how quickly could he get there. He could be there in a half hour, he said. Meant they'd be late for school so she almost set it up for later that afternoon, but she knew Tish would go behind her back and call Nan if heat wasn't soon to come.

They washed themselves over the kitchen sink in silence. Neena laid out Tish's school clothes over the backs of the kitchen chairs, Tish's favorite red velour hoodie, a white turtleneck, cuffed Jordache jeans. Neena didn't put on her school clothes though. She ran back up to Freeda's room and stood at the dresser and lotioned herself down with Jergens. Then she covered her nakedness with a pink velvety robe given to her by Freeda when Freeda returned this last time. She made her face up then, lipstick and eyeliner and rouge so that she would appear a decade older than she was. Though she had a mature look anyhow with her naturally shadowed eyes that seemed to fall under their own weight, her mouth that was fleshy and full, her cheekbones that jutted in a way that made her look as if she was caught between a blush and a come-on. She'd had her womanly shape by the time she was twelve. "That chile built up from the ground," people on her grandmother's block where she was known used to say. She moved her fingers through her hair, pushing its thickness toward her face to hide the truth of her age.

She fixed on Freeda's pink boxed set of dusting powder and perfume resolute on the dresser. She dabbed the puff into the powder that smelled of talc and then stroked it down her cleavage. The puff was so soft against her skin, the softness painful, and she wrestled back cries.

When Neena got back down to the kitchen, Tish was at the stove stirring around in the pot of oatmeal. Tish looked so vulnerable from the back, so small. Her braided hair hung over her shoulders and seemed to overwhelm her back with its thickness. Neena fought the impulse to go hug Tish. To hug her meant they'd be combining the abandonment that they each felt in drifts that came and went in manageable intervals. To hug her meant they'd both be overcome in a powerful gust of sadness that would knock them to the kitchen floor.

"You're my daughter when the heater man gets here," Neena said to Tish's back.

"So what," Tish said, as she turned and showed her face and Neena was able to shake the impulse to hug her. Tish had such a nice-girl face that was round and a mild-complexioned brown with wide eyes, a softly formed nose, and a cleft in her chin. They had different fathers. Freeda had been married to Tish's father for a time, a respectable man who owned a hat shop in South Philly who'd bailed early on in the marriage when Freeda's highs and lows asserted themselves. Neena never knew her own father. Though she had wondered over the years if she'd been conceived by one of the lowlifes who took advantage of Freeda during her deflated moods. Wondered if that's why she was born looking twenty-one.

Neena prayed that she looked even older than twenty-one that morning as she stood in the dark cellar next to the Jones heater-repair guy. She'd unscrewed the lightbulb and told him the light was out so their line of vision was limited to the swath of yellow oozing from his flashlight. She shivered as he threw the light at the heater and explained to her what the problem was, a bad starter. He handed her a written estimate of how much it would cost to get the heater humming again. She took the flashlight and pointed it at the estimate to keep her face in the dark. Eighty-five dollars, the estimate said. Was the heater even worth that. Neena focused on the PAID-IN-FULL ink stamp sitting upright in the top layer of the toolbox. She pictured the money she'd scavenged from her mother's purses and coat pockets and dresser drawers. Enough to keep them in food and tokens until she could secure a part-time job, not enough to get them heat.

"You kidding me." She forced a half smile. "Eighty-five?"

"Square business," the heater man said. "And that's only 'cause I know this model of heater. Lucky I do. This bad boy is a serious relic, got to be fifty years old."

She thought him to be in his early forties. Perhaps a looker in his youth but she guessed he'd worked on too many heaters because a crease ran the width of his forehead as if he was squinting to figure something out in the dark. Appeared clean at least, no black line under his fingernails that were illuminated by the flashlight.

"I told my ex he shouldda made the previous owners convert to gas before he settled on this house," she said, talking in fast whispers. "No offense, but you know you can't tell a black man nothing." She tugged at the belt of the pink velvety robe to show off her cleavage as she tilted the flashlight toward her chest. She let her mouth part slightly, her droopy eyes go even lower. "Though I bet you're an exception." She moved in closer and brushed his arm.

"Well, try telling me something and let's see if I'm the exception." He was smiling, a moistening like dew forming at the corners of his mustache, the crease though still folded along his forehead as if it had been ironed and spray-starched there.

"Damn, it's just that, you know, eighty-five? I mean, can we work something out?" She breathed into the moldy cellar air. "I'm a single parent and all, you know." She nudged the robe to part more. "My daughter will be leaving for school directly, mnh, good as you look—"

He touched her face and his fingers smelled liked the refineries on a cloudy day. "Come 'ere girl," he said. She tried to keep from gagging as she gently pulled his hand from her face and held on to his hand and said that she wanted to be good to him, but she needed heat first, it was too, too cold. She couldn't go any further without the heat.

A half smile was his response as he asked her to stand close to him and shine the light toward the heater. "I work faster when a fine chick is looking over my shoulder," he said. Neena tightened as she watched him jam a stubborn bolt into a nut. She wondered then where they would do it. No furniture down there, they hadn't lived there long enough to accumulate the old soft things that were stored in normal cellars. No couch with the fiberfill peeking out, no wobbly coffee table, not even the bags of old clothes that most people pushed into the cellar until they would be given or thrown away. Just the moldy air down there and the chalk-colored walls that were concrete, rough and cold; she figured she'd just lean against the wall. No sense in prettying it, softening the situation and trying to make it something it was not.

He was all over her when he finished with the heater, pulling at the robe and saying, Come on here girl with your fine self. She moved him toward the wall and tried to get into position, the quicker to get it over with. This would be her first time though she'd come close the year before when she was going in circles over Malcom, the sixteen-year-old boy who bagged groceries at the Pathmark not far from Nan's. As the heater man bit at her neck and struggled to free his manhood from his pants, she remembered how Malcom had run behind her after he'd bagged her elbow macaroni and can of sockeye salmon, jar of Hellmann's mayonnaise and sweet pickled relish. "You forgot your receipt," he'd said. "Never forget your receipt, Neena." She realized then that she needed a receipt for the heater repair. She was paying after all. But he was to that breathless, hard-to-stop stage of things. She made herself go stiff with him then; pushed him hard. "Wait a minute, I need the thing first," she said.

"I don't have no rubbers," he said.

"No, no, a receipt, I need a receipt, with your paid stamp on it. I need it or I can't be good to you, baby. I need it now," she said as she hurled the stream of light toward the toolbox.

He cursed as he went to grab the estimate from the top of the toolbox. He pounded the receipt with his PAID stamp. He handed the receipt to her as he kicked off his shoe and pushed one leg completely from his pants. Neena folded the receipt and put it in her robe pocket.

Her grandmother had insisted that the robe was hard luck when Neena had shown off the robe and danced around the house in it when her mother returned the last time. "Hate to imagine what your mother had to do to get that robe, to even hold on to that job with that married Wendell, and that house she's moving you to. Unconscionable what she probably had to do," Nan had said. The pocket of the robe felt so warm and safe as Neena dropped the receipt inside. Plus the furnace was singing to her in the background of the cellar and the steady spurts of heated air were building closer and closer to where she stood. She watched the heater man coming at her, dragging one pant leg behind him. She focused on the crease in his forehead as he squinted at the light going right for his eyes. She balled her fist inside the robe pocket and decided that she wasn't doing anything with him.

She held the flashlight up as if it was a nightstick and she was a traffic cop and had the power to stop a determined man. "Come on, girl, don't play with me," he said as he tried to pry the light from her hand and deciding instead to put his effort at pulling the robe from her shoulders. "Fair is fair."

"Only if you got a thing for jail bait," the defiance coating her words, such a contrast to her purring as she'd asked for the receipt. "And the girl upstairs is my sister, not my daughter. And you making me late for school anyhow." The school part got to him, she could tell as his face caved in on itself, the crease on his forehead throbbing as if it was about to separate. He jerked back then as if he'd taken a knee to his groin, looking at her as she allowed the yellow swath of light against her, the truth of her age sinking in on his face, his face getting more contorted the longer he looked at her.

"You little—" he said finally. "I ought to—I don't believe—shit I never touched—"

Neena tried to imagine him translucent so that she could stare right through him. Her stare had the affect of making him back up, stooping then to pull up his pants, cursing as he did.

He was still cursing as he stomped up the steps and walked through the kitchen. Tish was at the kitchen table slurping her oatmeal the way a much younger child would since she was supposed to be Neena's daughter right now. "You need to tell your sister or whoever she is to you that she could get herself hurt playing around with grown-ass men," he said to Tish.

Tish dropped her spoon with a loud clang against the bowl. She ran across the kitchen hollering, "Neena, Neena, are you all right?" She took the cellar stairs in two jumps and was sobbing by the time she got to the back of the cellar, not even trying to muffle it though her crying usually garnered a "stop being such a baby" from Neena.

"See," Tish said, her words hacked up by her sobs. "See, Neena, we can't do everything by ourselves, we can't."

Neena didn't answer, just stood there staring into the cellar's dull emptiness as Tish moved closer in to where Neena was. She took the flashlight from Neena and placed it on the cement floor. Then she pulled Neena's robe together and reached around to her back to grab both ends of the belt.

"Don't be trying to hug," Neena said.

"Girl, nobody trying to hug you," Tish answered. "I'm just trying to fix your robe all coming all off of you." Her voice was muffled as she rested her face against Neena's shoulder while she kept reaching for and then dropping the ends of the belt. The plush velvet warm against her face.

Neena gave in to the press of Tish's face and yielded to the hug, telling herself that it wasn't a hug because then the sense of loss would feel insurmountable. Knowing that Tish felt it too, the loss. They stood there like that and listened to the heater's steady hum that was keeping pace with their sighs.

Then the tender air down there was fractured by the sound of footsteps on the porch and Neena felt Tish's body stiffen. "Maybe the heater man forgot his nasty-looking thing," Neena said, trying to relax Tish by making her laugh. The declaration having the opposite effect, Tish horrified instead.

"His thing?" Tish screeched, pulling her head from Neena's shoulder. "You saw his thing?"

"What do you think?" Neena said, suddenly ashamed as she looked beyond Tish, though enough of Tish was caught up in the beam from the flashlight on the floor. Tish's cute mouth loomed around the edges of Neena's peripheral vision, Tish's mouth curled to one corner as if she'd just whiffed vomit, or dog shit.

"You mean he actually pulled his thing out on you, Neena? Daag. What? Were you gonna do it with him?"

"Do we have heat now? Quit whining," Neena said as she walked past Tish. "Anyhow, that's probably just the junk mailman. Come on, we're gonna be late for school."

"But he pulled his thing out on you, Neena." Tish's voice shook. "See, now I'm glad I called Nan."

Neena was halfway to the stairs, contemplating whether to skip school today altogether and take a long hot bath and rid herself of the feel of the heater man's fast breaths. She stopped but didn't turn around, said to the steps, "You better be lying to me, Tish. Tell me you're lying."

Tish's reply was her silence. And then the confirmation, the doorbell, the three rings the way her grandmother always did. Neena stomped up the stairs, saying shit, damn, fuck. Tish ran behind her. "I'm sorry, Neena, daag, but, I had to do something. We can't just live here by ourselves until Mommy decides to come back home. I'm sorry, Neena, okay?"

Neena kicked the cellar door opened. "Be sorry," she said. "Be sorry and tell her that I disappeared."

She went into the shed kitchen then. Folded herself on the cold dark floor and nestled inside the pink robe, the robe buffering somewhat her grandmother's voice as she moved through the house calling for her. "Stop with the foolishness, Neena," she said over and over again. "You coming home with me, now. Come on. Come on now and let's go."

Chapter 2

REEDA APPEARED IN swatches after that, a phone call here, a sneak in through a window to peep in on the girls there, but no more of her hot pink expanses, her exuberance as she dazzled one man after the next and showered the girls with hugs and attention. Not even that hollowed-out, zombie-like stare that took her over when her down moods hit. That February in 1984 became her last extended stay. Made every February after that a dreaded month for Neena, for Nan too. Sad, like the color pink for both of them was sad.

Right now Nan tried to keep her footing here in 2004 as she shooed the slant of pink and yellow light from over her sewing machine where she sat the way she did every morning from four thirty to seven. Her yielding time this was, the space surrounding the rising of the sun when whatever she worked on seemed to bend to her wishes. Her bobbin threads never popped; needles never broke; the most ornery fabrics cooperated and allowed the intertwining of the most elaborate stitches. She pasted her attention to the rumba of the sewing machine, her pleasure and comfort during her yielding time, tried not to offend the special softness of the hour with worries over what she could not control. Couldn't control that Freeda hadn't been able to stay put and raise her girls herself. Couldn't control the way that Freeda's coming and going had sculpted the girls, the women they'd turned out to be as a result: Neena's obsession over finding her mother causing her to be a rudderless underachiever with man-hungry ways; Tish just the opposite, treating her mother like she would an infected tooth and excavating her pulp and all, then relying on Nan and church and school to blunt the pain, so Tish prospered as a result. And Nan surely couldn't control that this was February and her past and present would fuse like every February mimicking the iridescent blue-green fabric she'd used for the two dozen choir robes she'd made last week; the fabric was such that she couldn't tell whether the green was the base color or the blue. It all depended on how the light hit.

She accompanied the sound of the sewing machine with her own soft hums. She was attaching a cream-colored satin border to an ocean blue brushed wool that would make a nice swaddling blanket for the baby Tish might or might not have. Tish, the good one, the well-married college graduate with the prestigious on-air news anchor job, was six months into a pregnancy racked with complications. She'd started spotting and cramping the day before and her husband, Malik, had rushed her to the hospital and they'd kept her, though at last report Tish was comfortable, the cramping and spotting having subsided. Nan was hopeful, though not to tempt fate she told herself that the blanket would be her donation to the fund-raising silent auction her church was having. The first Saturday in March, like they'd done since Nan joined there decades ago, the church rolled out a grand flea market that drew crowds numbering in the hundreds. The donations over the years growing in value and sophistication to match the upward march of the congregation: woven pot holders from the Five and Dime Store years ago, a pair of glass candle holders from Tiffany's last year. Nan visualized the blanket she worked on now folded on the display table in finished form. Might go for as much as a couple of hundred dollars, she thought, since the event brought back all the prosperous sons and daughters who'd been raised up in the church. She pictured them as she worked, the many lawyers and educators, a few medical doctors, PhDs, even a sprinkling of judges on the Common Pleas court. Though many had long since moved out of the neighborhood, some even while they were still children because their parents were actually the first generation to get college degrees en masse—Freeda's generation—most, like Tish, still claimed membership in the church, all willing to pay top dollar for that unique something they could bid on, stroke themselves in the process that in so doing they were giving back. She did such a good job focusing her attention on a positive outcome for the blanket that her ears were blotted to the sound of footsteps walking across her porch. She didn't even hear the doorbell until the second insistent ring. And even when she did, she told herself that she must be imagining things. Then there it was again. The doorbell.

She lifted her foot from the pedal of the sewing machine as her breaths caught in the top of her throat. No good news could be coming this early, she thought as she moved through the dining room into the living room and said, Sweet, sweet Jesus, have mercy please don't let it be her grandson-in-law come to tell in person what he couldn't say over the phone, that Tish had lost the baby. She was simultaneously weakened and manic-like from the prospect as she peered through the blinds at the front door. She didn't see anything, just the dew shimmering on the gray bricks of the church across the street, just the ice crystals dotting the tops of her razor-straight hedges, just the snow-speckled newness of her front steps that she'd had resurfaced before the winter set in. She wondered then if this was a scam, someone trying to get her to open the door and then rush her. Her middle-of-the-road neighborhood was not above such an occurrence caught as it was in the war between lushness and decay where the hedges stayed trimmed but there were bars around windows; no drug wars in the immediate vicinity, but there was the sense that any day now the sound of that car backfiring might instead be a gun going off.

She checked to make sure the dead bolt was intact, then looked through the blinds again. Still nothing. Thought about phoning Charlene across the street to ask if she saw anything on her porch, though Charlene was probably down in her basement pulling her boys' school-uniform shirts from the clothes dryer. In less than an hour Charlene would be bolting from her house like a bronco, late for work again, yelling for her boys not to miss the bus. Though Nan would see to it that they did not. Had marched across the street many a morning and used Charlene's emergency key to go inside and yank the boys, fine-looking, eleven-year-old badass twins, out of the house by their shirt collars, daring them to complain. "I'm old-school," she'd say. "I'll give you something to complain about hard as your mother works to give you a decent life and you got no better sense than to lollygag. Get on that corner and stand straight and tall and wait for that bus."

She wouldn't call Charlene, nor would she open her door. She just stood there in her vestibule for a minute. A chill raced across her arms even under the flowered duster she wore and suddenly she got a sense of Neena's presence, Neena the prodigal granddaughter who fourteen years ago when she was nineteen dropped out of college and left here in search of Freeda. Nan had seen neither hide nor hair of Neena in over five years now, though she did receive regular Happy Birthday, Mother's Day, Easter, and Christmas phone calls, the calls whenever possible coming on a Sunday during Nan's church-service time. Polite calls that felt like sand. Except for last night when Neena called. Called Tish's house while Nan was there tidying things for Malik. Nothing polite about the way Neena had clicked the phone off in Nan's ear. Nan couldn't fathom why Neena had so much hate in her heart. She moved to the edge of the vestibule and looked out. Then peeped through the blinds again, almost expecting to see Neena standing there. Saw nothing resembling Neena, saw a trench-coated man out there looking in through the blinds as she looked out. Their eyes met for a second and she muttered Get behind me Satan as she unlocked, then opened the door, though she kept the storm door closed and latched.

He smiled. He had big white teeth, a thick gold watch on his wrist that peeped from beneath the trench coat sleeve as he bent his arm to tip his hat. The tipped hat an old school move, though he looked to be under forty. She couldn't tell his race. Hair on the straight side she could see from the edges, skin color a blanched yellow. He could be white just back from Florida, she thought; or Arab; Puerto Rican; light-skinned Indian; could be a high yellow black man. Had the thought how both small and large the world had become; was a time for her anyhow when it was just a matter of black and white. Though standing here trying to guess his heritage wasn't telling her a thing about what he wanted, halfway afraid to ask what he wanted. Even as she did. "What do you want?" she blurted through the storm door.

He was still smiling and she remembered years ago a man standing on her porch smiling like that, that one had tipped his hat too. That one had come looking for Freeda. Thought history might be doubling back to slap her like an unexpected ocean wave when this one asked for Neena.

"Excuse me?" she said, as if she'd not heard right.

"I'm looking for Neena. Might she be here?"

His voice had the inflection of a network newscaster without even a hint of regionalism so that she couldn't even pick up an accent, though there was a trace of blackness in his tone, right at the ends of his words when he said Neena's name. "Can you tell me who you are?"

"Can you tell me if she's here?" He put his hand on the storm door handle and turned it. The move scared Nan. She closed the door all the way, then folded her arms across her flowered housecoat in a how-dare-you stance.

He raised his shoulders and his eyebrows, held his hands out as if to say, I'm harmless. "Please, can you open the door so I can talk to you?" he asked.

"Nothing to talk about," she shouted from her side of the door. "Neena doesn't live here, lives nowhere near here, won't be here. So don't come 'round here looking for her." Her breath made a circle of fog on the glass.

"But I'm Nathan, from Virginia, don't you remember."

She looked at him through the fog; his face was a blur. "Don't know you, don't want to know you," she said. Then she pulled the cord to the blinds to make him disappear. She stood in the vestibule and held her breath and listened for the pulse of footsteps leaving her porch. Peeped through the blinds when she heard the brush of shoe against concrete going down the steps. She watched his back as he turned and walked out of her line of vision. Now she went to the bay window that gave her an expanded view. He must have parked around the corner because the cars out there now were all familiar to her. Wished that she'd come to the door with a handful of salt to throw behind him, to make sure he wouldn't return. Asked out loud what had Neena gone and gotten herself mixed up in to have people ringing the doorbell at six o'clock in the morning looking for her. Angry now, and worried. Thinking now about all the people who'd shown up looking for Neena's mother, Freeda, over the years. Thinking of the one who'd stood out most in her mind.

Thirty some years ago in the early days of Freeda's vanishing and reappearing as if that was a normal way to live, a refined-looking man, oak-colored with beautiful straight teeth and a hint of silver running through his hair, had walked up on the porch and smiled and asked for Freeda. His smile was so disarming that Nan hadn't even snapped at him when she said that Freeda wasn't in at the moment. Truth was that Freeda hadn't been home in over a year. She was twenty-two by then and had left a note telling Nan not to worry, which in Nan's mind amounted to telling a fish not to swim. She'd call every month or so and in a flourish of sentences that didn't allow a response from Nan say that she was wonderfully okay, don't worry, please Mother, don't worry after me.

The man inquiring about Freeda that day had said, "You must be Nan," and Nan nodded, grateful that he'd first asked if Freeda was at home, because it had now been more than a month since Nan had heard Freeda's voice and otherwise Nan may have suspected that he was from the city morgue coming to tell her that her child was dead. He handed Nan a long white envelope then. Asked her if she wouldn't mind making sure that it got into Freeda's hands. Nan nodded again, easily deciphering by the feel of the envelope that it contained cash money. Nothing else had the soft springy feel of cash money captive in a long white envelope. He turned to leave and she called behind him,

"Your name? I need to tell her who this is from." He smiled again and she thought he might cry instead because his smile had such a sadness attached to it. His eyes were sad too as he said that Freeda would know exactly who it was from.

She propped the envelope inside the China cabinet. She turned the light on inside the China cabinet and left it burning even though she was conscious about things like wasted electricity. She paused every time she walked through the dining room after that and looked at the envelope and said a prayer that was filled with expectation of good. Felt in her heart that the man, the envelope were a good sign that Freeda would turn up soon.

And sure enough, a week to the day of the refined-looking man's visit Nan almost fell off of the stepladder where she was swiping away dust from the traverse rod that held her gold brocaded draperies. She stopped her dusting to see who owned the suitcase and shopping bags coming out of the trunk of the cab in front of her door. Hadn't heard mention from neighbors on either side that they had family coming in. Took the rungs of the ladder slowly then, clutching her chest as she did to still the palpitation when she realized it was Freeda bursting from the back door of the cab. Not just Freeda. Freeda with a pink and black psychedelic scarf tied around her mound of an African bush, Freeda in dungarees patched with smudged American flags, Freeda in flip-flops with each of her toes painted a different color. Braless Freeda in a white cotton gauze button-down shirt, the shirt open to halfway exposing her breast. Lord have Mercy, Freeda with an infant attached to her breast.

By the time Nan snatched open the front door the cabdriver had set her bags on the porch and Freeda was paying him. Then she grabbed him with her free hand to hug him. The cabby's expression caught between stunned and amused as he walked off the porch and Freeda stepped into the vestibule exploding with joy almost singing—there was such a lilt to her voice as she said, "Mother, there's so much to tell, too much to tell, I don't know where to start. Paris maybe. I've seen the Eiffel Tower, do you believe it. It was so remarkable, more remarkable than the Himalayas."

"You've been to the Himalayas?" Nan asked slowly, clutching her chest. Her voice felt like a corrugated box dragging out of her.

"Oh, Mother, of course not," Freeda said. "Not really. I haven't *really* been to Paris. Though I've been there in a figurative way," Freeda said as they moved through the vestibule into the living room and her voice expanded to fill the room. "It was all a state of mind anyhow," she gushed. "Everything was as real as it needed to be and as false. But this baby, Mama, this life, this is more real than any place I've been, and larger, her heartbeat is the most magnificent thing I've ever heard. More magnificent than Coltrane, Mama, or the sound of your pincher shears when you sew just before dawn. Listen, Mama, put your ear to her chest and you can hear the angels drumming their fingers against the Good Lord's throne."

Nan was frozen in place next to the vestibule door that Freeda had just walked through. Her hand had somehow moved from clutching her chest to covering her mouth to catch the silent scream bouncing around inside her mouth. Had been bouncing around for some time waiting for her to reach that hard spot where mothers sometimes ended up: that after all of the shrugging it off, the rationalizing that it was just a phase, the thinking over and over about how so and so's child also acted out and she made out fine; after the preacher's assurances that the Lord never put more on you than you could stand, and the root-worker's promise that there was a spell also for fixing Freeda's little behavior problem, Nan stood there looking at Freeda, her gorgeous dark-eyed cherub-cheeked daughter with the head full of hair that Nan would pull into ponytails and tie satin ribbons at the ends to match the color kneesocks she wore. That hair was wild under the psychedelic scarf like her eyes were wild. Her breast exposed as the baby sucked and Nan allowed the thought to see the light in this bright, airy living room. Her child's mind was gone. Sick her child was. Her tall slender perfect child was sick in the mind. What a hard tight place for a mother to be, as if the air around her was suddenly coated with varnish that had hardened and she couldn't even punch her arms through to grab her child to shake her or hold her as she listened to Freeda ramble on and on about the sunrise over the equator, the power of the rapids as she'd sped down the Amazon.

Then a part of Nan asserted itself from deep inside her chest, made itself into a thick stick and banged in a run against the bones of her rib cage, as if her rib cage was the xylophone Freeda played in third grade. Nan remembered the feel of each strike against the metal slats of the xylophone as Freeda sat on the stage; it was during Freeda's solo part and she'd hit each note so perfectly until almost the end. Nan had sat in the audience and closed her eyes and prayed you can do it Freeda, it's 1, 2, 3, 4, 5, 5, 6, 6, 6, 6, 5, 4, 4, 4, 4, 3, 3, 2, 2, 2, 2, 1, just like we practiced, Freeda, do it baby, please, do it for Mommy and Daddy. Freeda had paused with the balled stick suspended, then looked out into the auditorium and smiled the most gorgeous smile to ever shape a little girl's cheeks. She was dressed in the school-requested white blouse and dark skirt made by Nan's own hand. Nan had put pleats to the navy skirt, a trio of pearls on the tips of the blouse's collar; she'd pressed out Freeda's thick hair and hot-rolled it into soft curls that grazed her shoulders. She was the epitome of what a little girl should be, sitting there center-stage cross-legged in front of the xylophone. Then she landed the stick in a run across the metal slats back and forth sending up a melody not even close to the one she'd rehearsed. Played something that sounded more like esoteric jazz, a scratchy, unbalanced tune, unmoored, nothing to anchor the notes to the stage, to Freeda as the people filling up the seats swallowed their confusion, their embarrassment for the gorgeous child beating up on that xylophone. That's what Nan felt inside of her as she stood there looking at Freeda with the baby latched onto her chest, felt the disharmony of the hard irregular sticks against her rib cage.

And yet, Nan still tried to convince herself that no, Freeda's mind wasn't gone, not really. After all, black people don't go crazy, she told herself. It's the devil. Or it's someone wishing her hard luck and putting a temporary tangle on her mind. It's the confusion that sometimes follows childbirth. She needs a little rest, a little prayer. Needs to hear a little Mahalia Jackson singing "God Put a Rainbow in the Sky." Needs some homemade applesauce with hot buttered yeast rolls served from a good saucer. I can do what needs to be done to bring her back to herself, Nan thought as she moved her hand down from her mouth because her hand was beginning to shake.

She folded her hands around her chest; she rubbed her rib cage. Oh how it ached as if it was succumbing to a hard case of pleurisy. She was thinking now about that episode when Freeda was in her late teens; she'd heard voices and Nan had taken her to the doctor. The doctor offered to refer her to a specialist at Friend's Hospital and Nan thought no, that's where people go who are seriously disturbed. And anyhow the voices never resurfaced. Lord Have Mercy, Jesus. She wanted to scream. And a baby. You've lost your mind and come home with a baby. But you haven't lost your mind. We don't lose our minds.

We lose money on the numbers or when it slips from under our bra when we're taking out the trash; we lose husbands because they cheat or die; we lose best friends because they talk about us behind our backs because they're jealous of the new coat or ring or couch we just got; we lose jobs because in crunch time we're always the first to be let go; we lose our joy, our fineness as we age, sometimes we even lose our faith. We don't lose our minds, though. My God. And a baby. Whose baby. Please tell me, she wanted to say, that you've stolen this child. We can take her back, tell them you're not well, your mind is sick, not sick, no, yes, it is. Please don't tell me that this baby really belongs to you.

Though Nan could see that the baby did belong to Freeda by the unmistakable pout in the bottom of Freeda's stomach. Plus the baby was certainly pulling on more than air as she sucked and Nan wanted to close her ear to the sound. And then Freeda pushed the baby into Nan's arms and said she had to bring her bags in from the porch.

Nan received the child as the contraries swirled around. A softening on the one hand that this was her first grandchild, but then a hardening that the child had come without the benefit of a marriage as far as Nan knew. She touched the child's forehead but the baby recoiled feeling assaulted from the sudden loss of her mother's breast. She made sucking motions with her mouth calling for Freeda's breast by turning her head from side to side to find that sweetness she'd been drinking; she howled and stretched her hand. Nan tried to console the child as she leaned in to shush her, thinking as she did that the baby looked like something possessed by the devil the way she was contorting her face. That thought taking hold when the child's hand swiped at air and landed right in the ball of Nan's eye. Nan screamed from the sudden thunder of pain rolling out from her cornea. The child reacted to the sound of Nan's screaming and hollered louder still. Nan and the baby tried to outdo each other: the baby crying for milk, and to be returned to the only arms she'd known since her entry into the world; Nan crying from the erosion happening in her eye and also in her chest, as if the baby's finger had also gone right through Nan's chest, pushing into the raw meat of her heart turning like a corkscrew going deeper still.

Nan ran to the kitchen to run water to put to a cloth so she could soak her eye. She held the hysterical baby close, had to hold her close or she might throw her across the room, blaming the baby for the pain radiating out from her eye, blaming the baby too for the fact that Freeda's mind was gone, not gone, gone, it is, it is not, is, is, is so too. This baby her chickens come home to roost. This baby her punishment for dabbling with the devil when she was trying to make Freeda's father, Alfred, her own. "Damn you baby," she said out loud. Then shuddered that she'd said such a thing. This was after all just a baby. Her only child's firstborn. Just an innocent infant she thought as her eye settled into a duller, more continuous pain and she ran warm water over the cloth and instead of putting it to her eye, wrapped the cloth around her finger and dipped it in the sugar bowl and eased it into the baby's mouth. The baby sucking hard, frowning as she looked at Nan, Nan with one eye open, and the other red and swollen and shut.

Nan swallowed her questions that afternoon about where and how Freeda had spent the past year and allowed a relief to settle into her muscles over the fact that Freeda was alive. The relief took hold in degrees and she realized how tightly she'd held herself the past year as the muscles in her neck and shoulders and stomach became slowly unhinged. Even with the tug-of-war then in her mind that persisted up to today about whether Freeda was mentally incapacitated or not, was it a chemical imbalance or the devil trying to get to her through her child. Convinced herself for the balance of that day that Freeda's mental health was indeed intact once Freeda's thoughts seemed to settle as she unpacked her bags and handled the newborn with what Nan saw to be amazing deftness. She stopped talking about Paris and the Eiffel Tower and concentrated fully on the baby. Told Nan that the baby's name was Neena and Nan swallowed her questions about the origins of the name, strange name to her especially the way Freeda spelled it.

That evening after Freeda had bathed the baby down and dressed her in pink and yellow footed pajamas, had spread a cotton diaper over her shoulder and turned on the soft glow of the goose-necked lamp and settled into the armchair in the corner of the living room to nurse, such a calmness had passed between Freeda and Nan that Nan felt equipped to broach the subject about the baby's father. Who was he? What was his circumstance? How did she allow herself to have a baby without the benefit of marriage? Remembered the envelope then, the silver-haired man with the magnanimous smile who'd stopped by the week before.

"Almost forgot," she said, "gentleman came past looking for you, left an envelope."

"Pretty teeth?" Freeda asked.

Nan nodded.

"I only asked because I know what a stickler you are for teeth. Remember you used to make me brush mine until my gums bled."

"Now, Alfreeda," Nan said slowly, "tell me one time I actually made your gums bleed. You had sensitive gums that had a tendency to bleed and that doesn't have a thing to do with me making sure you cleaned your teeth well." Nan held herself as she walked toward the dining room. Wanted to say, so I guess you called yourself punishing me for your sensitive gums by running away like you have. She retrieved the envelope from the china cabinet as she tried to rein in the storm waiting to burst through her lips. Turned the light out in the china cabinet and closed the door. Closed the door softly though she really wanted to reach in and grab plates and start shattering them against the floor. Imagined the blue and white shards of tree branches and Chinese roofs strewn like pieces of an impossible jigsaw that the frustrated would-be solver could never complete. She was trying not to cry when she returned to the corner of the living room where Freeda nursed the baby. The gooseneck lamp drizzling down a soft yellow glow. Freeda looked up at Nan and smiled and Nan wondered who was the suspected crazy one here, Freeda looking calm and sanctified, Nan the one with her fists balled trying to hold her rage in her palms.

"Mother, could you open the envelope please," Freeda asked as she stroked the baby's forehead. "My hands are full. My life is full too," talking now in baby talk to Neena. "Finally, finally, you've filled my life you have. My doll baby. My little doll baby."

Nan slipped her finger under the sealed flap and pulled out the contents that she'd expected all along, cash money. She started counting the money, hundred-dollar bills, and her jaw dropped lower the longer she counted. She could scarcely pick her jaw up from the floor to ask Freeda, who, who was he, why'd he leave money like that. Called Freeda's name three times before Freeda finally looked up from the gushing she was doing over the baby's face.

"Just some guy," Freeda said.

"Just some guy does not leave a person two thousand cash dollars. What? Is he the baby's father. Man up in his thirties like he appeared likely got a wife. How you do this, Freeda? You weren't brought up like this. God knows you weren't. What goes through your mind, Freeda? Huh? Look at me and tell me what the hell goes through your mind."

Freeda looked up at Nan; she tilted her head, a tender concern swathing her face.

"Did your eye go down, Mama, from where the baby poked it? Do you need more ice?" she asked.

"Lord, Jesus, Freeda," Nan said, her balled fist going up and down, hitting herself in her side. "Don't do this. Don't pretend not to know what I'm asking you, Freeda." She shouted this last part so loudly that Neena dropped her mother's breast from her mouth and began to whimper.

Freeda lifted the baby up to her shoulder. She gently patted her back, encouraging her to belch. She closed her eyes tightly then. "He told me I needed medication. I told him all I needed was him. And he was all I needed at first. But then I needed Paris, the Eiffel Tower—"

"Stop it with the Eiffel Tower, Freeda. Just stop it." Nan rubbed her temples with her fists.

"So we didn't get married, so what. None of it makes this baby's heartbeat any less real. Did you even listen? Did you even put your ear to her chest? It changed me, the sound of her heart. It made me good."

"When were you not good, Freeda?" Nan asked, crying openly now.

"You yourself said I had the devil in me."

"That's a manner of speak—"

"But he has been after me—the devil. That's why I left. He came into my room with his hooded cape and Doberman Pinscher eyes and bamboo cane and told me he was coming back—"

"Freeda—"

"But it's okay now, Mama, because Neena's heartbeat has changed everything. I'm good again."

"Freeda—"

"Just listen, Mama, please." She cradled Neena in her arms again.

"Just listen to my baby's heart. Please listen to her, Mama. Don't you understand, I'm good again. If you listen to her heart beat, you'll know."

Nan would go to all lengths to appease Freeda when she cried like that, especially since her crying seemed to come in seasons generally following months, even years of giddiness and right living that Nan would congratulate herself for raising this creature so blessed with a joyful spirit. So particularly at the beginning of what turned out to be a season of crying for Freeda, Nan worked overtime to neutralize the cries by doing whatever she could of whatever Freeda asked. Like now. As Freeda cried and begged Nan to listen to Neena's heartbeats. Nan pushed through the air in the living room weighted down with Freeda's cries. She leaned all the way in and put her ear to Neena's chest. Felt the baby's heat rising through the pink-and-yellow-footed pajamas. She couldn't hear the heartbeat though, her ears too filled up with the desperate sound of her own sobs, indecipherable from Freeda's; the baby's crying mixed in then too.

Nan was back at her bay window where Charlene's boys were wrestling each other down the steps fixing to dirty up their navy blue school uniform pants. Nan stuck her head out the door and yelled for them not to make her have to come across that street and get them to behave; they gave each other one last push and then straightened themselves up and took turns calling out to Nan, it was him, not me Miss Nan. Now her phone was ringing and she told them to hurry to the corner because the bus was due. Then she closed and locked her door and rushed to answer the phone. Heard Malik on the other end saying he'd just spoken to Tish. The cramping had subsided and that was a good sign. He was headed back down to the hospital to take her a robe. Did Nan want him to stop by for her? Did she need anything otherwise? She pressed her eyes shut thinking how life slaps you down, then extends a hand like a good neighbor to pick you up. This boy was such a prince to her. She told him no thank you, said she'd either arrange for the senior transport van or catch a ride from any of a number of people on the block. She told him then about Neena's phone call the evening before, that Neena was in town, that she would probably call again. Took a deep breath and then in a flurry of sentences verbalized to him her fear: that the surprise of Neena's appearance might have devastating consequences for Tish's pregnancy. "She gets so excited over her sister, might be better if Tish doesn't know, if she doesn't speak to Neena until she and the baby are out of the woods."

"You saying don't let Neena talk to Tish? Are you sure?" he asked. "You getting ready to have me sleeping on the couch for the next year, Nan," he said, and Nan could hear how hard he was trying to bring levity to the situation as she walked back to the window to check on Charlene's boys. They were headed toward the corner and she told Malik to hold for one second as she put the phone down and ran out onto the porch and called out to them to put their caps back on their heads, did they want to catch the grippe out in February with their heads bare. They both pointed to each other as they shouted across the street, he took his off first, Miss Nan, no he did, even as they reached into their coat pockets and pulled the caps out and pushed them on.

She went back into the house and took a deep breath before she started speaking into the phone again. "Now, Malik," she said, rushing her words. "Just think about what you yourself told me that the doctor said about how important it is that Tish remain as calm as possible. I know for a fact of a woman down home who lost a baby after a sudden clap of thunder struck the magnolia tree in front of her house and her water broke at only six months, like Tish is six months. And just last year right around the corner on Pine Street a young woman miscarried after her father reappeared in her life some fifteen years after walking out of it; she was six months too and even younger than Tish, don't think she was even thirty."

"But, Nan, this is her sister."

"Now, Malik, I'm not saying never let her speak to Tish, I'm just saying until Tish and the baby are out of the woods, they could be out of the woods by this time tomorrow, Lord willing. Am I right?"

"Yeah, Nan. Sure, it's just that—"

"It's just that right now Tish's frame of mind has got to be the priority. Anything frayed as a result can surely be mended afterward, but right now we got to keep Tish's environment calm, so that she can keep the baby's world calm. Am I right, Malik? Huh?"

"You're right, Nan, sure," Malik said on a sigh, and Nan was satisfied that Malik was convinced. Then she told him that should he speak to Neena to please give her a message. "Tell her that her grandmother's concerned about her, really and truly I am. Tell her that I said that it's later than she thinks."

She hung up the phone, then reached into her flowered housecoat for a tissue. Felt a deep-down sadness about having to deny Tish and Neena the pleasure of each other's company as she dabbed at her nose. Though she'd decided years ago that if it came down to choosing between the welfare of Neena and Tish she had already decided her affection would point to Tish. Forced to make that decision when she was trying to raise the girls and stretched to the end of her emotional capability dealing with the roller coaster of Freeda's comings and goings and she'd had to determine how best to parcel out what was left of her good attention. Her good attention seemed wasted on Neena, who was proving time and again that she just didn't have a do-right constitution. The only thing to do was to put her resources into the child who'd likely benefit. And Tish had benefited well as a result. Settled in Nan's mind. Though far from settled really as she thought about time running out. She knew about time running out, knew what it felt like to try to hold time captured in her hands as if time was a wren chick and would lay there soft-feathered, its tiny heartbeats pulsing against her palm. Knew how the reality felt too, time more like a bird of prey, sinking thick claws into her flesh to free itself, to fly away according to its schedule, taking what she loved in its sweeping upward motion, leaving her with empty hands scarred. Felt that way about time and her mighty love, Alfred. Met Alfred the same day she met her best friend, Goldie.

Chapter 3

AN MOVED TO Philadelphia in an exodus north from Albany, Georgia, in 1947. Followed cousins here who were prospering; Nan prospered as well working two jobs: one for the government where she sewed sleeves to army dress blues; the other for a dress shop in West Philadelphia where she made dresses and suits and blouses that the owner then claimed to have imported from France. Nan even embroidered the label, MIMI, that was affixed to the garments she whipped up. She was instructed to come and go through the back alley, to say that she was the girl should anybody ask. Drastically reduce the salability of the clothes she made if the customers knew they'd been created from concept to final hem by the colored. Nan acquiesced because she was paid handsomely for her talent, her complicity. Made almost as much there from six in the morning until noon on Saturday as she did working all week her nine to five for the government. Able to grow the savings account she kept at the post office to the point that her dream house was almost in reach: a brick-faced double-wide row home with a

hedged-in garden and sit-down-a-spell-type porch on a shady broom-swept street. She'd see versions of that house every Saturday as she walked through West Philadelphia on her way to and from her second job. Prayed fervently for such a house; prayed too to fill the house with a husband's loving arms in the main bedroom under the triple bay window that would surely attract the silver beams when the moon was full; prayed also for a child to play under her feet afternoons in the backyard while she hung clothes on the line. The times weren't in her favor though because the section of West Philly where she wanted to buy was all white. But she was a young woman, not even twenty, her youth helping her to see possibilities over obstacles. Saw signs of the possibilities when she stopped one day in front of the store on the corner of Chestnut to wait for the bus in the shade, Sam's Delicatessen where the canned goods in the front window were arranged in an equilateral triangle.

Nan was drawn inside the store by the contrasting aromas pushing through the screen door, the soft brown pumpernickel breads and mammoth dill pickles swimming in the barrel and the jug of fresh made lemonade conjured up no doubt by the colored help, Goldie she said her name was. Though Nan perceived immediately that Goldie was more than the help. Could tell by the way she propped herself on the stool behind the counter with her big legs crossed, sandals dangling from her pretty brown feet, toenails painted bright red, lips bright red too. Hair hard-pressed and pinned up in a French roll, slightly bored expression when Sam brushed past her to pull a box of Carolina Rice from the shelf above her head. The way she turned and looked out the window it was as if he worked for her and not the other way around, as if it was his job to satisfy her and keep her attention on this side of the storefront window. She did, though, pour the lemonade from the jug and handed the plastic cup to Nan as they waited for Sam to assemble Nan's order: liverwurst, cheese, two tomatoes, half a loaf of Jewish rye, and a quarter pound of sweet butter.

"You work near?" she asked Nan as she wrote on a brown paper bag the prices of the items Nan had asked for.

"Do a little day's work around the corner," Nan said, lying per her boss's instructions. "My main job though is at the Quarter Master, seamstress."

"You got you a good job. They hiring?" Goldie asked throwing her voice in Sam's direction. "I might be looking."

"Not so much right about now," Nan said as she looked at Goldie in a girl, are you crazy kind of way.

Goldie winked at Nan. "They'll probably be hiring directly," she said, "once they get another war started. That white man will keep something going, won't he now? Son of a bitch."

Sam let out an Ah shit, goddamn slicer, and then pounded the liverwurst he'd been cutting back into the chilled display case. "Goldie, I need you to get the guy out here about this got damn slicer. Got damn machine trying to take my goddamn thumb off."

"Sure thing, Sam," Goldie said, a yawn to her voice, then put the eraser end of the pencil to the figures she'd jotted on the brown paper bag and told Nan her lemonade was on the house. "Your whole order gonna be on the house in a minute if Sam don't hurry up. You fixing to catch the D bus, right?"

"Sure 'nuff," Nan said.

"Where abouts you live?"

"Downtown, Mole Street. Though I do love this part of Philadelphia. Want to buy in this part but it, you know, they wouldn't, what I mean is, nothing selling right now, you know, to me." She let her eyes go in Sam's direction signaling to Goldie that she really couldn't say what she wanted to say.

"Yeah well, you just hold on a little while longer," Goldie said. "Change coming to this part of Philadelphia too. Hear tell a colored man looking to buy right around the corner, on Spruce. Hear tell the owner actually considering it. And you know all it takes is one of us. You know white folks gonna be like crabs trying to get out of a basket, stepping all on top of one another, underselling their own mamas to get the hell outta here. You know that white man ain't letting no colored folk get but too close, not close in that way anyhow. Son of a bitch. Ain't it so Sam."

"You know what, Goldie, don't talk to me," Sam said as he cut orange cheese in thick slices with a mile-long serrated knife. "I'm trying to concentrate on what I'm doing, please. Plus I treat you too good to have to listen to your bullshit."

"You get good too, baby," she said. And Nan couldn't believe she was hearing what she was hearing. She knew such relationships existed, but she'd never seen one up close. "Plus you used to could take a joke," Goldie went on. "You not going crotchety on me, are you?"

Sam tore a sheet of wax paper from the roll, cursing under his breath as he did, wrapped the liverwurst, then the cheese, then the butter, and slammed them on the counter in front of Goldie. Goldie laughed. Then pointed out the window at a suited-down man standing in front of the store. "There he go. That's the one trying to buy around here. Negro likely lost again. Once a week he end up outside there trying to get downtown. Came in here one day asking directions. At first I thought he was trying to ask me for a date. I told you 'bout him, didn't I, Sam?" Sam didn't answer as he threw things around in the display case to get to the tomatoes. "I said to him, 'Baby, right now the man I got is more 'n enough man for me. Almost too much for me.' I didn't tell you that part, Sam, did I? Can't have you 'round here getting no big head on me."

Neena couldn't believe Goldie was making this white man blush as his face turned as red as the tomatoes he dropped into a small-sized brown paper bag. "These are on the house today," he said as he placed the bag on the counter. Placed it softly compared to how he'd slammed the meat down. Allowed the side of his arm to rub up against Goldie as he did. Then asked Nan if she wanted a piece of dry ice to keep her things fresh until she got where she was going. Nan barely heard him though. The heat building up in the store between Goldie and Sam made Nan desire some kindling of her own. Made her swallow hard to get rid of the saliva accumulating in her mouth as her attention turned to the man on the other side of the window and their eyes met through the window and he smiled at Nan and tipped his hat. He had the softest eyes she'd ever seen on a man, a sandy-toned complexion, a stevedore's muscle-bound upper body that showed even through his suit jacket, a good-quality seersucker. Plus he had black silky straight hair, meant she'd be spared the torture of the pressing comb should they be blessed to have a girl. She chided herself for letting her thoughts skip across seams that hadn't been attached. Even as she felt such a swoon in her stomach that she had to put her hand to the counter to steady herself. Here were two signs at once, that this neighborhood might be getting ready to change over, that the man looking to help the change along, fine man, was outside smiling at her.

"You courtin'?" Goldie asked her then. " 'Cause that Negro look like he could use some direction in life."

"Aw Goldie, you and the matchmaking. A real Cupid this one thinks she is," Sam said as he squeezed the back of Goldie's neck and she let out a little moan and bent her neck and said, "Right there, Sam, it's stiff right there where your thumb is pressing, mnh, you really know how to do."

Nan hurried into the bottom of her vinyl bag for her purse. Such a scene down home would mean a brick coming through the window with a stick of dynamite attached. Then Goldie said, "Uh oh, that Negro look like he getting away. He fixing to cross the street and I didn't even finish totaling you. Let her pay next week, Sam."

"Yeah, yeah, next Saturday's fine." Sam rushed his words as he ushered Nan to the door, then closed the door, locked it, and before Nan could turn around to thank him he'd flipped the door sign from the side that read COME IN, to the one with the clock that indicated BACK IN 30 MINUTES. Nan said glory be, to herself as she half ran across the street. Wanting to ponder the differences between the mixing of the races up here and down home. But she was on the other side of the street now and the man was tipping his hat again and asking her if the bus stopped there that would take him near to Fourth and Kater.

She looked at his left hand to confirm that the wedding band finger was clean of a circled imprint though he was wearing a pinky ring, a tarnished silver something. He seemed to sway as he stood there the way a drunk man would and she sighed, ready to release all expectations that he might be the one she'd been praying for as she listened to him explain that he'd gotten turned around. "Just finished my shift down on the waterfront where I been since before daybreak," he said. "And my sugar must have gone too high, or too low, because my head started spinning and my mouth went dry, even my eyesight doubled up on me. Next thing I knew I was on the wrong bus though surely it must have been the right time because it led to this pleasure for me of beholding you. Alfred, Miss Lady, my name's Alfred."

Nan blushed as she told him her name. She was rarely complimented so. Her looks she knew were mild rather than impressive. She was short with a high waist and straight hips, had neither big legs nor a remarkable chest, small wary eyes, blunted nose, round face with no cheekbones showing. Though she did have a pretty mouth, thick and formed and looked like a heart opening up when she smiled. Now she reclaimed the hope that he could be her answered prayer. High sugar, that was his problem, not inebriation. She told him that to get to Fourth and Kater he needed to be stepping up on the same bus that was squealing to a stop where they stood. He extended his hand for Nan to go first though the steps turned into a sliding board on him as he followed her up and he ended up sprawled out right at the bus driver's feet. The bus driver, a silver-haired fat white man, shook his head in disgust as gasps and then ripples of laughter moved through the bus from the front to the back.

"Well, somebody help the man. He's got sugar diabetes for goodness sake," Nan said as she leaned and tried to hoist him up from under his arms. The bus driver shifted the bus into a rough neutral and the sudden back and forth caused Nan to fall on top of Alfred; her mouth kissed the shoulder of his tan and bone seersucker jacket and left her heart-shaped lip print. A half dozen people got up then to help Nan. She dusted the front of her pale blue cotton dress and said to the driver that he was doing Satan's bidding jerking the bus like that though she could scarcely be heard over the sounds of Alfred's grunting as he was helped to standing. Nan guided Alfred through the bus, "high sugar," she said feeling the need to defend him each time she caught the eye of a woman who looked like her in age and situation, feeling somewhat exalted right now because she was leading this good-looking, straight-haired man by the arm.

When they came to an open double seat Alfred said, "Beautiful ladies must go first," though Nan insisted that he take the window. She was beginning to pick up the traces of alcohol hanging to his breath so she told him that the breeze might help his disorientation.

Alfred slid first into the seat and tried to keep his head up. He didn't want to pass out on this bus. The part about him being diabetic was true enough, and he really had gotten to work before dawn, he was a hard worker. He was also pissy drunk right now, and embarrassed because drunkenness had not been his goal when he'd ordered a shot of whiskey with a beer chaser to wash down his stewed fish platter. Getting drunk was never his goal. A soothing buzz was all he was ever after. Just something to smooth out the choppy situations in his life that often had to do with a beautiful woman breaking his heart. Like the one he was trying to get to now on Kater Street. Signs were that she was running on him the way the last two had and he was determined to catch her in the act. The motion of the bus though lulled him to that state that passes back and forth between nausea and euphoria. He let his head have its way and it fell like a sack of rocks and twigs against Nan's shoulder, thinking on the way into oblivion that this woman with the unremarkable features and stubby figure had the most pliant shoulder upon which he'd ever had the pleasure of passing out.

Nan thought a similar thing about the weight of his head as she gently slid his hat from his head so that the nice quality straw wouldn't be crushed, thought how bearable the weight of his head was. Wanted to slow the pace of the bus that it seemed to her had never reached Fourth Street so quickly, though she did have enough time to pull a pen and a small tablet from her white patent leather purse. Wrote what a pleasure sharing the bus ride with him was, and to please call so that he could arrange to get his jacket to her so that she might clean the lipstick stain that happened when they fell. She signed her name and the telephone number of the store up the street from her apartment where most people on the block took their calls. She slipped the note into his lapel pocket, then touched the sleeve of his seersucker jacket to rouse him. He was dead to the world so she put her entire hand around as much of his arm as she could, his arm so thick and solid and warm, the thought of that arm holding her turned her insides to liquid. He sat all the way up then and immediately she missed the weight of his head against her shoulder. She put his hat in his lap, told him she was getting off here, the next stop was his.

Though Nan had left Alfred on the bus, he was with her constantly in her daydreams. Her daydreams were usually accompanied by her humming some worldly music; Johnny Hartmann singing "You Are Too Beautiful" seemed stuck in her head. Sometimes her daydreams expanded to include the daughter they would have, assuredly a pretty girl given Alfred's good looks, a piano-player Nan thought, seeing the dresses with crinolines attached she'd make for the child's recitals. And when Alfred wasn't with her in her daydreams, he was present in her conversation as she chattered about the bus episode to her church lady friends, the women who sat at sewing machines on either side of her at the Quarter Master where they attached sleeves to the Dress Blues, her neighbors up and down Catherine Street, Goldie who'd she'd visit with every Saturday after she left her second job.

But after a month of not having heard from Alfred, Goldie told Nan to stop talking about him. Cautioned Nan that people might become envious seeing how happy the telling of the story made Nan, people might commence to wishing her hard luck.

It was a stormy Saturday and Nan doubled the length of her visit with Goldie to try to wait out the rain. Sam had gone in the back of the store to take his nap and Nan and Goldie ate egg salad sandwiches and sipped iced tea and Goldie asked Nan to describe the ring again that Alfred was wearing.

Nan smiled in spite of herself as she pictured Alfred's strong-looking manly hands, imagined those hands tilting her face for him to kiss until Goldie's voice pulled her back.

"The ring, Nan. Tell me again about the ring."

"Oh, it was just a silver something, not at all garish—"

"Tarnished though, right. Didn't you say it was tarnished?"

"Well, I did, but what—?"

"Was it tarnished to black or bluish, or did it have a hint of red around it."

"Near as I can recollect it had a hint of red," Nan said, face caught up in a worry frown over Goldie's line of questioning.

"See, I don't like that."

"What? What you talking 'bout, Goldie?"

"The ring. I don't like your description of that Negro's pinky ring."

Sam stuck his head in from the back room and told Goldie, "Don't try to use the slicer. If anybody needed a cut something, come wake me."

"Go count your money, Sam," she said on a laugh. "I know when to call you."

She turned her attention back to Nan and explained to Nan that when the metal's worn against the body turn color, usually silver goes to red, it means somebody has put something on that person.

"Put something on him? You mean like roots."

Goldie came from behind the counter and stood right in front of where Nan sat and adjusted Nan's pearls that had latched around the collar of her polka-dot blouse. She talked right into Nan's eyes as she did. "That's exactly what I'm saying, baby. Somebody done already rooted your man. And whatever they put on him is fixing to work because his silver is turning red. Wasn't you, was it? You didn't fix him, did you?"

"Come on, Goldie, I don't know nothing about working no roots. You know I'm in the church."

"Well, in the church or outta the church, you still got to fight fire with fire. You got to work fast to counteract whatever somebody else is already doing. The first thing you got to do is get a strand or two of that Negro's hair—"

"No way, Goldie, I don't dabble in that mess. And if I did, I sure don't know him good enough to be pulling on his hair."

"Suit yourself then. But I guarantee you the most you gonna get from that Negro from here on out is a tipped hat, and a howdy do Miss Lady, if you even get that."

"See Goldie, that's where we differ. I believe that the Lord delivers the desires of the heart in His own time and His own way."

"The Lord also helps those who help themselves. And the lady I used is from Virginia, and my mother used to say people from Virginia can cause you to crawl on your belly."

"Why would I want someone to crawl on their belly?"

"That's just an expression, Nan. You know, just to describe how potent—I'll tell you how potent," Goldie said as she walked to the window and looked out on the rain falling in slanted squares. "Sam and me started out the typical way, me doing days work, cooking and cleaning and ironing. Him showing up in the middle of the day when the wife and the kids were outta the house making no mistake about his intentions. I was young, about the age you are now. I denied him for the most part. Then Miss Eule who worked two doors down from me, would come and sit on the back steps and smoke her pipe when we took our break after hanging the wash on the line, told me how she handled her lady's husband. Said her auntie from Virginia fixed him so good that his mind went blank to her. Said she became part of the woodwork to him and he left her 'lone from then on. So I told Miss Eule I didn't know if I wanted to fade into the woodworks far as Sam was concerned, I wanted to be seen, but not seen as just some faceless body for him to take his pleasures with, shit, see me as a total woman same way you see your wife.

"I remember Miss Eule laughed so hard her pipe fell from between her teeth. I remember her digging her toe into the dirt below where we sat on the steps making a hole to bury her pipe ash. She told me I was young to the ways of the world, but give her a strand of my hair and his hair and two dollars as soon as I could come up with it and as much as possible put my bare feet inside of his shoes. Then she went to visit her aunt and came back with a special solution for me to mop down the floors with, gave me special bath crystals, gave me candles to light, I 'clare it wasn't a month later before Sam started bringing me ladylike gifts, perfumes, a charm bracelet. Bought me a weekend in Atlantic City, then strutted himself over to Kentucky Avenue where I was staying as if he was colored himself. Came loaded down with stuffed animals and toy windmills and chocolate-covered cherries and saltwater taffies. Lord have mercy, Nan. You talking about gentle. That man more concerned with giving me pleasure than taking his own. Mnh, mnh, mnh. Treated me like I was the most precious specimen he'd ever beheld. Still do. He talk gruff, but it's all for show, Lord have mercy."

"So maybe he just felt it anyhow, maybe the roots didn't have a thing to do with it."

"I have wondered about that. Though I had my final convincing when Miss Eule gave me a special soap for washing the bedsheets where Sam and his wife slept. A week later that woman packed up her and her kids and said she was moving back to Brooklyn. Said she hated Philadelphia, hated working in the store, missed her own people too much. So what are the chances of such a thing happening unprovoked like that?"

She stopped talking then because Sam stuck his head in from the back. "You okay, Goldie?"

"Fine, Sam, thought you was taking a nap."

"Can't sleep. Close up for a half hour when it gets empty out there."

"See what I'm talking 'bout. He can't get comfortable if I ain't close by."

"And what about you, Goldie? You comfortable when he not near? Seem like they put something on you too."

Goldie laughed as Nan gathered her things to leave. Nan could still hear her laugh when she crossed the street and saw the sign in the window turned to BACK IN 30 MINUTES.

Goldie's musing on the power of a love potion wore Nan down. The circumstances helped. Alfred had not called and Nan's preoccupation with the why not had ballooned so that she imagined him killed in his sleep by a leaky gas stove, or unable to move his neck after eating half-cooked pork. She dragged through her well-ordered days burdened with the weight of missing him as if they'd been attached for decades. She finally yielded when she spotted Alfred on Fourth Street where she'd gone for zippers and a new bobbin head and there was Alfred strolling down the street. Nan waved and he looked at her as if she was part of the blue and yellow of the summertime air. She cleared her throat then and called his name and when his eyes focused on her he asked, "Yes, Miss Lady? I don't believe I've had the pleasure." She was too devastated to remind him about his fall up the bus steps, her lip print on his seersucker jacket, her shoulder that became his pillow.

"See they made his mind go blank," Goldie insisted when Nan related the details of the encounter. And though Nan refused to go see the lady Goldie used herself because she was afraid of the devil and what the Lord might do to her for going to such a place, she did provide personal items for Goldie to take so that the lady could work with the essence of Nan, provided her hair brush, a handkerchief that she'd recently cried into, and her signature written three times in red.

Goldie returned with instructions and candles and powders. Told Nan how to sweep her house daily from front to back, gave her the contents to mix a solution for mopping her floors, a dime to wear against her ankle, and when Alfred still didn't come around she told Nan that they were dealing with some strong mess that required a direct approach. Alfred needed to drink a special concoction, Nan had to be the one to get it down him.

They were sitting in the dining room of Nan's two-bedroom apartment. Sam had gone to the dock to buy spices in bulk and he'd dropped Goldie off. Nan had just finished making dress pants for Sam that Goldie was giving him for his birthday. She was cleaning up the scraps of gray all-weather wool from around the sewing machine. She wished she'd treated Alfred the way she treated most everything else she'd ever wanted. Picture it, claim it in the name of the Lord and if it wasn't delivered, then it wasn't to be, just that simple. Wished now that she'd followed her mother's approach about things: "Don't start nothing, won't be nothing," her mother always said. But she'd started something for real, an obsession the likes of which she'd never experienced.

She'd directed her own hand to paint the outcome she desired. Her desires, though, had spilled outside of the margins, bled on off the entire page, and sprouted hands and feet, a bear-sized body that she couldn't see beyond, couldn't think beyond; could barely breathe because of its hot, heavy presence in her face moving with her from side to side, up and back so there was no getting around it. Nothing to do but feed it. Feed it or watch it come after her with its big bear paws and tear the skin from her short cube of frame, crush her bones to the gristle, all the way to her soul that she didn't even know who owned these days. Devil himself might own it by now. No sense in even thinking it preposterous what Goldie was suggesting. Goldie suggesting that Nan perch next to Alfred on a bar stool where the lights were low and his logic likely faltering. Goldie even producing the situation: the boyfriend of one of her cousins, who used to work as a stevedore before a hundred-pound can crushed his foot and he ended up losing the foot, had just settled his insurance case and was throwing himself a scotch and chitterlings birthday party at the bar on Bainbridge Street. "I know your Negro gonna be there, Nan."

Nan protested that she'd never even been inside a beer garden. Wouldn't know what to say or do or even think inside of one. Goldie told her she would go with her; she'd have to think of a nice-like lie to tell Sam to explain her leaving the house dressed up on a Saturday, but she would do it for Nan.

Nan had no choice but to relent. The bear-sized obsession stood in front of her with its thick immovability and dared her not to, then stroked her hair with its oversized claws as she thought about the dress she'd make from the red satin fabric she'd bought when she'd seen Alfred that first time. She'd give the dress a wide sash and a low open back to replicate a waist line that would also create the illusion of curved hips. She'd edge the hem of the dress with black lace and wear black silk stockings with seams up the back. She'd never worn seamed stockings before, black either, never went darker that Puff-of-Smoke though cinnamon was her main shade.

She put the cloudy-colored liquid concoction per Goldie's instructions in an empty vanilla extract bottle, was supposed to add a single drop of her own sweat though she wasn't sure whether her sweat went in the bottle or ran down the side. She hadn't asked Goldie what made up the contents otherwise. She didn't want to know. From minute to minute didn't even believe this was her, Nan, good-raised southern Christian girl going to these lengths to get the man of her obsessions with whom to make the daughter she was desperate for.

But here she was in her red belted dress and black seamed stockings, her hair in loose longer curls and not the tiny ones rolled tight to her scalp that she usually wore. Here she was getting out of the Yellow Cab as Goldie pulled her toward the door marked LADY'S ENTRANCE on the side of the Bainbridge Street bar. Here she was dizzy from the low-hanging blue lights and the smell of whiskey and chicken and pork. The crowded room revolved on her as the drum beats from the live band thumped in her chest. The laughter was strong and sad and drifted in wafts like the steam rising from the bowls of chitterlings and rice. She tried not to look around and gawk like a country girl in New York mesmerized by the city's bigness. But she was mesmerized. And she was repulsed too. Had the simultaneous urges to both giggle and vomit as she followed Goldie past women in painted-on clothes—that's how tight their apparel—and men with shiny processed hair and suits cut too loud to wear to church. Then Goldie turned abruptly; her mouth formed in a wide **O**. And when Nan said, What? Goldie said she didn't believe what she was seeing but there was Sam's brother playing the keyboard with the band. "Lord Jesus," Goldie said, "what they doing bringing in a white boy from New York. Shit. That's all Sam needs, he'll swear I'm running on him. God. Sam don't deserve that. Damn. I got to go, Nan, I'm sorry baby. Shit." She hesitated, looked at Nan as if Nan was her child and she was leaving her for the first day of school in a bad neighborhood.

"Damn," Goldie said again, and Nan could see the tussle over whether to leave or to stay play out on Goldie's face. Saw the leaving win out as Goldie blew Nan a kiss and said, "You gonna do just fine, baby," then moved farther and farther toward the door where they'd come in. Nan tried to follow Goldie, determined not to stay by herself, but then the room stood still for Nan because there he was. Alfred.

His stool was turned away from the bar and looked out on the center of the room where big butts and balloons and blue and white crepe paper wiggled to the beat. His face had an intensity about it that shocked Nan; in all of day-dreaming over him she'd only pictured his smile. Plus he'd cut his hair, though the remnant strands were still silky and black, still charmed Nan. His whole presence charmed her, from the width of his shoulders under the gray pin-striped jacket, to the way his leathers matched on his belt and his shoes, both burgundy with a lizard cut, even the way he swayed, almost imperceptibly from his waist to the beat of the drums. She had the thought then that she would go to any lengths to make him hers. She'd dance with the devil if that's what it took. She put her hand to her mouth at the image that conjured. Thought the smell of drink so pervasive in here that it was sifting into her pores and she was getting drunk just standing here, just watching Alfred, wanting him, Lord Jesus did she want him. Pushed past her temerity in this bar with her support, Goldie vanished and said, "Good evening, Alfred, do you remember me? Can I sit with you a minute and tell you how we know each other?"

Alfred was drinking hard. Didn't know any other way to drink once he got started. Envied his peers who could stop at two or three or while they could still make their hands and feet behave. Had promised himself he was walking, not staggering out of here tonight, that he would wake in his own bed in normal sleep-garb of boxer shorts and T-shirt, not in his clothes where he'd pissed himself, or worse in an alley with his pants pockets turned inside out, stripped of his watch and wallet and his emergency half pint with no recollection of how he'd gotten there. But he was to that no-stopping serious stage, and now it appeared that somebody was ready to start some shit. Fighting in bars was not uncommon for Alfred. Sometimes he'd catch a saucy lady sneaking peaks at him, and out of respect he'd wink back and garner the wrath of her man. Other times it was all a misunderstanding because of what he did with his eyes. He had a feel-things-deeply nature that he kept to himself because such a quality in men he thought sappy. He'd perfected a hardened look with his eyes to disguise how emotional he was but with his pretty-boy eyes, if you didn't know him, you'd swear he was glaring at you; a problem in places where liquor was being poured and men with diminished judgment mistook his practiced tough-eyes as calling them out for a fight. His own diminished judgment, though, was the real problem tonight as he eyed Frank who worked first shift at the dock. He'd suspected Frank of carousing with his last woman even while Alfred was still giving her half his pay. Another woman sat on Frank's lap right now whispering in his ear and Alfred watched Frank throw his head back and laugh with an open mouth. At that moment Nan appeared in front of Alfred and blocked his view. Her lips, their heart shape vaguely familiar, were moving but he couldn't understand what she was saying. "What? I can't hear you, what?" he said, shouting so loudly that even with the high volume of foot stomping and laughter and music, the people in his vicinity turned around to look at him, and at Nan.

Nan rubbed her hands up and down her bare arms, reacting first to Alfred's unfocused stare then to his booming voice telling her to speak up and now the sense that all eyes were on her. She felt threatened by the sudden attention. Felt naked. Wished right now that she'd used the leftover red satin fabric to make a cape so that at least her back could be covered. Torn between repeating what she'd just said, or mumbling out never mind and scurrying through the smell of chitterlings and rye to get the hell on out of here. Except that Alfred was up from the bar stool, now his hand was on her back, his hand thick and warm, and she had to steady herself as he leaned in to whisper in her ear. "You're right Miss Lady, I ain't got to take that disrespect from Frank, I'm do just what you suggesting. I'ma put my foot up his—'scuse my French, Miss Lady—his ass."

Nan tried to respond that she hadn't suggested anything like that but there was a disconnect between her brain and her vocal cords, all her neurons it seemed crowded in that space on her back where he had his hand, and jumping then to her ear, his breath pushing in her ear as she felt his spit droplets against her cheek, wished she could capture the drops, preserve them for Goldie's lady to use, forgot all about Goldie then, her lady, could barely remember her own name as she listened to Alfred tell her to take his seat at the bar. "Pretty that area up a bit with your red dress, Miss Lady," he said.

She didn't know what was happening anymore as she lifted herself up on the bar stool. Disoriented first over the fact that she was actually sitting on a bar stool, then over what Alfred had just said about some

Frank? Kicking Frank's ass? That *she'd* suggested he do it?! She tried to piece through the crowd to follow Alfred's pin-striped suit jacket. Stopped herself suddenly, then swiveled around ever so slowly to see if it was there. It was. Brown-colored liquid in a short glass, no ice. His drink. She was staring down at his drink.

She pulled back the clasp on her satin clutch purse and fingered the warm smooth glass of the vanilla extract bottle thinking this is too easy. She looked around her; the man on one side of her thoroughly engaged in loud talking about how a building had collapsed on him and he'd walked away unscathed, the man on the other side of her speaking love to the bowl of chitterlings he was gobbling. She put both her hands inside the purse to unscrew the lid but then she heard a voice say, Choose your poison, and she jumped and almost screamed. It was the bartender. "Whiskey sour's on the birthday boy tonight. You want that or something more'n that?"

"What's on the birthday boy is fine," she said as she closed her purse and thought it made a sound like a gun going off, then opened it again when the bartender walked away, hurrying to remove the bottle cap. She fitted the bottle in the palm of her hand and brought her hand up to scratch her cheek and in one quick motion lowered her hand and dumped the contents of the bottle into Alfred's drink. She dropped the empty bottle back into her clutch purse. Alfred's drink was now to the rim of the glass. It was too full. He would notice. She leaned her head in and gently raised the glass to soup up a bit. Her heartbeat was competing with the drums in here as she swallowed and then breathed deeply to try to settle herself though she felt the need suddenly to gag. The bartender returned and slid her drink down in the space next to Alfred's. She almost drained her own drink in several swallows, trying to douse the urge to spit up. She was surprised at how easily the drink went down. She felt warm suddenly, and pretty. Stifled the impulse to giggle as she angled herself on the bar stool and crossed her legs and looked out on the party time glad that she'd added the touch of black lace to the hem of her dress. Dresses worn by half of the women in here could have benefited from a redesign, she thought. Smiling now that Alfred had told her to pretty up the area. She did giggle now and let out a small belch that made her laugh even harder. Saw Alfred walking back in her direction. Was certain his eyes went soft for her as she lowered her lashes Josephine Baker–style and when he was standing right over her she let go with, "Hey, good looking, what you got cooking?"

"That depends, Miss Lady, what you wanting to be served?" he said as he reached in behind her and took his drink and held it in his hand.

She leaned in close to him the way she imagined Dorothy Dandridge might do. She liked the feel of him standing over her, so strong and sturdy, the sense of mutual proprietorship as she told herself that he didn't even need whatever were the contents of that vanilla extract bottle; hadn't his eyes just gone soft for her just like they had the day she peered into his eyes through the window of Sam's Delicatessen. She hadn't done any hocus-pocus that day. He turned the glass up to his lips and she held her breath while he swallowed, despite what she'd just told herself about not needing for him to drink it; she felt her whole chest open up when he put down his glass, his glass empty. But now he grimaced and motioned for the bartender.

"Why you watering down my Southern Comfort?" he barked at the bartender. "That's right. And don't look at me like I'm crazy. You the one crazy if you think I don't know my own Southern Comfort."

Nan pulled at his arm. "You know, Alfred, it just occurred to me, I might have drank yours by mistake and you, well maybe you just drank mine."

The bartender slammed another short glass of brown-colored liquid in front of Alfred. He glared at Alfred, then said, "Just to keep the peace, my man," and walked away.

"Now you see, Miss Lady, that's no respect." Alfred talked in Nan's ear. "Like Frank over there showing me no respect. I'm glad you called me back over here though, 'cause Frank ain't worth me bruising my knuckles over. Though I did promise him he's got an open invitation to meet my fist. What's your name, sugar?"

"Nan," she said, confused again about him saying she'd called him back over as she watched him empty this drink too and then motion for another one. "You might remember me from a few Saturdays ago at the bus stop on Spruce. Your sugar was high and well, I got lipstick on your jacket."

He smiled. "Yeah? Lipstick on my jacket. What? Were we dancing?"

"Yeah," she said. "We were dancing. I'm sorry you don't remember. You a good dancer, Alfred."

"Well, dance with me now. I swear on my dead momma's grave I won't forget this one."

He extended his hand to help Nan down from the bar stool. His hand, its vastness swallowed hers up and she felt dizzy from the heat of his hand, the heat of his entire large self as he covered her in his arms. He moved into her and then away, then back into her and she picked up his rhythm and followed him as if she'd been born doing this. The small space of a dance floor was crowded and they were jostled about but Nan barely noticed, so caught up in the feel of Alfred's arms caging her like this. She understood the nature of sin right now, thought sin nothing more than pure pleasure stretched to its extreme. This dance with Alfred, she thought, the purest, most pleasing thing she'd ever done. She let her head press against his chest, her head swimming, her equilibrium nonexistent, her ability to stand up straight right now totally dependent on Alfred's arms. She let herself go completely against him, was about to tell him that the room was spinning and she thought she might faint. Or fall. She was falling. She screamed and tried to hold on to Alfred but he was being pulled away and she ended up grabbing for the red and blue air. The air let her down. She hit the floor that pulsed like prairie land beneath a stampede. This was a stampede, she thought as she covered her face from the high heels and the thick leather soles coming down from all directions. Screaming coming down too practically doused by the heavy grunting sounds of men fighting, the umphs and ows and mother-fuck-shit-you-bast-I'ma-kick-your-ass sounds. A bar fight this was. She'd heard of such things from her unchurched cousins. Never imagined that she'd be caught up in one herself, praying for her life as she was now. Praying for Alfred too, hollering out his name. The floor quaked for real then. Alfred landed on his back next to Nan. A white balloon fell on top of him and bounced along his chest. It burst and Nan clutched at her heart and whispered, "Mercy Jesus." Alfred stared up at the ceiling. He made a laughing sound and then he was out.

Two ox-sized men dragged Alfred out of the bar by his feet. Nan followed behind yelling for them to watch his head, don't bang his head. He had high sugar anyhow and the whole thing with Frank, she was sure, was a misunderstanding. They left him on the ground on the corner of the Bainbridge Street bar. The ground intermittently red and blue from the flashing neon lights of the bar. Nan sat down on the ground next to him and put his head in her lap. She loosened his tie and fanned him and called his name. She pulled her lacey handkerchief from her purse and wiped at the trickle of blood under his nose. His lips were busted, his eyes on the way to swelling shut. She needed ice, witch hazel. The Sun Ray across the street long since closed this late on a Saturday night. She thought about trying to hail down a red car but that could get him arrested for public drunkenness. A trolley pulled to a stop on the corner. Its squealing brakes sounded like silver pellets hitting the pavement all around them, then the rumble as it rolled away leaving people like tree branches shaken loose after a storm. The people walking past them now feeling the need to comment and Nan wondered what gave them the nerve as they said things like: One too many, huh? and I'd send that nigger back where he came from, and Damn, somebody got their natural ass kicked tonight.

She rubbed his hair and kissed his forehead as if he was already the acknowledged love of her life. He started coming to then, squinted up at Nan. "Hey there, sugar, what's your name?" he asked.

She just shook her head back and forth. Didn't even matter that he didn't remember her name. She believed he knew her name. Could almost hear him calling her name from some nonintoxicated place burrowed deep inside of him and covered over with so many layers that even if whatever she'd poured into his drink had any power, it was impotent in the face of what Nan believed to be his goodness. That's what she thought she heard calling her name right now. His goodness.

"Doesn't matter what my name is," she said. "What matters is why I'm here."

"Why you here, sugar?"

"To help you change your ways."

"My ways are mine. Don't concern nobody but me."

"Your ways gonna be the death of you, Alfred. I can help you. I can save you, I know I can. Me and Jesus can save you."

Through the slits his punched-out eyes were becoming he took in

Nan, remembering the image of her on the bar stool, the scarlet-colored backless dress that formed her hips, the black seamed hose, the heart-shaped mouth, her hair unloosed around her face, and she bore, he thought, a striking resemblance to Lena Home. Looked like Lena Horne now with the blue and red light flashing down on her. No way he could deny Lena. No way he could continue on the route he was traveling either. She was right about that, it was killing him the hard way, over and over, every night a new awful death; every morning a head-in-the-toilet resurrection. He started to cry then. "Save me, Lena, please baby, save me."

Nan flagged down a cab and took him home to her apartment on Catherine Street that smelled to him of bleach and cake batter. She put ice to his lips, salve to his eyes, washed down the open cuts with peroxide. Then spooned him up the pot liquor from her mustard greens to help him fight off infection. No alcohol though. In the morning she left him a cup of strong black coffee on the end table next to the couch where he'd slept. Told him she was on her way to church, she'd be pleased to fry him a mess of eggs, when she returned, and layer it between buttered toast and salt pork, though she doubted he'd be able to keep it down. He confirmed that he wouldn't by clutching his stomach and she hurried for a pot for him to vomit in. Though he could barely lift his head because of the feel of hammers falling alternating from the front to the back, he managed to motion for her to come closer, whispered out that he was thirsty, please, please, could she leave him something to drink. She produced a pitcher of ice water, pulpy orange juice in a glass bottle. No alcohol though. He touched his head, his barely opened eyes, his cheekbone that throbbed to the beat of the hammers in his head. Gasped out that he was in pain, could she leave a little taste of something for pain. She said of course, what was she thinking, of course he needed something for the pain. Promptly offered Anacin tablets in a tin, the tin opened to make it easy for him. No alcohol though. When she returned from church she fussed over him, checked his forehead for a fever one minute, brought him ice chips sprinkled with ginger the next. Even whipped up two pair of pajamas from left-over blue fabric from the choir robes she'd made so that when he sweated through one, there was a crisp clean pair for him to change into. No alcohol though.

The second dry day at Nan's, Alfred was sure he would go into the shakes and end up in a sanitarium as he maneuvered the hallway to enter the healing parlor she had set up for him in the back bedroom where he took to the four-poster bed and collapsed all over again. It was a cozy room the color of cream from the ribbed bedspread to the lacy coverlet to the tuxedo-striped wallpaper to the velvet fainting chair to the boxy victrola for playing LPs. The coziness was lost on him at first but by the third day his eyesight had cleared and his stomach had settled and his senses opened to the rhythms of the house, the clean and quiet order of things, the smell of bleach early morning as she washed down the concrete of the backyard, the early morning rumba sounds her sewing machine made. He became accustomed to her sweet comings and her goings when before she left for work she'd offer him a Bible to thumb through, a *Tribune* to read. In the evenings she'd prop on the edge of the fainting couch across from the bed as he ate the meal she'd prepared that had progressed through the week from clear brothy renderings to stewed chicken and dumplings with homemade apple-sauce on the side.

She'd tell him about her day, how many sleeves she attached, the spats between coworkers. She'd relate the headlines, pieces of dropped gossip she'd picked up as she tunneled through the block home. Had only pieces to relate, not whole stories because she didn't tarry as was her usual custom from house to house. Didn't get her daily updates about the progression of this one's pregnancy, that one's mother-in-law travails, the other one with the bad-seed son. She was in too much of a hurry to get in her own front door. Enthralled as she was by the feel of opening her door in the afternoon knowing he was up here, the house seeming to know too the way the air sighed so contentedly from the living room to the kitchen, and especially as she'd move through the hallway and approach the back bedroom where he was tucked away, the pink pansies on the hallway wallpaper winking at her because his being here was a secret after all, not even Goldie knew that he was here.

By Friday Alfred's true coloring had returned and his robustness, Nan noticed as she sat on the edge of the fainting couch and chattered in a soft voice and watched Alfred enjoy the butterfish and rice. She was telling him about a dog she'd seen on her way to work. Described the black and white dog that she said had spooked her. Something about the dog's stance, the way he tilted his head reminded her of her dead uncle. The dog even tried to follow her onto the bus and when she called the dog by her uncle's name, said Uncle Latch, stay, stay, the dog put his head down, his tail between his legs, and slithered on around the corner. She said she practically cried the whole ride to work missing her uncle suddenly.

What Nan didn't say as she looked up at the frosted glass of the window with the hand-stained diamond in the center, keeping her focus on the sky-blue colored diamond instead of on him sitting up in the bed, his pleasing features having returned as the swelling went down, his manliness bursting through the hastily made pajamas, is how many times of the day she thought of him here, wanting to take her foot from the sewing machine pedal and rush home even as her workday was just beginning. Nor did she say right now that she guessed he'd be feeling his own strength soon enough and would leave here and head on home. Hoping as she thought it that he wasn't strong enough, not that she wanted him weak, she just wanted him here.

Alfred listened to the dog story; he was touched by the story. So much about Nan touched him since he'd been here. Strengthened him too. He even thought he might be able to tolerate a little jazz music this evening though he couldn't remember enjoying music without a drink in his hand. Thought this would be his test of making it as an on-the-wagon man, his ability to enjoy his music through undiluted ears. He cleared his throat and asked what kind of music did she have around the house, and if she had none at all that was fine. Wanted to say that her voice was music enough though he didn't say it; this too was something he was unaccustomed to doing without benefit of strong drink, acting on his impulse with a woman. Though he felt moved to be impulsive with Nan right now. That she wasn't beautiful moved him most of all, the purity of that. No having to question a beguiling smile for authenticity, no distracting nymph-like frame all up in his face clouding his logic as his pants pocket were emptied of his substantial end-of-the-week wages, no knock on the door followed by a guilty expression because she'd gotten her times with her men mixed up. Not that there weren't beautiful women who were honest and true, just that they had not been part of Alfred's repertoire. Thought how calming it would be to spend man-woman type time with someone of Nan's leanings as she left the room and returned shortly with half a dozen long-playing albums. The Dixie Hummingbirds was expected, Mahalia Jackson too, but glory, glory she had the Billie's, Billie Holiday, Billy Eckstine. She put on "Everything I Have Is Yours" and Alfred drummed his fingers and craved a closeness with Nan. Though right now he also felt the craving for drink as an ant crawling up his throat trying to reach his tongue to incite his taste buds into a revolt. He swallowed hard to get rid of the craving but it caught in his throat and gagged him. Nan ran to get the pot that he'd used earlier in the week when he was in the throwing-up stage. He didn't throw up now as Nan leaned over him with the pot. She was wearing a white cottony housedress trimmed in pink eyelet lace. Her innocence astounded him as he allowed her nearness, the effect her nearness was having on him to grow larger than the craving for drink. He stroked her arm. "I don't need that," he said motioning to the pot. "All I need is you."

"Well, well now, is that so?" Nan said as she stood straight up wondering suddenly what to do with the pot. The whole week he'd been here she'd imagined herself ripping through her handiwork of the blue pajama top to get to the broad thickness of his bared upper body, to rub big circles on his chest, to slide her mouth along his collarbone, to pull the pajama bottoms down and straddle him. And here he was stroking her arm, turning the skin on her arm to butter, melting her arm to cream with just the back and forth of his hands; his eyes were focused and starved for her; his manhood rising for her beneath the blue fabric. Here was the essence of her imaginings as she'd hit the pedal at work to start the sewing machine and twice almost lost a thumb, her concentration so fully on him. Here were the imaginings come to life, gathering sight and sound, smell and touch and taste for the culmination in real life and Nan was stymied. Though it wasn't her religion stopping her right now, nor was it that the window was open to halfway and anyone happening to be sitting on the back steps of houses on either side of her might be privy to the Lawd, Lawd, Lawd sounds; she wasn't even stopped by the fact that she had no diaphragm, no jelly, no rubbers; stopped right now by the simplest thing, the got-damned pot. Its speckled oversized circumference caught between the bed and the wall. She tried to keep her movements subtle to nudge it up or down and finally used her knee to pop it up, almost said Fucking pot, though she wasn't the cursing kind as she flung it to the other side of the room. She never heard the cymbal-like sound as it clanged against the wall because Alfred took over once she was free of the pot.

He was both gentle and ferocious as he lifted her short self onto the bed and slipped his hands under her housedress and squeezed her to him. He told her that he needed her but she was so pure and he had blotches all up and down his soul, the things he'd done, but oh did he need her. His hands were hot against her back and then he moved his hands in big sweeps and started a fire wherever he touched her. Made her cry, made her holler Mercy in ways that redefined the word. Felt herself opening in places that she didn't even know were places. Pictured suddenly a maple tree with its startling crown in full leaf, its trunk so wide she couldn't get her arms all the way around, its bark coarse and layered all the way through to the pith, to the core to where the sap was rising so full of itself that it needed just a tap, some pressure on insertion, then the gushing could come, thick, so sweet, shaking the forest floor with its coming, or was that the bed shaking, the cream-colored coverlet tossed high and caught on the bedpost waving like a flag signaling surrender, yielding then, giving in.

"My, my, my," she said as she collapsed against him and rubbed her fingers through his hair that was thin and fine. "Mercy. Mnh, mercy, mercy, me."

Saturday, a week to the day of his arrival, Alfred was dressed to leave. His pin-striped suit pressed to Nan's high standards, his shirt crisply starched, a shine to his shoes. He was going to pick up his paycheck, he said, make sure he still had a job to go to come Monday given that he'd been absent for a week. Would she like barbecue ribs for dinner? he asked, fried fish? a quart of something from Chinatown. Just name whatever she had an appetite for and he'd make it appear; he swore he would.

Just you walking your strong, fine self back through my door will satisfy what I got an appetite for, Nan said, blushing, unaccustomed as she was to talking like this. She'd talked like this at the Bainbridge Street bar when she had whiskey sours swimming through her head, though again she pushed the details of that night from her mind because she did not choose to think again about the potion she'd slipped in his drink, did not want to wonder whether the fact that he'd slurped down the contents of that vanilla extract bottle had everything to do with him being here. Told herself again that whatever he'd drunk that night had come out from both ends in his massive excretion of bodily fluids. She never believed in the power of root-working anyhow. Still the thought that she now owed the devil for delivering to her Alfred hung in her mind, swayed there like a hem coming undone on a curtain valance, the threads dropping, no longer holding the billowy bottom in place.

Chapter 4

AD NATHAN, THE blanched-colored man who'd just left Nan's house looking for Neena, known where he was going, he would have parked at the other end of the block, and in doing so would have run right into Neena.

A sitting duck Neena was the way she was glued to the corner this morning, unable to continue up the block to Nan's house. Needed a rock hard stomach to say, Nan, things have happened and I need a place to stay for a night or two. Her stomach was tender though. Her entire self was. This being February for her too. Missing Freeda too.

Her real intention anyhow had been to go to Tish's house, but Tish had moved recently to a redone Victorian somewhere in historically certified Overbrook Farms and the new address was in the condo where Neena had been living in Chicago. The unit padlocked the day before by the man who owned it. Luckily Tish's cell phone number had not changed and Neena had been calling Tish since then. Had even tried to reach Goldie at her assisted-living facility, but was told that

Goldie was part of a group sickened on a bus trip to the casinos and the group was under quarantine for the next several days. Finally yesterday evening, a live voice answered Tish's phone. Neena was unaware that Tish's cell phone calls had been transferred to her home phone, and that Nan was there, so Neena ended up speaking to Nan—the absolute last person she wanted to speak to. Worse still, she learned that her sister was threatening to miscarry.

Since Goldie and Tish were it for Neena in the way of help: no girlfriends, no extended family with whom she was close enough to call; she lumbered here to ask her grandmother for help. But now she faltered. She'd only gotten this close to Nan's house because of what the man she'd met last night had said to her about a living bridge. Neena always in the state of having just met a man. Nice men mostly, married with pretty wives and reputations to protect; the soft-type man who'd been close to his mother making it easy for Neena to fake adoration, making him quick to pay when she'd shake him down in the end. That's how she'd supported her nomadic lifestyle as she hopscotched from city to city tracking down dead-end leads to her mother. Though the man who'd encouraged her here was atypical.

It was last night. She'd just landed back in Philadelphia—not landed as in a plane touching down on a runway at Philly International, landed as in body and soul hitting the ground at the end of a nosedive. Eighteen hours prior she'd returned to the Chicago condo from a trip to San Francisco, an ophthalmology convention where her eye-doctor boyfriend Cade was receiving a humanitarian award for his work with seniors. Cade's wife had decided to accompany him at the last minute and when Neena said, Not a problem, that she would just hang in Chicago and see him when he returned, he'd insisted that Neena come along, though on a different flight, a room arranged for her in a nearby hotel.

The experience was disconcerting for Neena, meant that Cade was getting careless. Decided to end it with him that weekend over dinner at McCormick & Schmick's while his wife enjoyed a ladies-night boat ride up the San Francisco Bay.

She manufactured tears and dangled him the line that had garnered her payoffs other times: that an ex-boyfriend had gotten into her apartment and hidden a camera in her bedroom and wanted ten thousand dollars to keep the pictures of their naked selves off the Internet. Cade was eating lobster tails and his lips were glistening from the butter sauce, thin lips, and it suddenly occurred to Neena that lips that thin on a black person meant that he was stingy. Plus he was red-complexioned and her grandmother always said that red-colored Negroes were mean. She felt a thump in the pit of her stomach as she watched the butter on his lips glaze over, lips so shiny that they reflected the candlelight and it appeared as if a rainbow had spread out over his thin lips; his skin tone so red at that moment that it was as if she was watching the sun set. Knew right then that he wasn't going to pay. Even as he nodded, and said, "Okay, ten thousand," woodenly, his mouth moving as if it was being controlled by a puppeteer. "I'll get you the money, Neena, okay."

She knew then that when she got back to Chicago she'd have to pack up what she could and head for Detroit. Though when she did return she was met in the hallway by Cade's brother Tito, delivering to Neena a get-out-of-town-by-sundown message. Said what he ought to do to her for trying to extort money from his brother. Said he ought to make like her face was a frozen-over lake and he was an ice fisher trying to get at a silver trout. The threat scared Neena and she didn't scare easily. That he'd been so descriptive meant to her that he'd actually visualized himself slashing through the skin on her face. And she had a nice face. Not classically beautiful but odd in a way that was hard and soft and sultry with its asymmetrical arrangement as if her features had been shaped more for artistic interest than for prettiness with the heavy severe eyes and the gushy smile, the molded cheekbones, the subtly formed nose. Shaken, she'd asked if she could just get into the apartment for a few things, personal things.

A half laugh was Tito's response, not unlike the heater man's half laugh all those years ago when Neena had asked him if they could work something out in exchange for his getting the heater going. This Tito was even more of a bottom feeder, a nonaccomplished slot-machine addict who humped off of his brother's success. Collected a nice paycheck for a couple of hours a week of shuttling Cade's half-blind elderly patients to and from appointments. He touched Neena's face; he had soft hands like his brother Cade had soft hands. Neena remembered suddenly stories she'd heard about her grandfather's hands, Freeda's father. He'd been a stevedore on the waterfront and all that manual labor had left his hands callused and rough as tree bark. But they were magic hands, Freeda used to tell Neena, when he pinched your cheek, or touched the center of your forehead with his thumb, or swung your hand inside of his on the way to get cherry water ice, all you felt was the softness, as if his inside goodness came out through his hands. Neena thought that this one's hands were the antithesis of her grandfather's. This one's hands had the feel of his inside meanness, felt as if a steel wool pad stroked her face right now.

The people who lived across the hall from Neena were having dinner. An older couple, refined, the husband a retired anthropology professor, the wife a botanist. Neena could hear the gentle tinkle of metal against glass coming from their apartment. Nancy Wilson singing "You've Changed" floated into the hallway on air weighted with the aroma of baked manicotti. Neena willed them not to look through their peephole. She'd told them that she was a student at Harold Washington College majoring in political science. Believable enough since was always taking a course albeit noncredit somewhere or another. Always with a book or two protruding from her bag. Right now her tote held *A Short History of Nearly Everything* that she'd been reading on the plane ride back from San Francisco. Couldn't stand the shame of what she really was: a failed daughter who hustled married men.

Tito's soft, rough hands pulled at the silk scarf atop her coat. She thought she might vomit though she swallowed hard and told herself to just do what she had to do to get into the apartment and at least scoop up her jewelry, pictures of her and Tish with Freeda when Freeda was happy. She knew without having yet checked that the credit cards Cade had opened for her would be dead now, the bank accounts that he'd controlled where she'd foolishly put money that was legitimately hers, her cell phone too she was sure would be without service.

Tito's fingers rubbed her neck, making circles toward her throat as he drew his boxy face toward hers to kiss her. She tried to tell him that they should go inside, but the sound that came out of her was more like a screeching half cry, followed by three short gags.

He pushed at her shoulder then. "What's that about?" he asked, his voice ricocheting from one side of the hall to the other. "You trying to say I repulse you or some shit?"

Before Neena could reply, the door opened to the apartment across the hall. The couple stood there side by side, she in a black velour lounging set dabbing her lips with a white cotton napkin, he in brown corduroys and a tan sweater. They looked like someone's concerned mother and father. They were childless, Neena knew, and now she thought what excellent parents they would have made. Wished right now that they were her parents, even as she wished that the floor beneath her would give way so that she wouldn't have to stand here so filled with shame in the path of their concern.

She forced a smile. "Evening," she said, then turned and started down the hall. Walked away from the contents of that apartment just like that. All those things: the gold and silver, the leather and cashmere and silk; the designer's name stamped or etched or sewn or painted on the label or lining, the strap or flap or sole. The accumulations of a lifetime. Pathetic when she thought about it.

She didn't know if Tito would follow her so once she was out on the street she started to run. Ran all the way to the bus station. Found an old debit card in the back of her purse from a bank in Newark with a $183 balance. That would more than get her to Detroit. Except that when the ticket agent smiled and asked where was the pretty lady headed, and she looked at his eyebrows, eyebrows like Mr. Cook's who used to own the store at the corner of Nan's block, Detroit never came out of her mouth. "Philly," she said instead. "I'm headed home to Philly."

She felt like such a cliché sitting on the bus, sweating in her black-on-black designer garb, her overpriced knee-high boots, her leather bag. Kept hearing the Lou Rawls song about living double in a world of trouble as she rocked herself the whole bus ride, telling herself not to cry. She rarely cried.

It was snowing when the bus pulled into the Philadelphia station at Tenth and Filbert. About seven at night and Neena was glad for the snow. Always thought that the snow softened the city. Made Philadelphia feel charming and safe like a storybook of a town where every house had an unlocked door and a frolicking spotted pet dog.

Bow Peep, the man who would talk Neena into going to Nan's,

thought a similar thing about a nighttime snow in Philly as he stood outside of the bus station and scanned the faces. A street corner musician, a flutist, he mostly fancied himself a prophet-type healer. Looked like a prophet right then with his long woolly hair and leather sandals like Jesus wore. Strapped on the sandals even on snowy days, which made him look half crazy. Though crazy, he would say, would be pulling on wool socks over the jungle rot that he'd picked up in Vietnam more than thirty years ago. The snow's cold wetness was wonderful against his feet as he pushed his trained breath through his flute and competed against the wide swaths of city sounds, the car horns and road rage–type cursing and loud talking in dialects from highbrow to hip-hop. He didn't mind that he was generally ignored out here. Understood that most prophets had low approval ratings in their own lands. And anyhow there was the occasional audience ripe for a prophet encounter who'd stop and stand in front of him. So he played against the elements. Played "Tenderly" as the oblivious people rushed past. And here she was, an audience stopping to listen. She was under forty-young, he guessed. Odd-looking in a pretty way with wild fluffy hair and features that stopped short of too prominent. He bent way back to hit a high note and tried to send her a healing vibe through the music, then pulled his flute from his mouth and asked what was her name.

"Neena," she said. She reached into her purse and pulled up a five-dollar bill. Broke as she was, she was still touched by how hard he was working out here so she let the money flutter down into the faded green, snow-speckled lining of his flute case.

"Well it's gonna be all right in a minute, Neena."

"Yeah?" she said. "Define minute."

He was about to talk about the relativity of time and circumstance but now here was Cliff in front of him, his like-a-brother homey from way back reaming him out about being out here in the snow without proper foot gear. He didn't tell Cliff his rudeness was disrupting a transformation in the early stages. The first stage was always the stopping to listen the way this young lamb just had, meant that the receptivity was already in place. Trying to explain that to Cliff would mean an interrogation about his meds. Instead he introduced them. "Neena, please meet the finest civil rights attorney in all of Philadelphia, and the best friend the universe could ever bestow on a naked-toed musician such as me."

"Neena," Cliff said, extending his hand, looking beyond Neena. His attention pulled to the other side of the street. Neena shook his hand, sizing him up the way she'd been sizing men up since the heater man in the basement. This one in a nice cashmere coat, meticulously shaved mustache, strong features though incredibly sad eyes. She looked away from his eyes, had a weakness for men with sad eyes that she guessed she'd inherited from her mother.

She looked down at his hands. "You should have on gloves," she said.

"I don't need them. I've got tough hands," he answered, as he turned his attention from the other side of the street. He started to say something about tough hands meaning a tender heart but stopped himself. Too much of a line; too true for him these days given the situation between him and his wife. The situation unnamed, just an unsettled murkiness between them.

More out of habit than the desire to know him more, Neena asked Cliff for a card. He reached beneath his coat into his breast pocket. "You haven't been denied access because of your race or gender lately, have you?" he asked, trying to make a joke.

"Not tonight, but the night is young," she said as she fingered the card, and then slipped it into her purse heavy with the weight of the dead—dead cell phone, dead credit cards, dead checkbook. She smiled at Cliff, thanked Bow Peep for the music, then hurried off.

She was still posttraumatic from her encounter with Tito and for a second she thought that she saw him in her peripheral vision. Told herself that she was being silly as she tried to lose herself in the crush of the after-work foot traffic, looking around for a pay phone to try again to reach Tish.

She was on Broad Street in front of the Ritz-Carlton that used to be a bank. She approached the coated Ritz-Carlton doorman, slipped under the oversized umbrella he held, and smiled her gushy smile, and when he smiled back and said, Ma'am, good evening, she went into a story of having just left her cell phone in a friend's car. Could she please use his to make a thirty-second call. He glanced at her hand and she went down into her purse, found a single dollar bill, and pressed it in his mammoth hand, thinking with hands that large he needed to be playing football instead of opening doors for thankless people to come and go and taking her needed dollar when his minutes were probably free anyhow. She sat on the bench and held her breath and dialed Tish's number. Hoped Tish and not her husband would answer. "Tish?" she said as soon as she heard the nonmale "hello" on the other end. The "hello," though, hadn't come from Tish. The "hello" was in that flat, airless tone. Nan's tone. Had she dialed Nan's number just now by mistake. No, she was sure she had not.

A pause, then, "Neena? Is this you, Neena?"

"It is, yes, Nan? How are you, Nan?"

"I'm doing, I'm doing. How are you is the question? Where are you? Are you in Philadelphia?"

"Just passing through, just wanted to say hello to Tish," Neena said imagining that Nan's face was opening and closing with that look of irritated relief, relieved that Neena was alive, but irritated nonetheless to have Neena's voice pushing in her ear.

"Just passing through?" Nan asked. "Headed from where to where?"

"I'm just, just headed to a meeting for my job, a conference." Neena tried to keep a lift to her voice.

"Are you sure you're all right, Neena?"

A forest sprouted in Neena's throat suddenly and blocked her reply of, yes I'm sure. She tried to push her voice through the thorny denseness, the thicket. She heard her grandmother calling her then from the other side of the trees, Nan's voice fading in and out, an urgent voice her grandmother used that snapped the end from Neena's name and sounded like a sharp breath. She cleared her throat. "I'm here, yes, Nan. I'm all right. I'm fine."

"You sure? You gonna stop past so somebody can get a look at you and see for themselves if you're all right?"

"It's—you know, if there's time, there's this meeting thing—I really wanted Tish's new address—"

"You not lying, are you?"

"About wanting Tish's address—"

"About some meeting—"

"God, Nan, why do you always have to assume the worst about me?"

"Well, you will lie. Am I right? Your mother would run off but she—"

"God, Nan, please! I didn't call—God, I called for Tish. May I speak to my sister, please."

"Well, now, Neena, if you kept in touch the way you belong to do, you'd know your sister's not well. In the hospital. Threatening to miscarry—"

"Threatening to miscarry?" The panic-driven spike in Neena's voice drew the Ritz-Carlton doorman's attention as he turned from helping a couple into the back of a cab and hunched his shoulder and motioned his hands to Neena in a yo what's up with my phone kind of way. Neena signaled to him with a raised finger just a minute, then asked Nan what hospital.

"Not a good idea to tell you that, Neena—"

"What are you saying, Nan—"

"Not the best thing for Tish to be shocked by your presence all of a sudden, too hard on her in her delicate condition, she's got enough to do to try to hold on to the baby."

"I can't believe you're saying this to me—"

"I can't believe you wouldn't have thought it already, if you thought about more than yourself sometimes and your own devilish desires—"

Neena pressed the phone off. Walked it back over to the doorman and just nodded because she couldn't talk. He wasn't trying to talk anyhow as he dropped the phone in his pocket and opened the door to the town car that had just pulled up. Her feet were weighted suddenly as she stood on the corner thinking about what to do. She tried to slow her breathing. Tried not to feel anything right now because anything she felt would be too imprecise, too muddled to call by a name the way a psychiatrist she'd been with said was necessary to do. Give what you're feeling a name, he'd insisted, and then the emotion will be manageable. She started down the alphabet: afraid, blue, conflicted, deflated, effaced, fucked, was that an emotion? How about gored? Hope, she hoped with everything in her that Tish would hold on to the baby.

Stuck at H now, Hate. She hated Nan. Blamed Nan for the way her mother would disappear. Abandoned the alphabet but at least her breathing was coming under control.

She started walking. Turned onto Market Street and tried to console herself with the fact that although she had no arranged place to sleep tonight, at least she'd made it here during a nighttime snow so that the city was more a silhouette; its hardness shadowed in muted outlines forming a picture pretty enough to be in a storybook. She looked up on City Hall under a coating of snow, imagined the *clop, clop* of horse-drawn carriages. Walked now through City Hall courtyard. Now she felt trapped in a gothic tragedy the way shadows were falling overpowering the snow. She curled her toes in her boots to keep them back from where the cold moisture seeped in as she walked closely behind a woman carrying a bag from Miss Tootsie's gourmet soul food. The woman talking on a cell phone saying that dinner was lovely, and oh what nice portions, and she was bringing home a doggie bag good for a whole 'nother meal. Neena followed the woman down the steps to the el—often found herself following random women who looked to be about the age her mother would be, fantasizing that it was, that she'd call out "Mommy!" and Freeda would turn around and turn on that beatific smile and say Hi doll, how's my doll baby. The fantasy scrambling like a bad cable signal when the women turned around, like this woman was doing now, warily at first, relaxing when she saw it was Neena behind her and not some purse-snatching thug, Neena having the thought that given her dire situation she could become just that, or worse. Become a she-wolf waiting for the moon to rise.

She walked the length of the platform. The el that would take her to she had no idea where was coming like a silver bullet kicking up the urine-scented air down here. She got on the el. She tried to settle into the train's clackity motion. Looked around the el to distract herself. The assemblage of commuters dotting the seats made up an international brew that surprised Neena: Asian, African, Middle Eastern, probably a few Latinos that she guessed she was taking for black. A police woman leaned against the pole, the gun in her holster expanding her hips to plus-size. She was saying something about Fifty-second Street to an old cat in a leather Sixers bomber. Neena got an image of Fifty-second Street then, remembered when it was a bustling retail strip by day, a partygoer's paradise by night. The devil's trap, her grandmother called it. "You go down there on a Friday or Saturday after dark," Nan used to say, "and the devil gonna have you in his clutches, have you doing his bidding until the day you die and you join him to burn up in hell for all eternity."

Neena knew Nan was just trying to scare them; it had worked with Tish. Smiled now remembering how Tish wouldn't venture onto Fifty-second Street even during the day when it was dense with normal people banking at Provident National or buying lemon pound cake from the Cookie Jar, a Baldwin novel from Hakim's. Neena, though, walked the strip regularly in the aftermaths of her mother's perennial disappearances, trying to find her from among the women propped on bar stools laughing with too much fervor. Her mother's bottomed-out moods always sending her down here to grovel with people she would barely acknowledge when she was up. When she was up she'd socialize with respectable men who'd take Freeda and the girls to wholesome places like the Franklin Institute where they'd walk through the giant-sized heart. Neena's mother telling her that whenever Neena crossed her mind, which was a thousand times a day, her heart would feel as large as the one they tiptoed through at Franklin Institute.

Suddenly Neena wanted to be on Fifty-second Street as the el pulled into the station. She got up abruptly and slid through the doors just before they closed, and walked down the steps from the platform onto a desolate stomped-to-the-ground corner that was so far from her memory of the area that she just stood there at first, gasping, feeling as if she'd just stepped across the rotting threshold into an abandoned house. Wondered how much worse it would look without the softening effects of the snow. Developers obviously hadn't refound this part of West Philly yet, hadn't sent the explorers, the pioneers, in to resettle the way she'd heard they were starting to do even along Ridge Avenue in North Philly. She breathed through her mouth because the corner smelled like mold. A fried chicken place across the street did little to erase the smell, but at least it sent up a cracked swath of light and she could see beyond the steel-grated building of what had been a booming Woolworth's, up the street to a broken neon sign with only the apostrophe lit. The orange-red apostrophe soaked up the snowflakes as soon as they landed and seemed to say something possesses me, just don't ask what. The idea of the broken sign fit so with what the area had become that Neena walked up the street and on inside.

Neighborhood bars were generally not her preference and this one appeared to have outlived its usefulness. It was warm in here at least. The light, though, was as shallow as what she'd left on the outside save circles of sky blue that bounced around an old-fashioned jukebox right now playing Otis Redding. A rail-thin bartender seemed half asleep when she walked up to the bar and asked if there was a pay phone she could use. He motioned to the back of the bar and she dug in her purse for a quarter to occupy herself so she wouldn't appear to be looking around the bar, even though she was looking around the bar. Picked out the man wearing a burgundy cable-knit sweater as the one most likely to hit on her. Would have to be him, he appeared to be the only man with any life moving through him from among the three or so other unattached men in here who seemed zombied out at tables barely illuminated by candles so small they weren't even threatening to the plastic red carnations sprouting from shot glasses.

She was at the back of the bar now, her hand finally on that near-extinct specimen, a pay phone. She dialed her sister's number hoping for Tish's husband, prepared to hang up the phone should Nan answer again. Then there it was, Tish's voice in prerecorded form saying, "This is the day the Lord hath made, I rejoice, am so glad that you called." Neena swayed from the sound of her sister's voice melting in her ear. Imagined Tish with a rounded stomach, Tish with her God-loving disposition, her sunny compliance to whatever the rules were, her petite cuteness that never garnered the type of attention from men that Neena's appearance had. Tish pregnant. Thought back to when Tish had told her. It was in the fall, Neena remembered, because Tish was rushing off to a Halloween party sponsored by her sorority for children living in a homeless shelter. Only nice costumes, Tish had stressed. Fairy god-mothers and angels and puppy-dog type costumes. "They've seen enough monsters in their young lives," Tish had said, and then started to cry. Tish was always easy to cry. So unlike Neena who rarely did. Neena didn't leave a message. She called information to try to extract her sister's address, had tried also before she boarded the bus in Chicago. Got the same response now, a private listing. She waited for an operator to try to convince the live voice that since she knew the phone number, she should be privy to the address. To no avail.

She swallowed the desperation trying to edge up her throat as she walked to the bar and took a seat. Counted to ten. By the time she got to nine there he was talking in her ear, the man in the burgundy cable-knit sweater. "Hey lady," he said. She exhaled softly, wishing for a mint against the roof of her mouth to overpower the smell in here of bad whiskey and overwrought cologne. "My name is Ramsey," he continued, "and I don't mean to intrude if you just want to sit here and be with yourself, but I just gotta say that you are the finest thing that's walked through that door in all the years I been coming in here, and I been coming in here a lotta, lotta years. What's your name, doll face?"

She angled slightly the swiveling bar stool so she could see him. He had a dark mouth, and a neatly trimmed mustache, a broad nose and chin, wide shoulders. A wedding band, of course. He leaned in closer and she could see the blazing white shirt collar atop his sweater. The collar line was pressed and clean and she hoped the shirt had been laundered at the cleaners and not at the hands of some hardworking wife doing double time. When her mother had had an ongoing relationship with the married man Wendell, Neena had been hyper for it to end. Though Neena had always been able to reconcile her own time with a married man.

"Doll Face," she said then to his shirt collar.

"Excuse me?"

"You said, 'What's your name, Doll Face,' and I'm telling you my name. It's Doll Face." She focused on his mouth, the way it took its time pulling back to a full-throttle grin. He had long, straight teeth, too white to be his own.

"Oh, you a kidder, huh," he said on a laugh. "Well, I like to play."

"No, no. For real," she said. "That's really my name. My last name is Face. My daddy named me Doll. I have a sister named Sweet and one named Baby and my brother's name is Bold."

His lower lip folded and unfolded itself several times as if that's where his brain was, as if his lip was charged with determining whether or not she was just messing with him. His lip deciding to go with it, she could tell, as his tongue quickly wiped away the residue of thought and he was smiling again. "What you drinking tonight, Doll Face? Whatever your pleasure, I'm here to make it happen."

"I'll just have ginger ale."

"That's all, nothing stronger?" he asked, disappointment hanging on the end of the question as he made hand motions to the stick figure tending the bar. "You don't drink?"

"I do." She played with her fingers. "I'm just going through a thing right about now and I need to feel what I'm feeling."

"Might help a pretty lady to tell a stranger all about it? Care to join me at my table?"

He extended his hand and she looked at him under-eyed, feigning shyness.

"I swear I don't bite," he said and she hesitated and counted three beats in her head and then allowed him to help her down from the bar stool. She followed him to a table in the back of the room. Red miniature lights framed a heart-shaped wreath on the wall behind his head and made it look as if he had donkey ears. Wondered then if that was a sign that he was a jackass. She suppressed the sudden need to laugh at the thought as she unbuttoned her coat and slid her arms out, unzipped the ankle boots, and lifted her feet back so they could dry. She could feel him staring at her, trying to get her to look at his eyes. She refused. Folded her hands on the table instead and furled and unfurled her fingers. He grabbed her pinky finger and squeezed it and she looked at his wedding band, a thick solid gold; her eyes then traced the hair on his hand to his watch, a black-face Movado.

"You from 'round here?" he asked.

She shook her head, no. "Georgia," she said.

"Oooh, a southern girl, they grow them pretty down there. I been there plenty of times. Atlanta. The Big Peach. Had me some hot times in hotlanta."

She looked up beyond his head to the wall and those red lights again shaped like donkey ears that fit his head so exactly. Even when he turned to acknowledge the bartender as he set their drinks down, the lights seemed to turn with him. She tried to think of the sound a donkey made, a hee-haw sound. That was a mistake because everything he said now resembled that sound. Now she was going to laugh. She bit her lip. Felt so mean to sit up here and laugh at the man. He was raising his glass in a toast. "Here's to Georgia," he said, though she heard hee-haw and she couldn't hold it in. She covered her face with her hands and the laugh caught in her throat and came out like sobs. He squeezed in the chair next to hers. His arm wrapping all around her shoulder telling her to let it out, might help to tell ole Ramsey all about it, if he was anything, he was a good listener.

She manufactured tears, then let them slide melodramatically down her face. Sipped her ginger ale and put a tremble to her faux southern accent as she told him that she was sad and lonely. Her husband had just left her for her best friend and she felt incapable of trusting another human being ever.

"You can trust me. Baby, I'm for real," he said. As if on cue the Dells crooned from the juke box, "Stay in My Corner," the longest slow-drag song on the planet if you were caught dancing with the wrong person. "Come on, doll face, I think they're playing our song," he said as Neena sniffed hard and yielded to his pull on her elbow. He sang in her ear as they danced just a foot away from the table. She closed her eyes as he held her tightly and gently at the same time. She felt nothing.

Ramsey whispered to her in that man-about-to-burst-begging voice that they needed a more private corner for her to stay in. Asked her then if she would like to go for a ride over the Ben Franklin Bridge? He'd just gotten an E-ZPass and had nowhere he needed to be for the rest of the night. Didn't have the confines of a day job either because he'd gotten a generous early-out deal when the naval shipyard closed down in the nineties.

Neena interrupted him to ask about the wedding band.

"Oh that," he said, "means nothing," going on to explain that he was in the midst of separating from his wife.

She assumed that he was lying though she couldn't tell for sure because she never looked in his eyes. Didn't look in his eyes now as they sat again at the table and he talked about his two grown daughters. His voice went soft and innocent when he told her how much his daughters looked like his mother. She figured he wouldn't be rough or violent as he asked again if she'd like to help him christen his E-ZPass.

She kept her eyes on the table, rubbed her finger around his wedding band. "On one condition," she said.

"Name it," he said, and she heard the excitement in his voice shaping his words so that they sounded like gunshots.

"I have a weak stomach in a car," she said. "And those God-awful stick shifts are the worse. I do declare you'll be stopping every other block for me to lean out the car if you drive a stick shift. So if you don't drive a stick, I do believe I'm inclined to go for a little ride."

He laughed with an open mouth as he frantically dug his hands in his pocket and pulled up a slim wad of cash and pushed two fives down on the table. "I drives a Ford Tempo, baby. And my ride is as smooth or as hard as you want it to be." He helped her with her coat, then ran his fingers through her hair all the way to her scalp and said that he loved her hair, he hadn't seen hair like that since he'd marched with Angela Davis in Montgomery.

"Huh?" Neena asked, turning to face him. She knew that Angela Davis was too young for Montgomery; she assumed he was joking.

"Angela Davis," he said. "You know who she is, don't you? She was a fine something back in the day with her militant self. Yeah, that Angela Davis had a head of hair, hair didn't even budge when they turned those fire hoses on us."

She looked down again, at the worn vinyl flooring, and said Jesus to herself. Then suggested that they stop at one of the thousands of liquor stores on Baird Boulevard so that he could get what he liked to drink, thinking the quicker for him to pass out with. He told her, no need, he carried his pleasures with him at all times, right in his car trunk. She was relieved that at least he didn't say in his pants.

He turned into the parking lot of a roadside motel that boasted twenty-four-hour cable. "Lovely rooms at this place," he whispered in her ear as he checked in with a debit card, then once inside the room that smelled of Lysol and bug spray he tossed his coat on the bed, barely giving Neena a chance to hang hers in the closet before he was grabbing at her, pushing his fingers through her hair again, telling her how much he loved her hair. She held him tightly and sniffled and when he pulled himself back to look at her, to ask her what was wrong, was she thinking about that two-timing husband of hers, she looked down at the wheat-colored carpet and mumbled out that she had just had a female procedure done the day before and she was limited in her womanly abilities, forcing the tears again, "but oh, my, my, my, we can improvise," she said, as she pulled him in a slow drag and used her knee the quicker to bring his essence down, which badly spotted her skirt, thank goodness it was black, wool.

She went into the bathroom and wiped the skirt and while she was at it washed her stockings with a thimble-sized bottle of shampoo. She tried to focus on everything outside of herself: the emerald green of the shampoo seeping into the nylon, the sweet minty smell; anything so that her interior would remain integrated, so that she wouldn't separate from herself and start floating around in this bathroom and see herself with an objective detachment, that she'd just gone into a ghetto bar and allowed herself to be picked up and brought to some roadside dive. She hung the skirt and stockings from the showerhead even noticing the graceful way the neck to the showerhead curved, like a swan's, she thought, as she went back into the bedroom and sat in her turtleneck and panties next to Ramsey while he ha ha-ed at the television. "A *Green Acres* marathon on tonight. I swear this is some funny shit," he said. He seemed so wide awake, so sober, she wondered if it was just water in that bottle, not vodka.

She sat there for a full two hours watching the unintelligible banter, trying not to think about her mother; when her mother was buoyant she would sometimes talk in an accent like that, calling Neena and Tish darling the way Zsa Zsa was saying it now; whatever else she was saying had Ramsey shaking the bed, he was laughing so hard. She rolled her eyes up into her head, thinking he was intentionally trying to spite her by not finally passing out.

She got up to go to the bathroom. She locked the bathroom door and sat on the side of the tub and asked herself what was she even doing here. She'd not done anything this low-budget ever. She tried to convince herself that she'd only gone into that little neighborhood bar in West Philly because of the lit apostrophe, because she felt that's what her life had come down to as well, the nomenclature blacked out, the apostrophe still glowing orange-red though. Told herself that she'd only left with Ramsey because he had wide shoulders and she thought that he'd be content to let her lay her head close to his heart for a while. She told herself she'd just wanted to fall asleep counting heartbeats. Wondered if that was even possible anymore, did such softness even exist.

The stockings were swinging as they hung from the showerhead. She felt them. They were damp, but dry enough, she thought, deciding she'd tell him she was ready to go. Go where? Where? Nan's!? She felt a scream edging up her throat. She certainly couldn't go to Nan's in the middle of the night like this. Couldn't go there period now that she'd acted like a common street whore. Nan would smell her wrongdoing the way she always had. She jammed a fist into her mouth so she wouldn't scream. Sat down on the side of the tub to try to focus on her breathing. The stockings swaying from the showerhead made shadows on the wall and she was getting the picture of a fresh-killed piglet swinging over the sawdust-covered floor of a Ninth Street butcher shop. The image making her think of her mother, the way her mother would sometimes stop at the butcher shop window and stare in at the piglets swaying and twirling, blood dripping from their mouths frozen in midair. Freeda would point to the mouths. "It's so sad," she'd say. "They're smiling; probably thought they were headed for a romp in the mud."

Neena tried to shake the image. Did now what she'd always done when she needed to distract herself from thinking about her mother. Blamed Nan. Nan with her tightly curled hair, her oversized patent leather purse swinging from her arm, her look of bewildered sadness during Neena's growing-up years when Freeda was hours overdue for retrieving Neena and Tish and Nan would slant her chin toward the traverse rod as she closed the gold-brocaded drapes for the night at her living room window. "Looks like your mother won't be right back after all," she'd whisper. "Look like y'all here with me for a spell." So many times Neena had felt a brick drop inside as she heard those words, and she'd fault Nan for her mother's failure to return. Faulted Nan right now for her circumstance of sitting on the side of this tub. Had Nan just given her Tish's whereabouts, she could be with her sister right now. What she wouldn't give to hear Tish's voice in the real. To be so close, too close, and unable to feel Tish grab her with such a ferocity. My sister, Tish would say, and then pull Neena in a tight hug. And Neena would pretend that she was above such sentimental gushing, even as she'd yield herself so completely to the closeness. If not for Nan withholding Tish, Neena could right now be rubbing her hand over Tish's stomach, encouraging the baby forming there to keep up the fight. The baby would sense her goodness, her worth. The baby would know that Neena didn't have the devil in her like Nan always said. Tish knew it too. Nan was really the one with the devil in her. If not for Nan she could right now be turning down the covers in her sister's guest room. Imagined a leather pull-out sofa, satin-trimmed blanket, flannel sheets with pink pansies.

Damn you, Nan, she said out loud even as she heard Ramsey on the other side of the door gawking at *Green Acres*. Damn you, she said again, feeling that boulder come up in her chest that often surfaced as a result of Nan, separating her from Nan.

She'd first felt that separation when she was only seven, Tish not quite four, 1978 and Freeda had been gone for about a year. Nan called Neena and Tish in that urgent voice, interrupting their game of jump rope in their cutoff jeans and fraying canvas sneakers. She had a hot bath waiting for them and she scrubbed them down herself with Ivory Soap as if she didn't trust them to get themselves clean enough. She slathered their elbows and knees with petroleum jelly. She hard-pressed their hair with VO5 that added a sweetness to the acrid scent of burning hair. She clothed them in white cotton blouses that had been freshly line-dried, starched, and ironed, and newly made pink and white gingham skirts with kick-out pleats. It felt like Easter to Neena because she was wearing a nylon slip and her barely walked-in patent leather shoes.

She and Tish looked like Kewpie dolls as Nan paraded them out for a nice long ride on the D bus to Wanamaker's department store in town. "These here are my grand," she beamed in response to the multitude of comments from strangers on the bus of how cute the little girls were, how well-groomed. Repeating it over again as they walked along Chestnut Street, and even as they spread out at the counter in Wanamaker's basement and Neena and Tish laughed as they swiveled on the red leather padded counter stools and Nan ordered them each a vanilla shake and a foot-long hotdog on a hoagie roll. Afterward Nan said they would walk some to help digest the meal. They walked for what seemed like miles south on Broad Street, walked so long that Neena's church shoes were beginning to rub against the backs of her feet and she could feel holes forming in the heels of her lacey anklet socks. "Where we going, Nan?" she asked. "My shoes hurt. Will we be there soon?"

"We're going where we're going and we'll be there when we get there," Nan said and Neena clamped her lips together then because she knew when Nan talked like that it could mean a back hand against her mouth if she kept pressing Nan. She tried to ignore the feel of imitation patent leather against her heels even as she wanted to remind Nan that she herself had said the shoes were just for church, that they were cheap shoes with a plastic lining and would mess up their feet if they kept them on for too long. She wanted to ask Tish if her feet hurt too but

Tish was on the other side of Nan swinging her arm happily as she walked, and anyhow Neena was now distracted from the feel of the tender skin being rubbed away from her heels because now they turned one corner after another and the streets got smaller and smaller until they were like alleyways that could hardly contain the oversized cats that kept jumping from the steel trash cans, and even turning the cans over so that Neena and Tish and Nan had to step out into the street to avoid the strewn contents that smelled mostly of fish.

Nan stopped finally as they walked through the tiniest alley of a block. She stood in front of a narrow house that looked to Neena as if it wanted to collapse, probably would have fallen long ago, Neena thought, if it wasn't connected to the houses on either side that appeared to be holding that one up, the front door a marred board of splintered wood, a hole where the knob should be.

"Come on," Nan said as she pulled both of them by their hands; her voice sounded so cloudy as if she needed to clear her throat. They walked up the three short steps, the steps smooth and depressed in the middle. Nan knocked hard on the door with the foot of her balled hand and then looked at her hand and then looked around as if trying to find something to wipe her hands on. Neena noticed all of a sudden then that the orange-red-tinged air was being overtaken by the night, either that or this tight alleyway of a street was just darker than the rest of the world and her stomach started turning in on itself and she was about to risk a backhand to her mouth and ask Nan where had she brought them. Plus Neena was worried about Tish; Tish was starting to hum the Winnie the Pooh song and Neena knew that Tish only hummed like that when she was afraid. But before Neena could say anything the door crunched open and a man stood in the doorway looking at them, and then looking away and then saying, damn, dragging the word out.

A thick gold cross swung from around his neck and kept hitting against a splatter of a grease stain on his pale blue tie, his suit also pale blue, a white handkerchief bunched into his lapel pocket that he pulled out now and rubbed across his brow, his brow dripping with sweat and no doubt, Neena thought, the thick pomade that sat on the top of his badly processed hair. Neena noticed then that his pants zipper was undone, and she guessed that he became aware of it in the same instant because suddenly a briefcase appeared right there, obstructing Neena's view into his nasty manhood.

"I'm looking for Freeda, I'm her mother, a lady from my church said she heard that Freeda was spotted living over this way," Nan said and Neena's heart stopped beating right then because Neena had not seen her mother in over a year. Neena had wished for her mother's appearance whenever there was a chance a wish might come true, like right before she blew out the candles on her last birthday cake, or when a star seemed to shoot across the sky, or she caught a whiskered dandelion, even before she fell asleep on Christmas Eve. Please let my mother be standing here when I open my eyes, she'd wish. And now here was Nan calling her mother's name as if her mother might be as close as the other side of this greasy-headed man slopping his false teeth around in his mouth. Neena pushed past him. "Mommy, mommy," she cried as she ran into the house. "Mommy, it's me, it's Neena."

A short hallway ended on a wide open room that smelled of turnips and whiskey. A rotating fan chopped at the air in the corner and Neena's eye followed the sound to the other side of the room beyond a mountain of rumpled bedclothes. Then she saw the mattress, the slight woman on the mattress breathing to the beat of the fan; her lacey full slip was rolled all the way up to her waist. Her nakedness glistened and made a screeching sound in Neena's head like a fork hard-scraping a plate. Neena rushed to cover her with one of the crumpled sheets. She smoothed the sheet over her just as Nan and Tish ran in. Nan calling frantically for Neena, Tish holding tightly to Nan's hand while her other hand covered her eyes, saying that she was afraid in here. "Let's go, Nan. I'm scared, I'm scared," Tish pleaded.

Nan and Neena just stood there looking at each other, the woman snoring on the floor between them. Nan was breathing hard and choking back sobs. "I wanted her to see you and your sister," she said. "I wanted her to see what she was losing if she didn't turn her life around. But she's of the condition to see nothing right about now, already lost you and your sister far as I'm concerned. Come on, Neena." Nan reached out her hand. "She's dead to us, let's go, let's go."

"She's not dead," Neena said. "She's breathing, Nan, don't you hear her, she's not dead, she's only asleep."

"She's drunk—"

"She's not drunk either. She's only sleeping and I'm staying here 'til she wakes up." Neena kneeled on the mattress and shook her mother.

"Neena, get up from there, you don't know what kind of germs living in that mattress," Nan said, tugging with one hand the tail of the starched white blouse that Neena wore, holding fast to Tish with her other hand. Tish with her eyes still closed, whimpering, working herself up to a cry.

Neena pulled herself from her grandmother's grasp. "Come on, wake up, Mommy, it's me, Neena, your little girl. Wake up and see how cute I look with my hair pressed out. It's me, Mommy. It's Neena, your little doll baby." She pushed at Freeda to make her turn around, then leaned in so she could kiss her mouth the way she'd always kissed her mother's mouth. Except that now the face was in full view and Neena could see that this was not her mother's face, the mouth curving back into a smile certainly not Freeda's gushy smile, the arms reaching for Neena, pulling her all the way onto the mattress not Freeda's arms. The arms held her so tightly she could barely breathe. The voice in her ear saying, My baby, my little girl, you came back to me.

"Lord, Jesus," Nan said on an extended whisper, "you not Freeda," yelling then for the woman to turn her grandbaby loose, turn her loose right now.

Neena struggled against the woman and the woman held her harder still. She called Neena baby and sweetie and honey and Neena listened for a real name, thinking that if she came across a little girl with that name she could ask her where her mother was and if the girl didn't know then Neena could tell her. Maybe too that little girl might know where Freeda was; perhaps she'd also been taken to the wrong house by her grandmother just like Neena. Now Neena gave in to the woman's arms. If Freeda mistook another little girl for Neena, Neena would want that little girl to hug Freeda as well. Now the woman cried, and Neena said, "Don't cry, Mommy, it's okay," even as Nan pulled and yanked and tried to peel the woman's arms snaked around Neena's back.

"Neena, you lost your mind, that's not your mother. Get up from there," Nan screamed, and Neena wished that there was some way that she could give Nan a signal to let her know that of course that wasn't Freeda; she was only trying to make the woman feel not so sad. She kissed the woman's chin and then Nan landed her open hand against the side of Neena's face. Neena didn't feel the sting of the slap, felt instead the woman's arms loosening from around her.

Now Tish let out an extended shriek at the sound of the slap. Tish with her eyes still pressed shut crying, "What's happening? Let's go, please let's go."

"Who's hitting her, why are you hitting her?" the woman asked, pointing her finger in the wrong direction toward the wall, her eyes open but unfocused. "Hit her again and I'll make you pay," she said.

"You need to pray to be delivered from this hell," Nan said as she snatched Neena up from the mattress. "And you need to know if you lay down with pigs you wake up smelling like shit," she said to Neena as she shook her by the arm. "How dare you kiss such vermin."

Neena glanced down at the mattress to see if Nan's words had made the woman cry harder. The woman, though, was already snoring again; Neena already missing the tight thinness of the woman's arms. Tish screamed inconsolably for them to leave, please could they leave.

They stumbled back toward the front door, Nan shepherding them out of the house onto the narrow alleyway of a street where night was starting to fall; the night somewhat kind at that moment the way the blue-gray air blurred the harshness of that block so that even the cats looked as if they could have been cuddly pets. Nan pulled Neena and Tish close under her arms as they walked, consoling them, and herself, with It's all right, thank God that wasn't your mother, it's all gonna be all right. "Neena, your mouth okay? I didn't mean to have to hit you like that but that was urgent. Lord Jesus, Neena. You too young to even understand."

Neena started with the questions. "Who was the lady, Nan? Where do you think her little girl is at? Who do you think her little girl is? What was wrong with the lady? Where do you think Mommy's at now, Nan? What do you think she's doing? Who do you think she's with? You think she's safe? Is she all right? Huh, Nan, do you think my mother's all right?"

Nan tried to explain the woman's condition by saying that she'd fallen into a badness of mind. That her mind made her do things that weren't the right things to do. Extended that explanation to Freeda, why they hadn't heard from Freeda, Freeda was suffering from a badness of mind. Tish cried then that she was afraid of Freeda, please save her from catching her mother's badness.

Then Nan repeated what she'd said back in that room that smelled of turnips and whiskey. Told them that the only way they were going to have peace about their mother was just to accept her as dead.

"But what about when she comes back?" Neena asked.

"Well, then, we can be happy that she's resurrected. But for now, she's dead, Neena, like that woman back there is dead. Let your mother be dead and ask the Good Lord to heal your broken heart."

Neena wanted to ask Nan if they could turn around and go back for the woman and help her off the mattress and take her home with them and give her a bath and feed her chicken and dumplings and resurrect her. They could help the woman find her own little girl and that child could feel the sun come up in her chest the way Neena felt whenever Freeda returned. Neena didn't ask though. She listened to Nan talk about the power of prayer. She retreated inside of herself and stopped with the questions. She put on her nice-girl face and nestled deeper under her grandmother's arm as they turned back onto Broad Street. She started to disbelieve her grandmother then. By then Neena was too familiar with the minty smell of her mother's sighs. Had too often felt her mother's backhand gently against her forehead checking for a fever, or Freeda's fingers aimlessly pulling at her hair when she laid her head in her mother's lap. By then she had curtsied for her mother too many Easters after practicing the recitation she'd say at the children's service at church. Had too many bubble baths drawn by her mother, had her knees and elbows scrubbed too much, her eyelids kissed, her bangs curled under into perfectly shaped barrels. Had shaken her mother far too many times to bring her attention back when that hollowed-out stare overtook her eyes. Had crossed too many big streets alone to find a store that sold Argo starch when Freeda was running low. She'd cried too hard each time Freeda went away, the-inside-of-the-skull crying that caused her head to pound for hours after. She'd jumped like the cow over the moon elated at Freeda's inevitable return. Because Freeda always returned. She'd return happy and able. Neena reminded herself of that as they walked. Too young to be aware that she was beginning the process of rejecting a lot of Nan's teachings: that good is always rewarded in the end; that you reap what you sow; that joy cometh in the morning; that hard honest work is the antidote for depression; that Jesus Christ is Lord. Neena was even beginning to disbelieve that. A little at a time as if all the imprinting of all the things she knew to be true were being slowly lifted from the grooves, the grooves filling in with sand. Felt like a silver pinball in the game machine at Mr. Cook's Hoagie and Variety Store when the lever misfires and doesn't send the ball up the column into the game so the ball slides backward until it finally drops with a clang into the pocket separated from the balls still in play. Even as Nan pulled her closer under her arm, Neena felt farther and farther away.

Ramsey had finally stopped with the hee-haw laughter as Neena stood from her seat on the side of the tub and hung her things on the back of the bathroom door. She ran the shower then and got in and washed up. Scrubbed herself as much as the minuscule bar of soap would allow. She finger-parted her hair and plaited it in two uneven cornrows. She dressed and swallowed three glasses of spigot water. She felt as if she might vomit when she opened the bathroom door and stepped back into the room. Though music greeted her when she did. Sweet music. The sounds of Ramsey's snores.

His keys were on the nightstand next to his watch. She snatched up both in one quick move, then retrieved her purse from the dresser, stepped into her boots, and grabbed her coat from the closet. She dropped the keys and watch in the coat pocket and headed for the door thinking she'd let him keep his wedding band. Stopped then and listened for the breaks between his snores as she tiptoed to the side of the bed and stood over him. She lifted his hand and brought it to her lips and kissed it, she tugged at his ring as she did. Not as if he was trying to honor what the ring represented. The ring was stubborn and she knew that she should just let it be. She'd lost a good ring once; her finger had throbbed for a week after missing that ring. His finger should throb too, she thought, as she looked at the bottle of Gordon's to measure how much he'd drank. Told herself this was indeed a drunken stupor as she tugged and twisted the ring and thought about rubbing the finger down with shampoo, remembering then she'd used it to clean his essence from the skirt. Angry now at herself for even being here like she was some common whore. She wasn't, she told herself, as she felt the ring loosen and gave it one more pull and it slid off into her palm. His hand, though, suddenly stiff and she blinked and then was looking into his wide open eyes. They were green eyes and that surprised her because he was a blackened complexion. Wondered if he was kin to the devil with eyes so light. The thought giving quickness to her movements as she backed up, said she was ready to go, was he ready to take her, wasn't that *Green Acres* hilarious. Talking nonsense now as she reached behind her to open the door, watched him shake his head back and forth trying to shake his consciousness into full existence. She was out of the room now, running along the stained orange carpet in the hallway, down the first flight of stairs, hoping these were the ones that led to the car, a burgundy Ford Tempo. Shit, they were all white from the snow. She barely remembered the car's shape. She heard him above her, on the balcony, really just a ledge outside of the room. She didn't look up as he yelled for her to stop, called her a lowlife thieving bitch. "You touch my car and I'mma kill you," he said. She slipped on the snow-slicked asphalt as she ran, recovered herself and hit the remote on the key chain, and ran to the car that flashed its head-lights, saying Thank you, Jesus, the irony of calling on Jesus in this situation banding around her chest and she could barely breathe as she jumped into the car and blasted the ignition, jerking the car into re-verse just in time to see him run from the stairwell. She took her time so that the car wouldn't go into a skid as she slid the transmission into drive, turning out of the parking lot onto the highway, coasting until it was time for her to get into the E-ZPass lane.

She parked the car in downtown Philly in a tow-away zone. Day-light was making pink and yellow noises overhead as she pushed through the lower-budget shopping district lined with dollar stores and wig stores; jewelry we-buy-gold-and-silver type stores; multipurpose stores that sold fake Versace jeans, and the latest underground rap CDs. The bus station too was in this part of town with its trundling lines: the too-broke or too-prudent to take Amtrak, the too-motion-sensitive to fly, departing; the view of their backs quickly interrupted by faces of the newly arrived. That was her plan right now. Claim a hard seat at the bus station until the pawnshops were open and ready to deal. Get what she could for the watch and ring and hope for enough to buy a hotel room for the night.

Now she realized she had passed the street where she should have turned off. Now she was on Race Street in Chinatown. The whoosh of traffic on Vine Street moved from intermittent to continuously flow-ing. The lights from the Ben Franklin Bridge poked into the sky, the sky loosening itself up and shaking out widening bands of pink and yellow. It was a spectacular sight and she got chills as she stood there watching the interplay of the bridge lights, the light pouring from the sky. She was often hyperperceptive in the dawn hour. Affected by sensory detail that would have ordinarily escaped her. Like now as she heard a sound that almost did make her cry. The flute. She couldn't believe this was the same musician from earlier, that he was playing "Bridge over Troubled Waters." Thought at first she was imagining the sound, imagining him, but there he was sitting on the steps of the Hong Kong Restaurant.

She watched him as he played, glad that his feet were fully covered this time in barely worn Timberlands. Same long green coat he'd had on earlier; a quality, plaid muffler draped over his shoulders. He had a mild-looking face, long, like his nose and neck were long, long line of a mouth she could see even with his lips pursed. His shoulder-length locks were pulled back in a ponytail, his face shiny as if slathered recently with Vaseline. He eased the mouthpiece from his lips and his last note held there shimmering in the air between them. Now his voice took up the space. "You got anybody laying down for you, baby?" he asked.

"Huh?"

"A bridge? You got a living bridge?"

"I have—a—yeah, I have a sister," she said emphatically, then wondered who she was trying to convince.

"Yeah? Where is she?"

"Uh, here, you know, in Philly, I'm on my way to get to her, she might be having a miscarriage—" She stopped herself. She felt challenged, felt silly.

"Sounds like she's in no better shape than you."

"I mean, well, I have a grandmother here too, you know, it's just—"

He raised his finger. "It's cool," he said. "I only asked 'cause it's important for a person to know where their bridge is. If it's your grandmother, you know, cool, so you go to your grandmother."

She nodded. She didn't know what else to say. And anyhow he put his breath back to his flute and resumed the song. The sound was like crystal curving through the air and Neena stood and listened until the end of the song. Then she rifled through her purse heavy with Ramsey's watch and ring to pull up her last five-dollar bill. He held his hand up then to stop her. "Let's keep it pure, baby," he said as he put his mouthpiece back to his lips and started to blow some more.

She sat next to him on the steps. The concrete was hard and cold against her. She had been asked many things of a man in the predawn hour. Never purity. She could feel the widening bands of daylight moving through the air. Now he played "I'll Be There." The music's largeness sucked the chill from the air. It was warm—the music, the air—as it seeped through her pores. She breathed deeply and took in the scent of car fumes mixed with dumplings frying. The music was inside her now, in her chest keeping time with her breathing. She didn't even realize that he'd stopped playing until she felt his arm around her shoulder, his fingers falling against her forearm in ripples. So soothing his fingers were. His hand squeezing her shoulder now the way a brother would, drawing her in until her head took up the space around his long neck and she was doing what she hadn't done since she was a teen. She cried. Big heaving cries that felt like drumrolls pulsing out of her as Bow Peep said, Yeah, yeah, yeah. And even that was to the beat.

Chapter 5

SO HERE NEENA was at the foot of Nan's block unable to push through the shimmering bands of daylight. Such a clean block. The cleanliness, the Nan-inspired orderliness such a contrast to how Neena felt on the inside. Felt dirty and jumbled. Felt heavy-laden too, as if Ramsey's watch and ring had grown inside of her purse and taken on the weight of concrete slabs. She remembered how light and innocent she used to feel on this corner when it was home to Cook's Hoagie and Variety Store, the corner store that had served this community from the late fifties all through the eighties. Though now, in 2004, the Koreans owned the space; renamed it Spruce Beauty and Health Supply, peddled things like synthetic hair and rubber cement glue for affixing acrylic nails. Taped display posters in the window showed off straight-haired, flawless-skin black women in sequined gowns and mocha-colored lip gloss. The store a travesty to Neena because, though not their fault, the more recent owners didn't understand the history, the realness of that place, didn't know that this corner was a holy land of sorts to Neena. Neena had certainly likened Mr. Cook to God during her childhood because of his eyebrows that were a bushy silver gray. Freeda had told Neena that although no one had seen the face of God in its entirety there had been reports of his eyebrows that were the color and intensity of an Atlantic Ocean tide at a hurricane's approach and Neena had blurted, Like Mr. Cook's, Mommy? And Freeda had laughed. Exactly, exactly, Neena.

The people around here used to call Mr. Cook's store the colored store to distinguish it from the one at the other end of the block called Whitey's. Though by the time Neena and Tish were growing up around here the owners of Whitey's—SMITH'S VARIETY was the name stenciled on the window—had long since let their store go, having been scared off by the Black Power of the sixties, plus by then they'd sold enough penny candy to the children around here to send their own children to medical school. Still the people called Mr. Cook's store the colored store, though Neena never did because it implied that his prices were high, his goods inferior. And he'd explained to Neena the race tax. He paid more for everything: more for insurance, more for his mortgage, more for extensions of credit, more per item since he bought in smaller quantities since credit was so expensive.

Neena liked Mr. Cook. Liked it down there in his basement store that smelled of roasted peanuts and hoagie rolls; liked the ripples of activity as Mr. Cook's wife waited on the customers and yelled at the children not to put their sticky fingers against the glass that showcased the candy they'd buy; Johnny Hartmann or Lou Rawls keeping time to Mr. Cook's hacking knife separating the done meat for his specialty cheese steaks from the still-needing-to-cook; the ring, chime, ring of the pinball machine interrupted by some young boy's profanity when the machine went tilt, that boy told to take his bad mouth out of the store. She especially liked that Mr. Cook would talk openly about her mother. Most people became preoccupied with their hands or the sky or a scratchy throat that suddenly needed clearing when Freeda's name came up, as if she was already dead. Mr. Cook, though, would cut right to the core as if he were logging off a hunk of salami to run through the slicer. "No inkling her mind would go," he'd say. "Sweetest girl you'd ever want to meet growing up, she would turn the lights on in here with her smile, like your smile, Neena. Never underestimate the power of a beautiful smile," he'd say.

It was six months after the heater-man incident and Neena was perched on the cracked red leather counter stool listening to one of Mr. Cook's Freeda stories as he folded scrambled steak and onions into a long roll. "Yeah, Neena," he said as he squirted catsup into the meat and then arranged waxy white paper for wrapping the cheese steak in. "There was this one day, Lord, let me see now, must have been 1971, cold, real cold, kind of cold that snuck up inside of you and did its damage from your bone marrow and then spread out from there. Well, Freeda blew in here this particular day wearing two winter coats—one she had on the way a person normally wears a coat; the other she had tied around her like an over-the-neck apron. So she came in here turning the lights on with her smile. Telling me as she untied the coat from around her how people were looking at her like she was crazy. And I said, 'Well now, Freeda, that might be a little understandable seeing as how you are wearing two coats.' 'Mr. C.,' she says to me, 'crazy would be allowing my perfect creation to be exposed to the elements.' Then she gingerly undoes the second coat. Come to find out she was swaddling you up under that second coat. She unbundled you from all the layers she had you wrapped in. Handled you with such tenderness, she did. Finally when your little face come into view you was looking at your mother just-a-smiling, and she looking at you smiling, and I heated the bottle she handed me, thinking I'd just witnessed what Coltrane blew his horn about. A love supreme."

Neena blushed at the telling. She felt innocent down there amid the swirl of Mr. Cook's stories: not the same person who months earlier had almost done it with the oil man to get the heater repaired; not the same person who'd started charging the pimple-faced boys around there a dollar a minute to grind up against her in the alley—she was trying to save enough money to run away to find Freeda if Freeda wasn't soon to return—she'd laughed when she'd told Tish about the boys, how not one boy had lasted an entire minute so it felt like free money, then tried to swallow her shame when Tish's cute girl face collapsed in disappointment.

She looked at Cook's eyebrows now cupped in a question mark as he focused his attention beyond Neena and Neena didn't even have to turn around to know that Tish had probably just stuck her head in the door. It hadn't failed yet that within twenty minutes of Neena nestling atop the red leather counter stool, her grandmother would summon her. And sure enough Mr. Cook said, "Neena, your sister's trying to get your attention."

Neena sucked the air in through her teeth, would have said, "Awl shit," if Mr. Cook hadn't been in hearing range. "I was about to ask you how long my mother stayed in the store that day," Neena said instead.

"There's always next time," he said, as his wife called out that Mackadoo was on his way down for a hoagie with everything, and Cook began spreading mayonnaise on a roll, his eyebrows dipping like a child's drawing of birds in flight. Neena braced for Tish to tell her that she was wanted at home, Neena irritated that Tish so easily referred to Nan's as home where the gold brocaded couch matched the gold brocade of the draperies that matched the gold matting in the framed art of Jesus ascending. The smells from dinner probably still hanging in the air, fried liver smothered in onions and gravy. Neena never could tolerate the taste of liver. Though really Neena had to concede that this was home for Tish. Tish was a joiner; she had friends here. Already a member of the scout troop that met around the corner, the youth group that met in the church so conveniently situated across the street, the Future Teachers/Doctors/Lawyers/Leaders Society, whichever Tish planned to be this month because her aspirations changed as frequently as the doilies on the arms of Nan's brocaded couch. Good student Tish was, Neena too for that matter. Both in the mentally gifted school downtown that drew students from every section of the city. Neena glad for that, meant that when Freeda came back and moved them away from Delancey Street, they wouldn't have to change schools.

"Tell Nan I'll be there in a minute," Neena said as she watched Mr. Cook line the hoagie roll with shredded lettuce, then salami slices, then ham.

"Nan doesn't want you," Tish said as she swiveled the counter stool in a circle, laughing that it felt like the cup-and-saucer ride she'd gone on when she went to Wildwood last week with the dodge ball team. Neena thinking again, like she'd thought when she'd first heard about it that only Tish could find and *join* a dodge ball team.

"Okay, Mr. Cook," Neena called out to him, "I can stay. You can finish the story."

"Story?" Tish said, a widening smile taking over her face, such a classic face with the pert nose and cleft in her chin and Gerber-baby brown eyes. "Ooh, I want to hear too, Mr. Cook."

Cook was spreading sliced tomatoes on top of the cheese that covered the salami. Now he moved onto the onions. One eyebrow was slightly higher than the other as he worked, and Neena knew that meant that he was in deep contemplation so she hit Tish's thigh to hush her persistent begging for a story. The store was in the middle of a lull. Not even the *ring-chime-ring* of the pinball machine so that they could almost hear the sounds as Cook pressed hot and sweet peppers and pickles on top of the onions and then sprinkled the creation with oregano and salt and pepper. He rolled the hoagie in wax paper and slipped it into a long brown paper bag. "Mackadoo's with everything," he called out to his wife.

Now he stood in front of the counter where Neena and Tish sat, both looking at him with anticipation. His dark, round face, usually shaped for laughter, was pointed, serious. "Well there was this one Halloween night," he began slowly, "when your mother brought you girls in for trick or treat."

"Trick or treat? You sure?" Neena asked. "My mother doesn't believe in Halloween."

"I know that to be so, but that wasn't always the case," he said, as he went to the sink next to the grill and squirted liquid soap on his hands, then rinsed them. His eyebrow settled into place and Neena nestled against the cracked leather back of the counter stool.

"Well, Nan believes in Halloween because we trick-or-treated every year that we lived here on a Halloween," Tish said.

"We're not talking about Nan, we're talking about Mommy," Neena said, an edge to her voice.

"Daag, girl. Take the boxing gloves off, please," Tish huffed.

"Now the Halloween I'm thinking about," Cook rushed to say, as he looked from Neena to Tish, then went to the ice-cream bin and reached in with his scoop and commenced to filling a silver canister with a mound of chocolate ice cream, then vanilla, then chocolate again. "You were still in your mother's arms, Tish."

"*I* was? My mother had *me* in her arms?"

"Sure nuff. Why surprised?"

"I guess I just don't remember stuff about her like her arms, you know, her holding me."

"That's sad, Tish, that's really, really sad," from Neena.

"It's not my fault if I don't remember, Neena, okay. Isn't that right, Mr. Cook? Anyhow Nan says some things are better unremembered."

"And you'll never catch me disagreeing with your grandmother, baby girl," Cook said, winking at Neena as he poured milk and vanilla extract over the ice cream and set the canister on the blending machine and started it whirring. "Now if I recall correctly, the night I'm talking about was before your mother stopped observing Halloween. Just after sunset and the store was crowded with masqueraders holding out their bags. 'Trick or Treat, Mr. Cook, Trick or Treat.'" He made his voice go high.

"Neena, you couldn't been no taller than the seat of that stool you sitting on. You were a princess if I've ever seen one, a long sequined gown your mother had you in with a silver crown on top of your head and sparkles all along your cheeks."

"What was I?" Tish asked.

"Only the cutest bunny rabbit to ever hop out of a cabbage patch. Your mother had even glued pieces of cabbage to your white furry costume. That Freeda was a creative something. Very artistic. Like your grandmother is artistic when it comes to a needle and thread.

"You were just a bouncing in your mother's arms, Tish, having a grand old time, and you, Neena, were grinning like you always grinned when you were at your mother's side. Then suddenly the store went black, pitch black, and at first no one said a word because everyone was so stunned. What's the likelihood of a power failure on a Halloween night, like a bad *Twilight Zone* episode, like any second we'd hear Rod Serling say, 'Submit for your approval,' but anyhow, there we were, a store filled with people and no electricity. Then Tish, you broke the silence by crying—"

"Boy, that's a surprise," Neena said.

"But Mrs. C., the always-prepared, gets a hurricane lamp going, so people could see their way clear if they wanted to leave because at that point we didn't know if the blackout was citywide, or just in the store. Come to find out it was just inside of the store, 'cause the porch lights all up and down the block were glowing bright. So the store emptied in a hurry, save for you girls and your mother.

"So Freeda was bouncing you, Tish, and holding you close trying to comfort you, telling you it was okay. Neena, you was even on your tiptoes encouraging your sister not to cry. Then you tugged your mother's arm and told her that it was the wolf that was scaring Tish and she said 'What wolf?' and I was looking too 'cause I thought everyone had left, but sure enough, in the shadows of the corner of the store back by the pinball machine was the most realistic wolf, as realistic as a wolf could be standing on two legs.

"Sure nuff. So your mother hands you over to Mrs. C., Tish, and I'm holding my breath 'cause I know Freeda, you know, what she's capable of. So she walks right over to the wolf. 'You get a kick out of scaring little babies, huh? Why don't you come out of that mask and really scare someone,' she says.

"Now mind you, the store was being lit by Mrs. C.'s hurricane lamp that gave off a cha cha kind of light that made everything in the store at that moment take on an eerie feel. Especially when the wolf reared back and swiped its paw through the air, I'm telling you, that paw looked so authentic I wasn't even surprised to see blood rush out of your mother's cheek where the paw landed—"

"Blood?" Neena shrieked. "It bloodied my mother's face? Is that where that scar came from on her face?"

Cook stopped the blender and squirted in a thick line of chocolate syrup, then stirred in the canister with a long-handled spoon. "But your mother grabbed the paw, Neena. Then grabbed the hood of the costume and yanked it off. And there was a grown woman standing there, short woman, not too bad to look at even beyond the scowl hung over her face that could have been its own mask, as entrenched it was. Then she started to cry. A defiant cry as she shook and raised her fists up and down. Freeda stood there at first with her mouth hanging, the line of blood thickening along her cheek, and I'm expecting her to go at the woman, Mrs. C. too, 'cause she gasped. Then you know what your mother did? She took the woman in a hug. Yes she did. Then this teenage girl runs in hollering, 'Mom. Mom!' And meanwhile her mother is struggling to break free from Freeda's hug. 'What's happening in here?' she asks. I guess it took a few seconds for her eyes to adjust to the dimmed view coming from the hurricane lamp. Then she sees the blood coming from Freeda's cheek. 'Mom, what did you do?' And she nudges her mother away from Freeda. Freeda telling her it would be okay, it was just a little scratch. Well, by then, Mrs. C. had put you, Tish, into my arms, then she was over there dabbing your mother's cheek with peroxide, but Freeda waved her away and followed the girl and her mother out of the store."

Cook put a widemouthed glass between Neena and Tish, a straw and napkin on each side of the glass. He poured the milk shake into the glass, then stared off into space. "And then what?" Tish asked on a whisper.

One of Cook's eyebrows was raised again, even as he resumed. "Well," he said slowly, "you were screaming inconsolably at the top of your lungs by then, Tish. And Neena, you tried to run outta the store behind your mother but of course we held you back. Then your mother returned, and like magic, the lights came on. And I said, 'Freeda, you always could turn the lights on in my store with your smile.' So she sat you right over there in that booth, Neena, and she arranged your arms for holding your sister, then she put Tish in your arms. And Tish, you settled right down with Neena holding you, you were just a-gurgling with contentment. And Mrs. C. went to work cleaning up that cut on your mother's face, it was a nasty cut, near as we could tell the woman must've been holding a hook of some kind. But anyhow, the night settled in and I commenced to satisfying the trick or treaters that filed back in once the lights reappeared, though in between I made the sweetest, thickest milk shake that I'd ever concocted to date, it was so thick, you had to slurp it down with a spoon, Neena, and every so often you put a spoonful to Tish's mouth and she would just squeal with excitement." He laughed then. "I sure do miss those days, surely, surely I do."

"Well, what about the woman and her daughter? What did Mommy do when she went outside?" Neena wanted to know.

"Ah," he said, shaking his head, "no story there. Drink up, girls, drink up."

Neena persisted though. "Mr. Cook, she made my mother's face bleed. You saying no one knows why?"

"Near as we can tell," he said, as he concentrated on removing the blending sticks from the mixer, "the woman had a grudge against Freeda for some long-ago something. I can't say really."

"You can say, Mr. Cook. Please," Neena begged.

"Well, baby girl, I do remember hearing that at some point your grandmother had to get involved and convince the woman that your mother's mental health was sometimes on shaky ground. I never got much of the detail. And anyhow, I just told you the story to explain why I'm always saying that your mother would turn the lights on in here with her smile."

"So that's why she didn't take us out for Halloween after that?" Tish asked. "Because of the lady and her daughter?"

"No," Neena rushed to say. "Because she said people had enough real monsters in their lives without pretending to be monsters too."

"But that's the point, they are pretending," Tish said, a question to her tone.

"Yeah, but think about it, Tish, who knows what images Mommy lived with in her head."

Tish nodded. She listened to Neena and leaned in to sip at the milk shake. They both did. The chocolate syrup was prominent and they took turns saying, "Mnh." In between Tish conceded how it was sad that she couldn't remember the feel of her mother's arms; Neena saying that she wished she'd been old enough to kick that wolf's butt. And Cook left them be. He turned around to clean off his grill to get ready for the nightly round of steak orders, because people who ordered cheese steaks for dinner tended to eat them late. Then Nan stuck her head in the store. Said that she was ready to fit Tish for the semiformal cotillion dress she was making. Said she needed Neena to hand her the straight pins so she should come in now too. Tish jumped down immediately from the counter stool. Neena said she'd be right behind them. She wanted the chocolate remnants of the milk shake to linger for as long as possible, so she stayed at the counter scraping her straw against the bottom of the wide-mouthed glass.

She thought about the woman. She didn't need Mr. Cook to draw for her a map of who the woman was. The woman obviously enraged because Freeda had been with her husband. Wondered if the husband was her father, the girl who came to get her mother her half sister. But then she covered the wondering with a wool blanket the way she'd been doing for several years since that Saturday afternoon when they were living with Freeda.

She was twelve, Tish eight. Tish was around the corner that afternoon at her Brownie meeting so Neena had her mother all to herself. They were playing pick-up sticks on the blond-colored Formica kitchen table and Freeda's pile of red and yellow and blue sticks was much larger than Neena's; a good sign to Neena because that meant that Freeda's dexterity was appropriate, her hands were neither shaking the way they would when her mood was about to make like a cannon ball blasting, nor were her fingers thick and clumsy. Neena was chattering away, on that mountaintop where she'd perch when all was right with Freeda. She was telling Freeda about a girl who lived on Nan's block who she couldn't stand because the girl thought she was too cute for her own good. Plus she turned double-handed when they played rope, always keeping Neena from getting to ten-ten. "And guess what, Mommy," she said then, "her father's on drugs anyhow and who was my real father, Mommy?" The question just sneaked out like a jailbird making a break, as if the question had been sitting there in the corner of her cheek waiting for that exact moment to free itself. Neena didn't even realize the ramifications of the question's escape until she moved her tongue around, feeling the vacuum in her mouth where the question used to live. She looked at her mother then. But Freeda turned her face from Neena. She'd never done that before, turned her face from Neena. Even when she was in the throes of depression eating Argo starch by the boxful for hours at a time, Neena could still depict on Freeda's face that unmistakable look of adoration for Neena. It would feel to Neena that Freeda could never tire of looking at her. But that Saturday afternoon as Freeda sat with her winning pile of pick-up sticks on her side of the kitchen table, she turned her face away. Her hair was pulled up in a thick roll and her profile with the dramatic cheekbones and set-back eyes looked as if it might shatter right there over the kitchen table like a smashed porcelain sculpture.

Neena rushed her words then. "Never mind, Mommy, you don't have to say. It's okay, it's okay. Isn't it okay, Mommy? Huh? Please Mommy, it's okay?" She was crying in spite of herself, her words wobbling and barely able to stand as she vacillated between convincing Freeda that all was still well, and begging her for it to be.

Neena got up then and pushed through the air that suddenly sagged over the kitchen. She tugged Freeda's shoulder. "Look at me, Mommy," she said. "Come on, why won't you look at me?" She tried to turn Freeda's chin in her direction, couldn't stand the feel of her mother's resistance so she fell into her chest, crying, begging until she felt Freeda's hand against her back, patting her back. "It was a mistake," Freeda said, "just a mistake. It's okay, Neena, it was just a very bad mistake."

Neena didn't ask her mother to define the mistake. Was he, the man her mother had spread herself for, the mistake? Had he been some worthless doo-wopper with processed hair that he kept tied under a red and white bandana. Or maybe a whiz at calculus who'd gotten a free ride to MIT, his parents daring Freeda to try to claim their genius son.

Wondered if he was a sleazy married older man who'd taken advantage of her mother. Or was the mistake that Neena had asked, that she'd even wondered. Decided that day as her mother patted her back that she'd never wonder again, she'd strangle the need to know, throw a wool blanket over the need to know and twist its neck until its thrashing stopped.

Tish was back in the store calling to Neena's back, "Nan's getting impatient for you to help her with the straight pins," she said.

"You better go to your grandmother, baby girl," Mr. Cook said. "Always go to your grandmother when she calls."

Chapter 6

NABLE TO FORCE her legs to move beyond the space that used to be Mr. Cook's store, that was now Spruce Beauty and Health Supply, to push further up Delancey Street to ask her grandmother for help, Neena caught the 42 bus back into town. She walked into the first pawnshop she came upon. This one called Gems Bought and Sold: We Pay Top Dollar for Gold and Silver Boutique. Business was popping in here and Neena was next in line, thankfully because she was exhausted. Thought back to when the last time was she'd slept reclining. Hadn't slept at all last night, and the night before that had been spent on the Greyhound bus where her sleep was raggedy, a snatch here and there until her neck threatened to snap and she'd wake in a panic. Wondered how long a body could go without sleep before the imagination just took over and pulled the curtains to make the room dark, fluffed the pillows, turned down the bed like so much maid service. Never mind that you were really standing up in a line in a jewelry/pawn shop, head filled with crag-shaped worries about what to do from here; Grand-

mother's voice telling you that you will lie; flutist's voice asking you about a living bridge, Ramsey's hardness trying to make itself felt in that West Philly bar, you laughed in that bar. And this bed looks so good, the gold-foiled wrapped chocolate on the pillow, easy-listening classical music whispering through the speakers, knees about to bend to fall into this bed, when he, the jeweler, says, "Next."

Neena blinked to bring herself back to here. Glad that a man's voice had brought her back from the brink of the delusional bed she was about to fall into. She was hoping for a man from among the jewelers, two women and two men servicing this line. Her guy was South Asian brown with gray and white wiry hair springing from around his mouth, a pretty mouth, she thought, looking at him close-range now as she approached the counter and put Ramsey's watch and ring on a felt square. He studied the watch and ring. She studied his mouth. She looked away because he was eyeing her now. "Whose?" he asked, dangling the watch between his fingers as if it were a dead mouse.

"My late brother's," she answered.

"Ring late brother's too?"

She nodded. "The good die young."

"ID?"

"His?"

"No, your own?"

"Oh, of course," she said as she pulled up her wallet and flashed her Illinois driver's license.

He patted the felt pad and she laid the open wallet there as he looked at the picture, then at her, then copied the license number down at the top of a yellow call slip. He walked away then, hit a buzzer on the wall, and went through a door. She stood there looking straight ahead, couldn't see on either side of her because of dividers that kept the transactions private. She could hear spurts of the conversations though. A young brother sniping that this wasn't supposed to be no donation, yo, just give me my shit back, he said. White girl on the other side angry too, though not at the associate, as she said, Whatever, I just want all vestiges of him gone, I'll take whatever. Neena remembered reading how the jewelry was the thing first to go during the dot-com skid. Pawnshops became a cottage industry in Northern California. She had thought back then how stupid people were to assume that those good times would continue to roll. Maybe roll like an ocean giving and then taking back. Thought how stupid she herself was not to have secured her possessions in a safety deposit box outside of the apartment Cade kept for her. She pushed her coat sleeve back and looked at the gold cuff-type bracelet she wore. She pulled it from her arm and put it on the green felt square; did the same with her gold hoop earrings. She thought about adding her watch to the skid. Reasoned that she needed to know the time of day as her man walked back in her direction. Movements fluid like a tiger's, strong like a tiger's too.

"More?" he said as he looked at the bracelet and earrings on the felt square. "Dead sister's?"

"Dead self," she said, biting the corner of her lip, feigning shame, except that she really felt the shame.

He inspected the bracelet and earrings with the clinical finesse of an oncologist, no indication from his face how much the cancer had spread. He cupped his hand over a sheet of tablet paper and wrote, scratched out, turned the page, then wrote again, tore the page from the tablet and slid it around so Neena could see. "We give this amount," he said. "Final. No haggling here. You take?"

"I take," Neena said. She watched him hit the buzzer on the wall and disappear again. The few hundred he offered at least gave her the illusion that she had options. Enough money now to catch a bus back to Chicago to try to reason with Cade, try to talk Cade out of what was legitimately hers. Sighed on the thought, knew that the very thought was a land mine poised to explode in her face should she try to put it into action. Knew she needed sleep before she crafted her next move.

He was back. She signed four contract-sized sheets of paper, not even bothering to read them. What could they say anyhow, you're a broke ass, take what we're offering and then go on and get your broke ass on outta here. When her man asked her if he could help her with anything else, she said that she needed a phone, could he direct her, so hard to find a pay phone anymore. Put on her gushy smile as he stood there looking at her deciding. "You come with me," he said finally as he motioned her to the end of the counter, then pressed a buzzer to lift up a square of counter for Neena to pass through to get to the other side.

She was in his office; he pointed to a cordless phone almost hidden on the desk cluttered with coffee-ringed sheets of paper. "Local?" he asked.

"Definitely," she said as he looked up at the ceiling; her eyes followed his. A camera pointed at her head like a cannon, its red light blinking as if to say, Don't try shit. Realized then that this wasn't even his office; the camera watching him too as he stared back at it with a longing hanging from his face; face seeming to say that he wished he could punch the lights out of the camera. "You press buzzer when you finish, I let you out," he said. She nodded and picked up the phone and walked over to the window. She dialed Tish's number and counted the rings as she watched the people on Eighth Street in that rush-to-get-to-work stampede, such hostility on their way to work. A break in the phone rings matched the break in her breathing as she hoped for Tish's voice, braced herself for Nan's. Tish's voice again saying, "This is the day the Lord Hath Made, I rejoice and am glad that you called." She didn't leave a message. Part of her wished that she was religious right now. If she believed just a little in the power of prayer right now she would pray for Tish, that Tish could hold on to the pregnancy. Had the thought then that wishing she believed—at least for the moment—and actually believing might be the same thing. Said into the camera pointing at her head, "Bless my sister, would you please." Said it with arrogance, but said it.

She pressed the phone off and placed it back on the desk. Hit the buzzer on the wall and looked at her feet as she waited for her man to let her out. Decided that a pair of vinyl-type snow boots would be among her first purchases with her newly acquired cash. Concentrated on that thought, the thought reassuring.

When her man opened the door she thanked him profusely. "We both have color," he said, looking beyond her to eye the camera as if it was a monster that might pounce. Looked as if he was about to cry. "Next time you help me, or somebody who look like me."

"God, I would so love to," Neena said as he led her back out into store/selling area and she pushed through the door onto Eighth Street, thinking that he should watch what he says, all the surveillance in that store he could get shot for suggesting that black people and brown people get together. The blast of cold air as she started up the street reminding her how tired she was.

She knew of a cheap hotel that used to be on Arch Street. Walked in that direction, stopping along the way to buy a wool cap from a stand on Market Street; clearance underwear from Big K at the Gallery at Market East; and from the Salvation Army Thrift Store, a secondhand peach-colored sweater, black corduroy pants, and a pair of rubber-soled vinyl boots. Never imagined that she'd be shopping thus accustomed as she was to sinking into the designer collections at upscale department and specialty stores. Could see herself over and over in the everyday people as she walked through town. The people shopping with that look of fanaticism that said that it didn't even matter what they were buying as long as they were spending because to consume was both an opiate and a speed, a snort, a skin pop, a simultaneous rush and nod intended to divert the everyday people. Neena had succumbed to that euphoria over the things she'd buy. Meaningless things; overpriced excesses.

Not today, though. Every purchase today a necessity. In addition to underwear and secondhand clothes, she added to her haul Dollar Store soap—Dove, who knew you could buy Dove soap at the Dollar Store—deodorant, cocoa butter lotion, and Alberto VO5 for her hair. She was left with enough to buy a week of nights at the Arch Street Hotel.

She fought dizziness as she looked around the hotel room with its cigarette-burned particle-board furniture and framed Dollar Store art that was in such stark opposition to how she had lived. Like she'd worn nice things: she'd surrounded herself with nice things. She wished right now as she looked at the limp pillows on the bed in here that she had at least enough money left to replace them with feather down. Knew that she was being excessive though she did buy new pillowcases, reasoned that her face, her nose and mouth and eyes deserved at least assurance that the pillowcases were not infected with the germs of those forced to lie here prior to her being forced to lie here, germs that couldn't be washed and tumble-dried out.

She thought of germs most of the first night in the hotel. Though consoled herself that at least she could wake in the morning without the likes of a Cade's breath all in her face. Felt an unhinging in her legs and arms the way she'd feel on Fridays when she worked a day job and right before she fell asleep would remember that the next day was a day off. One of the hardest parts about living the way she had of late came when the likes of Cade gave his wife a preposterous line so that he could spend the night with Neena (once he'd told his wife that he was participating in a sleep study), which meant that he'd be pulling on her first thing in the morning and she cherished her mornings alone. The morning air was like pink eyelet lace, floating and innocent. Not heavy and dramatic and slow to move the way it would be when the night lumbered in and Cade would walk through the door with a three-pack of condoms and his cell phone on mute.

She tossed and turned the first night in the hotel and woke up every hour or so with a racing heart. Even got tangled up in the chasm between deep sleep and wakefulness and thought that she saw Cade's brother standing over her, laughing the way the devil laughed in Rod Serling's *Night Gallery* when he'd tricked a child into doing wrong. Thought he was coming at her with a pitchfork, heard her grandmother's voice then saying to Cade's brother to just go ahead and take her, she was tired of fighting for a demon who just wasn't made up to do right; heard Tish screaming, then saying No, no, Nan, don't let the devil take Neena, please Nan, I'll pray, I'll pray for Neena too. She rocked herself then to help ease herself back to sleep. Rocked herself the way she did when her mother would leave. Rolled herself up into a ball and hugged the pillow and rocked and finally fell into a good dreamless sleep, thought she heard the melodious chime and whistle of Bow Peep's flute as she fell asleep. Slept continuously for two nights and days straight. She was sure she must have gotten up to go to the bathroom, to sip the God-awful spigot water, but she didn't remember. Remembered only the rocking.

Neena woke the third morning to a blast of sunlight rushing through the dingy sheer curtains. She showered and pulled her getting-denser-by-the-day hair into a puffy ball. She walked around the corner to a WaWa and bought a phone card, a large coffee, and a breakfast sandwich. Her money was melting but she consoled herself with the thought that at least she had a bed for the next few nights. She'd surely reach Tish in that space of time. Tish would provide her a room in her lovely new home until she found a job. She jumped at the thought. Had not considered really that she was here to settle down. Why was she here? Mr. Cook used to say that when you find yourself in desperate straights, that's when you become who you really are. She sat on a bench on the Parkway and sipped her coffee and thought about that as she devoured the sandwich.

It was warmer out today, the snow from the night she'd arrived long gone, and as she looked up and down the block she saw that every other bench was occupied. Looked closer and noticed adjacent to the occupied benches shopping carts showing plaid and shoes and pillows; stuffed green trash bags; crates covered over with blankets and coats. She finished her meal and walked the length of the block and listened to the listless bench-dwellers call out the times and locations of the food give-aways. She felt herself being eyed. Wondered if they could see through her cashmere coat that this is who she was, one of them right now too.

She stopped at the pay phone in the hotel lobby and once again tried Tish's number. Hung up as soon as she heard the click of the answering machine.

Back in her room she slept some more. It was mid-afternoon when she woke. Woke famished. Counted her money. Twelve dollars and sixty-five cents. She ripped the name of the designer from her black cashmere coat and wore the coat inside out and found one of the places the people occupying the benches on the Parkway had called out. She stood in a long line with other suffering people: drug addicts and alcoholics, schizophrenics, casualties of the jobless recovery. Though some standing in line she was sure suffered from plain old indolence, sloth, most it seemed had legitimate claim to a meal. Mostly young, mostly black, mostly male. How did this happen, she wondered? All this energy, the accumulations of so many mothers' prayers and tears, all this hope on hold standing out here waiting in line for a soup-kitchen meal. Did they all happen to be in the same vicinity when a despairing fog settled and turned them into this. Where were their families, their communities? She could explain away her own situation. Fell through the net, she had. But there were too many men out here to have just fallen through a net. Figured the net had been intentionally cut to facilitate whole piles of young black men falling through.

Today's meal was a tomato bisque soup, a chicken and rice dish, half a Kaiser roll. She left the chicken untouched as she considered the possibility that the government was not above experimenting with bird flu, its transference from cooked chicken to disposable humans. She was still hungry when she finished. Looked around the cramped room, actually generous to call it a room, more like an unfinished breezeway between the street and the alley out back with tables crammed in and fold-up chairs with their legs interlocking so it was hard to get up once squeezed in at the table. An altar made of a milk crate atop a table covered with white plastic, an oversized Bible on the crate. Two bud vases with paper carnations stood up front where a thin-faced man had blessed the food for a full half hour before anyone could eat. "It is fruitless," he'd interrupted himself mid-grace to say, responding to the muttered complaints, "to nourish a man's stomach without first feeding his soul." Neena thought it a nice idea that flew like a wingless bird in this room as she pushed against the back of her chair trying to get a couple of inches so that she could wiggle herself up. Just three seats in from the aisle, though, it seemed like an acre when she considered she'd have to ask six people to move. She felt a thick finger against her shoulder, looked around, and saw the bear-sized man who sat next to her pointing at her Styrofoam plate. "Can I finish that if you're not?" he asked. At first Neena thought that he was joking, that he was on clean-up and charged with clearing away the garbage. She looked in his eyes then. Wished she hadn't seen it, the bottomless hunger, the shame. That kind of look could keep her up at night, could make her cry, and she didn't cry easily.

She swallowed hard, forced a smile, and said, "I'll cut a deal with you, you help me get up from here and it's all yours." Before she could check his face for a response, she felt herself being lifted, chair and all, clearing the heads of the three sets of people who'd had her trapped, wondering from on high how he was going to set the chair down. His arms couldn't be that long, she thought, as she felt a shrill in her stomach on the descent, then the landing as the chair came to rest—all four legs at once—softly in the aisle. By the time she'd recovered herself enough to thank him, he'd already set her plate in the space in front of him, his profile intense as he tore into the chicken.

The thin-faced man who'd said Grace for a half hour stopped her at the exit, handed her a pamphlet, a religious tract, and said, "Jesus loves you, sister." She took the tract and nodded more at the penciled face of Jesus on the tract than at the man standing in the doorway smiling. She walked out the door, folding the pamphlet into where her coat pocket should be. It fluttered to the ground and she remembered that she'd turned her coat inside out. She stooped to pick up the tract; saw about a half dozen others strewn where she leaned. She picked those up as well. Even as she moved up the street, she bent to pick up the tossed tracts and piled them into her purse.

She headed into town then. The night air, though cool, was absent teeth and soft to walk through. She went into the chain bookstore and browsed the new releases. Thought about and then abandoned the thought of stealing a couple of books. She felt the security guard's eyes like a laser beam in the center of her back as if he'd just read her thoughts. She looked up at him and winked. Then realized that her coat was still turned inside out. "Oh well," she thought, "like I care." She told herself that she'd have to soon get a library card, reminded herself that first she needed an address.

She took what looked interesting up to the café area and bought a cup of tea and tried to nestle in the hard seat. The tea was disappointing, for all that money it was no better than a cup of Lipton. She sipped it slowly, hoping for it to at least take the edge off her hunger. The most it did, though, was to remind her that dinner had been a cup of tomato bisque soup and half a Kaiser roll. She walked over to where the oversized windows looked down on Broad Street. No available chairs, of course. Wanted to ask the people sitting there didn't they have twenty-five dollars to buy the books they were reading? Didn't they have homes with sinkable armchairs where they could curl up and read instead of hogging all the seats here with their cheap, privileged selves? She let go a sigh and looked out the window, and when she did, saw on the other side of the street, Bow Peep, the street-corner musician whose arm had tapped her shoulder while she cried the other night. She put the books on the ledge and headed out of the store. Held her arms up when she passed the security guard in a mock frisk-me move and then she laughed. He didn't laugh, though a young boy on the way into the store thought it hilarious.

Bow Peep was immersed in his playing when Neena stopped in front of him. It was high tide on this corner as people splashed around: the young brothers strutting as if they owned the streets with their coyote-trimmed hooded coats wide open, their side-to-side footfalls matching the bass rhythms throbbing from every other Cadillac Escalade. Various pin-striped hustlers from lawyers to bankers to wannabe CFOs; newly minted city dwellers buying up the sky and turning the city white again. Middle-aged motherly types hightailing it up to Lord & Taylor for stockings for tomorrow and maybe a blouse on the 15 percent off coupon. People on their way home from work, or stepping out to a dinner, a happy hour, a show at the Kimmel or the Academy.

Neena thought Bow Peep could be on a stage himself with what he could do with that flute, the clarity of each note that hung in the air until it was joined by the one that followed. He was playing "What a Friend We Have in Jesus"—a song Neena knew well, would have to know well considering that she'd mostly grown up in Nan's house—and though Neena had long since stopped believing in the Jesus that had been defined by Nan, by the church, as she listened to Bow Peep play, she thought, Man, what a hell of friend that must be.

Bow Peep pulled his flute from his mouth and smiled at Neena. Extended his hand that she took. He was wearing blue and white knitted gloves with the finger tips cut off. Reminded Neena of the type of gloves Nan would have knitted with their perfectly even alternating rows of knit and purl, blue and white, decent and in order like everything Nan did.

"How goes it?" he asked as he set his flute in the case propped on top of a milk crate. He reached into the pocket of his long green wool coat, pocket large enough to hold a fishing boat. He pulled out a small silver tin and opened the tin and rubbed his naked fingertip inside, then smoothed a balm across his lips. The insides of his lips were cracked and swollen.

Neena hunched her shoulders. "I'm well, I guess."

She was being jostled standing there by the to-and-fro foot traffic so Bow Peep touched her elbow and pulled her closer in. "Did Granny show through?" he asked.

"I uh, I uh," Neena struggled with a response, thinking of how he'd prompted her to go to Nan's as he'd played "Bridge over Troubled Waters" the other the night on the steps of the Hong Kong Restaurant in Chinatown. Thought of how she'd been unable to push herself up her grandmother's block.

"No need to say. You know, it's cool, it's cool," he said as he closed his tin of lip balm and slipped it back into his mammoth coat pocket. "I was only wondering because when last we met our hero, she was going over the river and through the woods to grandmother's house she goes. No wolves, I hope, threatened our little lamb, little lamb who made thee, Dost thou know? Because the big bad wolf waits and waits and waits, nothing to do but sit and wait. He sits and waits."

He kept repeating himself then and Neena felt as if the lights had just been dimmed on the corner. She fervently did not want Bow Peep to be truly crazy in an incoherent way as she listened to him ramble on and build elaborate castles in the sand with his sentences that seemed as if they would hold until he'd add a thought and the whole idea collapsed into an indecipherable mound. Though she'd come to accept that her own mother was mentally ill, Freeda's logic had always remained intact, at least in Neena's view. Right now Bow Peep quoted the words to a Chaka Khan song about you reminding me of a friend of mine, and how seldom you find a face that's so kind, moving on to Jon Lucien, as he half sang the part of that song about oh lady where you know me from, asking Neena if it could be before when the world was just begun. "Could you be my soul mate?" he sang, repeating it three times, then reached down for his flute and moistened his lips with his tongue and started playing that song. Neena listened until the end of the song. She took in the aromas from the plethora of restaurants around here: garlic and butter and grilling beef, the smells reminding her of her hunger. She could hear the drum of the subway underfoot; pigeons flapped overhead. A thin line of dejection started to move up from her toes because she'd had hopes. Hopes for what? That Bow Peep might be a help to her? The dinner smells were overwhelming and she thought how foolish to have such hope. She lowered her eyes to tell him good-bye and turned and began to walk away.

He called out to her. "Neena," he said, "Oh Neena," stretching her name out, imitating Timmy calling for Lassie.

Neena turned around and when she did he started to riff up and down the scale, his fingers going spastic as he blew out high and low notes. He leaned back and then he bent forward. He was making music, attracting an audience from among the heretofore oblivious foot traffic. People began dropping dollars into the faded green lining of his flute case. When he was finished, applause came. He didn't acknowledge the applause, reached in his pocket and pulled out a swatch of fabric and started wiping his flute. The crowd soon dispersed, all except for Neena and an old woman with Kinte cloth wrapped around her head, a white cloud of puffy hair growing out of the center of the cloth. The woman wore a gray down-type jacket that was too small, a child's jacket because she herself was a slight woman. The jacket hung open; a gray scarf crisscrossed her chest like an Ace bandage. "Power to the people," the woman yelled to Bow Peep. "Blow baby, blow some more."

"All things in their time," Bow Peep said.

"The time is now; you better seize it while yet you still can," she said, and Neena looked from Bow Peep to the woman and wondered if they were on the same medication. Watched as Bow Peep picked up the cash money that had been dropped into his flute case and pointed the money toward the woman. "For you, my lady," he said.

"I can't take candy from a baby," she said.

"For gloves, please my lady, go buy your many selves some gloves."

"Well now, this little piggy did go the market," she said, waving her little finger. It was bent, Neena could see, as if from osteoarthritis.

"And it should never go alone," Bow Peep said, pushing the money into the woman's hands. "You know I'm right."

They volleyed back and forth like that, Neena fascinated that the one so easily followed the illogic of the other. The woman finally accepted the money. Neena had the thought then: this is how the pharmaceuticals would take over the world, through stealth-type drugs that dictated who could communicate with whom.

Now Bow Peep looked at Neena, his long face pointed, serious. "That little number I just played was for you, my tiger, tiger burning bright. That was your healing vibe. My notes of scale shall set you free. It's cool, baby. It's cool."

Chapter 7

EENA TOOK THE long away back to her hotel. She stopped once again at the pay phone in the hotel lobby. Knew by now that Tish's answering machine picked up on the fourth ring. Held her breath after the second when the ringing stopped. Damn. Not Tish though. Again, not Tish. Tish's husband answered, Malik. Neena had never met Malik. Knew only that he was raised in Willingboro, New Jersey, and that he was a cameraman for the local news station where Tish was the noonday anchor. Neena remembered hearing about how they'd met in graduate school. She'd seen pictures, wedding pictures from a year ago. They'd gotten married in Hawaii, Tish had said, because they just knew too many people, wouldn't be able to cut the guest list below five hundred. She remembered how ebullient Malik and Tish appeared in the picture as they cut their wedding cake. What a cutie you married, Neena had said in the note that went with the Waterford goblets she'd sent. She imagined his cute face now as he said hello, his light brownish eyes and light-colored skin and head full of throw-back nappy hair.

Tish had said the wedding hair was a compromise; he usually wore corn rows.

She fixed on a laminated parson's table holding an artificial potted peace lily as she introduced herself to Malik, said she had spoken with Nan a couple of nights ago and she was calling again to check on how her sister was doing. "Is Tish there? May I speak to her, please?" she asked, trying to keep the desperation from her voice. She listened to his pause, how heavy it was.

"Hey, yeah, Neena," he said, and she could hear how hard he had to work to lift the pause, voice sounding like someone in the midst of weight training. "Yeah, it's good to finally hear your voice, yeah, Tish talks about you nonstop."

"Is she all right?"

"We're praying, Neena. Yeah. Been running her back and forth to the hospital and she's there now, you know in the hospital—"

Neena sucked her breath in hard and quick as if her pinky finger had just been severed, grabbed her finger because it really did throb all the way up to her chest. "And what?" she said, when she could talk again. "I mean, their prognosis? You know, what are they saying?"

"It's like neutral at this point. The good news is that Tish should be okay. They're trying to save the baby though, you know, trying to help her hold on to him for four more weeks. You know, it'll still be touch and go, but they say if she can hold on to him for four more weeks he can be viable. So that's basically where it is. We're just trying to help her get there. You know every day he's with her is like you know, I'm celebrating and praising God."

"Him. A boy?"

"Yeah, a boy," he said, and Neena heard his voice crack.

"A boy." Neena repeated it, felt dizzy from the sudden surge of emotion. "What hospital?" she asked. "Can she have visitors?" That heavy pause again. "Or at least phone calls?"

"Yeah, like this so awkward, Neena," he said, and Neena concentrated on the tweed couch in the hotel lobby; it was cream-colored and leaned to one side as if a heavy body sat there sleeping or already dead. She guessed another month at longest before the Queen Anne–style couch leg broke finally under the invisible weight. She'd rather play with that idea than listen to what Malik was saying; she could have finished his sentences for him but she allowed him to continue.

"But yeah, you know your grandmother, Nan, I mean of course you know her, but she's got it in her head that any kind of surprise is gonna force Tish into a labor that they won't be able to stop. Anyhow, I'm not entirely convinced, but you know, what do I know? And your grandmother's citing all these midwifery type stats so I'm not trying to go up against all of that on the off chance that she could be right. So, I guess what I'm saying is that whatever I can do, I mean for you to be kept up with how Tish is doing, you know, just give me a number and I promise, you know, God, I feel like such a sellout doing this 'cause I know how much you mean to Tish. I know I'ma catch hell when she's back in the black and has a healthy baby and hears that I got in the way of you seeing her. God, I'm just, you know, kinda scared, Neena."

His voice cracked again, wider this time. She couldn't fault him for keeping Tish unreachable to her. Though she couldn't console him right now either. "Listen, thanks for your time," she said. "My sister married well, I'm glad for that. I'll call again soon to check on how she'd doing."

"Well wait, Neena," he said. "Do you want to leave a number? That way, as soon as there's, you know, any change in her condition, I can call you."

"No thanks, really, I'll be in touch," she said as she started again to move the phone toward the base. Then she heard him calling her again to wait.

"Uh, your grandmother said if I spoke to you to give you a message, she said—"

Neena cut him off. "Tell my grandmother to go to hell." She hung the phone then repeated it into the lobby air. "Go to hell, Nan," she said over and over; "Nan, go to hell." Said it even as she pulled the coffee-stained yellow pages from the ledge below the phone. Looked up the entries for hospitals. Didn't realize how many there were in the area. She hated to waste her phone card minutes but she would call each one until she located Tish. Scanned the list and narrowed it down to the four most likely. She started with HUP. Her grandmother was brand loyal and had proclaimed more than once that should she ever become incapacitated, don't take her anywhere except the University. Surely she would insist that's where Tish should go. And Tish had always done whatever Nan suggested of her.

Neena's heartbeat stepped up as she was connected to patient information and gave them Tish's name. Bingo. Tish was there. Her condition, please, she asked, her voice shaking. Fair. Thank Goodness, not critical or grave. Fair. Average. The phone number, please, yes, are you crazy, of course connect me, she almost shouted into the phone. And there it was. Tish's voice in her ear just like that. Such a weak voice, as if she was eighty and had just had a triple bypass. Not a fair-sounding voice at all. Neena got the thought then that Tish might in fact be close to losing the baby, the thought wrapping itself around her larynx thwarting speech. "Hello," Tish said again and Neena tried to pull up her own voice before it sank further into what was now a pit of quicksand filled with her second-guessings. Suppose Nan was right.

Suppose the shock of hearing from her right now did in fact cause Tish's uterus to contract and push the baby out too soon. She should have called more than a few times a year so that her voice on the other end of a phone line was part of the normal routine of Tish's life. Should have called daily. "Hello, hello," Tish said again. And Neena was picturing again what she imagined to be the guest room in Tish's new home. The slant of the morning sun hitting the side wall the way it did in that childhood bedroom she and Tish had shared at Nan's. Selfish of her to put Tish in jeopardy for the chance to soften her own situation. Should not be Tish's emergency that she, Neena, had only two nights left in this fleabag hotel. Now there was another voice in her ear. Nan's. Who is this please? Nan's voice demanded and Neena tried to fix a rock in her stomach to anchor her to get the words out, to say to Nan, Happy now? She heard a click in her ear before she could utter a mumbling word. Then a silence fractured by her own hard breaths.

Now she rifled through her purse looking for that lawyer's card, the one who Bow Peep had introduced to her the night she arrived here. She'd told herself on the bus ride from Chicago that she was finished being a confidence woman, she'd even visualized herself sprinkling talc over that part of her life the way she would over a grease splatter on good silk to lift the stain so that even the heavier jagged outlines of the stain disappeared. But now she had to admit that even then she'd been holding the idea in a dark crevice of her brain of pulling in just one more man. Knew when she'd asked for the lawyer's card that she had this very thing in mind. Just one last time she told herself now. Just to get enough money to legitimize herself for good. Then she could move to a place like North Carolina where the cost of living was cheaper than here, where she could buy a little town house on a new development and put up a swing set in the backyard for the children she was sure Tish would have. Allowed the idea of one more hustle to peek its head outside of the crevice, allowed the dingy light in this lobby to enlarge the idea even as her insides grew teeth and gnashed at the lining of her stomach. She pulled up the Jesus Loves You tracts and bunched them in her hand. Dug some more through her purse looking for the card, the nice heavyweight linen with raised lettering.

Her heart was beating double-time as she talked herself in and out of calling him. The pencil image of the sad-eyed Jesus stared up at her from the brochure. "Do you know that he loves you?" the caption on the brochure read. She smoothed the edges of the tracts and placed them in a neat pile on top of the coffee-stained yellow pages phonebook. Remembered then that she'd taken the card out and slid it under the lamp on the particle board nightstand. She headed to her room to retrieve the card. She walked across the lobby and got into the elevator, a tight four-person-capacity crypt with faded red indoor/outdoor carpet for wall covering, a scuffed vinyl on the floor. She wouldn't go for an outrageous amount from him. Just enough to start her new life in North Carolina. She was picturing already the boy-books and baseball mitts she'd buy for her nephew. She could return to school, she told herself. She could maybe combine an arts degree with psych courses and counsel black women living in shelters, maybe teach them how to bend wire for bracelets and earrings, how to glue chips of Austrian crystal, how to market the handmade jewelry to local retailers. Imagined the internal glow she'd get from helping the down-and-out women to positions of restored dignity.

She imagined how her mother would smile. There it was, her mother's smile. The power of its absence had hung over her and directed the course of her life as she'd moved to those places where she thought her mother might be. No indication of Freeda in North Carolina, though.

She braced herself for the way the elevator rocked from side to side on ascent. Held her breath so she wouldn't inhale the musty air as she walked the few steps to get to her room. Allowed her chest to open finally once she'd unlocked the door. The inside of the room smelled like her, like pink Dove soap and cocoa butter lotion and the VO5 conditioner that had dressed her hair since she was a child.

Chapter 8

LIFF WAS THINKING about his wife, Lynne, when Neena called. He was sitting in his downtown law office where the ceilings were nine feet high but suddenly felt like those dropped ceilings in the basements of his youth with the recessed lighting and the brown stains from the shoddy plumbing. He'd partied hard in those basements back in the late sixties. A real lady's choice back then with his oversized 'fro, and good weed in tow, and his acceptance to the Ivy League. But he was tall and the dropped ceilings were oppressive, like the faux wood that paneled those basement walls, the wall-to-wall carpeting in the smartly done upstairs portions of the house, the living room suites covered in custom vinyl to protect the likes of him, he guessed, the truly poor, from coming in contact with the upholstery fibers.

He hadn't been truly poor for decades, though. He and his wife lived in an old-wine part of the city where its age meant value, not decline. The homes were mansion-sized brick, though not garish displays, carved into stunning topography and set back amid specimen plantings from a century ago. The interior spaces were voluminous, rooms to get lost in. Though the basement had low ceilings because of the piping, so Cliff refused to finish the basement, determined that if they had children they'd party upstairs so that some teenage boy in the middle of a growth spurt wouldn't have to suffer as he did. So far, though, there were no children; he and Lynne had been married for fifteen years so that it looked as if there would be none.

The law office was empty when Neena's call came through. It was after seven and that's why Cliff had been thinking about Lynne, because of how late it was and he'd not heard from her all day. He was thinking that he should have heard from her several times by now. She should be a little melancholy since her Alzheimer's-suffering mother was living with them now, she should need to cry on his shoulder or at least hear his voice during the course of her day. Then the phone rang and the caller ID flashed OUT OF AREA and he assumed it was Lynne since she was always losing, leaving, her cell phone somewhere and having to use a pay phone. He was irritated when he heard a voice other than Lynne's; he would have let the call go into voice mail.

"Who are you? We met where?" he asked, interrupting Neena, an edge to his voice.

"On Filbert Street. Not far from the bus station," she said. "Remember your friend was wearing sandals in the snow and you chided him."

He tried to picture Neena. He couldn't, though he remembered the night. Remembered that at the point when Bow Peep introduced them, Cliff had been distracted by a woman across the street laughing very hard at something a man was saying in her ear. The woman's laugh was that of someone thrilled to be alive because she was so in love with the man whispering in her ear. At first Cliff thought the woman was his wife, Lynne. It wasn't Lynne and he was both relieved and disappointed.

He remembered, too, feeling a sting in his own toes when he'd seen Bow Peep's exposed feet. He and Bow Peep were closer than most brothers. They'd grown up next-door neighbors on a broken-down West Philly block back when broken-down blocks in West Philly were the exception. The kids on his block set apart as a result, ostracized by the parents who threw their children sweet sixteen parties in the finished basements. Though Cliff was given a pass because of his smarts and his charm and his looks, Bow Peep too because they were inseparable until Cliff went to college and Bow Peep to war. Cliff suffered a type of survivor's guilt when Bow Peep returned with only a portion of his sanity intact. He became Bow Peep's guardian of sorts. Bow Peep would insist that it was the other way around, that he'd been on the point in the jungles of 'Nam and to this day could sniff out danger after dark; he had Cliff's back, he would say.

Cliff tried again to picture Neena's face, couldn't, though he did remember that she'd dropped a five-dollar bill into Bow Peep's flute case and the gesture had softened him. Now he apologized to Neena for his rudeness just then by cutting her off. "It's been a grueling day," he said, "but that doesn't excuse my poor manners." He didn't say that he was mainly irritated because it should have been his wife calling. "So what can I do for you?" he asked Neena.

She replied that she had a somewhat unusual case, was there a fee for his initial consultation.

"You've got my ear right now," he said, "for free."

She laughed. Made him think again about Lynne's laugh. That crystal laugh that he'd had in his head all day today. He'd just told himself when the phone rang that he wouldn't tighten up inside if it was Lynne and she said, "Hello, Cliff," and then the laugh. It was just a laugh, for goodness sakes, that's all, nothing representational about the laugh, no metaphor, no joke, as in joke's on him.

He banged his fist against the desk to stop himself. Asked Neena to excuse him for a second as he pushed the hold button and grabbed his fist and stood and yelled out, fuck, from the pain in his hand. Hoped he'd not broken his hand. Though he deserved a broken hand, wished he could kick his own ass for allowing this emotional implosion.

He massaged his hand until the throbbing subsided. Was about to switch back over to Neena's call, but the red light no longer blinked, meant she'd hung up. Just as well, he thought, as he gave up on trying to picture her, thinking instead about the other events of that night. On his way home his car had skidded on Lincoln Drive, an omen, he thought, because when he finally arrived home the front door was ajar from where his mother-in-law had gotten out again. She'd gotten out last month and he and Lynne accepted that they couldn't leave her alone. Switched off their schedules so that someone was always with her. That had been Lynne's night, he was sure, as he'd hit Lynne's cell phone on the speed dial. "Is Babe with you?" he'd yelled into the phone at the sound of her perky hello. Could tell by her pause that Babe was not.

He remembered that he'd lost reception then because he was down in the cellar, calling out for Babe, then out the back door. Dialed 911 as he ran through the yard and gave the police dispatcher her description, light complexion, could almost look white, silver hair, no idea what she was wearing, a bathrobe, one of my suits, she could be naked, she could be on her way to freezing to death.

He remembered rushing through the park that bordered their house, thinking how much he hated his life. Though he had enormous affection for his mother-in-law, he hated this new layer of obligation to her. He hated practicing law anymore, hated this city anymore, hated that his wife was so absorbed in whatever the hell was absorbing her these days that he could no longer access that cottony part of her, that come-to-me-baby durable softness. Hated that he would be fifty-three his next birthday and that his knee was gone as he could feel what was left of the cartilage being ground to a fine dust as he ran through the park, hollering for Babe, trying not to concentrate on the knee.

Remembered feeling on the brink really of letting it all out, his rage. Rage about what? About the plight of the black man in America that hadn't changed much since his days as a token black in the Ivy League? No, that rage was familiar, a global rage that had been simmering all of his life; he knew how to manage that rage, live with, thrive in spite of that rage. That was a shared rage, communal. Could look at a version of himself, the judge in a courtroom perhaps, and know that when they peeled back the civilities, the rage was there; or at a board meeting for some foundation, across the table, just one other black man, the eye contact, yep, same rage; on the golf course, though it was a public course, fore, yeah brother, I'm pissed off too; the same rage, really when he was honest with himself, as the rapper's rage. This rage, though, pacing back and forth in his chest like a lion in a zoo trying to figure a way out, was a different rage. This rage felt too personal to share with the brothers, stamped with his name only.

He remembered the rage thinning out some when he found his mother-in-law stretched across a bench in the park talking to the sky as if she was talking to Cyrus, her doctor-husband who'd died not long ago. Remembered his relief as he tenderly wrapped her up in his coat and carried her into the house. Remembered that she'd told him a joke about a man and a woman having coffee in the woman's small kitchen after a night of passionate love-making and the man is sitting there dressed in the woman's pink robe and they hear a sound like thunder, but it's not thunder; it's a banging and the man asks, What the hell is that? And the woman just looks at him as if she's lost her speech. And he says again, What the hell is that? And she blurts out, My husband, my husband, he's early, he's been at sea, he shouldn't be back this soon. And he looks at himself sitting in the pink robe and says, No problem, where is your back door? And she says, I don't have a back door. And he looks at himself again in her pink robe, and he says, Okay, so where would you like a back door?

Cliff remembered that he'd laughed. Laughed so hard until his eyes ran. Laughed so hard until Babe laughed too. Laughed until Lynne rushed in, demanding to know why he'd hung up on her just then. He remembered how her coat had fallen from her shoulders when she grabbed her mother in a hug and he looked at Lynne squeezed into the clothes she wore. Tight jeans, tighter top, high-heeled leather boots. An extreme look compared to how she usually dressed. Usually dressed in loose flowing silky things; tunics, and layers of sheer over satins. Though it had been the curve of her hips that had first attracted him, and he'd tease her that he thought rich girls were supposed to be thin; she was built like those down-the-way sisters, he'd relaxed into the unstructured fit of her clothing. She was an artist after all—mixed media—flighty and sweet. He'd tried to tell himself that he was being ridiculous, that there was nothing outrageous about the outfit, really. But then she turned around, the stretchy red top she wore showed cleavage, her breasts had a pinched look. He was close to asking her who the hell had been pulling on her breasts. Remembered swallowing the thought, almost choking. Where had such thoughts come from anyhow? This was Lynne, his pure-to-the-bone Lynne, even as her face held that speechless expression like the woman's face in the joke Babe had just told. "Where you been?" he asked.

"I was at a reading, one of my students at the Germantown Y," Lynne had said out of breath. "And why'd you hang up in my ear?" she demanded.

He remembered watching as she wiped her hands over her face in big circles, leaving splotches of red because her skin was light, thin, showed everything, stretched even tighter it seemed with her hair pulled back beneath her characteristic scarf/headband, her light brown curls falling every which way to the rhythm of her neck going side to side. "I hyperventilated all the way home thinking Mother was lost. And where were *you*? This was your night, after all. God, the least you could do is to be here on your night," she'd said on an extended glare as she stood under the archway between the living room and the foyer.

He remembered that it was as if he was seeing her the way he had not seen her in years, through eyes unencumbered by the day-to-day married people's ramblings: the what to eat for dinner, where; the game tonight or *The Sopranos;* your turn with Babe, no yours; the case lost, won, dentist appointment today, colonoscopy next week, am I the only one who loads, empties the dishwasher around here.

He remembered that he'd had to turn away from her because her look was uncontainable at that moment: her shallow lips plumped suddenly, slicked with a cherry-tinged gloss; her raw soft beauty usually covered up with the swatches of spats and irritants and familiarity breeding contempt, exposed. Remembered that he became aware that he was seeing her the way another man—not her husband—would see her. Remembered how suddenly desirable she appeared. And then his rage erupted like a sudden-onset toothache and he said, "You know what, Lynne? I'm sick of this fucking shit." And she demanded that he be specific, that he say exactly what *fucking shit* he was sick of. And he didn't say because he couldn't say.

He remembered that Lynne was so angry that she slept downstairs in the room with her mother that night and he sat awake half watching *Law & Order* reruns, half reading Randall Robinson's *Quitting America,* then falling asleep, then waking in the middle of the night hot and itchy, tangled in his sheets, his manhood throbbing. He got up to turn down the thermostat, to pull the sheets tight on the bed. To go to the bathroom. He remembered looking around for water to pour. Lynne usually left a picture of ice water on the nightstand to satisfy her middle-of-the-night thirst. The cubes hitting the glass had always been such an erotic sound for Cliff, a prelude when he and Lynne were new together; when she'd wake at about two in the morning and sip her water and then reach for him, her mouth so wet and cold as she put it there and there and Lord-baby-yes, even there and he'd feel flattened, as if he was on that Hell Hole ride at Wildwood Beach of his youth that spun him around so fast that he was plastered to the walls, liquefied and turned inside out to a giddy dizziness. No ice cubes chimed that night, no crystal picture in there with lemons floating on top, no water goblets on the matching crystal tray.

He remembered that the house was quiet as falling snow as he tiptoed downstairs for water. He ran the water from the faucet and stood in the middle of the redone kitchen with its hard stainless steels and opulent woods. He drank back-to-back glasses of tap water. The taste of the water reminding him of childhood on his broken-down block of Ludlow Street where his mother would call him in from his hard playing and make him drink two glasses of cold faucet water back to back because she'd lost a nephew to dehydration. Actually sunstroke but

Cliff knew that his mother went out of the way to use big words around him when he was growing up. Credited her for his heightened verbal skills.

He remembered that on his way back upstairs he'd stopped in front of Babe's door. Had the thought suddenly that Lynne might not be in there. That she'd put her tight clothes back on for a rendezvous with the night. He'd put his hand on Babe's doorknob, eased the knob around, quietly opened the door to Babe's room.

He remembered that the air was warm and smelled of rubbing alcohol and baby talc. There were two lumps in the bed for sure. Told himself he'd not expected otherwise. The gooseneck night lamp was angled toward the bed and drizzled Lynne with yellow light. His Lynne. He tipped across the Berber-covered floor and stood over Lynne, turned back the covers and kissed her cheek. He pictured the broad curve of her hips in the tight jeans, his throbbing increasing to unbearable at the thought. He pulled at her shoulder. She made sleep sounds, half yawns, half moans, and tried to cover herself up again. Then he lifted her, whispered in her ear to forgive him please for cursing at her like that, please. He tried to cradle her and carry her across the room. She'd put on weight. He'd not noticed how much until just then. He managed to get her through the door and out into the darkened foyer.

He remembered her frightened expression once she was fully awake. "I can walk," she said. "Cliff, your back's gonna go out, your knee. We're gonna fall. Put me down. I can walk."

"And I can carry you. What? You think I can't still carry you?" he said as he started up the stairs.

"You can, Cliff. Of course I know you can," she'd said, even as she reached out for the banister and let go a scream as he staggered midway up and almost fell backward. He righted himself, though, and made it to the second floor and into the bedroom where they dropped onto the bed like two wild geese just shot down out of the sky.

He remembered that he moved on top of Lynne, saying her name, saying please, Lynne, please, an anguish to his tone as he slid her nightshirt over her head, and then reached to turn on the light so that he could look at her.

He remembered that she grabbed his arm, preventing him from reaching the light. Then she called his name. Called him baby, saying Oh God, please as she pulled at him and grew him. Their clumsy shifting and groping eased into their familiar rhythm.

He remembered that with the approach of his dam-burst, he felt a ball in his throat, enlarging into a boulder-sized mass, an accretion of every suspicion he'd felt of late. Remembered that as his manhood exploded, he cried. He came and cried. He kissed Lynne and squeezed her and made cracked moaning sounds in her chest. He remembered that she held him; she held him and held on, her eyes pressed shut, he guessed, so that she couldn't see him cry.

The red light on the phone was blinking. He'd not even heard it ring. The caller ID flashed OUT OF AREA and he figured that it must be Neena again. Wouldn't allow his expectations to be raised that it might be Lynne. He answered and it was Neena and his stomach dropped. She apologized; she was on a pay phone, she said, and had to put more money in. "So do I still have your ear for free?" she asked, laughing.

He tried again to picture her. Still could not as he listened to her laugh, the laugh open and continuous, accessible, an invitation in the laugh. He knew a woman's laugh. Had been interpreting a woman's laugh since the young ones of his youth in those finished basements. Read laughs the way some men read a woman's lowered eyes, or subtly moistened lips, a blushed cheek, an exaggerated sway of the hips.

Throughout the fifteen years he'd been married, he'd heard the come-ons in the laughs, the I-know-you're-hooked-up-but-we-can-be-discreet laughs from all types of women. He'd returned those laughs with a smile that said, Yeah, but I'm committed to my wife *and* in love with her too, then a polite kiss on the cheek to salvage the woman's ego; a whisper in her ear, but if I weren't, we could make merry. Thought again about Lynne's laugh, the way it gushed of late like water from a spring that's found a new opening, free at last, it just flowed and flowed.

He still couldn't picture Neena, and before he could think further about what he was doing, he was telling Neena that actually, she had more than his ear, laughing himself as he said it. "I've got a fund-raising event tomorrow evening on Broad Street. I don't know how close you are to town but I'll be there at around seven. If you can stop in, please, make yourself known to me. Possibly we can talk for a few minutes there. You can tell me what makes your case enticing."

Chapter 9

AN HAD FELT Neena's presence through the phone line when Neena called Tish's hospital room. Knew that she was hanging up on Neena's hard breaths when she mashed the phone down. Now she moved the phone from where it had been on the cart next to Tish's bed. Put it on the small table on the other side of the chair where she sat. She swallowed hard, trying to stuff down the thick band of guilt rising up in her throat in the form of reflux. Told herself again that keeping Neena from Tish was the best course of action just until Tish and the baby were out of the woods. She tried now to concentrate fully on Tish. Tish looking very much like Freeda around the eyes right now. That dark hollowed-out look that went right to Nan's chest and froze there. Nan's prayer had been that the girls would be delivered from Freeda's legacy of highs and lows and voices. And though Neena seemed determined to repeat her mother's habit of dropping off the planet until she felt like realigning herself, both Neena and Tish seemed to have been spared the

perversity of their mother's ways. Especially Tish. Such a grounded sweetheart Tish had been to Nan.

"More ice?" she asked Tish now.

Tish shrugged her shoulders, then smiled. The smile gave life to her eyes and Nan was up in a second, walking the length of the hospital corridor to the lounge area farthest from here just to utilize her nervous energy. It was evening and she'd been here all today. Paced the floor while Tish endured a plethora of tests, and then a procedure to stitch her cervix shut. Kept Malik company, and his mother when she came, answered the phone and took messages from so many well-wishers, so many people knew Tish, loved her, especially with her memberships on so many boards and organizations, active in her sorority; her by-invitation-only tea-sipping women's groups; service organizations that did for those with less. Neena so much the opposite. Neena should have been a painter or writer, a monk, the way she kept to herself instead of what she'd turned out to be. What had she turned out to be? Nan didn't know, knew only that Neena had shown academic promise in her teens, industrious, worked her part-time job after school and on weekends at Cook's Hoagie and Variety, garnered a scholarship to Temple University, then disappeared in the middle of the night when she turned nineteen.

Nan was back in Tish's room. She reorganized for the tenth time the items on the tray table. She poured ice in a cup and offered it to Tish, though Tish waved it away.

"Remember," Tish said, "how Miss Goldie would never give Neena and me ice when we were small 'cause she said that's why she'd never had any children; she was always eating ice and it froze her womb."

Nan chuckled as she sat. "That Goldie full of stories, got a story for every situation."

"I guess I'll be hearing from her soon," Tish said.

"I'mma go visit with her soon as she recovers from that stomach flu she caught on that casino trip. Not letting anybody in or out from her wing of the assisted living 'til the weekend."

"I'm talking about Neena."

"What about Neena?" Nan asked, swallowing the ice chips herself, then coughing.

"She'll probably be calling soon," Tish said as she patted the mound that was her stomach at six months pregnant. "Never fails, whenever I need to hear from her, the phone rings and it's her. She gets annoyed because she's always hated to hear me cry, but as soon as I hear her voice I start crying and she thinks I'm crying because I've been worried about her and they're tears of relief, but really it's because I've been in the middle of going through something and my situation is making me tender and then her voice just, you know, makes me cry."

"No, I didn't know that," Nan said.

"I wonder if Neena even knows that, you know, how much she's done for me just by calling the way she does."

"Well, if she knows when to call like you're saying she does, she likely knows how much you're getting out of it, Tish. Now what else can I do for you before I head on home?" Nan asked, thinking about the blanket she wanted to finish for the grand flea market the church was having.

Tish hit the remote and flicked the channels on the television. "I hope the ratings don't go up this week while I'm off air. That perky replacement of mine would love nothing better. Did you ever hear the story about her running away?"

"Who? the chile filling in for you?"

"No, Neena."

"Neena? Running away? You mean when she was nineteen?"

"No, leaving at nineteen is not running away, Nan; that's *leaving*. I'm talking about when she was sixteen," Tish said as she turned the television off.

"Sixteen?"

"Yeah, remember?" Tish said, grimacing as she tried to sit up more, then waving Nan away when Nan stood to help. "I'm not even gonna relive by repeating all the commotion of that day after Neena's sixteenth birthday, and the night before, for that matter. But, yeah, Neena got up in the middle of the night, she sneaked out through the bedroom window, and took the bus downtown to Miss Goldie's."

"Hush your mouth, Tish," Nan said as she sat back down and twisted the ends of the scarf that hung from her neck. It was a royal blue velvet and silk burn-out scarf that Tish had given her for Christmas. "Goldie wouldda told me such a thing."

"Apparently not if you never knew it happened. Neena said that she curled up on Miss Goldie's purple velvet couch, remember that couch?" Tish closed her eyes and sighed. "I loved that couch with the brass nail heads. Remember how the back of it dipped in the middle so that the couch actually looked like a heart, and how plush it was, how sinkable it made your body feel."

"I do, of course, Tish. I helped her pick the couch out. Couch was good and lived on by the time you and Neena came along. Now, what about Neena running away to Goldie's?"

"Well, Neena told me that once she sank into that couch it was so easy for her to pour her heart out to Miss Goldie. Not that it was ever hard to talk to Miss Goldie, something about the way she looked at you, as if she was just a little bit amused by what you were saying, that, you know, was just encouraging, you know, even if you were admitting having just done some horrible thing, Miss Goldie's expression just took the sting out of it. But anyhow, Neena said that Goldie just listened to her without judgment or chastisement. Said that before long she could hear Sam banging around in the kitchen and at first Neena thought that Sam was irritated that she'd shown up past midnight like that. Then a bit later, Sam called Goldie and Neena into the kitchen and she said he had set a table like it was a holiday. Had their plates sitting on silver laminated place mats, their tea poured in the silver-rimmed china cups, and in the center of the table between two light blue taper candles was a steaming bowl of buttered hominy grits and a mess of fried silver trout. He held their chairs out for them to sit and she said that on his way out of the kitchen he patted Neena on the top of her head and then squeezed the back of Miss Goldie's neck. She said she could feel how much love they had for each other just by the way Sam squeezed the back of Goldie's neck and the way Goldie leaned into his hand, as if at that moment Sam and Goldie carried on a conversation that no one else could understand but them. A mighty love, she said she witnessed that night. She said that she herself would probably never know that kind of love, but that I had a shot at it, that I shouldn't settle for less."

"Is that what she said, Tish?"

"She did. I was only twelve, but I shall never forget that. Abided by it too. You know, I could have a much more dazzling husband than Malik, but I wouldn't have the mighty love we've got."

"Wonder why Neena thought she wasn't privy to such a love?" Nan asked. Asked herself more than Tish.

They were both quiet for a time, Nan still twisting then untwisting the ends of her scarf, Tish rubbing her stomach in slow circles. Then Nan asked Tish how was Goldie able to persuade Neena back home. Obviously that's what happened, Neena made it back home before the sunrise, before Nan was able to miss her.

"Well," Tish said, readjusting one of the several pillows at her back, again waving Nan away when she started to rise to help. "Neena said that her plan had been to spend the night at Goldie's and then start off early for Newark. That's the last place Mommy had called from and she felt it in her bones that Mommy was still there, in Newark. She had money saved from what she held back from her church dues and from her allowance. But then she ended up back home, anyhow. She half-joked that she thought that Sam sprinkled some go-back-home dust in her grits. Though really she said it was something about eating the fish, no offense, Nan, but she said it was the best fried silver trout she'd ever eaten, and she had to really concentrate on separating the bone from the flesh and that took her out of her own head for a minute. She said that it helped that Goldie didn't tell her one way or the other what to do. Didn't say that she was right or wrong for leaving. Though Goldie did say that Neena would regret it forever if she left without telling me good-bye. So Neena consented to do that, you know, sneak back in the house and tell me good-bye. Sam and Goldie gave her a ride home and she said that she took one look at me sleeping and said to herself, I really don't feel like listening to this girl cry tonight. So she blinked the porch light per Goldie's instruction if for any reason she changed her mind about leaving, and then she just got undressed and went on to bed."

"Well, now," Nan said, as she moved from twisting and retwisting the ends of her scarf to untangling the cord that hung from the phone on the table next to where she sat. "That's quite a chunk, I must say, that I never knew. I suspected that Neena was sneaking out of the house from time to time when she got in that hot-in-the-behind stage—"

"No, actually," Tish interrupted as she pulled one of the pillows from behind her and tossed it toward the foot of the bed, "most of the time Neena wasn't being hot in the behind, she was being her own private investigator trying to find Mommy."

"Well, whatever she was doing, Tish, wasn't right for a teenage girl to be trying to take matters into her own hands like that. Superseded her means, she did. Wasn't equipped at that age to be finding her mother on her own."

Tish shrugged her shoulders. "I guess," she said.

"You didn't, did you, Tish? You missed your mother every bit as much and you been able to find peace with her leaving. All Neena had to do was lean on the Lord like I implored of her. Nobody's suggesting it was an easy thing to do, but it was doable."

Tish sighed and closed her eyes again. She didn't dispute what Nan had just said. Though she also understood how differently she and Neena related to their mother. Understood it even more now that she was close to motherhood herself. Nan had been her mother, really. Unlike Neena, Tish had spent the bulk of her infancy and toddler years with Nan. She was accustomed to the rhythms of Nan: the cha cha sounds of the sewing machine floating through the early morning air; the soft humming as Nan cooked and cleaned; the way Nan swayed from side to side as she sat in church, always the same row, same spot on the pew. The rise and fall of her breaths when they spent summer evenings on the porch, Tish leaning against Nan while they listened to the street sounds of the hand-clapping rhyming games the girls played, and the smack of sneakers against asphalt as the boys relay-raced from corner to corner, and the swing-low-sweet-chariot-type moans as women in black veiled hats lined up to go in the church across the street for a nighttime funeral service. There was for Tish a calming predictability to life with Nan.

Time spent with Freeda was jarring in comparison, like riding in a prop plane during a thunderstorm and having to wrestle with the nauseating motion, the dips and hard wavers from side to side, the fear that the plane would hurtle to the ground and wondering if it would hurt when it finally did, would she feel it when her head crashed through the seat in front of her, when her knees pushed through the bones of her rib cage. Though even that wasn't the worst of it. The worst was the noise of it: the way that Freeda would talk back to the voices she'd hear, and then pull her hair and clutch her stomach as if she was getting tragic news from the voices. Her screams would wake Neena and Tish in the middle of the night and Tish would cover her head with her pillow and sob into the pillow while Neena ran to Freeda, Neena actually able to calm Freeda down as she almost sang to her mother in a soothing voice, It's okay Mommy, there's nobody there, see Mommy, it's okay. At times like that Tish would pray for Freeda to leave, and once she was gone and they were settled back on Delancey Street with Nan, Tish would pray that her mother would never return.

"Tish, Tish," Nan called. "You want more graham crackers from the pantry before I leave from here? More water? Another blanket? Pillow?"

Tish shook her head. "I'm fine, Nan. I got this thing to push if I really need something."

"Well, is the television positioned to your liking? No sense in bothering them sitting around the nurse's station if there's something I can do."

Tish didn't respond. She was back there at six years old in the second floor of the duplex where she and Neena and Freeda lived on Market Street. The bay windows of their bedroom looked out on the el tracks and Neena would run to the window when she heard the train's approach. "Here's another one, Tish," she'd call out excitedly.

Though Tish found the interminable rumble of the el annoying; at night the line of lights would rush past the window like a long silver snake interrupting her sleep. But the worst was that day that the el seemed to run nonstop. Tish was in bed that day because she was suffering from the flu. Suffering too because Neena had gone to school so that Tish was home alone with Freeda and she was afraid that if there was an emergency with Freeda she wouldn't know what to do. The walls of the room were hot pink and the color made everything more unbearable: how hot her skin was, how much her head ached, how loud the train was, as if the train was running through her head; even Freeda's closeness was unbearable as Freeda sat on the bed and leaned over Tish, attempting to feed her chicken soup. "Mnh, Tisha, it's so good," Freeda said as she blew on the spoon and edged the spoon toward Tish's mouth. Tish could smell the garlic and thyme coming together on the spoon. She clamped her mouth and lowered her head.

"But I made it just like Nan's," Freeda cooed. "I used the very same recipe that she used on me when I was your age. Come on, just take a couple of sips for Mommy."

Again Tish refused. "Well, would you like a Popsicle then?" Freeda asked. "A cherry Popsicle might cool you off. You have to have some fluids, Tish."

Tish pouted.

"Don't you want Mommy to help you feel better? Don't you think I can?" Freeda asked.

"No," Tish said. "It's poison."

"Tish," Freeda said as she chuckled, "Mommy would never hurt you. Please believe me. I would kill myself before I ever hurt you."

"Then why don't you just kill yourself then," Tish said. She didn't know why she said it, hadn't even known that she'd been thinking it until the words were out of her mouth.

Freeda put the spoon back in the bowl and set the bowl on the nightstand. She stared off into space for what seemed like hours to Tish and Tish listened to the el as she counted the rising and falling of her mother's chest because otherwise Freeda was absolutely still. When Freeda turned to face her again, Tish looked for signs that her mother had been crying. Once Freeda started with the crying she was soon to leave. She hadn't cried, though Tish could see that her eyes were different, as if they were sitting back farther in her head.

Then Tish started to cry, convulsively. "I'm sorry, Mommy, I didn't mean it, Mommy," she said over and over as she cried.

Freeda grabbed Tish to her and held her in a tight hug. She squeezed her so hard that Tish thought that she was preparing to crush her bones. Freeda was wearing a mohair sweater and the wool was both soft and itchy against Tish's face. Freeda rocked Tish. She whispered in Tish's ear. "It's the fever, Tisha. You're burning up with a fever and a fever makes you say things. I want you always to remember that, you were burning up with a fever; a fever makes you say things."

"It's the fever, Mommy, I'm sorry Mommy," Tish said over and over, even as her mother wiped her down with a cool washcloth and turned the air conditioner on, though it was wintertime outside.

Nan was up, standing over Tish's hospital bed. Now she was dabbing Tish's cheeks with a cool cloth, wiping Tish's eyes, telling her that it was okay to cry, go ahead, cry. Just hold on to her faith even as she cried. Tish nodded. She hadn't even realized until just then that she'd been crying.

Chapter 10

AN KNEW ABOUT holding on to faith. Thought her faith had been tested and retested to the point where, if she'd been the type to question God, the why, Lord, why, would have been her nonstop utterance.

She turned up pregnant as a result of her climbing into bed with Alfred that first time. The pregnancy itself was not the calamity it might have been since by the time she knew for sure she and Alfred were already on the track to get married: Goldie had agreed to stand in witness; Sam had already offered cold cuts and Manischewitz for the reception; the people at her second job offered her a wedding-day dress. The stormcloud for Nan was not the pregnancy, it was that in her mind the child had been conceived too close in time to her sipping at the contents of that vanilla extract bottle and Alfred gobbling down what she had not. Worried from then on that the root may have lingered in their systems and damaged some workings of the baby coming to be in her womb. Though the baby by all accounts was perfect.

Alfred certainly thought the baby perfect as he looked at the infant through the receiving window. He never thought that such beauty could exist in human form the way that it did in that newborn. Nor did he know that such a feeling could happen to him on the inside that was so large that it reset everything about him, changed him. "A girl," he said out loud to no one in particular. "Look at the mat of shiny black hair, look at the dark-as-midnight-eyes. I'm melting, I'm so very thankful." He was also quite drunk as he staggered from the receiving room into the maternity ward where the new mothers occupied the beds that filled the length of the room. He was so overcome with gratitude for Nan giving him such a beautiful daughter that his eyes did him wrong and he cried in front of the bed that was not Nan's and rubbed the foot of the woman who lay there. She woke and screamed. That started a commotion that rippled the length of beds until it got to Nan's bed and the story was that a crazed drunk just tried to chop off someone's foot.

Nan knew it had to be Alfred. The seven months of married life with Alfred had been filled to brimming with the embarrassing consequences of his love for drink. His putting his key in the wrong apartment door, and when the door didn't open, just passing out there anyhow. His getting thrown out of bars and some Samaritan fetching Nan so that she could patch him up and cart him home. He'd insist that the mailman was late with the milk, he'd argue with the milkman because he'd not gotten his mail. He'd show up for work dressed for church, gone to church dressed as if he was preparing to unload cargo from a ship.

So Nan couldn't even look at Alfred now as Nurse Ratched's twin led him to Nan's bed, telling him that if he showed up in that condition again he wouldn't be granted entry. Nan pushed deeper under her covers and faced the wall.

"Nan, please don't turn away, Nan," Alfred begged. Then he got down on one knee. "Please, Nan, I have something important to say, please, I need your eyes on me." Still Nan kept facing the wall and Alfred dug in his pocket looking for a ring. Why? he asked himself then, was he looking for a ring. They were married already, weren't they? He was confused. But since he found himself on his knee, it must mean that he was supposed to propose. "Marry me, Nan," he said. "I never loved any woman like I have you, please, Nan. Please be mine."

Nan could hear the snickers jumping from bed to bed and she told herself that the women were jealous; their husbands were neither as devoted nor as good-looking as her Alfred. She turned around then. "Get off that floor, Alfred," she said through her teeth, trying to salvage any tatters of his dignity. The tone of her voice, the demanding urgency of it, went farther than the chewing of coffee grinds did toward sobering him up. Now he remembered what it was. The baby, as he stood and took Nan's hand in his and started to cry all over again.

"These are tears not of a weak man, but of a changed man," he said. "The sight of that baby has changed me, Nan. My ways, my ways, I lift my hand to Holy Heaven. My ways from this point on have been changed."

Nan looked at him standing there. His nice royal blue handkerchief was tucked in under his collar instead of in his lapel pocket. His exquisite tan and white seersucker suit was buttoned wrong, the knot of his tie was turned backward. His beautiful dark eyes were bloodshot in the corners. His nose ran as he stood there sobbing. She was flooded with that same large feeling she'd gotten when she saw him that first time in front of Sam's deli on Chestnut Street. Here stands the love of my life, she thought. May the Lord have mercy on my soul. Then she asked him if he'd taken his insulin yet today. Had he tested his urine for sugar?

"We can get to me after hours. Right now we've got to give our child a name. How do you like Alfreeda. Please say you like Alfreeda."

"But your insulin, Alfred—" Then she stopped. "Alfreeda," she said slowly, considering the name. "It has a certain ring, I must say, Alfred, it does." She lay back against the pillows and allowed the idea of the name to settle.

Then Alfred began to sing to the tune of Maria, "Alfreeda, we've just had a child named Alfreeda"; he walked back and forth the length of the beds as he sang, endearing the other mothers to him with the grand affection he was expressing for his newborn baby girl. He was back at Nan's bed telling Nan that just the thought of his name attached to something as pure as the infant would seal the fact that he was a changed man, a better man.

And he did try. The day he brought Nan and the baby home from the hospital and the yellow cab pulled up in front of their South Philly apartment, Alfred leaned in and told the driver to keep going. "Keep going some more, my man, I'll tell you when to turn," he said as they went beyond Twenty-third Street, crossed the river, then beyond Thirtieth, beyond the University of Penn, and the grand castles of West Philadelphia, at least that's how Nan had always characterized them. By the time they passed West Philadelphia High School for Boys and Girls, Nan assumed that they were going to Sam's store. Sam and Goldie must have prepared a surprise welcome home luncheon, Nan knew. Then Alfred whispered in the cabdriver's ear and instead of turning right they turned left. Then left again and through a block that looked as if it was lifted from a storybook with its leafed-out trees and whitewashed concrete sidewalks, and lush hedges newly sheared.

Alfred hopped from the cab and helped Nan out, Nan holding the baby close. He walked her to the foot of the steps, then held her elbow and guided her to the porch. "Ring the bell, Nan," he said as he hopped back down to the curb.

"Ring the bell? Who lives here, Alfred?" she asked, but Alfred was too preoccupied counting out money to pay the fare so Nan walked across the broom-swept porch and rang the doorbell. Her hands shook and she pulled the baby even closer. Then looked through the blinds and saw Goldie and Sam walk into the vestibule and her heart dropped. Foolish of her to think that this was her house, that Alfred could even pull off such a feat without her assistance. This was the house Sam had bought for Goldie and himself. She fixed her face to smile, kissed her newborn's forehead reminding herself that the pleasure she held in her arms was worth ten thousand houses, and she was happy for Goldie, she loved Goldie like a sister, she reminded herself too.

"Congratulations, Goldie," she said as the door opened and Goldie took the baby from Nan's arms, Goldie cooing and welling up at the sight of the child, saying, Look, Sam, look, you ever seen something as beautiful as this?

Nan moved beyond them into the wide-open living room with the buffed-up hardwood floors and as if to confirm it for Nan, there was Goldie's couch, the gold brocade that Nan had helped her pick out last month. Nan was so large with Freeda in her womb that she was unusually short-tempered with Goldie that day at the furniture store as Goldie went back and forth between two or three models asking Nan over and over, Which one you favor, Nan, huh? You got good taste. Which upholstery will give me better wear, huh? You know fabrics.

Now Nan had to sit on the couch. She was exhausted. Of all the childbirth side effects she'd been primed on, nobody told her how plain tired she'd be. She sat on the couch. Almost wanted to put her feet up on the coffee table. The coffee table familiar, the brown and white tile shaped in a diamond that was at the center of the table. Her coffee table this was. The end tables and lamps hers too. And there over the mantel, the picture of Jesus ascending. Her picture, her house, her dream come true as she listened to Sam and Goldie still in the vestibule making bright exclamations over Alfreeda, then watched Alfred walking toward her. His chest as wide as the double-wide window centered on the living room wall. She told herself then to hold on to this moment, she would need this moment, would need to return to it time and again because happiness like this couldn't last, wasn't supposed to last. If it lasted, she told herself then, how would she know that she had faith?

Those early years were good during Alfred's sober times. Alfred and Freeda adored each other and he was always looking for a reason to parade her down the street, swinging her hand in his, both beaming when people stopped them. Oh how cute, the admirers would say. Oh look, what a perfect daddy's girl. And she was. From infancy on she lit up whenever Alfred was near. Goldie would tease Nan that she needed to have another child that was for her, because that baby girl is all Alfred's. Though Nan didn't mind. She enjoyed that father and daughter adored each other so. Encouraged it, in fact. Noticed that Alfred didn't even want the streets as much after Freeda was born.

One brilliant Saturday morning Alfred lumbered home sooner than usual after walking Freeda to the dance studio where she took ballet. Nan had been cleaning grout from the back splash over the kitchen sink. Had thought she'd timed it to how long it generally took him to walk the five blocks to the Fancy Feet studio and back. Didn't like for him to catch her cleaning. Goldie had cautioned her to never let her man catch her in the act of cleaning. Too domesticated a thing and a man's nature resists domestication. "Better you let the house go than look like a wife," she'd say. "The average man prefers a sweetheart to a wife." She hid her hands behind her back as she peeled off the rubber gloves she wore, then pulled the drawer open behind her and dropped the gloves in, the gloves still wet with ammonia. Then turned to wash her hands, trying also to disperse the smell hanging over the kitchen. Asked Alfred then what did he do? Fly back?

"She's too sad, Nan, not normal. I know what I'm talking about."

"What are you talking about?" Nan asked as she went to the refrigerator and pulled out their Saturday afternoon snack. Deviled eggs and sardines, saltine crackers on the side. She set down two napkins, plates and glasses, poured lemonade into the glasses. Alfred pulled her chair back so she could sit, then he sat, sighed. Bowed his head while Nan said Grace. Reached for her hand then.

"All I'm saying is that we might be in for a rough landing." He pulled her hand to his lips and kissed her hand and Nan hoped her hand didn't smell of ammonia. "We been fortunate to fly this high for this long." He continued talking while Nan served their plates. "I have anyhow, never thought life could be as good as the one you've made for me. But the air's holding trouble ahead, Nan. I hate to say, but it is. Freeda's too sad for a well-loved, cared-for eight-year-old child."

"What's got you talking like this, Alfred? Did Freeda have another one of her crying spells, normal thing for a child, especially a little girl."

"She didn't cry, but she did put words to her feelings as we walked past the fire station and I pointed out the pole that the firemen slide down. And she said sometimes she slides down a pole just like that but then she can't get back up. And I asked her to describe what she was talking about. And she said sometimes she's pulled down to the bottom inside of herself and she's stuck even though she doesn't want to be there. And I asked her what's pulling her down like that and she said a strong wind that has hands and eyes, big rough hands and Doberman pinscher eyes." Alfred's voice caught in his throat and he swallowed hard. "And so I asked her what it was like down there, and she said it feels like how the Reverend Mister describes where Satan lives. No joy allowed."

"Now, Alfred. The chile's got an overactive imagination, always has." Nan stuffed an egg into her mouth. She then arranged a sardine on a cracker just to do something with her hands, her hands wanting to shake. And she couldn't let Alfred see her hands shake, couldn't let her concern show, her concern might push Alfred's worry to proportions that he couldn't handle with a sober mind. Might start him drinking again and so far this time he'd gone for close to four years.

She'd become accustomed to protecting him from potential life blows. When she herself had had a cancer scare that turned out to be just a fibroid, she'd not even hinted it to Alfred for fear of arousing his taste buds for Jack Daniel's, or Southern Comfort, overproof rum. She never complained of a headache, or toothache, stomach sickness, agitation; worried that in order to take away her complaint, he'd first have to bolster himself with his own liquid panacea. And though Goldie had suggested that she was going about it all wrong, what's the sense in having a partner if you're still dancing alone, she'd say, Nan didn't want to take the chance that in her weakness, Alfred would himself become weaker still. So she held her hands from shaking.

Though she may as well have let her shaking hands show anyhow. May as well have allowed her entire self to go into convulsions because a few months later Alfred started drinking again anyhow. Nan couldn't say for sure if it was his worry about Freeda, had never been able to say for sure what the spark was that ignited his desire for drink. Though he did rein himself in the following month, for good, he swore. This time for good. For good that time lasted eight weeks, six months; once he went another entire four years without a drink and their sober life was idyllic, filled with a clean house and thick center-cut meats and the sounds of Freeda's laughter when Freeda was a happy girl. But inevitably Alfred would return to chasing down a meal with a beer and then chasing the beer down with rye. Nan would threaten to put him out, then she'd put him out, then she'd go find him and drag him back home. She'd pat him down with a cool cloth, help him roll into bed. She'd pour strong black coffee down his throat come morning so that he could go to work.

To his credit he remained a hard worker, brought most of his paycheck home. He was never violent or excessively argumentative with Nan. Didn't run around with other women that she knew of. He'd cry and sing " 'Round Midnight" and then pass out. Nan convinced herself he was the best possible of drunks, told herself that if this was the worst storm life was sending her way, she could weather it.

Except that she couldn't. Came to that realization one Sunday morning, a decade and a half into the stop-start-this-time swear-it's-for-good-never-could cycle. Nan got up early and took a longer than usual bath. Took extra time with her appearance that morning too. Combed her hair out in looser curls, put on eye shadow, and lipstick and rouge. She'd had the thought from time to time that if she'd been a prettier woman; if she'd been smarter; if she'd been more charming; if she'd been wittier, stronger, weaker, sexier; if she could dance, sing, play pinochle, play the harpsichord, the ponies; if she'd been anyone other than who she was: Nan, the well-raised southern girl with the beautiful mouth though otherwise unremarkable looks who could create old-time-religion-type transformations with a needle and thread and some fabric to cut, then she could have turned Alfred's lusting from the direction of those bottomless shot glasses and made him lust only for what was righteous, thought herself righteous.

Sat Alfred down that Sunday morning. Really sat down beside him on the porch where he'd landed the night before trying to get to his keys; his urine glistened as it trailed down the steps and seeped into the garden where pink begonias were on display. "Do you think you even have it in you to stop? Are you even able, Alfred?" she asked.

Alfred looked at Nan and in his mind she was smiling. She was all dolled up with lipstick and rouge, her hair out, her voice like honey with a hint of a rasp that made his manhood stir. He smiled back at Nan. "Hey there, gorgeous."

"Do you even want to? Alfred. Whether or not you're able, do you even want to stop?"

He thought he'd never heard Nan use such a nonjudgmental tone. The nonjudgment in her tone snipping through the layers of his inebriation. He cried and shook his head back and forth, "No, No, I don't have it in me to stop," he said. "I can't, I can't, Lord knows I can't. And I want to, Nan. I want to, for you, for Freeda. But I can't. I don't have it in me to stop."

Nan took his head against her chest and rocked him like a toy boy-doll. She could smell bacon sizzling all up and down the block. Could detect too that unmistakable aroma of raw chicken parts dressed in flour and paprika going into the army-sized skillets in the church kitchen across the street. She should be over there right now helping to prepare for the dinners to be served between the morning and afternoon services. She should be shaping her pretty mouth in the special smile she reserved for Mr. Edwards, the Sunday school superintendent.

A robust middle-age man with a balding head who'd lost his wife a year ago, Mr. Edwards hadn't sent the earth to moving under Nan's feet when she looked at him the way that the earth had shifted when she'd first seen Alfred, but there was a burp in the air that seemed to hint of possibilities. Mr. Edwards would hold on to her hand longer than most when he greeted her; of late he'd even started leaning in to give her a polite peck on the cheek, allowing his lips to linger as he whispered, Good morning my dear sister Nan. She'd not done anything to provoke the attention that actually made her feel less weighted on the inside, smiling on the inside. She'd not batted her eyes, not twisted her hips when she walked past him, not smirked her mouth in a come-on smile. And most especially, she'd not mixed her sweat in a brown-bottled concoction to persuade his attention, because that act all those years ago in that South Philly bar that smelled of chitterlings and whores' perfume still plagued her.

Alfred had fallen back asleep against her chest, had slobbered all over her dress, and she realized she'd have to change it. Realized something else as she sat on the porch floor rocking him. She'd have to let him go. And if he came back to her it couldn't be on staggered legs. Never was that she wasn't enough of all those things she'd tell herself she wasn't enough of each time he went down into the mineshaft of drunkenness. The list expanding the longer he remained down there. What she really wasn't was God. Realized then that nothing short of God would cure Alfred. She cradled his head and rehearsed how she'd say it. She'd tell him that she just couldn't go on with him like this. She didn't have it in her. And since by his own admission he knew how that felt not to have something in you, something that you were desperate to have in you but it wasn't within your power to put it there, he should be able to read her heart, and hold no malice against her for snipping the cord that had bound them.

Alfred was snoring against her chest and she rubbed the softness of his hair. She thought about how she'd explain it to Freeda. Goldie had asked if Freeda would like to spend the week on Coney Island with her and Sam, and Nan thought now would be a perfect time. She kissed Alfred's forehead and he smiled in his sleep. She thought she'd change into the black and white sateen dress to wear to church today, the one with the dropped waist that gave the illusion of curves to her hips.

Alfred moved back to South Philadelphia and Freeda, who'd always been a daddy's girl, shuttled back and forth between the two. She didn't take one parent's side over the other, though if she had her leanings, it would have been toward her father. She had huge love, affection, and respect for her mother, but she was devoted to Alfred because she understood his compulsion to drink. She thought that, like her, he had a dark bottomed-out place inside of him that tried to hold him mired but the drink allowed him to float back to the top. Saw his drunkenness as his attempts at being happy, at being good. In Freeda's eyes, his goodness always showed through.

By then Freeda was a pom-pom-shaking high school cheerleader for the West Philly Speed Boys; secretary of the Young People's Choir at her Baptist church; Saturday shampoo-girl at Miss T's Beauty Salon on Sixtieth Street. Except for Freeda's tendency toward happy-sad swings on her emotional pendulum, she seemed none the worse after the snap in her parents' union.

A year into the separation something solid inside of Freeda that had held her together at the core, even with her high-low moods, began to break down. She was seventeen and her menstrual cycle became erratic and she was afraid she was pregnant though she hadn't actually had sex by then. Her junior prom date had come on her clothes, a sky blue satin gown hand-sewn by Nan. And Nan had been preaching to Freeda since she was old enough to understand that a man's essence could in fact travel through cotton or nylon, or silk, or polyester, even wool, to get inside of a woman because that was the nature of a man's essence, that was its God-intended purpose, to get inside of a woman to plant the seed that would blossom into a baby. She was so sure that the prom date's essence had meandered on through the satin that she began swallowing Humphreys 11 pills by the handful because the girls on the cheerleaders' squad said that would bring on a miscarriage. She was relieved when she started cramping the next week and realized that she wasn't pregnant. Though she was also sad because she didn't know for sure whether or not she had been, whether or not she'd disrupted a life trying to form.

It was also about this time that she began eating starch by the boxful. She'd been introduced to starch when she was just eight years old by Lou, the wild-looking woman who rented the third floor of Sam and Goldie's triplex. Lou would sit on the stairwell licking mounds of starch from her palm and the sight of her fascinated Freeda. Freeda would drift out into the hallway as Goldie and Sam and her parents laughed and talked around the kitchen table while Sam prepared a gourmet meal. Freeda would pretend to be counting the banister spokes on the stair rail, or the bouquets of purple and blue pansies on the wallpaper as she stared at the woman with her explosive hair uncombed, her feet always bare, until one day she worked up the nerve to talk to her.

"What you eating, Miss Lou?" she asked.

"Starch, girl."

"Why?"

"Got acid in my stomach."

"Me too."

She laughed. "You too young to know what I'm talking 'bout."

"Does it burn in a circle?" Freeda asked.

"Mnh," she said as she studied Freeda. "Maybe you do know. Come'ere, stick out your hand."

Freeda did and Lou tipped the box over Freeda's palm and filled it with starch. "Don't tell Goldie I gave you this. I don't want no shit out of those people."

"I promise not to," Freeda said as she sat on the steps next to Lou, careful not to spill the starch from her hands, and licked the starch. The starch was powdery-soft as it filled up in her mouth and filled her up on the inside and even back then she'd gotten a surge of euphoria like a Christmas tree that's plugged in and elicits an aaah when the lights suddenly shoot into view.

The night a year into her parents' separation Nan was out for the evening and Freeda had gone through two entire boxes of Argo starch. She stomped on the boxes to flatten them so that she could put them in the bottom of the trash so Nan wouldn't know. She felt drunk by the time she climbed into bed and dreamed a vivid dream where she was at the Academy of Music sitting between her mother and father fascinated by the throbs of color and motion pulsing from the stage. Except that there was no sound accompanying the flashes of orange and red and purple that the performers wore as they jumped and glided across the stage. In the dream Freeda shook Alfred's arm, then Nan's to ask them where was the sound. Her parents didn't respond because they were too absorbed in what was happening on the stage so Freeda said to herself, This is a silly dream, I think I'll wake up. She woke to a soaked feeling under her back and realized she'd peed in her sleep. How did that happened? she wondered. She'd had no indication that she had to go the bathroom, not even in the dream; she should have had to go to the bathroom in the dream the way she often did and would wake at the last second and run down the hall just in time. She got up and began pulling her sheets from the bed. She'd wash them and try to get them on the line before her mother woke; otherwise how would she ever explain wetting herself at this age? Then she stopped. There was no sound. Not the rustling of the sheets, or the creak of her bare feet against the hardwood floor. She rapped her dresser with her knuckles, still nothing. She was deaf, she thought, horrified as she started for her bedroom door to run to her mother for help. But something was calling for her to stop, saying, "Wait, Freeda, wait."

She was relieved, she wasn't deaf after all if she could hear this voice. Whose voice? "Who are you?" she asked into the bedroom air.

"Sportin' Life," the voice replied.

"Sportin' Life? From *Porgy and Bess*?"

"Necessarily so," he said. And Freeda felt his voice coming from inside of her own head. The inside of her head transformed to the Academy's stage and there in the center was Sportin' Life, calling her by name. "Come on, Freeda baby, come go away with me," he said on a laugh.

"You must be crazy," she said. "I don't know you."

"Change your sheets, pee-bottom, then we'll talk."

"Fuck you."

"Okay, now see, I didn't want to have do this so soon, wanted to dance and romance you first, but now I'm forced to introduce to you our mutual, personal friend. Here he is, the one and only, the original, the devil."

Freeda had always been devil-phobic since she was a young child. Every time her mother mentioned the devil, which—Nan being Nan—was often with phrases like: get behind me devil, don't let the devil use you, nothing but the devil in her/him; Freeda would get a glimpse of the devil's eyes that were like a Doberman pinscher's eyes. The image would paralyze her with an icy shrill that moved from her toes to her crown and she'd be disoriented for minutes after. She surely wasn't trying to meet the devil in person. She screamed at Sportin' Life to leave her alone. She chased him around the room even as part of her realized the senselessness of it, he was in her head after all, not like she could catch him. Except that now he was in the room, he was sitting atop the radiator dressed in a plaid suit with a three-button vest and diamond argyle socks.

"Like my socks?" he laughed as he lifted the cuff of his pants and Freeda saw how thin he was, figured she could take him in a fight as she kicked at his ankle. He was quick, though, too quick as he moved around the room in flashes. She began throwing things: books, knick-knacks, jars containing lotions, a lamp. She aimed for his oblong head that was changing in color from red to green like a traffic lamp.

She hollered at him to leave her as she threw whatever she came upon, aiming in whatever direction he seemed to run. And that's how she was as Nan stood frozen in the doorway to Freeda's room.

Nan had just fallen asleep. She'd been tossing and turning in her head about whether to remain in the relationship with Mr. Edwards with whom she'd begun a discreet affair. Earlier in the evening they'd laughed through dinner at the Pub then Nan had accompanied Mr. Edwards back to his house, a spacious Mount Airy twin where she'd helped him remove from the walls some of his dead wife's pictures. He'd had pictures of the woman in every room from the vestibule to the kitchen, some even blown up to poster size so that it felt to Nan that the dead wife was standing over her everywhere she turned in the house ready to scratch her eyes out. Goldie had suggested to Nan that the need to overexpose the woman all over the walls like that meant that Mr. Edwards was likely weighted down with guilt. And when Nan had pressed Goldie as to the likely origins of the guilt, Goldie had conceded that she couldn't say whether or not it was rational guilt, whether he had done the woman wrong while she was alive, or whether he just felt guilt for not having the power himself to keep her breathing, but that if Nan had designs on Mr. Edwards she'd have to help him walk through the guilt.

Nan did have designs on him. She was in her late thirties by then and he was ten years her senior and she liked that he knew more. Not that Alfred wasn't intelligent, but Nan could never predict when the drink would erode Alfred's judgment so that she felt the need to always be a rung higher on the ladder when it came to her thinking. But with Mr. Edwards she could know or not know about a matter and if she knew he'd pay her a compliment; if she didn't he'd patiently break the matter down into digestible chunks. Plus she enjoyed the close caring they shared without the miseries that tagged along with being in love. She thought that once the caring turned to full-blown in-love she'd start to worry about him, was he eating right and taking the water pills for his pressure, were his car brakes in good working order so he wouldn't skid off of the Schuylkill Expressway. She knew that Mr. Edwards, being a man, would resist her attempts to check up on his well-being, which would cause her worrying to increase. Knew that once her worrying reached its height she'd begin to resent him for having to worry about him in the first place. Thought that nothing could kill the beauty of falling in love quicker than being in love. So since she was content with the status of their relationship she thought it worth it to do as Goldie suggested and help him through his guilt.

She asked him to accompany her to the Flower Show and as they walked through the Civic Center transformed into the brilliance of garden after garden, right as they got to the path that led through the tulips, Nan confessed to Mr. Edwards some of her inner turmoil over asking Alfred to leave. Said that she felt partly responsible for Alfred's unchecked drinking. "I declare, if I'd been more of a woman, I could have likely sobered him up all by myself."

"No, no, no, no, no," Mr. Edwards rushed to say as he pulled Nan to him right at the entrance way to the rose gardens. "You're woman enough, Nan. You're more than woman enough."

By the time they reached the lilies, Nan had gingerly turned the conversation back to him. Said that he was man enough too, at least to her eyes and to her heart. "Though I have the feeling," she said, "that you, just like I, am guilt-ridden for not having the power to change the outcome in the life of a mate."

Once that transom had been crossed, he acquiesced to Nan's gentle prodding about the poster-sized picture of his wife over the half-moon table that especially haunted Nan each time she'd stepped into his house. The wife, Alma, had a pipe mouth with inordinately thin, almost nonexistent lips that delighted Nan because Nan knew that her own lips were her best feature, so full and voluptuous. But this picture of Alma, besides being larger than life, made Alma's mouth appear as full as Nan's; her skin that Nan had known to be light and freckled was bronzed and smooth in the picture; even the veins in her neck that Nan remembered most about her because she was thin and the veins always seemed to be jutting, were flush, making her neck youthful. Plus, she was sans glasses in the picture, and her light brownish eyes had a flirty look, at least Nan reasoned that's what a man would see. Though Nan saw something else, something only her gender would pick up, it was a look of proprietorship that seemed to say, I dare you to go after my man.

So Nan was ecstatic that Mr. Edwards agreed that yes, that large one should probably come down; then he'd even suggested a couple of other locations from where pictures of Alma might be removed.

But as Nan took down an eight by ten from the mantel she was assaulted by a never-ending spiderweb spread around the corner of the frame; its silky threads grazed Nan's pretty mouth and hung there glued and she'd had the urge to spit the rest of the night. And then as Mr. Edwards lifted from the nails the poster-size photo with the thick wooden frame, it slipped from his grasp and just missed his foot—would have likely broken his foot—though it did hit the half-moon table, crashing the blue and white bone china bud vase Nan had given to Mr. Edwards to commemorate their six-month anniversary. Later that night, as Nan and Mr. Edwards languished in his bed enjoying the soft lies lovers tell each other as the glitter settles, there came a loud splitting sound, as if the foundation of the house was shifting and when they went downstairs to investigate, they saw a crack in the wall over the half-moon table where the nail that held the poster-sized photo had been; the crack lengthened and widened even as they stood there. On the one hand Nan had the thought that she was caught in the middle of an episode of *The Alfred Hitchcock Hour*. On the other hand, though she'd never believed in ghosts or visits by the dead, and though she rarely cursed even to herself, as she stood there watching the crack in the wall grow, she let the words reverberate through her head: *This dead bitch is trying to tell me something.*

It was past midnight when Nan returned home and Freeda was sleeping soundly. Nan had checked her forehead for a fever the way she'd done every night since Freeda was born, whether or not she'd shown indication of a cold. Then she'd gone to bed herself and her sleep was uneasy since her mind was wrestling with Mr. Edwards's dead wife. She really didn't want to sever what she had with Mr. Edwards, even as she tussled over the looming presence of the dead wife. Had added a request in her prayers before she fell asleep that the woman not ride her sleep the way that people down home talked about witches doing. And then as soon as she'd drifted into a tentative sleep, she woke to the screaming and crashing coming from Freeda's room.

"Lord have mercy, Jesus," she breathed into the bedroom air when she could unfreeze herself from the terror of watching Freeda. She ran to Freeda to try to both contain her and understand what was happening. "Freeda, Freeda, look at me and tell me what it is. Please Freeda. Sweet Jesus, please."

"Mother, Mother, I don't want to meet the devil. He's gonna make me meet the devil."

"Who, Freeda? Who?! Lord Jesus you're just having a bad dream—"

"It's not a dream, it's real, Sportin' Life is in here and I've got to chase him out."

"Sportin' Life? Freeda, look at me, you're half asleep. Look at Mother right now and wake yourself up. Wake up, Freeda."

Freeda started sobbing then. "I peed in my bed, Mother. What's wrong with me? I peed in my bed."

"You what? Peed?" Nan pulled Freeda to her. "It's okay, you're probably coming down with something. Come on, I'ma draw you a warm bath. It's okay. I'll make tea, chamomile tea—"

"But the sheets, Mother. Don't we have to hang the sheets on line."

"Right now we're tending to you, come on, Freeda. It's okay. Let's get you in a warm tub, let's get some tea in you. It's okay. Yes it is. Yes it is."

After the bath and then the tea, Freeda did seem to settle down. Nan tucked Freeda in to sleep in her—Nan's—bed. She lay down with her until she heard Freeda breathing easy, deep-slumber breaths. Then Nan slipped out of the bed and went into Freeda's room. She took her bedside Bible with her and turned on every lamp in Freeda's room and opened the window wide and read out loud verses that had to do with casting the devil out. She called Mr. Edwards's wife by name as she did. "Alma, you got a gripe with me being with your husband, you deal with me woman to woman. Don't involve my child," she said. Though deep down she didn't believe it even remotely possible that the dead had disturbed Freeda's sleep, just in case, she read the Bible out loud and stripped the bed and moved the furniture and swept every crevice in the room. She wiped the room down with bleach and then burned a vanilla candle, followed by one scented with cinnamon. Daylight pushed through the window when, exhausted, she was done. She called in sick to her government job and climbed back into her bed with Freeda. They both slept that day until well past noon.

That evening Nan took Freeda to their general practitioner family physician and related the details of the night before. He examined Freeda, meaning that he listened to her heart and checked her ears, and nose, and throat. He felt her feet for fluid retention, then palpated her abdomen, her back, the glands in her neck and under her arms. He asked about headaches, falls, any other kinds of trauma. Change in diet, routine, troubles at school. Concluded that as an isolated event, the episode of hysteria could be just a delayed reaction to Nan and

Alfred's separation. If it happened again, he said he could give Nan a name of a colleague at Friends Hospital.

"Friends Hospital?" Nan asked, slightly horrified. "Isn't that where the truly disturbed go?" Even as she was determined that Freeda would never need such a place. Already thinking of how she'd undo her separation from Alfred, and sever the soft caring ties she'd enjoyed with Mr. Edwards. Should she have occasion to credit herself for the damnation in her life, she didn't want another notch in her belt next to the one having to do with working roots to make Alfred love her: that by asking Alfred to leave and taking up with Mr. Edwards, she'd pushed her daughter into the devil's arms.

So Nan detached the hook and eye that had connected her to Mr. Edwards, then she asked Alfred back. She accepted that Alfred was her cross to bear, and what a heavy cross he became. The next several years were an overcast series of the drinking bouts lasting longer, the dry times shorter. The dry times taken up with Alfred's alcoholic-induced hallucinations, then came the sanitarium stays.

Through it all Nan prayed harder than the day before, prayed for forgiveness, for deliverance. Fasted, read her Bible, did for others with less than she. She counted it as a special blessing that at least Freeda had no more middle-of-the-night hysterics and she'd not found it necessary to follow up with the Friends Hospital doctor. Though Freeda still had the high-low mood swings, they were easy enough to rationalize away as something that all girls went through in their late teens.

Freeda did seem to settle into a normalcy except that Sportin' Life still came to call. He and Freeda would have whispered conversations late at night when the house was still. Freeda learned to keep his visits to herself. She figured out that as long as she did what he told her to do, he kept the devil from her view. When he told her to leave, she left. Left a note for Nan begging her not to worry. Then Sportin' Life would seem satisfied and vanish for a time and Freeda would return ebullient. And then the sadness would descend and there was Sportin' Life breathing in her ear again. Freeda acquiescing. Except for that night years later when he told Freeda to get the extra pillow from the dining room closet and start with Neena because Neena would be easier than Tish. Tish would kick and scream but Neena adored her so. It would be lovely, Sportin' Life insisted, how easily Neena would succumb.

That was finally where Freeda drew the line.

Chapter 11

EENA WORKED WITH her hair as she prepared to meet Cliff. She greased her scalp and platted her hair into half a dozen braids. She tore a brown paper bag into strips and twisted the strips to use as curlers and rolled each braid. She showered and then moved the blow-dryer around her head. She tried to ignore the circle of hunger in her stomach. She'd not eaten yet because she'd slept much of the day. Felt like a newborn all the sleeping she'd been doing since she'd been here. Sleeping and peeing, it seemed.

She dressed in the peach-colored sweater she'd bought at the Salvation Army Thrift Store, the good black wool skirt that had made the trip from Chicago; her black tights and boots. She made her face up with the ridiculously priced makeup she'd come here with. She remembered buying much of it the week before from a young girl training to be a cosmetics associate at Saks. "I'm hating on you sister-girl 'cause you know how to treat yourself," she'd said to Neena as she wrapped the already boxed items in tissue paper. When Neena replied that the cost of the bronzing powder alone could feed a Sudanese village for a week, she'd gotten a blank stare from the young girl; then the seven-foot-tall blond supervisor who'd been hovering around pretending to fix the display cleared her throat in a tone that demanded that the trainee respond. "Now see, this company supports the world's poor," the young girl rushed to say. "That's why I'm proud to work here." She nodded emphatically, even as she gave Neena that why-you-gonna-put-a-sister-on-blast look.

Neena looked in the mirror at the painted-up version of herself. Now she tore off toilet paper and wiped the lipstick from her mouth, now she washed her face of the sheer foundation, the bronzer, the blush, now she creamed her lids to get rid of the taupe-colored eye shadow. Her face was naked now, gleaming. She put Vaseline to her lips. Decided that's all she'd wear tonight in the way of face adornments. She unwound the twisted paper from her hair and undid the plaits, then picked her hair out into an oversized curly 'fro. She grabbed her coat, her leather purse, and was out of the door.

She stopped at the pay phone in the lobby and called the hospital's patient information to get an update on Tish. Fair. Okay, Neena told herself, she could handle fair.

The temperature had actually risen since she was last out and she slowed her steps to enjoy the feel of the night. The air was like a feather. She said into the air, "Be okay, Tish. Please. You and my nephew please be okay. Please, please, please." She repeated it louder as she pushed her voice into the silvery air. "Please be okay, Tish. Please, you and that baby be okay." Worked herself up to a full-scale incantation as she walked. Walking now past the fountain at Logan Circle; the fountain was shooting pink water into the air and she wondered who would do such a thing as turn the water pink. She thought about all those the pink walls of her childhood; remembered how Tish had grimaced at the one house on Sansom Street when they'd returned from school and Freeda greeted them, gushing, smelling of turpentine and paint thinner. Freeda had just covered the living room walls with the thickest color pink Neena had ever seen, so thick that the room felt smaller, the ceilings lower, and she remembered that she started to perspire. Then Tish began to cry. "This is ugly, I hate it. Who would do such a thing?"

"But, Tisha," Freeda had said, "I need it. I need the pink to be happy." Then Freeda's eyes went darker and Neena wanted to slap the shit out of Tish. Though now as she watched the pink sprays from the fountain interrupting the blue-gray night, she realized that the walls were hideous, really they were.

"Be okay, Tish, please," she continued to chant as she walked past the Four Seasons Hotel where a town car pulled up into the driveway lined with pots overflowing with nonnative plantings and emptied itself of short white women in minks. Neena called out even louder for her sister and the baby to pull through. She didn't even care that she looked certifiable out here talking to herself as she continued to pray through the air. She invoked Tish's name for the several more blocks as she entered the thicker part of downtown. Even as she crossed Market Street. Market Street right now still loaded down with people, all types of people that seemed as if they'd been flung from galaxies far and wide, a miracle that they didn't start a war of the worlds out here, or at least collide like meteors smashing into each other's heavens. She was almost shouting out Tish's name by the time she reached Broad and Chestnut and there in hearing range was Bow Peep at the same corner where'd she'd seen him last. Now she was suddenly embarrassed as Bow Peep looked at her, his long mouth upturned in a smile.

She felt like a high-brow Baptist caught dancing at a Pentecostal church as she put clamps to her mouth and shyly waved.

Bow Peep motioned her over. She started to ignore him and continue on but she was already within the range of his gravitational force. So she stopped.

"Whoa, the hair, I like," he said

She'd forgotten that she'd picked it out into a tall 'fro. "Thanks," she said. "I'm in a hurry, sort of, and don't really have time—"

"Yeah, where you headed?"

"Uh, somewhere," she said, deciding she'd not mention that she was on the way to meet up with his buddy. "We'll run into each other again soon, I'm sure—"

"You know somewhere there's a place for us, Neena, a time and place for us. Who is Tish?" he asked before she could pull away. "Isn't that the name you were just calling out?"

"That's my sister."

"Ah, the one who might be having a miscarriage," he said as he punctuated himself with a low note blown through his flute. "You told me, remember, the night you cried."

Neena nodded, of course she had. Not like he had special powers and could otherwise know. He began playing his flute again and then she did pull away, even as she felt the notes he blew pushing like a massage in the small of her back.

She stepped into the blue-colored air of the venue for the fundraiser. An upscale jazz club. She was bombarded by the sight of pink-leather-purse-draped women all pseudo-pretty in a Condoleezza Rice been to charm school but I'll cut you if you fuck with my man sort of way, the men in pin-striped designer suits. She thought that if Tish were well she would fit into such a place except that her sister was really pretty, really nice. A flat-faced woman with slicked-back hair and rimless glasses sitting behind a skirted table asked Neena for her name, then told her to stand off to the side because she wasn't on the list and someone would speak with her shortly. Neena ignored her and walked toward the main room, replied to the woman's "Miss, uh, please," that she was just going to use the ladies' room for goodness sakes, an oversight anyhow that her name wasn't on the list. Said bitch under her breath as she went into the bathroom and then commenced to sneeze from an overwrought bouquet of tiger lilies taking up the granite-topped vanity, granite the new Formica, she thought as she used the bathroom then stood at the vanity and took her time washing her hands though the lilies were making her eyes swell, her nose run. She lifted a cotton napkin from a stack folded in a gold-leafed basket and drenched it with hot water and held it to her face. Her inescapable reality mingled with the steam rising off the napkin and sifted into her pores: that she was destitute in her black on black designer clothes. She wondered how many times in the course of a day she'd encountered people who looked like her, normal-looking, well-dressed people. She'd never considered that they might be hungry, like she was right now, that they might be the end-of-the-week-away from homelessness. She got a chill at the thought. She heard someone coming into the bathroom so she dabbed her face dry and reapplied Vaseline to her lips. Her hair was standing wild and she pulled her fingers through to make it taller still, then patted the ends to shape it into a more even mound. She walked out of the bathroom and once again back into the blue air of the jazz club.

She edged past the woman checking names and moved toward the sounds of a vibraphonist warming up in the bar on the other side of the club's main room. Baby-stepped her way across the hardwood floor around the circles of people sipping wine and munching on political commentary. A tray of petite food floated past and she started to reach and pull away one or several, wanted to just tell the waiter to give her the entire tray so she could find a corner somewhere and stuff them two at a time into her mouth as empty as her stomach was, load her purse up with the rest to eat when she returned to her room. The tray was filled with crab meat; she could tell by the smell and she was allergic to shell fish. Another tray went by her head filled with shrimp. She wondered what was wrong with having a little cheese and crackers, some chicken wings. Hated the way some black people felt the need to overdo as she dodged the cell phones that waved through the blue air like silver minnows until she made it over to the marble bar area that was cast in a soft pink light. The sounds of the vibraphonist melted the pretense over here, the air over here creamy and quiet compared to the rest of the club. Excitement surging in the rest of the club because rumor was that Barack Obama was slated to drop in. A sparse assemblage of deal makers and men and women trying to get some physical release sat or stood in couplets around the bar and hung on to each other's whispers. Neena settled into a leather-clad booth. She slid her coat off and ordered a ginger ale. She sipped the ginger ale slowly. Allowed the lilting sounds from the vibraphone to work through her like so many fingers, so calming this music was. She had a clear view to the circle of light where the vibraphonist played. An old head. Complexion like a copper penny. He was playing "The Shadow of Your Smile," and Neena wondered if Cliff would even show up. Couldn't believe that she was preparing to do this yet again. She hopscotched through her memory and thought of the other men she'd conned, landing now on that first one.

He was a doctor, she'd met him while selling pharmaceuticals; she was in her twenties and shaking down a man had been the farthest thing from her mind. She'd actually felt something for that one. Not love exactly but a sweetening in the air when she was with him as if wind chimes were suddenly moved to sound. He was coal black with silky straight hair; told Neena over the lavish dinner paid for by the drug company so that he would write their prescriptions that his wife married him mainly because she wanted her children to have pretty hair. His wife was obsessed with hair, he'd said, and looked as if he was about to cry.

He was a gentleman. He didn't press his knees against her thighs at all during dinner the way that one doc had, nor did he slip his delicate surgeon hands beneath the stark white tablecloth to cop a schoolboy's feel as they shared a caramel-apple ice-cream dessert. And even though he did kiss her mouth good night at the dinner's end, it was a tenuous kiss that asked permission. Neena appreciated that he was polite that way. The night lasted then for a few hours more in a hastily gotten room at a Westin Hotel. A year-long affair ensued until it was time for her to move on.

For the occasion of breaking up she'd served him in the dining room of her one-bedroom apartment that she'd rented furnished. She loved the view that apartment had of Lake Erie that caught the fractured rainbows in the evening light. She'd prepared appetizers of smoked blue fish and crumbled feta rolled in phyllo, a spinach and orange salad, a main course of linguini under blackened tuna. She'd started off by talking about Freeda; she'd otherwise never talked about Freeda and even that night did so in metaphors. "My mother spun in and out of my sister's and my growing-up years the way that fabric did when we used to go with my grandmother when she'd buy material for the choir robes she was always stitching. The fabrics were wound on these huge bolts, rows and rows of bolts from the ceiling to the floor in store after store along Fourth Street in South Philadelphia."

He looked at her quizzically as she talked, wondering, she could tell, where the story was headed. His soft face scrunched mildly as he glanced at his watch. He was supposed to be at the board meeting for Black Men Making a Difference. The meeting would go until ten so he needed to leave by nine thirty so that he could fall in on the end of the meeting and be seen there. He rubbed his hand up and down her arm. "That doesn't give us a lot of time for, you know." He motioned toward the bedroom, then leaned in to kiss her arm.

She pulled her arm away. "This is important," she said.

He relented and dropped his delicate hands, reminding her that he had only until 9:30. She wasn't insulted; didn't feel exploited. She generally wanted to move against him as much as he did her. She was using him too. But at that moment she needed to say what she needed to say as she described the most spectacular bolt of all. The one wound up with hot pink silk. She stretched her arms and swept them wide. "My mother was like that pink-colored silk; she'd spread out in a grand display, just dazzling she was. But sooner or later her sadness would hit and she'd roll up into a tight button until—poof—she was gone. The thing is, though, once you've had that silk wrapped around you and been carried on a wild and riveting ride, you know, the love, the excitement, it's like you never get over it, you know, you just got to have it next to your skin, you know, so you do whatever it takes to track it by the threads left behind." She sat against the ladder-back chair exhausted after trying to describe Freeda, her attachment to Freeda, met his puzzled expression and then she sighed.

"The point I'm trying to make," she said, "is that when I was nineteen I withdrew from my sophomore year at Temple University and used my savings to come to Cleveland because this is where I'd heard my mother was." She paused to swallow and catch her breath.

"And?" he said, more than asked as he lightly drummed his slender fingers against the table. "Is she here?"

"She was here, she's gone now, but she was. Anyhow, I've been working with a private detective who located a woman who'd befriended her, and it looks like she's in Newark."

"Your mother or the friend?"

"My mother, who do you think. Would I be packing up to leave here for some anonymous friend?!"

"You're leaving?"

"That's what I'm trying to say, yeah. I'm leaving. I'm Newark-bound, you know, as soon as I can."

He didn't say anything, his disappointment visible in the way that he lowered his head and concentrated on twirling the linguini around his fork. She hoped he wouldn't cry. She had the thought that he wouldn't be able to go on without her given his apparent hunger for her that would spill all out of his skin as soon as she opened the door and she'd rush him inside so that his hunger wouldn't grow an ocean on the hallway carpet. She tried to keep the conversation upbeat as she told him that though the hunt for her mother was draining financially, work should be easy to come by in Newark. She ended her spiel with how glad she was that they'd never been found out. She knew how important that was to him, his marriage, his coveted position as the chairman of the Deacon Board at his church.

He raised his head when she got to the part about his marriage, his generally soft-featured face suddenly a hardened mold of itself. His fork hung in midair, his arm paralyzed, linguini strands tic-tocking from the fork splattering the sauce against his blazingly white polo. She knew enough to know that this was not the look of someone about to sing a Chi-Lites tune of "Oh Girl" (I'll Be in Trouble if You Left Me

Now)." Knew that this was the look of someone thinking he's being shaken down. She was smart that way in her ability to discern facial expressions. Too smart for her own good, her grandmother always said.

He started to cough; his delicate surgeon hands covering his mouth with a salmon-colored linen napkin; his eyes darting frantically as if she'd just said, Pay up or I'll send pictures of our naked asses to your wife, your pastor, your straight-haired kids.

She felt a rage building that he could so readily misconstrue their year together as her orchestration of some premeditated sting. She fingered the stem of the glass holding her ice water, thought about tossing it right where his eyes bulged. She combed her fingers through her hair instead, pushed its thickness toward her face to hide her rage. She'd had her hair flat-ironed the day before at an overpriced salon because he liked it bone straight. Realized then that it was him, not his wife, who had a thing for hair. Counted up all the money she'd spent on her hair the year they'd been together. All the money she'd spent period shopping the gourmet aisles to put together meals like the one she'd fixed that evening. Her rage flapped around in her chest like a caught bird as she considered the price she'd paid for clothes that tantalized like the hot pink off-the-shoulder drape-neck top that she wore right then that fell to one side when she moved a certain way. It fell halfway down her arm because she was rocking herself to settle herself down the way she'd always done. The rocking worked so well for her that day that by the time he stopped coughing and could straighten himself up in the ladder-back chair and get his mouth to work to ask her how much? How much did she want to go away quietly? She didn't throw her ice water in his face, didn't shout, Asshole, I'm not trying to extort money, I'm only trying to tell you about my mother! She fixed the dark severity of her eyes on him. Calmly replied then, "Five thousand. You know, I think five thousand should do."

She had been surprised how quickly, how easily that first one paid. And that had been in the early nineties before the proliferation of the Internet. The Internet changed everything. Even a married man who might admit to an affair would do whatever it took to prevent himself from actually being seen so compromised in the form of streaming video e-mailed to his prestigious Listservs. Cade had been the first man to actually take a chance that she'd been bluffing. She wished she hadn't been bluffing. Wished she had the video for real. Wished there was a way she could get into that Chicago condo. She wouldn't allow herself to think about all of her possessions locked up there. Had to imagine it all dead.

Neena drained her ginger ale, ate the cherry that adorned it, even chewed the cherry stem trying to pacify her stomach that was beginning to make its emptiness heard. She looked up then because she felt someone staring at her; there he was finally, Cliff. She tried not to look at his eyes, had noted even in that two-second glance the night they first met that he had sad eyes. She looked at his chest, he was wearing a pink tie; now she looked at his mouth; a dark, pretty mouth; a strong nose; back to his eyes. Now she didn't even guard against her hyper-empathetic predisposition and the sadness in his eyes sneaked up on her, gathered along the surface of her skin, oozed under her skin like a foamy cream, making her hold on to his gaze, smiling as she did.

Cliff stepped into the club with an attitude. As he'd turned the corner headed here he'd had to confront a gang of white boys—neophyte lawyers he could tell by snatches of their conversation—taking up the entire sidewalk as they practiced the art of making people walk around them. To walk around them meant Cliff would step into a puddle of water in the street so he barreled right for their center. The shortest of the gang said, "Hey pal, an excuse me would have been nice."

"No, you not clogging the sidewalk with your snot noses would have been nice, really nice," Cliff said as he pushed on through and continued walking.

"Sign that dude up for anger management," one of them said to Cliff's back. Cliff snuffed the urge to turn back around and escalate the confrontation. He was angry. He'd just lost a case today. Tempted to blame that loss on the fact that he'd worn pink. His wife, Lynne, had told him that pink was the color for 2004 and if he were really secure he'd wear the pink shirt/tie ensemble she'd given him for their tenth anniversary. He'd worn the ensemble today, though he was old school. Resisted now relating the pink to his lost case. Enough tension between Lynne and him these days, especially with her mother, Babe, there without making Lynne responsible for his losses. He shook off thoughts of his wife, her mother, the lost case, the white gang out on the street because he needed his game face for this fund-raiser, this one to tap the region's conservative-leaning blacks, the type who sipped sauvignon blanc at art shows and complained about the poor. Generally not Cliff's crowd since he'd been a poor boy until he'd started practicing law. And even for a time after he'd rejected material excess because back then to struggle was noble. He'd sympathized with the Black Panthers in his youth, demonstrated and raised his clenched fist as he'd shoveled his way through the Ivy League, for what? he'd been asking himself of late, to pave the way for this newest generation of black professionals to buy tank-sized Humvees.

Once he stepped into the club, the blue-colored air was actually a surprising relief, the sudden burst of warmth a relief too, as were the knowing sounds from a vibraphone, the smell of wine and designer perfumes. A long line of people chatted it up in front of him as they waited to sign in. He looked through the diminished light in here beyond the table gauging the turnout. Good turnout. Dove, the receptionist from his law office, sat behind the table checking names. Before Cliff could get to her, to say that a woman, Neena, would be showing up who wasn't on the list, Dove had already lowered her rimless glasses gesturing with her eyes for Cliff to look at her. "Just one, so far," she said as she scanned the foyer area. "You can't miss, very big sixties hair."

Cliff knew that was most likely Neena. That was how they handled people who'd not anted up in advance. Cliff would introduce himself, make nice, extract a card, send a gracious letter the next day acknowledging their presence at the fund-raiser, extolling the virtues of the candidates they'd endorsed, the expense of running campaigns, not to mention the cost of uncorking all that champagne. A check generally followed from all but the severely obtuse or destitute. He made his way now from the foyer to the main room, shaking hands and slapping backs. He followed the blue air in here over to the soft pink of the bar area. That's when he saw Neena. He still didn't remember her from the other night and he wondered what else his preoccupation with Lynne was making him miss as he looked at Neena's hair, thick and wild as if she'd just undone braids and not even finger-combed it, just let it stand and fall where it may. Bold of her, he thought, to wear her hair like this with this crowd that Dove called the St. John suit club. He liked that boldness. He thought that she had an odd-looking face, simultaneously soft and severe. Taken with the Crayola-black eyes, though, the tender, amorphous mouth; the mild brown complexion; the thick hair falling every which way; Cliff decided that she was in fact beautiful. Though he wouldn't bother making a pitch for a do-nation because she was also broke. How did he know that? he asked himself the way he often did when he'd drawn a conclusion based on a quick observation, the rationale for which hadn't yet leaked into his conscious mind.

A granite-topped serving table separated them. Cliff became aware of the table when he rammed his bad knee into its base as he tried to make it over to where she sat. He refrained from grabbing the knee and hollering out, though he was momentarily stunned from the jolt that radiated out from his knee all the way to his toes, his scalp. It took ev-erything in him not to grimace, not to limp as he walked toward her, extending his hand, taking her hand in his, saying, "Hello, Neena? Right?"

"Yes, I'm Neena, guilty as charged," she said as she tried not to look for too long in his eyes.

"As a lawyer, Neena, I'd advise you never to admit guilt, at least not right away. May I sit?"

"Please, feel free," she said.

"Feel free, huh?" he said as he eased into the booth. "I have to admit that's something I've not felt for a while now, free." He didn't know why he said that, hadn't even known that was the exact truth about how he felt until he'd said it. He laughed for levity's sake.

Neena continued to smile her gushy smile. "From what I can see of these people," she said, "you appear to be the most free person in here tonight."

"I have to admit it, these aren't generally my people here tonight."

"No? So what's it like with your people?"

"Ooh," he laughed softly, "that depends on whether beautiful women like you are gracing the crowd." He stopped himself. What was he, anyhow, an old man trying to get a rap going? Poor rap at that. He looked straight at Neena, about to apologize for bordering on the inappropriate. Her lips were smirked to one side playfully. He wondered if Lynne made such an expression when she sat across the table from whomever. His stomach tightened at the thought and he smiled so that he wouldn't grimace.

"So now, tell me about your unusual case," he said as the barmaid stood over him and he pointed to Neena's glass, and Neena said, Please, yes, another ginger ale, and Cliff said he'd have the same.

"Actually, I'm going to be perfectly honest with you, Cliff, since you can likely spot a liar at fifty paces. I don't really have a case for you."

Cliff raised his eyebrows. Now he saw what it was that told him that Neena was broke. The sweater. It had once belonged to his wife, he was sure, only because he'd given the sweater to Lynne, then shortly after he'd seen it in the top of the give-away bag headed for the Salvation Army. Lynne had apologized over and over when he asked her about it. "See, look what happened to it," she'd said as she stretched it out to show him. "I wore it to that Maya Angelou reading and the stupid huzzy on the door insisted that she couldn't let anyone in unless their name tag was prominent. So me, like a dummy, stuck the adhesive thing on the sweater knowing how delicate this kind of cashmere is. And then this happened when I peeled it off," she'd said as she showed him the rectangular-shaped scar of pulled wool. He focused on the rectangular patch now as he listened to Neena admit that she didn't really have a case to discuss with him.

"Actually, I'm working tonight," Neena said.

"Yeah? What do you do? May I ask?"

"Actually my employer sent me to seduce you, get you caught up in a scandal to bring you down. You're raising too much money for their opponents, you know."

Cliff hadn't expected that. He laughed out loud. A truly felt, unfettered laugh.

Neena played with her straw. Her stomach was growling louder now, embarrassingly so as she listened to his laughter mixing with the vibraphonist's competent strokes, the compressed energy spilling in here from the main room. His laughter so sheer and unclipped.

"They wouldn't have sent you," Cliff said when he'd recovered himself. "They would have sent a white one. They always send a white woman when they're trying to bring a brother down."

"Would that have worked with you?"

"What, a white one?"

"No, me?"

"Oooh," he said, his smile still hanging around his face, "that's a setup if I ever heard one. If I say yeah, I'm saying I'm a gullible charlatan who runs around on his wife. If I say no, I'm saying you're not irrestible. And I'm not about to say you're not irresistible."

Neena lowered her eyes, feigning shyness, though she actually felt shy. The barmaid returned with their drinks and Cliff turned to speak to a woman who'd waved. Neena sipped her ginger ale and focused in on the vibraphonist who was stroking a sultry rendition of " 'Round Midnight." That had been one of her grandfather's favorite songs according to Freeda. Once Neena, who had only heard the instrumental version, asked her mother what the words were and Freeda recited them and midway through Neena was sorry she'd asked and told her mother to stop. Thought the words too sad for her mother to be repeating since holding the sadness at bay was their greatest challenge.

"Midnight is always sad," Freeda had said. "Too many miles to travel 'til the sun rises. Unless you're well enough to sleep, and fortunate enough to dream soft dreams."

Neena didn't want to give herself over to thinking about that here and now. She'd thought much about it over the years during her own waking midnights, many sad. Though she'd also had her times for dreaming softly. Couldn't bear the idea that her mother had not.

Cliff's attention was back. "So you were telling me about how you're setting me up for a scandal, Neena." He laughed.

"No," she said. "You were telling me how you're not about to say that I'm not irresistible, though I'll have to diagram that sentence to figure out the double negatives."

"No need, two negatives always make a positive, right?"

Before she could say anything else Dove was standing over Cliff, telling him that the mayor had just come in.

"Tell him I'll be over in five," Cliff said.

"You're joking, right?" Dove said, looking from Cliff to Neena, pausing to look Neena up and down, pursed her lips together then, her lips thin, colored in a muted pink shade of gloss.

"I'm not joking, no," he said, trying to keep the edge from his voice as he gave her that what-the-fuck-is your-problem look. She stashed right back over her rimless glasses.

"It's okay, really, I'll be here," Neena said. "You've got business, got to free the people." She smiled at Cliff as she said it, darkening her eyes, though, as she glanced up at Dove thinking that Dove took her for a know-nothing in an Afro. She knew things. Smart. If she'd wanted, she told herself she could be dangling from the side of that same mountain that many of the people in here were dangling from right now. Trying to make it to the top. She'd recognized long ago that the top was a cruel illusion, especially for people like her. A mountain for Sisyphus to climb is all it was.

Cliff got up then and bowed in Neena's direction. He resisted the urge to reach out and stroke her face. He pivoted on the wrong foot and turned to walk away and felt another searing jab move up his knee, limping for real now, thinking, Fuck it, his knee was gone; he was fifty. No sense in trying to hide it.

Neena took his limp to be a swagger and she smiled as she watched him walk away. She liked him, she had to admit. Though she couldn't like him, not yet. Cloud her judgment if she gave over to liking him. Though right now her judgment was already clouded by her hunger. Her hunger really rumbling now without the distraction of conversation with Cliff. She'd have to get something to eat before the night slunk much farther along. Depending on how long Cliff would be, she might have to slip out of here before he even returned. There would have to be fast food nearby. A Wendy's she remembered on Fifteenth Street, a McDonald's on Broad on the other side of Market. Didn't they have a dollar burger special going on now? She was salivating as she thought about a hamburger, a shake. God, what she wouldn't give for one of Mr. Cook's milk shakes with the thick chocolate syrup that wouldn't allow itself to be mixed in so that it came up through the straw all solitary and potent and hung in her mouth and there it would finally blend with the thick cream of the shake. Or the chili he made in the winter that they'd have on Saturday nights after her shift was done and they'd close the store and she'd help him cash out and they'd sit in a booth exhausted and he'd call to his wife, "Okay, Mrs. C., time for you to do a little work for a change and serve me and baby girl." The jalepeños would bring tears to her eyes but she just let the tears roll because she couldn't stop eating the tender beans, the chunks of onions, the perfectly seasoned beef. She thought she would cry for real right now as she even pictured her grandmother's chicken and dumplings, more than pictured, she could actually smell the pepper and the dough coming together in the pot, imagined how the chicken would just fall off the bone. Wondered if her grandmother still cooked like that. She was getting up there, seventy-six her last birthday. God, why did they have to so dislike each other, she wondered as her mind jumped from one of her grandmother's specialties to the next: the sweet potato pies, the corn bread she made from scratch, the apple-sauce that she'd prepare in extra large quantities because people all the way at the other end of the block would smell the apples boiling, the cinnamon and nutmeg and butter going in, and suddenly they'd appear at the front door, starting a conversation with Nan, asking ca-sually if that was her applesauce they smelled. Neena thinking now that Nan's applesauce could give someone religion, thinking that she'd try Jesus all over again if she could have a bowlful right now, hot, with a couple of straight-from-the-oven buttered yeast rolls on the side. Her desire for food at that instant was so intense that she could barely catch her breath.

And then Cliff was back, looking at Neena's face in the candle-light; her face was flushed and he thought that the look was one of desire, thought that Neena wanted to be with him. He wasn't sure what he wanted, knew what he didn't want, though. Didn't want to go home like a loyal puppy dog, panting after his wife, yelping for her to bring her head down out of the clouds, and once she did, look-ing at Cliff as if he was the troll that had just replaced the prince. And here was Neena with her palpable desire, her wanting that was so ef-fusive that it seemed to hit him right at his throat, making him swal-low first, then clear his throat, then grab at his tie because suddenly the tie was too tight, too heavy, though it was a light-weight silk. Suddenly the knotted pressure of the tie against his neck made him feel that he might gag, made him acutely conscious of the pressures in his life like his dementia-suffering mother-in-law living with them now, and the pressure of being middle-aged, presumably successful with his Italian leather briefcase and hand-stitched shoes, and over-sized house in Chestnut Hill, while at his core a circle was spinning around and around fueled by a feeling of purposelessness. And there was Neena's wanting that right now in the blue-lit air at this jazz club was better than church the way it zeroed in on his need to make an immediate adjustment in his life, loosen the damn tie so that he wouldn't choke.

Neena's brows curved in a question mark as she watched Cliff undo his tie completely and just let it hang from his neck. She laughed then, a free fall of a laugh, and her oversized hoop earrings made circles of the blue light in here as she laughed.

Now he was back to thinking about Lynne's laugh as he eased into the booth. Wondered if this is how Lynne laughed when she sat across from whomever it was she was having an affair with. There it was, finally. He'd let the feeling take form, attached to it congruence, three simple words: she's running around. Who was it? Who had moved in on his wife, moved against her with a compelling slow grind? Would have to be compelling, he was no slouch himself, he thought. And he'd been faithful. The whole fifteen years, like a hundred-yard punt return, he'd woven around the big-legged, curved-hipped temptations, the temptations so heavy with his own desire that he'd even had the breath knocked out of him once or twice. But he'd stayed on his feet. The goal line in sight, Lynne the goal line, he'd carried, carried rushing always back to her. Felt like such a fool that he had as he listened to

Neena laugh. Felt like a mother-fucking, son-of-a-bitching fool. There was that rage again, that Cliff's-only rage that stood alone. And here was Neena affecting him.

He didn't know what is was about her, if it was the secondhand sweater, or the boldness of the nappy hair, or her quick wit, or that she'd put money in Bow Peep's case that night in the snow, or even that he was being cheated on and Neena was here and available. How available, he wondered, as he looked at Neena directly? No play to his face, his voice, as he got in between her laugh and said, "Okay Neena. So why'd you call?"

"Why'd I call?" She stopped mid-laugh and repeated the question. Pretended to be thinking about her answer as she picked up her glass. Though she'd known already what she would say.

"Yeah," he said. "Since you're not a prospective client, what are you looking for from me?"

She cleared her throat, then swallowed. "Actually, Cliff, I called because I'm just back in Philly after some years away. Not a lot of friends here anymore." She pushed the sweater sleeves up to her elbows, then pulled them back down again. "And I have a possible job offer here, with Merck, pharmaeutical sales, so I'm thinking about settling here again and I just thought I'd put myself out there and follow up with people I've been meeting, you know."

"So what? You just randomly calling people or should I consider myself lucky?"

"You know, I have to tell you, Cliff, no offense, but I'm not usually into lawyers, it's really your friend, Bow Peep, who made me want to get to know you."

"Bow Peep? What'd he say?"

"It's not what he said, it's just the fact that you know, you'd have him as a friend. It gives you a whole 'nother dimension. I've had huge affection for people like Bow Peep who the sane and proper might consider close to the edge, and I could tell a lot about a person by the way they responded to her?"

"Her?"

"Yeah, a cousin, we were close?"

"Is she still alive?"

"No," she said. She didn't know why she said it, felt small explosions going off in her stomach reminding her that she was starving. "Anyhow, you know, I'm back here in Philly, and trying to make new friends, and then I was moved by Bow Peep's flute playing and I could just tell that he has this really generous spirit and then I could tell, you know, that you really care about him. So I thought, here's this lawyer, probably thinks he's, you know, a real gift, yet his heartstrings are obviously pulled by someone who plays a flute while wearing sandals in the snow. It's hard to explain—"

"No, I get it, Neena. Really I do. And I really appreciate you saying that," he said. "The guy is like a brother. Got messed up in Vietnam so I do what I can. Smart guy too."

"I've noticed. He's kinda profound."

"Oh, so you two been talking, huh?"

"I ran into him on my way here."

"Uh oh, he counsel you?"

Neena laughed. "Well—"

"You know that's what he does. He believes that anybody who stops to listen to him play has a heightened sensitivity, you know, an evolved awareness. He believes he can help get them to the next level. And honestly, who am I to say he can't? I know people tell him stuff, personal stuff that he never repeats because it's like he respects a type of—what would you call it? A musician-listener confidentiality, I guess you'd call it."

"I saw him give a woman all of his money—"

"He does that too. And I'm like, Come on Bow Peep, word get out on you and you're gonna have every freeloader in Philly on your corner."

"I think he knows who to give it to, though."

"Hope so," Cliff said, thinking now about how Bow Peep had always been a bone of contention between Lynne and him, Lynne once telling him that with all he did for Bow Peep it was as if he, Cliff, had a son whose existence she wasn't privy to until after they were married. Now he let his eye search for the rectangular scar on the cashmere sweater Neena was wearing to make sure that he hadn't imagined it. There it was, evident under the soft pink glow of the candlelight, its presence making him realize what it was about Neena that was affecting him most of all. That she wasn't Lynne was affecting him most of all.

The vibraphonist was playing "Moody's Mood for Love" and Neena sang a bar: and then she unleashed that free fall of a laugh, made Cliff laugh too.

"You're too young to know that song," he said.

"I'm older than I look."

"And I'm married."

"And?"

"And I don't mean to sound inappropriate," Cliff said. "I mean, I'm not coming on to you, at least I don't think that I am, I'm just, mnh, what am I doing here? I'm just, just saying, you know. I wanted you to know that." He cleared his throat. "That I'm married."

"So I know that," Neena said, and then she was quiet; they both were as the sounds of the vibes made circles over their heads.

When the song was over Cliff looked at Neena and raised his eyebrow. He didn't know what he was asking of her with his raised eyebrow. Neena could tell that he didn't know. She was mildly surprised by his awkwardness.

"So does your wife know?" she asked.

"Know what?"

"That you're married?"

"Ooo, you've got jokes, huh?" Cliff said as he watched her pretty mouth unfurl into a demure smile. Then he looked away, down at the globe covering the soft pink of the candle. "Listen, Neena," he said. "Would you like to get out of here? We could go somewhere. Where would you like to go?"

"Mnh," she said, working hard to sound nonchalant. "I guess we could grab a bite to eat. Are you up for something like that?"

"Always up for something like that," he said as he extended his hand and helped her up. She reached back for her coat and he held it open as she pushed her arms through the sleeves.

They weaved around the throngs of donors; many were laughing in earnest now, the alcohol beginning to peel away their facades in layers. They made it to the other side of the heavy wooden door where the night air was the color of smoky silver. They walked beyond the circles of people lighting cigarettes and then stood there as if realizing suddenly that they were strangers. Neena thinking that she hadn't even gotten to a library yet to google his name.

"So, Neena, do you have any place in mind?" he asked.

"No, you choose. I told you I've been away for a while." She avoided his eyes, looked at his mouth instead, his solid rock of a chin. She counted the gray hairs in his mustache.

"Mnh," he said. "My buddy's got a restaurant near South Street. Did you drive?"

"No. I'm staying not too far from town. Over on the Parkway with my great-aunt?"

"Well, the place I'm thinking about is five blocks away. You mind the walk?"

Neena said that no, she didn't mind the walk, even as her head made its objection known, light-headed from hunger, though she walked anyhow.

Chapter 12

HEY ENDED UP at Hugh's Restaurant. UPSCALE, DOWN
HOME was stenciled on the window below the name. Cliff
telling Neena that he came here every chance he could because the odds were against black restaurants, particularly
in the first two years, and Hugh's just opened six months ago.

"Black businesses period," Neena said, "shoot, a black corner store
is hard-pressed to make it." She thought about Mr. Cook's store, how
he was open from seven in the morning until ten at night, and always
did just a little better than breaking even. The race tax, he told Neena.

"Black corner store?" Cliff said, as he held the door for Neena to
walk through. "I thought they went the way of the Buffalo. Do you
know where any are? Tell me, I'll go there." A white-shirted host met
them at the door and Cliff and the host exchanged pleasantries, then
Cliff squeezed Neena's arm and excused himself, he was going to find
Hugh, he said, to make sure they were treated right.

The host took Neena's coat and led her to a table in the corner near
the back of the small room. The tablecloth was white muslin like the

young man's shirt, the walls were peach stucco, matching, she noticed, the color of the sweater she wore. The chair the host held out
for her was bamboo with a red and orange flowered seat cushion. A
ceiling fan whirred overhead and pushed the warm air down, and
then there were the aromas, the air bulged with aromas: mustard
greens, turkey wings, bread baking, fruit. Melted candle wax fell
into a holder fashioned from a lemon half and added even more complexity to the smells in here. Nina Simone's voice issuing down from
the speakers mounted high up on the wall added complexity too.
Neena sighed as she took her seat. Said, "Smells good in here." The
host smiled, then excused himself, leaving Neena to look around. A
mixed bag of diners in here: the after-workers still in suits and pretense; the looser artsy type; the boyz from the hood, or at least
dressed to impress that way.

Now water was being poured in her glass, a menu tipped in her direction, and she said thank you to the waiter, though she didn't actually see the waiter, saw only the row of laminated black buttons down
his white shirt because she was too preoccupied with the menu. Everything about her physical being, her eyes, her tongue, her skin, even her
feet that she flexed inside of her boots, her tingling scalp, her nose that
she feared might be opening and closing now, everything about her
intensely focused on the meal as she studied the menu. She'd start with
the vegetarian spring rolls, or maybe the fried catfish tenders, she'd
ask if the gumbo contained shellfish, then a mixed green salad, the
roast turkey with the sage stuffing for her main course, steamed cabbage, okra and tomato, hot buttered corn bread. A dessert of, of what?
She turned the menu over. Oh my God, she almost shouted, coconut
cake, a five-layer tower of power it was described on the menu. Her
eyes were welling up. Wanted to signal the waiter that she'd go ahead

and order without Cliff, but that would be unacceptably rude, and any- how here was Cliff walking back toward the table.

He sat and unfolded his napkin and put it in his lap. "What looks good?" he asked.

"Everything," Neena said, unable to hide the excitement in her eyes, the look in her eyes charming Cliff even more.

"Then you should order everything," he said on a laugh.

"Don't tempt me."

"I'd like to."

Neena feigned a blush. Though she really felt the need to blush. She kept her eyes on the menu so that she wouldn't look at Cliff. Now he was excusing himself, said he'd be right back, he had to take a call. Neena looked up wanting to scream out, Please, Cliff, in the name of all that is sacred, please hurry, I'm going to pass out if I don't soon eat. "Sure, no problem," she said instead.

To Neena's relief, it was a quick call. Her stomach was kicking up a cyclone as Cliff walked back to the table. He walked fast, then stood there. Why was he just standing there? Why wasn't he seated so that the waiter could come back over, leave a basket of hot bread when he did.

"Neena," Cliff said, then paused and she knew whatever it was it couldn't be good, devastating whatever it was because it would mean yet another delay in her meal. "I am really, really sorry about this," he continued, "but things are happening all of a sudden. I have an emer- gency, my mother-in-law suffers from dementia and I just got a call, something's happened at home and I need to get there."

"Oh God, no," Neena said. "My God, I'm so sorry," and she began paraphrasing Langston Hughes in her head: What happens to a meal deferred, does the hunger sag like a heavy load or does it explode. She couldn't look up at Cliff. She thought that if she looked up at him she might cry.

Cliff was surprised that Neena seemed so genuinely distraught over him and his situation. "Will you promise to call me tomorrow? Please, Neena. We could try again for tomorrow," he said as he pulled the back of her chair out so that she could stand. She nodded as she reached around to the arm of her chair to retrieve her purse.

"Can I put you in a cab somewhere?" he asked.

"No, it's a nice night, I'll be fine."

The host appeared with her coat then, and helped her coat on, followed by the waiter with a black handle bag saying that Hugh insisted that they not leave empty-handed. Cliff handed the bag to Neena. "Why don't you," he said. "For you and your aunt. My family drama has made short work of my appetite."

Neena called on her restraint so that she wouldn't snatch the bag. "Only if you're sure," she said. Allowing the bag to hang loosely from her fingers. "And I hope things at home aren't too serious, I hope they're quickly resolved."

Cliff opened the door and Neena stepped back out into the night.

After Neena and Cliff said their rushed good-byes, Neena turned off Broad Street and walked west. She passed a development of new town houses. She'd noticed so much new construction since she'd been back here, hundreds of thousands of dollars for the square footage of a bread box, it seemed. The development she walked past now had a small park in the making. Unplanted trees with their root systems still wrapped in burlap stood at evenly spaced intervals. She pondered how long the trees could live like that, trying to stay curious about something outside of herself so that she wouldn't tear into the shiny black bag. Though right now pondering the meaning of life wouldn't keep her from the bag. A sign pointed toward the builder's model, behind it a small bench almost hidden by one of the soon-to-be-transplanted trees. She walked along the short cobblestone trail to get to the bench. A security guard on the other side of the minuscule lot smoked a cigarette. Neena pointed to the bench, flashed her hand in a question mark, he lifted a couple of fingers telling her to go ahead. She sat. She slowly opened the bag, praying that it would not contain a seafood gumbo–type dish loaded with shrimp. She gingerly undid the foil on the top plate. Hallelujah, short ribs of beef and string beans and mashed potatoes in the one plate. She picked up the beef by the bone, didn't know whether she raised her hand to her mouth or leaned her mouth to her hand. The result the same once she bit in. Heaven. Tender, succulent heaven. In between she ate the string beans one by one with her fingers as if they were fries. Licked the mound of mash potatoes as if it were an ice-cream cone. Didn't even stop to belch before she'd unwrapped the second plate. The second plate the roasted turkey platter. How did they know? How did they know?

The smell of the turkey rising from the plate reminded her of Thanksgiving, of the night before Thanksgiving really, when Nan's turkey was slow-roasting in the oven and the dining room table was filled to overflowing as she and Goldie and Sam and Tish and Nan packed the baskets that would be given away to the families in need. Goldie telling story after story that had them hysterical with laughter. The soft aroma from Nan's own turkey in the oven sifting in from the kitchen, swirling around their heads, smoothing out even the erratic air that most often filled the space between Neena and Nan. She pushed a thick slice of the turkey into her mouth, this turkey almost as good as Nan's.

She was drunk by the time she finished the second platter though still she poured into her mouth the contents of the two small dessert cups, one, a peach cobbler; the other, bread pudding. She smacked her lips. She pulled napkins from the bottom of the bag and tried to clean her hands. The napkin stuck to her hands and she peeled it off and told herself not to touch her clothes until she could wash her hands. She scrunched the plates in the bag and with some effort pulled herself to standing. She couldn't remember ever consuming such a volume of food at one time. Not even spread out over an entire two days had she ever eaten this much. She felt as if she was waddling as she walked back to Broad Street and tossed the bag in the first trash can she came upon. Now she was thirsty.

She started walking in the direction of her hotel. She was still thinking about Nan as she walked. She was remembering one of those night-before-Thanksgivings when the turkey-scented air in the dining room was floaty and filled with laughter. They had an assembly line working that night. Tish was in charge of the canned cranberries; Goldie, the boxes of rice; Sam, the eight-to-twelve-pound turkeys; Neena, the packaged greens; and Nan, the candy canes taped to her jars of applesauce with a note that contained a Thanksgiving Day prayer. Goldie had just told Neena that maybe they should switch, because greens meant money and she, Goldie, could sure use some money, tight as Sam was with a dollar, said that Sam still had his kindergarten lunch money in his pocket. The dining room bulged with their laughter. Then Sam said, "Well, I must have used my first grade lunch money to buy you that new Bulova watch wrapped around your arm." They laughed some more, deep, rich laughs as Goldie and Sam went back and forth with their playful banter.

Then the doorbell rang and Nan looked at the jar of applesauce in her hands, said more to the jar than to the people in the dining room, "Anybody expecting company?" Then she looked directly at Neena. Neena still remembered the expression that had come up on Nan's face because it so mimicked what Neena felt at that instant. A hope that it was Freeda. A hope that was too large to be contained even though it would have to be contained because if it wasn't Freeda then the plummeting that followed would feel unbearable.

It had not been Freeda that night. It had been Cook bringing bagged nuts to go into the baskets. Neena remembered that although Nan joked with Cook that he better just drop his coat right along with the box of nuts and get to loading the nuts in the baskets, Nan's face had a collapsed look, like an empty balloon waiting to be filled, and Neena could see that the vein in her grandmother's throat appeared suddenly engorged and she could even see it throb. Neena understood that look too, because again it mirrored what was happening inside of her. It was all that contained hope over it being Freeda at the door just sitting in Nan's throat with nowhere to go. Neena remembered too that Nan was agitated suddenly with how Neena was packing the greens, said that Neena was crushing them; Be careful, she'd snapped at Neena, or let Tish pack the greens.

Neena couldn't believe how warm it was out here for a February night. She unbuttoned her coat. She tried to belch so that she could open some room in her chest and breathe better. She was in the mixed-bag part of town that was part black heading to white, on the fringes of the moneyed part of Center City. A group of young black men transported a set of drums into the side entrance of a church for a night service, Neena thinking that if developers had their way this church would be condominiums this time next year. A trio of teenage girls now went into the church; their jackets were wide open and she could see that they were dressed in navy skirts and white blouses, the youth ushers. They giggled and whispered and pointed at the boys. Neena had been an usher at that age. She'd been complimented often about her posture when she ushered, what a nice straight back she had.

She wondered if there was a water fountain close to this opened side door of the church, maybe a ladies' room where she could wash her hands. She walked inside, down some stairs. She followed the ushers through the empty, darkened lower sanctuary, no doubt the girls were headed to the bathroom. A water fountain gleamed at the front of a hallway, a sign marked RESTROOMS pointed down the hall. Neena stopped at the water fountain. The girls' chatty voices reverberated from farther down the hall. "He crazy if he think he getting some, I don't care how cute he is," one of them said. The water was ice cold and Neena drank and drank more, still seeing Nan's face, now that vein in Nan's throat, that hope-contained caught in her throat that Neena recognized when she would return for visits in the early years of her leaving. Back then she was holding down a legitimate job as a pharmaceuticals sales rep and was not ashamed to show herself to Nan and Tish. Nan would never say with her mouth, I hope you got news about your mother, I hope you gonna tell me she's alive and well, or at least alive. Her face said it, though, the skin stretched tight, her throat, the vein that throbbed, even her voice that came out sounding restricted, locked.

Neena stood from her lean over the water fountain. Something was wrong. A shift had happened suddenly and she felt as if she'd been turned upside down. Now right side up again and the brown ceiling above her was spinning round and round, the floor too, and now all that food she'd just eaten changed its course, headed up instead of down. She held the wall and made it through the dim hallway into the ladies' room. The young girls were in the mirror combing their hair and putting gloss to their lips. Neena rushed past them into a stall as one of them said, "Ooh, a Gucci bag. I wonder if it's real."

All of it came up then: the cobbler and bread pudding and turkey, the string beans, the potatoes, the short ribs of beef. Came up roughly, as if someone had forced a hand down her throat and yanked it up. Much of it missed the mark and landed on the floor, her boots, the edges of her coat. When she was finished she just leaned against the door and moaned. Empty again. Here she was empty all over again.

The ushers looked at one another and hunched their shoulders about what to do. They were eleven, twelve, and thirteen; the youngest and oldest first cousins, the one in the middle best friend to the oldest. The youngest, LaTeefah, said, "Eeil, gross." Her cousin yanked her arm, telling her to be quiet. The best friend tapped on the door and asked Neena if she was okay.

Neena straightened herself up. The floor and ceiling had returned to their rightful positions, the spinning of both had calmed and was coming to a slow stop the way a roulette wheel stops. "I'm okay," Neena said as she looked at the fallout and began unwinding toilet paper, to do what with it she didn't know, toilet paper with this situation about as effective as cleaning chemical waste with an alcohol swab. But at least she wiped her mouth. "Is there a janitor around?" she called through the stall.

"We don't really have a janitor," said Breanna, the oldest. "Everybody does everything."

"Well, is there a mop I could use, some kind of soap or Clorox? At least some paper towels?"

"Teefah, go get paper towels," Breanna said to her cousin. "There's some under the sink in here but that's not hardly gonna be enough." She handed Neena the thin roll of paper towels over the top of the stall door. And Neena did what she could with them, at least along the toilet seat.

Then the best friend said, "She's gonna need a bucket for real. Look, Bree, it's gonna slide all out here in a minute."

Neena shook her purse from her shoulder and took off her coat and hung both on the hook in the stall. She rolled up the sleeves of the peach Salvation Army sweater. She unzipped her boots and stepped out of them, stepping over the pond of her retching into the outer area.

The girls had dispersed. The bathroom was old with fixtures from the fifties but it was also blazingly clean, Neena could see as she scrubbed her hands at the sink, then used her hands to rinse her mouth, then washed her entire face. The youngest returned then with more paper towels. "You're lucky," she said to Neena. "Kyle, that's the pastor's son, just went to BJ's this afternoon so we have plenty of paper towels." Then the middle one, KaShandra, came in dragging an industrial-type bucket on wheels though the wheels didn't really roll, a mop in the bucket, behind her Breeanna with a no-name pine oil cleaner saying that she tried to tell Aunt Maddie what happened but her aunt said she didn't want to hear nothing about nothing, that people would be filing in here soon and she wanted the bathroom restored to the way it was when she'd scrubbed it down earlier.

Neena took the pine oil. "I guess I better get busy," she said as she unwound paper towels and used them to sop up what she could from the floor. She then went into the stall next to the one she'd ruined and poured the pine oil in the toilet then pushed the mop in the toilet. She mopped the floor then, using the other toilet to clean the mop in between, saturating it with more pine oil. She wiped down the toilet seat, the back of the toilet, the wall inside the stall. She knew how to clean, her grandmother had seen to that. Her grandmother used to tell her and Tish that even if they reached the station in life when they could pay somebody else to get rid of their dirt, what good were they to themselves if they didn't know how to do such a basic thing for themselves.

The oldest girls disappeared again and the youngest stood there talking to Neena as she worked. Asked Neena if she modeled, she looked like a model she'd seen on an Web site for girls who want to model.

"With these hips." Neena laughed as she cleaned off her boots and put them back on. "Be careful on those Web sites, they have a tendency to exploit people."

"Everybody exploits everybody," LaTeefah said.

"I don't know if everybody does," Neena said, as she removed the now-filled trash bag from the can and replaced it with one from under the sink.

"That's what my mom says," LaTeefah insisted. "She says she can't hardly get an even break because it's all about do unto others before they can do unto you. So she said she doesn't give up breaks because she doesn't receive any."

"Your mom goes to this church and talks like that?"

"No. She doesn't belong to this church. I don't live with my mom."

"Well, I bet you don't exploit anybody," Neena said. "I bet you try to treat people fairly."

"Depends on how they treat me."

"For real, yo," Breeanna said. She and the best friend KaShandra had returned, looked around the bathroom amazed. "When I heard what my aunt had said about this bathroom being restored, I was like somebody is really gonna take a butt kicking over this bathroom."

Neena tied the trash bag and sat it in the doorway between the bathroom and the lounge area. Asked where they dumped the trash.

"There's a Dumpster out back," Breeanna said. "But don't worry, I'll take it out. Yo, I'm just relieved that's all I have do. You sure you're okay?"

Neena nodded. "I'm sure, sweetie," she said as she retrieved her coat and purse from the back of the hook on the stall door. She stood over the sink cleaning the coat and bag.

Breeanna moved in closer and fingered Neena's purse. "That's a real

Gucci," she said. "See, Shown"—she pulled the best friend's arm—"you can tell by the clasp. Kadia's doesn't have that, I told you Kadia's was fake."

"It's just a purse," Neena said.

"And you sure can't live in it," LaTeefah said. "My mom says what's the sense in spending that kind of money on something if you can't live in it."

"Your mom's right about that," Neena said.

"Her mom lives in a shelter," Breeanna said and the skin on LaTeefah's face pulled back some soft brown skin. "But it's not the worst thing," Breeanna added quickly. "Teefah gets to live with me because of it, right Teefah?" She put her arm around LaTeefah's shoulder and kissed her cheek.

"And right next door to me," said KaShandra. She put her arm around LaTeefah's other shoulder and Neena looked at the three girls standing there arm in arm; cute girls with their clear eyes and thick braids and starched white shirts for ushering in. Again that feeling rolled in on her that she wished that she believed in the power of prayer because she would pray that they be protected, that they be loved extra hard by whomever was charged with their care.

Neena asked LaTeefah how often did she see her mom as they walked into the bathroom's lounge area, a moody room with an old-fashioned French Provincial–type couch and glass-encased end tables that lit up on the insides, throwing a soft yellow light over the couch. A calendar on the wall was centered over the couch with a picture of a pretty brown girl clasping her hands in prayer, her cheeks rounded in a smile.

"Saturday afternoons, I'll see her tomorrow," LaTeefah said.

Neena emptied the contents of her purse on the couch and asked for a trash bag. She put the contents of her purse in the trash bag and then handed the purse to LaTeefah. "I want you to give this to your mother," she said. "Tell her if she doesn't want it, there's a big flea-market thing at my grandmother's church two weeks from tomorrow, on Delancey Street in West Philly. They've been having it the first Saturday in March since the beginning of time. Tell your mom to ask for Nan, and to tell Nan that Neena said it would be okay to sell it from her booth. She should be able to get a couple hundred for it if she sells it from Nan's booth."

LaTeefah held the purse spread out between her palms and looked from the purse to Neena and back to the purse again. She was unable to close her mouth. Breeanna and KaShandra volleyed a set of extended whoas back and forth.

"Can you remember all that?" Neena asked. And LaTeefah nodded her head up and down.

"I'll help her remember," KaShandra said. "We go with Teefah anyhow when she goes to see her mom."

"We'll have to hide it though; they steal there," Breeanna said. Said it to Neena's back because Neena was already walking out of the bathroom lounge, down the hallway, past the water fountain, and through the lower sanctuary. The lights had been turned on down here and a piano was starting up upstairs; she could hear strikes against cymbals. She wrapped the ends of the trash-bag-turned-purse around her wrist and then hurried through the lower sanctuary and out the side door of the church. She didn't want to recognize the song that was coming together upstairs and once the piano got going she knew that she would.

Chapter 13

WEEK AND A half later and Neena asked herself why was she still here. Had asked herself that every morning since the morning after Cliff's abrupt departure from Hugh's Restaurant. She'd not called him at all that day like she'd promised him that she would because she'd left her room just long enough to get to the store to buy ginger ale and graham crackers since her stomach was still queasy after that vomiting episode. And then she'd not called him over the next two days because she'd vacillated about whether to even go through with it with Cliff. When she'd finally called she'd learned that he was out of town. He was due to return today. Now she was back to *no*, she wouldn't go through with it. Back to asking herself: So why was she still in Philly?

Told herself again this morning, as she had every other morning that she was staying for Tish. Convinced herself that Tish was more than enough of a reason to remain in Philly. Neena was still afraid to speak to her in the real, fearing still that the shock of the sound of her voice might do harm to Tish and the baby. So she'd decided to wait until Tish's condition was upgraded to good, then she'd go see her. Then she could leave Philadelphia. To go where, to do what, she didn't know. Continue her search for Freeda? She'd been aware—though made a conscious decision not to dwell on, the fact—that she'd avoided punching in her mother's name each time she'd used the library's computer. Generally the first thing she did when she sat down to a computer was do a search of her mother's name. She hadn't since she'd been back here. Though she had punched in Cliff's name. Pulled up a recent item in the *Inquirer* that included a picture of Cliff and his wife. Wife looked just as Neena had expected, that soft pampered look with the spa-treated skin and silky straight hair, big eyes, big teeth. According to the picture caption, they were at the wife's artist-loft—an open studio event. The picture was crowded with people milling around in the background. In the foreground Cliff smiled with his arm around his wife's shoulder, his hands bunching the fabric of the tunic she wore. Her face was turned toward the camera but the rest of her was not, not even her eyes. Neena imagined that her demeanor was that of someone thinking, Hurry up please and take the damn picture, I need to be over there or there, anywhere but here with this man pulling my shoulder off. Neena told herself then that her interpretation of the picture could be entirely wrong, the wife might have been gazing at Cliff in the most adoring way a second before the camera flashed, then someone called her or maybe one of her pieces had fallen off the wall, distracting her. Neena hoped that was the case. Hard to proffer money from a man by threatening to go to his wife if the situation was such that his wife didn't give a damn. But the day she'd pulled up the picture her decision-meter was at "no" in terms of pursuing a relationship with Cliff, so his wife's demeanor was of no consequence one way or the other. And Neena asked herself again that day, Why was she still in

Philadelphia? Reminded herself that day that she also wanted to visit with Goldie before she left. But as with Tish, she wanted Goldie to get stronger too.

Today yet another reason for her being Philly-stuck chiseled itself through to her conscious mind: the Arch Street hotel was beginning to feel like a home. That fact nearly horrified Neena when she was finally able to admit it to herself. The night before she'd fallen asleep thinking how the lumps in the mattress had seemed to shift so that they were no longer rocks under her back; now they surrounded the print of her body, nestling her. And this morning she'd noticed hints of yellow in the dominant gray of the bedroom air. The scratchy sounds of the television in the lobby had become familiar, comforting almost. Even the emaciated desk clerk, who must live here because he seemed always to be on duty, had begun nodding a good morning to Neena and pointing at the old-fashioned coffee percolator on his side of the desk, offering Neena a cup. This morning she accepted and asked his name as he poured the coffee.

"Dexter," he said, without looking up. "Cream? Sugar?" he asked then.

"Please, a little of both, thanks," Neena said as she took in the coffee's smell. "This is so nice of you, Dexter, really. I'm Neena, by the way."

"Know that," he said when he handed her the Styrofoam cup. "Checked you in twice, remember?"

He had, that mid-morning when Neena arrived over two weeks ago, and then again two days ago after Neena returned from the pawnshop where she'd gone her first morning here, where this latest time she'd unstrapped her watch from her arm and let it fall on the felt pad yielding her enough cash to extend her stay another week.

She took the cup and sat on the lopsided couch and sipped the coffee. She hadn't had perked coffee in years, her coffee mostly coming from automatic drip–type machines. It was fresh and strong and reminded her of Nan. She wondered if Nan still took her coffee from an old-fashioned percolator. She shook the thought. Didn't want to dwell on Nan. "Granny" is what Bow Peep called her. Now she smiled in spite of herself as she thought about Bow Peep. She'd seen him practically every day, sometimes two, three times a day. She'd start out walking in the direction of the library or the bookstore, only to end up at Bow Peep's corner. Twice when it was early he'd taken her to breakfast at the Reading Terminal. Once in the evening they walked to Whole Foods—because Bow Peep raved about their oyster crackers—and shared half a rotisserie chicken and sweet potato wedges. His conversations went the gamut from barely intelligible to remarkably sterling. His long line of a smile gave Neena a surge that caught her off guard the way that it snaked inside her and filled her up with a sensation that approached giddy.

She drained the coffee and tossed the cup in the trash can and called out a thank-you to Dexter as she walked across the lobby. He barely raised his index finger in acknowledgment.

The air outside was bright yellow and sharp. Neena pushed her hands into her coat pocket and fingered the dollar bill she'd put there for coffee—thanks to Dexter she could hold on to her dollar. She fell in line with the other walkers. She'd do four miles at a good clip around the Parkway, then back to her room to shower. By then the library would be open and she would read until lunchtime, then around to Broad Street to visit Bow Peep. This had become her routine. Lunch was generally a soft pretzel with mustard and she even had her preferred vendor on Twelfth Street because his pretzels were extra doughy at the center. She'd browse the bookstore shelves after lunch. She'd stand while she read the magazines: *Newsweek* one day, *Time* the next, *Essence*, *The New Yorker*. That way she could appreciate the seat when she got one finally and she'd settle in to turn the pages on a meaty something, a complicated literary novel or a scientific tome about the formation of the universe. When it started getting dark out she'd use the pay phone to call patient information to check up on Tish. Tish's condition as of yesterday was still fair.

Today as she walked through the hotel lobby after her morning routine, she heard mention of her sister on the noon news. She stopped, paralyzed. There on the screen was a clip of her sister from a prior newscast. Had something happened to Tish? Why were they showing her? A different clip now. Tish smiling. Such a gorgeous smile.

"Dexter, please turn that up, please," Neena asked, out of breath as she ran to stand right in front of the television.

"She would like to thank all of you for your cards and get well messages and looks forward very soon to spending lunchtime again in your living rooms," the substitute anchor said. Neena had to sit on the lopsided couch to gather together the pieces of herself that had come unbolted at the thought that something had happened to Tish.

"You 'kay?" Dexter asked.

"I am, yeah," Neena said as she allowed the terror she'd just felt to dissipate into a fine mist until it was gone. Now she was dizzy with another emotion. She flicked through the Rolodex of feelings to give this one a name. Pride. Damn, her sister was the damn noontime news anchor in a market as large and competitive as Philly's. Damn. You go, Tish, she said to herself, you fucking go, girl! She laughed out loud. Acknowledging as she did how opposite they were. Acknowledging something else as she sat there: she would call Cliff. She headed for the elevator to go back to her room for his card. Didn't try to analyze the intersection of thoughts about Tish, how well Tish had done for herself, and this sudden resolve to pursue a course with Cliff; to get what she could as quickly as she could and then move on, move out, up and away like a hot air balloon that's unable to land. Like her mother.

She was back in the lobby and she rushed to get to the phone before she changed her mind again. She pulled her replacement purse—this one a leather-look vinyl that she paid eight dollars for on the corner of Fifteenth and Market—high up on her arm as she used her shoulder to prop the phone. She'd thought often about those cute little ushers. Wondered how LaTeefah made out giving her mother the purse. Wondered if LaTeefah's mother would keep the purse. Neena had barely noticed its absence from her life. Surprised herself at how easy the purse had been to let go, especially the way she'd burned to have it. She started to punch in Cliff's phone number, knew her preoccupation with the purse right now was a delaying tactic. But now she stopped before she hit the last number. She just stood there holding the phone against her shoulder. She took in the dull gray air of the hotel lobby that had begun to feel like home. The lobby was filled with her yearning. No pretense to this lobby to distract the yearning. No brocaded draperies at the windows, no claw-footed couch, no velvet wing chairs. Just the drafty air ignoring the space heater on this side of the check-in counter, just the lopsided couch and two aluminum folding chairs with gold and green tie-back seat cushions; no side table lamps to set a mood, just the overhead ceiling fixture that emitted a steady buzz; the phone on the wall across from the sign-in desk, the television against the opposite wall. Neena's wanting was naked in this dowdy hotel lobby. She just wanted to be good, a good girl, that's all she'd ever wanted to be. Just Freeda's good girl so that her mother would stay. She felt the gap widening between what she'd yearned to be and what she'd become as she hit the last number and listened to a voice say, "Law offices. May I help you?" She asked to speak to Cliff. Told the woman that Cliff was expecting her call. Said it with authority. Then there it was, his voice exploding in her ear.

She could hear the pleasure coating his voice, taking his voice lower, throaty, getting all inside of her as he said, Hey, extended the hey, drew it out like a song. "I gotta say I am thrilled to hear from you. I figured you'd probably dumped the very idea of me the way I had to rush out of Hugh's."

She laughed from deep inside herself. "I was under the weather, that's why I didn't call the next day. Is everything all right at home?"

"Everything is everything, Neena. I was actually out of town all week."

"I know, I called—"

"Really? See. I checked in every day. Did Neena call? I asked—"

"I didn't leave a message—"

"Okay, I'm relieved. I was thinking maybe it was the tie."

"Huh? Tie?"

"I was wearing a pink tie the day we met, and I'm usually not into pink ties, and in retrospect I had a rough day in that pink tie." He coughed. "Until I met you—"

"What color is your tie today?"

"It's—well, let me look at it, what color is my tie? That's a catchy book title, you think? Some guy made millions on a book about the color of a parachute. I should write one about the color of ties."

She knew the book about the parachute. "And the tie would represent?" she asked. "What? Choices?"

"Exactly, "Cliff said. "Choices that men make, middle-aged men who feel that they've gotten the butter from the duck in terms of, in terms of what? In terms of fulfillment from you know, from jobs, family, you know the civic responsibility-type things, you know, and one day somebody asks you what color is your tie and you have to stop and look because you don't even remember, because chances are the tie was probably a gift, so you're walking around in somebody else's preferences for you, and you probably got dressed in a semi-fog anyhow, so of course you don't know the color tie, and, and, damn, I've spun way out there, haven't I. Whoa, Trigger, let me pull the reins on this horse right now before he starts a stampede." He laughed.

Neena laughed too. "So, what color is it?"

"Striped, actually, let me see, there's gray and navy and a light green."

"Lime?"

"I guess that's what you'd call it, yeah, lime. I don't really know colors."

"You'll have to know colors for your book, though."

"Do you know colors? You could help me write it."

"I mean, their names, yeah, but there's a whole psychology around color, you know, which colors look good on you, how colors make you feel, you know, affect your mood."

"I guess that's why psych wards have light blue walls."

"Been there, have you?"

"Felt right at home too."

They both laughed. Neena felt the laugh deep in her stomach. Now Cliff was stammering, trying to invite her out. Again she was caught off guard with how awkard he was; it was reassuring. Not like that last one, Cade, whose finesse should have been warning enough.

"I'm done at about six today," Cliff was saying. "Can I make it up to you this evening for the way I had to bail on you last week?" he asked.

Neena said sure, six worked for her. He told her where his office was; she said she'd be in the lobby at six.

Cliff's substance reminded Neena of her first boyfriend, Richmond. There was complexity there, unpredictable variations of gray that were provocative in ways that the what-you-see-is-what-you-get black-white formation of most of the men she'd been with could never be. She'd thought most of them simpleminded strivers; trying to get something on the side without consequence, intelligent for sure, but essentially dim about the big themes that moved below the surface. Their hungers were so conventional, their egos so easy for her to satisfy: make this one feel young, that one handsome, the other one adept at pleasing a woman. She wasn't sure what Cliff was starved for, though, didn't know, given her current situation, if there was time for her to discover it. Still, she was intrigued by him, the way that she'd been intrigued by Richmond.

She was turning sixteen the year she met Richmond. She wasn't pretty in a classic way like Tish was pretty with the nicely shaped forehead, the soft nose, the blushable cheeks, and the cleft in the chin. One had to decide for himself if Neena's features came together in a pleasing way: the droopy eyes that had a wildness about them, the pouty heart-shaped mouth, the asymmetrical cheekbones. Most men deciding her look was pleasing when taking into consideration the way her hips jutted despite her tall slender build. Her grandmother accusing her of walking in ways to maximize the slant of her hips. "God don't like ugly," Nan would say. "I saw you switching right in front of Joan's husband with that hot-in-the-behind look plastered to your face."

Neena wasn't hot in the behind, really. Though she also wasn't oblivious to how her look affected a man, older men mostly. Thought the boys her age silly and trite. So she was surprised to find herself actually attracted to Richmond. Richmond wasn't his real name but that's what everybody called him because he lived in Virginia but spent summers here with his aunt who lived around the corner on Spruce Street. The aunt's backyard looked into Nan's backyard.

Richmond was light with a face full of freckles. A loner, like Neena was a loner. Well read and headed to college like Neena too. She'd see him at the library summer afternoons and felt sorry for him. Couldn't fathom why a teenage boy would be leaning into books instead of splashing in a city-run pool, or shooting hoops, or sneaking into the movies, or bagging groceries at Thriftway to save up for a new Atari game machine. She knew why she was there. She was there reading daily newspapers from Newark, from Cleveland, from Detroit, from Chicago. Cities from where Freeda had called in the past, cities to which she may have returned. Neena was drawn to newspaper accounts about anything having to do with a black woman in her mid- to late thirties. Had even called the Auburn Hills police department inquiring about an unidentified body but that corpse was only five foot two and weighed two hundred pounds. Freeda was five foot six and slender. At least Freeda had been slender the last time Neena saw her.

Richmond was political, Neena discovered by the books she saw him devouring: *The Autobiography of Malcom X, The Miseducation of the Negro,* even Mao's *Red Book*. They started walking home together, taking the long way from the library on Baltimore Avenue around Cobbs Creek Park, even following the trail down into the park over to where the brick-faced guard station was. Neena told him how one of the park guards had been killed there in the early seventies. Said that her mother had described for her the evening that erupted with the sudden sounds of sirens and booted SWAT teams running through the streets of West Philly so that it felt more like a war zone. "A little girl was knocked off her tricycle and had to get eighteen stitches in her forehead. My mom said that she would carry that image forever of that little girl's head splitting open. Said that the child was wearing a yellow dotted Swiss sundress with the cute little matching panties underneath and the force of the police barreling through the street actually flung her through the air. From then on that little girl could never walk in a straight line. Walked zigzag from then on."

"Collateral," Richmond said. They were at the edge of the creek that smelled of honeysuckle and sewage and he looked away from the creek, looked up at the sky and squinted, and Neena thought he had the saddest eyes.

"Meaning?" she asked. The dirt was soft under her rubber-soled flip-flops and she tried to keep her footing as she watched him twist and untwist his watchband.

"Meaning they weren't intending to hurt her, but hell, in war they accept that the nontarget sometimes goes down too."

"You say that like you know what you're talking about, you know, like it's personal."

"Yeah, my pops and shit, yeah."

"He was collateral?"

"Naw, he was a target," he said, slowly. "You know, a Black Panther, so you know they wanted him dead."

"How?" Neena asked on a whisper so soft that it blended with the sound the leaves made as they twirled on the breeze and she had to ask it again.

"Heroin," he said, matter of factly.

"What, they strung him out?"

"No, not even that," he said. "My pops never did dope, didn't even smoke weed if you can believe it. But they tried to say he died of a heroin overdose. It's all such bullshit."

"Well, didn't they do an autopsy? Wouldn't that have shown that he never used."

"See, that's the thing. He did die from heroin, but he was murdered; the police, you know, they cold-bloodedly killed him. They tightened a belt around his arm and then shot him up because otherwise he had no track marks, just that one red dot where they'd plunged the needle that killed him. Plunged it in his left arm, and my pops was hopelessly left-handed. No way he could have shot himself up with his right hand." Richmond had stopped twisting his watchband. Now he twisted his hand around his arm. He left red marks on his arm. His veins were green and bulged underneath the red and it was hard for Neena to look at his arms because she thought how easy it would be for someone to kill him that way too. Now he balled his fists as he spoke. His voice, though, was steady, his face placid, that look of internal hysteria that Neena understood.

Neena's flip-flops were losing the battle with the soft dirt and she grabbed Richmond around the waist so that she wouldn't fall. He pulled her to him and kissed her. She had been kissed by boys in the alley behind Nan's house before but they had been too eager and out-of-control, laughable kisses. She wanted to cry, though, when Richmond kissed her, the way he held back. She wished that there was a patch of grass underfoot where they could lie because she wanted right then to touch him at the center of his sadness, wanted to uncoil the sadness for him, for herself as well.

The following week, the day after Neena's sixteenth birthday, she was out hanging sheets on the line. Richmond came over to help and Neena was full of complaints. Complained that Tish got out of the grunt work by belonging to a thousand different groups. At that very moment she said, Tish was with Nan at some kind of mother-daughter tea for one of the bourgeois societies Tish belonged to. Complained about Nan paying all she did for a clothes dryer and still insisted on hanging bedsheets on the line because she was superstitious. Complained that Mr. Cook had offered her a job in his store as his assistant sandwich-maker and Nan said she had to be sixteen first, and when she'd reminded Nan of that this morning, having turned sixteen the day before, Nan insisted that Neena first had to prove herself over the fall months by bringing home straight A's the first report card.

Richmond held the ends of the sheets while Neena pressed the clothespins in place. The sun was high overhead and the air was yellow and soft. Richmond was close against Neena's back. He covered her hand with his each time she affixed a clothespin.

"Tell me about your mother," he said into her ear.

"My mother? Like what about her?"

"Anything. Her habits, her look, what do you miss?"

No one had ever asked Neena such things before and she felt her heartbeat climbing. Where to even begin: with her mother's habit of hunching over the kitchen table cramming her mouth with Argo starch, her shoulder blades like knife points pushing through her paisley robe; or the stark look of Freeda's eyes when she was too happy, unsustainable such happiness was, and it was as if her dark eyes understood that and refused to play along; or the screeching sound her mother's nakedness made on the mattress in that room that smelled of turnips and whiskey—but no—that had not been Freeda on that mattress. That woman had been a stranger, vermin, Nan had called her, though Neena still missed the feel of that stranger-woman's arms, the hunger in that woman's arms; wondered if Freeda's arms were similarly hungry for her. "Um" is all Neena could say then. "Um, um, um."

"It's okay if you can't, Neena. For real, for real, I understand," Richmond said. His breath was hot pushing in her ear. He kissed the back of her neck then, allowed his body to brush harder and harder against hers. Neena still saying "Um, um, um," even as she squeezed her thighs to contain the yearning. The yearning confusing. Yearning for what? To be finally filled with a feeling that was larger than that of being a motherless daughter. Was there a feeling larger, or just another kind of shattering.

The sheets were yellow like the air, fully hung, and Richmond turned Neena around to face him. His eyes starved and begging and Neena pulled him along the side of the house and they climbed up the fire escape that led into the bedroom she still shared with Tish. Tish's bed lined with her stuffed animals, her bureau like a fragrance counter at Wanamaker's, organized rows of perfumes and colognes and body creams in pretty atomizers and gold-topped jars. Neena's dresser bare, save a carved wood jewelry box that Alfred, Freeda's father, had made; her bed absent adornments too, just the yellow ribbed summer-weight bedspread that she rolled away, then she took the top sheet off too.

Neena thought Richmond so clumsy and fast that this must be his first time; it was her first time and she wasn't even sure if she felt anything, though she did sense that Richmond cried. But then they did it again and he took his time. He said her name and used his fingers and his mouth as he moved against her and Neena thought that she could hear the el; she always loved the backdrop sound of the el because it seemed that every house that they lived in with Freeda was close to the sound of the el. Though Nan lived many blocks from the el. But there it was, she was certain, the rumba el sound getting louder now, squealing as it came to a stop inside of Neena, the brakes giving off white sparks that held before they went away.

After Richmond left, Neena had to once again strip the bed down, though when these sheets were washed she put them in the clothes dryer. She remade her bed and turned the fan in the room on high to air it. She took a bath and put on the same clothes she'd been wearing when Nan and Tish left, cutoff denim shorts and the T-shirt that Nan detested that was emblazoned with the phrase IT'S A BLACK THANG. She arranged her thick puffy hair the way she thought it should look after an afternoon of doing mundane chores, a nonchalant bun. She had a full half hour to spare before Nan and Tish walked through the door. And after all of that, when Nan looked at Neena, it was as if she knew, as if she'd caught Neena and Richmond naked and tangled on the bed.

Neena was sitting on the back steps reading *The Color Purple*, absorbed so that she jumped at first when Nan called her name.

"Why you jumping like a guilty party?" Nan asked, no play to her voice.

"Ma'am?" Neena said as she got up and felt the sheets. They were dry and she began pulling the clothespins out.

"What have you been doing all afternoon?"

The sun was a ball of fire in the back of the sky and the air in the yard had gone from the soft yellow of earlier to orange and red with a hint of night. Neena pushed her breath into the sheet so that she wouldn't turn around and glare at Nan. "Just reading and otherwise what you asked me to do," she said. "The sheets, stuff like that."

"Stuff like what? All I asked you to do were the sheets. So don't go trying to come off like some Cinderella. You wouldn't have had to do those had you consented to come along with your sister and me. Such a beautiful tea that was. You need to claim membership in similar upstanding organizations instead of hanging back idle letting the devil use you. Now I'ma ask you again. What were you doing all afternoon?"

The sheets were off the line. Neena inhaled their aroma as she walked them over to laundry basket resting next to where Nan stood on the top step. The sheets smelled like the corner where the Bond Bakery used to be, like the smell of flour and butter and sugar rising through the air. The bakery was right below the el tracks and she focused on the memory of that el sound, now the feel of that sound inside of her when Richmond had made the brakes squeal. She didn't answer Nan. She pushed the sheets into the laundry basket and walked past Nan into the house.

Nan was at her back, demanding that Neena not ignore her, who did she think she was ignoring her. They were in the dining room. Neena placed the laundry basket on the dining room chair that sat next to the buffet. That chair and the one on the other side of the buffet were rarely used, only on holidays or special Sunday dinners when Goldie and Sam came up from South Philly or Nan's church ladies, or Tish's cute-girl friends for whom Neena would help Tish cut bread slices into perfect triangles to spread with water cress, or shrimp salad, or strawberry cream cheese. The punch bowl, similar to the chairs in its lack of everyday use, was centered on the buffet. It was heavy; took two people to carry it in from the kitchen when it was filled with 7UP and sherbet. She looked at Nan standing there in her white straw hat, her single strand of pearls, her white laced gloves. She wondered how heavy the bowl would be now if she picked it up and threw it at her grandmother. The idea of the punch bowl crashing into her grandmother's head stopped her. She didn't really want to hurt Nan, she just wanted to shut her up.

"Who was in here today? Did you have company in here while I was gone? Be just like you to have company in here when nobody's home. Too much like doing things decent and in order to have company when I'm here so a proper acquaintance can be made."

"I didn't have company," Neena said through her teeth. "I hung the sheets, I tidied up otherwise. I sat out back and read my book. What is wrong with you anyhow?"

"You big liar, you—"

"I'm not lying—"

"You will lie, I know that about you."

"Jesus, Nan."

"Don't use the Lord's name in vain in this house."

"Well then, shit, Nan, how about that? Nothing to do with the Lord. This is bullshit."

"No you didn't, you dirty-mouthed little heifer, you." Nan went at Neena then with her open hand. Hadn't really hit Neena since she turned twelve, and then it was no more than a single backhand to the mouth. But now she hit Neena as if she was fighting a woman out in the street. Slapped Neena over and over on her face, her arms, her back when Neena tried to run. Grabbed Neena so she couldn't run and slapped her some more. Slapped her even after Tish rushed into the middle of the scene, Tish in only her strapless training bra and nylon panties from where she'd just been changing out of the clothes she'd worn to the tea, worn a Nan-designed strapless nude-colored taffeta dress that cinched in at the waist then spread out ballerina-style.

"Nan, please stop. Why are you hitting her?" Tish cried, as she jumped up and down to the rhythm of the slaps. "What did she do, Nan? Please, don't hit her anymore. You're hurting her Nan, please. What did you do, Neena? What did you do?"

Nan stopped more out of exhaustion than from Tish's hysteria. She peeled the white lace gloves from her hands, the irony of their delicacy not lost on her. She plopped into the for-company dining room chair and covered her face with her hands and sighed into her hands. Her straw hat tilted from her head and fell into the punch bowl.

Tish pulled Neena up the stairs, Tish moaning as if she'd been the one who'd just taken the ass kicking. "What was that about, Neena? Come on, let's get some witch hazel on you so welts don't come up. Is Nan all right? Why'd she go off on you like that? You think she's okay? Are you okay, Neena? I'm so sorry. What just happened, Neena? What?" Tish cried. Tish crying proxy for Neena because Neena didn't cry. Neena thinking that her grandmother trying to get to that part of her that was like Freeda, trying to beat that out of her. Neena determined that Nan never would.

Chapter 14

LIFF AND NEENA ended up at a diner in New Jersey not far from the Walt Whitman Bridge because when he'd asked her what was she in the mood for she'd answered, Soup, thinking as she said it that she needed to fill herself in degrees. She'd not repeat last week's mistake of trying to gorge herself.

"Soup," he said, as if the very notion struck something in him. "Soup it shall be."

They sat at the counter because that was Neena's preference. A coconut layer cake leaned in front of them, its cherry on the top slightly off center. The aroma of burnt coffee was prominent and reminded Neena of early mornings at Nan's; she could almost hear the gentle cough of the sewing machine, could almost see the yellow-pink light against the bottom of her bedroom wall.

She ordered the turkey with rice soup, Cliff the beef and vegetable. Cliff was well into his soup, spitting out cracker crumbs as he talked fast and animated, telling Neena about a case he was working

on. "Classic profiling. Young black male on the New Jersey Turnpike—"

"They're notorious, aren't they?" Neena said, allowing the steam
from the soup to hit her nose.

"You know it. One of the worst roads in the country for driving
while black. So this kid is stopped at two in the morning, doing nothing wrong, when he's pulled over, his license, insurance, registration
are all in order. At this point they're probably pissed because they're
itching for a bust so one of them says the kid was zigzagging, though
they'd not mentioned anything about his driving when they stopped
him. Asks him to step out the car, notices TOP paper on the seat, now
they're happy. They handcuff him, and then they shackle his feet, believe that? They take him to the hospital to have blood drawn for toxi-
cology. Marijuana shows up in his blood. So now they're high-fiving
each other. Another young black male in the system."

"But doesn't marijuana hang around in the blood for a couple of
days?" Neena asked.

"Absolutely it does. So its presence is not definitive in terms of a
DUI. But even before we get to there, it was a bad stop." He angled
himself on his stool and leaned in closer to Neena and told her the
ramifications of even a seemingly benign punishment like a driver's
license suspension. "If this kid can't drive in a garden-type state like
New Jersey, he can't get to work, you know the rest of the story once
he's unemployed," he said as he talked about other ramifications from
a sociological as well as legal perspective. He felt more alive right now
than he had in months. Had stopped talking about his work with
Lynne. Her increasing disinterest augmented his own sense of purposelessness. He'd even ask her about specifics of her projects, down
to curiosity about her mix of colors, hoping to elicit in her a similar

attention to the minutiae of his day. Thought that if she cared he himself might be revived. Realized now as he watched Neena blow on her soup spoon that that had been unfair of him to make Lynne responsible for filling him up on the inside.

"So this kid is a poster child for profiling, you know what I mean, Neena? Good student, from a good home, raised by both parents so they can't throw around that no-father-around-drug-dealer-in-the-making bullshit. Hell, my father split on my mother the year I turned ten—"

"And look how well you did."

"Anh, you know what they say, pressure either busts pipes or makes diamonds. I had a fill-in dad, though, in the form of a good uncle, my dad's brother. He'd show up on Saturday mornings, always in a nice fedora, taught me how to wear a hat. He'd hand my mother an envelope, never said whether it was coming from my old man or from his own pocket. I suspect it was from his own pocket. Excuse my profanity, but my old man wasn't worth shit."

Neena swallowed the first spoonful of soup laden with a tender chunk of turkey. She could taste paprika and garlic and thyme. "Well," she said, "maybe it was better that he left. Nothing worse than having shit around that's not even worth shit."

Cliff laughed. Felt the laugh. He scraped the bottom of the bowl with his spoon. "Mnh, soup was incredible," he said as he signaled the waitress. "Can I get a slice of that cake, please? And a glass of milk."

He looked straight ahead; they both did as they watched the waitress cut the cake. It was a healthy slice and Neena said to the waitress, "I bet you only cut them that big for the cute guys."

"You know it, doll," she said as she set the milk down and Neena watched Cliff cut into the cake with his fork, then swallow the milk, traces of the milk and the coconut clinging to the top of his mouth. Now he was saying how unbelievably good the cake was, offered Neena a taste.

"I'm still working on my soup," she said.

"Yeah? Were you an only child? They say only children eat slowly because they can."

"As of matter of fact, no. I have a sister," she said. "Yeah, a younger sister. She's pregnant and she might lose her baby. And I can't go to her right now."

"What? Is she far from here?" Cliff asked.

"Yeah, she's far from here," Neena said.

"And what? Is that the only reason you can't get to her?"

"Unh, my situation, it's kinda complicated right now? I'd rather not go into it."

"Are you in a relationship, Neena?"

"No, thank God," she laughed. "It's not that kind of complicated."

"Children?"

"Ditto."

"Me either, I mean the children part, by default I guess initially because after so many years it hadn't happened. And then after that by mutual decision, you know that if it happened fine, otherwise no heroic measures to make it happen. You know, she, uh, my wife, my lovely wife and I came to that understanding."

"Ain't understanding mellow?" Neena said.

"Ooh," he said, "she's going old-school on me. Who would've thought she'd know from Jerry Butler."

"You kidding me? I know from Jerry Butler, the Chi-Lites, the Intruders, *Cowboys to Girls*, you remember that?"

"Uh-oh, you taking me back to my knucklehead days. I see it now, me in a crowded basement of a house party, pretty young lady across the room lowering her eyes every time I look her way begging me to ask her to dance, and bold me with my boys egging me on to take that long walk across the basement that amounted to all of five feet, pushing the crepe paper and the balloons out of my way, extending my hand Billy Dee Williams—style, she looks at my hand, looks at me, looks back at my hand, turns to her girls, and they all break out into a laugh. Me having to walk back across the basement, my boys already saying, Ooh, that was cold, she put your—well, I won't say exactly what they said, because they, we, were kinda crude."

Neena laughed throughout the telling. Then said, "Silly girl, she didn't know who she was turning down, huh? I'd have danced with you, Cliff."

"Yeah?"

"Oh God, yeah."

They were both quiet then. The waitress put the coffeepot back on its heated skillet. The coffee that had been dripping down the sides of the pot sizzled into foamy brown bubbles as it met the heat. The burnt coffee aroma was invigorated in here, mixing now with the sugar and coconut of the cake. Neena had always loved the smell of burnt coffee, and of coconut, thinking now of the lavish coconut cakes her mother would make in the wintertime.

Now Cliff's voice got in between her thoughts. His voice was tight, almost a whisper. "So Neena, you know I honestly don't know what's appropriate, you know. And I really like you," he paused. "What I'm saying is I'd like to spend some time with you." He stopped again. "Okay, let's see how many more clichés I can throw out in the next sixty seconds. You want to count them or you want to be the time-keeper?"

Neena took hold of his hand that was hanging from the side of the counter. "Actually Cliff," she said as she squeezed his hand, "I've yet to hear a cliché."

"That's very sweet of you," he said. "You're very sweet." He pressed a twenty-dollar bill down on the check the waitress had slipped in front of him. He was looking at Neena. His eyebrow raised again.

She looked down into her bowl. The bowl empty save a few grains of rice, a nub of celery, a shallow pond of liquid. "Yes," she said into the bowl.

They were in the parking lot now. The moon and the sun were together in the sky, one on the way in, the other on the way out. The air was changing too and Neena buttoned the top of her coat and Cliff opened the car door so that she could get in.

Cliff lost his nerve. He'd reserved a suite at a Cherry Hill inn but now he couldn't get his car to go there. Thought it raunchy, disrespectful to pull into the inn's driveway, no bags for the bellman to check, answering the "How long will be with us sir?" with a cleared throat, so that the reply, the just one night would be scrambled. Would it even be a night? Could just be an hour, could not even get as far as the elevator because Neena might be outraged that he'd been so presumptuous as to assume that she was a willing party to his, his what? His revenge against Lynne? How dare you be so sure of yourself, he imagined Neena saying, that you can feed me soup, then bring me somewhere to screw. But he'd never been sure of himself, he'd protest. Sure he was smart, he'd concede, sure too that he had a decent look, knew how to pull out a semblance of charm when the situation demanded, but sure of his essential self? He'd never been. Never been able to track the uncertainty to its genesis. Was it that his father left, or that the ceiling in the living room always leaked, warping the wood floor below so that the bulges matched—the one hanging from the ceiling, the one pushing up from the floor. Or that his younger brother had bladder issues so that the whole family got teased for smelling like pee. Or that look that passed between the mothers chaperoning those parties in those well-appointed homes when he walked in—nice kid, they'd say with the look, but you know what block he's from, right?

Neena reached in to turn up the heat on her side. "Cold?" he asked.

"A little," she said as she looked at him and smiled. "But it's February, should be cold." She laughed, then explained that that had been her grandmother's response if they complained about cold in the winter, heat in the summer. "You may not like it, but it's as it should be. Grave consequences to pay if it were otherwise," she said mimicking Nan.

"She was ahead of her time," Cliff said. "Right on the money too with all the bleak forecasts global warming has stirred up."

"Yeah, like Florida and Los Angeles falling into their respective oceans."

"And palm trees in West Philly. Imagine that, Neena, you could have fresh coconut milk every morning."

"And the Schuylkill would be like a Caribbean waterway."

"All-inclusive resorts would sprout up on West River Drive."

"And alligators would become the new rodent to exterminate for."

"I can see the ads: GOT CROCS?"

"Though they'd probably have five legs."

"And become unextinguishable, like your grandmother said, grave consequences."

They bantered like that as they zoomed up the Jersey Turnpike, going from the laugh-out-loud outrageous to the scientific truth that was

sobering. Now they were riding past the inn where Cliff had reserva-
tions. He asked Neena if she had to be somewhere, or if she was able to
spend some time with him this evening.

"Mnh, I'm able to spend some time," she said.

"Well, there's this jazz house in Delaware, about an hour from here.
Love to take you there since you claim to have a good ear."

"Oh, I've got a good ear, let me tell you," she said. "I know from
jazz too. Don't let my young looks fool you. I'm an old soul, Cliff."

"And a pretty one too," he said. And it didn't even feel like a line.

At the jazz house in Delaware Cliff drank wine, Neena ginger ale.
They ate buffalo wings and celery sticks. Neena laughed at Cliff's
rapid-fire jokes until her eyes ran. They talked between sets about
books they'd read, movies seen, the eccentricites of Bow Peep; agree-
ing as they did that they'd not mention their budding friendship to
Bow Peep. "He's territorial," Cliff said. "An associate from the firm is
good enough to check up on him for me, you know, when I'm out of
town or otherwise can't get to his corner to make sure he's got money
for dinner and shoes on his feet. But he's decided that she needs his
healing, so I dare not mention her name in his presence for fear of disrupting some vibe in the air."

"Awl," Neena said. "His spirit is so honest, so generous."

"We all should be as good," he said, then raised his glass in a toast.

When the set started again, a Gloria Lynne–type on vocals singing tunes like "I'm Glad There Is You," Cliff moved his chair in close
and allowed his hand to make slow circles up and down Neena's
back. At one point he leaned in, leaned in like a soft shadow, and she
wondered if he was real, was she imagining this because she needed
this? He kissed her cheek and made a sound from the bottom of his
throat that was part moan as if he was saying, Damn, this feels good;

part too a small crying sound the way a baby cries because it can't say exactly what hurts. She turned then to face him, a thin film of perspiration glistened on her lips, her lips her most prominent feature, like Nan's lips and Tish's and Freeda's too, they all had in common the lips. He moved his mouth to cover hers, though she lowered her head at that second so that his mouth pressed her forehead instead. And then he made that sound again, that two-tiered sound that said this good feeling hurts so bad. And Neena wasn't sure what to do next. She'd never been here with a man before. So she didn't do anything. She let herself be still. She wasn't the aggressor, she wasn't feigning innocence. She let his mouth mark her forehead with the sound he made. Then the vocalist started to scat, started a run of those unintelligible mumblings, except that tonight Neena could actually hear the words.

Neena got dropped off, at his insistence, in front of Park Towne Place where she'd said she was staying with her aunt. He kissed her good night. It was a full kiss that wanted more. Then he asked for her number. "Mnh," Neena said. "Can we keep it so that I call you, just for right now? I'm comfortable with that if that's okay with you."

Cliff had his hands on the steering wheel. He stared straight ahead. "May I ask why?"

"Anh, like I said earlier, I'm in a really weird place right now. You know, without going into the details."

"So there's no man up there that you're living with, huh, Neena?"

"No man up there, no."

"Then I guess it'll have to be okay with me," he said. An edge to his voice when he said it.

"I'll call you tomorrow if that works?" she said.

"That works," he said as started to get out of the car to open her door. And she stopped him.

"No need, Cliff, really," she said. Then she walked into the apartment building as if she lived there. Even waved to the half-asleep man on the desk. She turned a corner and waited for a few. When she figured Cliff had pulled off, she went back outside and walked through the new frost in the air down to the Arch Street Hotel.

Chapter 15

EENA WISHED THAT Cliff was more like Cade, linear, predictable, almost a pleasure to shake down. No emotions to have to contend with, no heaviness of desires. Or even like that one from Delancey Street, Ted. She hadn't thought about Ted in years. Hadn't really hustled Ted for money; back then it was simply, purely trying to get to Freeda.

She was nineteen then and working in Mr. Cook's store, a student at Temple University on a full academic scholarship where, though her major was undeclared, she took a course load heavy on psychology. That job was a refuge for Neena. The way Mr. Cook's eyebrows cupped when he saw her did for her what two church services every single Sunday never could, made her feel innocent.

"Here comes my best worker" was Mr. Cook's standard greeting when Neena walked into the store. She'd hit his forehead playfully and then kiss the spot she'd hit and pretend that he was her father for as long as the kiss took. Any longer and she'd start to wonder about her real father, which would spiral into thoughts about Freeda, indictable thoughts and she had enough self-awareness to know that she was constitutionally incapable of holding on to any thought that might indict her mother. She and Tish were so unalike in that way. Though Tish was still Neena's soft spot. The only reason Neena was still living at Nan's, the only reason she'd gone to a local school, was for Tish. Tish had made Neena promise that she wouldn't leave until she, Tish, graduated high school. Tish was on schedule to graduate in two days.

Though Neena told herself that Tish was the only reason she stayed, she also stayed for Freeda. Stayed on the long odds that Freeda would return like she had once on Neena's sixteenth birthday. Stayed so she'd be there to greet Freeda, to tend to her if she needed looking after because surely no soft welcome would come from Nan or Tish. Stayed and endured Nan's chastisements that came at her like rocket fire: Why you always swaying back and forth like you calling to a man? Nan would say when Neena rocked herself to settle herself down. I know you not keeping company with some married man, she'd say if Neena smiled a hello to the men on the block. Where you going with that hot-in-the-behind look plastered to your face? she'd ask every other time Neena headed for the door. Neena so relieved when she walked down in Mr. Cook's basement corner store.

Neena double-tied her apron and took up her spot behind the counter to help Mr. Cook prep for the forty or more hoagies he'd make tonight. It was a Friday and all but the die-hard southerners relinquished activity in their own kitchens on Friday nights, opting to send their children down here to pick up hoagies and cheese steaks, quart-sized bottles of Frank's orange soda that they'd enjoy in front of the television as they laughed at Steve Urkel saying, "Did I do that?"

Neena had just finished slicing tomatoes and was moving on to sweet pickles when she looked up and saw Joan's husband, Ted, smiling at her, the one her grandmother had been accusing her of even back when Neena was infatuated over Richmond. "Your boss tell you I was looking for you earlier, Neena?" he asked, his smile wider than it needed to be.

"He did, yeah," she said, concentrating on the pickle.

She'd gotten an earful about him from Mr. Cook. "Watch out for that old Ted, Neena," Mr. Cook had said. "Watch out for any old married man who knows something about everything that has to do with something a young pretty girl like you needs to know. You could be talking about the man in the moon, Neena, and suddenly either Ted worked on the moon, or got a buddy who worked on the moon, or he knows whoever is hiring on the moon, or he can tell you the composition of the moon. Let me mention the man in the moon, or let eighty-year-old Hettie mention the man in the moon, or three-hundred-pound Vera, let even his own wife mention the man in the moon, suddenly he don't even know for sure if the man in the moon exists. He's full of his own droppings, he is."

Neena already knew this about Ted. For some time now she'd been aware of his gaze like so many groping hands as he stood on his porch and watched her walk. She had exaggerated the sway of her hips once or twice. Didn't know why. To get back at Nan, maybe.

"Yeah, well what I stopped to tell you about, Neena" Ted said, "is that I've got a buddy in Cleveland."

"Mnnmh," Neena said, smiling up at him, thinking about how she'd tell Mr. Cook that Ted's buddies didn't end on the moon, they were in Cleveland too.

"Yeah, Neena, so my buddy Ralph was telling me about this woman whose acquaintance he'd just made. Said she's from here, grew up on

Delancey. So I said I must know her, or if not her, least I must know her people. Sure enough, you not gonna believe what her name is, Neena. Name is Freeda."

Neena let out a small shriek. She'd just moved her thumb back before Ted mouthed her mother's name. Would have otherwise lost the tip of her thumb in the crush of pickles, though it was such a close call she wasn't sure she had not.

Mr. Cook called from the other end of the counter. "You all right, Neena?"

Neena took a deep breath and held up both her hands and wiggled her fingers. "Still got ten, Mr. C.," she said forcing a laugh.

"Be careful, how 'bout it. And anyhow, Ted, don't be distracting my people while they're using knives," Mr. Cook said, no play to his tone as he looked from Neena to Ted.

Neena scooped the pickles from the cutting board into a container and set it next to the one overflowing with sliced tomato. Her heart was beating both inside and outside of her chest at the mention of Freeda, that someone was claiming to have recently seen her mother in the flesh. Felt displaced suddenly, as if she had climbed out of her body; felt here and not here, part of her already halfway to Cleveland.

"I'm sorry, Neena." Ted took his voice down, leaned his head in, and Neena watched his mouth move to read his lips, his mouth dark and full. "I'm real sorry just springing that info on you like that. But, you know, I mean, I mentioned my buddy running across your mother to Joanie and she said whatever I do, don't tell your grandmother, said no one with any sense breathes Freeda's name in Nan's presence, so I figured I'd mention it to you."

"No problem," she said. "I'm glad you did. Unlike Nan, I can generally handle hearing my mother's name."

"I figured as much." He was smiling again. "And I thought, you know, maybe I could relate the details of what he told me, you know, not here though." He cleared his throat.

"Yeah, the details. I'd very much like the details." She breathed more than spoke, her words came out in whispered gasps. She felt tingly, as if she was about to go into chills, or break out into a sweat, her body unable to decide which. She was afraid. Afraid to hear about mother, afraid that her mother was in that flattened state, her life force slow-leaking out of her in a steady stream of sadness. Though she couldn't *not* hear about her, couldn't pass up the opportunity to know exactly where she was, to tangle with the idea of getting to her, wherever, however, she was.

"I'd tell you to ring the bell on your way in tonight but Joanie is out for the night at one of her sorority gigs so that wouldn't look too cool, you know, you coming past when she's not home."

"For sure."

"There is this sweet little tavern on North Broad where I go sometimes called the Rum and Coconut, though you're not twenty-one yet—"

"Been passing for years," Neena said. She had in truth sat on bar stools in Fifty-second Street clubs where she'd gone looking for Freeda in the aftermath of Freeda's last surfacing in Philadelphia. After hearing the nighttime click of Nan's bedroom door and watching Tish's ritual of saying her prayers and kissing all of her stuffed animals good night, Neena would dress herself to be older than she was, then creep through the night into red-air places where the men offered to buy her drinks. She'd tell them she was looking for her cousin, she'd show them Freeda's picture and ask if they recognized her, said that her aunt was sick over her only daughter's disappearance and she was doing what all she could to find her. "She's on that stuff," she'd say. Though to her knowledge Freeda wasn't on anything except for the massive mood swings. The men would swivel their chairs around to face Neena. They'd be willing to help her find her cousin, they'd say as they pressed their knees against her. She could see, though, that they were useless to her as she'd decline their offers of car rides to this or that neighborhood. This one though, Ted, was different.

At thirty-eight Ted was twice Neena's age, his hairline already pulling back, strands of gray mixing in with his meticulously shaped goatee, his face hinting at the places where wrinkles would form. Nice strong-featured face, mild brown complexion set off by the orange and red T-shirt he wore. JAMAICA NO PROBLEM blazed across the front, like his desire for Neena was blazing too, so uncovered, the muscles in his face so slackened that Neena was embarrassed for him, wanted to throw him a towel so he could cover some of his desire for her. She looked away from his face. Focused on the thick gold chain he wore almost hidden under the T-shirt, then on the developed muscles bursting beneath the cap sleeves as if his arms were already flexed, already around her.

"So when will you be there? At the Rum and Coconut?" she asked as she wiped a dishcloth along the cutting board, rubbing hard into the wood at the spot where she'd almost lost her thumb.

"'Round eleven." He said it more as a question than a statement.

Neena looked straight at him then. The severity of her dark eyes caught him off guard and he coughed. "I hope you're not making me waste my bus tokens," she said. She folded the dishcloth into a perfect square. Was about to move on to dicing onions but now Mr. Cook was standing over her.

"I need you on the register, baby girl," he said. "Mrs. C. feels a headache coming on like she does every Friday about this time. Maybe

Ted is up to cutting onions since he seems to like that spot where he's standing, and I ain't yet heard him order a sandwich to go."

"Yo, Cook, ease up," Ted said and Neena felt the tingling sensation recede from the surface of her skin. Recognized that the tingling had not just been fear about Freeda's condition, but that she'd just been aroused by Ted. She was surprised that the likes of a Ted could affect her so. Although she was glad that she was aware. As long as she was aware of her desires, she reasoned, she could control them. Unlike Freeda who never could control her desires, who'd go dreamy-eyed time and again over man after man with whom she'd have no future. Now Neena felt the arousal drain down to the soles of her feet. Felt like a little girl again with Mr. Cook standing next to her. Pretended for the moment that Mr. Cook was her father as she laughed at what he'd just said.

The Rum and Coconut was a tavern-type place during the week where people sipped mixed drinks and listened to rhythm and blues falling from the ceiling speakers. Conversations could be carried on in whispers without interruption unless the waitress stopped by to point out the fried wing, or hot roast beef, or peeled shrimp specials listed on the free-standing laminated menus. On Friday, though, the night Neena met Ted here, the tavern became an old-school party spot billed as an after-work set for the mature professional. Women in control-top hose and push-up bras and the men who'd like to relieve them of the same crammed the circular dance floor and shed the workweek skins as they moved to Earth, Wind & Fire singing "Got to Get You into My Life." Neena and Ted squeezed into a table against the mirrored wall; they were both wearing black, both their black shirts unbuttoned showing the neckline jewelry they wore: Ted with the thick gold link chain, Neena with a heart-shaped pendant given to her by Tish as a consolation for the ring Neena lost that Nan had presented to Neena on her sixteenth birthday. Ted reached in and fingered the heart and mouthed "nice" because they otherwise had to shout to be heard. Neena nodded. She got a surge from his finger against her throat, like she'd gotten a surge when she'd walked up the subway steps into the sudden flash of Broad Street neon and there Ted was on the corner, a worry line etched up his forehead as he leaned in to light a cigarette. She thought either that he was worried that she wouldn't show, or worried that his match wouldn't catch; it didn't matter to her really which it was, it was more the intensity of the expression that gave her the surge, his face set, so molded.

She leaned in and fingered his chain and he jerked, surprised by the move. She relaxed into the move as she took her time running her fingers across the gold links, then tracing a U along his collarbone and enjoying the feel of his pulse beneath her fingers, his pulse speeding up the harder she pressed. She used to do that same thing to Richmond. She hadn't seen Richmond since last summer. He hadn't come to Philadelphia this summer because he'd gotten a summer job in Atlanta where he'd gone to school. Neena had told him that he should take advantage of every opportunity to be happy, even if it meant loving someone else. "It's not like we go together anyhow," she'd insisted, though she herself hadn't been with anyone else.

The music slowed from the Earth, Wind & Fire tune to Michael Jackson crooning "Oooh Chile." Neena looked at Ted and raised her eyebrows, used her eyebrows to ask him to dance. He cleared his throat and coughed and then took her hand and helped her up to standing.

"What y'all drinking?" the waitress shouted just as they freed themselves from between the table and the mirrored wall. Ted pointed to the bar indicating they'd order there, their seats quickly taken up by a pair of women with big frosted hair.

Ted was a polite dancer; their bodies barely touched as they swayed to the beat. He sang some of the song in her ear; he had a nice voice, though he couldn't hold a note for long, his breaths coming too quickly, Neena could tell. Now she whispered in his ear. "The joint is jumping in here. I was expecting a quiet little bar set."

"It is, usually, you know quiet. I apologize, you know, I'd forgotten how this place changes up on a Friday."

"Well don't think you getting out of telling me about Freeda."

"Never, of course not. You think we need to find a quieter spot?"

"Actually I can hear you just fine long as you talking directly in my ear."

"Not a problem then. I'll talk directly in your ear. I guess we just have to keep dancing. Guess I'ma have to hold you a little closer too. You know how long I been waiting to hold on to you, girl?"

"No. How long you been waiting? Tell me. While you telling me about Freeda. Tell me how long you been waiting to do this."

He let out an involuntary moan and pulled Neena closer in. "My buddy, yeah, he works for a private social service entity in Cleveland that runs community living arrangements. He prescreens the prospective residents, yeah, and that's how he'd come to be acquainted with Freeda." Ted leaned his forehead against Neena's, then fingered her chin. "I knew for sure that he was talking about your mother when he described her eyes. Said she had wild dark eyes. Mnh, you got some eyes, you know that, Neena. On the one hand they can scare the mess out of a brother; on the other hand, damn, they turn me on. You turn me on, Neena."

A fast song was playing now and Ted still held Neena in a slow-drag pose. They were jostled by the hips and arms flapping and swaying, the intermittent shouts of "Party" getting in between their conversation, threatening to disrupt their conversation altogether. Neena wrapped both her arms around Ted's neck. Like she'd been surprised down in Mr. Cook's store when she'd first recognized a desire for Ted, she was surprised right now at how aroused she was, her arousal moving from the nape of her neck like a slow hot hand down her back. Her arousal felt dangerous right now because there was no Mr. Cook standing over her to call her baby girl and return her to innocence. The sense of danger mingled with the fear about her mother, what she was about to hear, needing to hear it, dreading it too.

Ted had Neena's face in his hands. His fingers traced the outline of her lips. He kissed her right where they stood on the dance floor. She thought it a bold move. He led her then from the dance floor crowded with bodies in various stages of getting it on. Led her right to the front door of the club. The door was glass and fogged over; fingerprints at a variety of heights looked like decoration. Ted added his own large prints as he pushed the door open and Neena stepped first into the night.

It was three o'clock in the morning when Neena walked up on Nan's darkened porch. She could see through the slice of opening between the drapery panels that the living room lights were turned on. Unusual for the lights to be on since Nan turned the downstairs lights off by ten most nights. The living room had in fact been black when Neena had tiptoed through on her way to meet Ted. She wasn't entirely surprised by the lights. She'd had a feeling that she'd return to lights. Sirens in fact would not have been a complete surprise. She had after all lived out her grandmother's prophecies tonight. She'd been a hot-in-the-behind heifer, the kind of girl doing ugly that God didn't like. Took down a married man like the Jezebel that she was. In the process Ted promised to call his buddy and get answers to Neena's dozens of questions about Freeda because he'd drawn blanks on the specifics. Didn't even know for sure if Freeda had even been accepted as a resident in the community living program, didn't know how functional she was, where she'd been the past three years, how she'd been living, was she on medication.

She turned her key in the front door and walked into the vestibule. Both couch lamps she could see now were turned on to their highest brightness. Company-type lighting. She wasn't completely surprised to see the lights, nor was she entirely stunned when she stepped into the brightness of the living room to feel her grandmother's hand hard against her mouth, though her grandmother hadn't hit her since that evening after Neena had been with Richmond for the first time. Her lip was blossoming as she stood there, spilling blood, and she cupped her hand to catch the blood and caught the sight of Joan, Ted's wife, tall and dark and slender like an African model with her close-cut curly 'fro. Pretty woman. Neena didn't have anything against Joan. She was able to stand there catching the blood dripping from her mouth and look right at Joan without shirking, though she'd just been with her husband. She didn't want Joan's husband. She'd enjoyed his sturdiness and how weak he'd gone. Enjoyed how he'd brought her to a silvery place. But she had no future aspirations that included Ted; she was no threat to Joan. She was searching for the proper way to say that but she was more concerned with her lip. Plus now Joan was coming at her with her fists balled. "Got to nerve to look at me all calm," she said, her voice catching in her throat and she sounded as if she was choking. "I got to get two separate phone calls from my best friends telling me what they saw at the Rum and the Coconut tonight. I got to hear them describe him and describe you and you gonna look at me all calm. I'm gonna kick your natural ass, you dirty little whore."

Nan got in front of Joan. "I'll deal with Neena," Nan said. "You best get back down the block and see to your husband. He's surely not blameless. He's more wrong than Neena if you want to know the truth of the matter."

Joan tried to reach around Nan to get to Neena. And now here was Tish, pulling Joan from behind. Tish in her lavender and yellow pajamas that almost matched the wallpaper in their bedroom. A dozen evenly spaced sponge rollers in her hair. "Please, Miss Joan, just go home, please," Tish said, and Neena could tell that Tish was trying not to cry as she, Neena, ran past them all into the kitchen so that she could spit out blood in the sink.

She was holding ice to her lip by the time Nan came into the kitchen. She stared beyond Nan at the copper canisters stacked on the counter. They were empty canisters; Neena had given them to Nan for her birthday and for once Nan seemed genuinely touched by something Neena had done. The following week, though, Neena told Nan that she'd read that the copper might leach into the flour or sugar or cornmeal. "Takes you to give me something nice, then hinder me from putting it to good use," Nan had said.

Now Nan pushed at Neena's shoulder. "I'm not even gonna ask you to explain yourself. No explanation exists for you bringing this whole household to shame."

Neena focused on Nan's quilted robe, the orange print against white, the ruffles around the neckline. "He had news about Mommy," Neena said to the ruffles.

"He's full of the devil," Nan said, then stopped and swallowed, Neena's words just now registering. "News about your mother?" Nan's voice higher suddenly, tighter, as if the ruffled collar had reached around to strangle her. Face looked as if she was being strangled too.

The color rushed from her face and seemed to settle in her throat, the veins in her neck jumping. She put her hand to her throat. "What he say about her anyhow? Huh? No-good nigger man like that will use anything he got to use to get a young girl into bed. And you got no better sense than to fall for it. She alive? Was he even able to tell you that? Huh?"

"She's alive. She is. In Cleveland."

"In Cleveland, huh?" Nan said. And Neena could hear how Nan's voice opened some when she said it. "So now I guess you got it in your mind to try to track her down in Cleveland?"

Neena hunched her shoulders, as if to say she didn't know what she had in her mind to do. Though she did know. Knew she would have to leave now. Had really left earlier tonight when Ted stood in front of her in Mr. Cook's basement store and said that her mother was in Cleveland. Had seen the balance on her savings account statement, close to a thousand dollars she had in the bank. Had planned out what she'd take, what she'd allow to remain. Hadn't realized until just now that she'd already left.

"She's your one-way ticket to hell, Neena," Nan said, and Neena looked at her grandmother, her scarf covering her tightly rolled pin curls, white film of Ponds cold cream shaping her hairline, clear thin liquid draining from her nose. Neena knew then that's how her grandmother cried, through her nose.

"Why you can't just get her out of your system is beyond me," Nan went on. "I birthed her and I've been able to do it. It can be done. Unless you just want an excuse to let the devil use you. What impact you think your behavior has on Tish? She's trying to live the life of an upstanding Christian girl. How's she supposed to walk through the block with her head held high knowing her older sister's now got a reputation for busting up a marriage. Huh? Something sacred, Let no man put asunder, and what do you do?"

Neena let Nan's voice fade into the background the way she always did when Nan started quoting scriptures. She was thinking about Mr. Cook, how'd she tell him good-bye. She missed him already. They'd played pinball after they closed up the store tonight and one game turned into two turned into a best of five series at Mr. Cook's insistence. Neena relented even though she had that date with Ted. Mr. Cook was a masterful player; only his fingers moved, he never shook the machine or cursed, and Neena had never won against him before. She did tonight, though. "Well baby girl, that's one to carry with you through life," he'd said. "You beat the socks off of me and I taught you the game." He seemed shorter as he walked her to the door and when she turned around halfway up the street she saw that he was still watching her. She wondered then if he'd done that every night. Watched her until she got safely to Nan's. She wanted to cry at the thought. She rarely cried, though. She rocked herself back and forth instead, the way she'd always done to calm herself.

Nan had stopped talking and was refilling the ice tray Neena had left in the sink. "Do you need more ice for your mouth?" she asked Neena.

Neena shook her head, no.

"Move your hand so I can see your mouth," Nan said, and Neena did. Nan pulled a handkerchief from her robe pocket and dabbed lightly at Neena's mouth. Then she pulled Neena to her in a hug; it was an awkward hug. "The swelling should be down by morning, Lord willing. Turn off the lights when you're through in here."

Nan walked out of the kitchen then. And Neena thought nothing more for her to do. Just turn off the lights and leave for real.

Chapter 16

Y THE TIME Neena had gotten to the part of her day when she sat in the bookstore and read, which meant it was mid-afternoon, Cliff still had not taken her call. She'd called three times and each time the person answering said that Cliff was not available, suggesting that if Neena didn't care to leave a number, it would be unlikely that she would speak to him this day. She glanced up every now and then and looked out of the wall of windows onto Broad Street below. She could see Bow Peep down there and his presence was comforting. Now she gave up her prize seat at this window and went downstairs and out of the store.

It had turned unseasonably warm yet again and the streets were loud with the sounds of teenagers just let free from schools. They laughed and squealed and cursed and made cat calls back and forth across the streets. Many were coatless and Neena stomped on the impulse to say something. Nan had drilled into her the importance of not changing into lighter fare when the winter temperatures rose. Winter air was still winter air and would sneak inside of you and give you consumption if you tried to play around with it, Nan insisted. Neena realized that she still didn't know what consumption was, though she never changed out of winter garb until after mid-March. Warm as it was today, she was wearing the peach cashmere sweater under her black wool coat. She wondered then what determined whether she rejected or accepted her grandmother's admonitions. Wondered if she'd been better off wearing thin cotton in January and clinging to her grandmother's Jesus instead.

She was across the street from where Bow Peep was. She strained to hear his flute above the midday clatter turned up high. She readied herself to follow his tangle of conversation as she raised her arm to wave. Now he was talking to a woman. At first Neena assumed that she was probably the same caliber woman as the one from a couple of weeks ago whose head was dressed in Kinte cloth, the one to whom Bow Peep had given his earnings, probably someone with whom he'd shared in-patient status on the psych floor at HUP. Neena watched as this woman kissed Bow Peep on the cheek and Neena could see from all the way on this side of the street that Bow Peep was blushing; his cheeks were high as mountains suddenly and his long line of a mouth lengthened more in a smile. The woman was crossing the street now, walking in the direction of where Neena stood. By all accounts she looked normal, like Neena looked normal. She was not a bad-looking woman either, Neena had to admit. Why did she have to admit it? Neena asked herself as the woman walked right past her now, the woman reaching into a good leather bag, pulling up a razor-thin cell phone, saying, Hi there, how are you? An accomplished tone to her voice. Having to admit it meant that she didn't want to admit it. She was stymied as she followed that thought because she'd never had such a thought, never had such a feeling as this feeling rising up from her toes as she looked at Bow Peep across the street and he was still smiling even as he shined his flute. She smelled buttered popcorn suddenly, didn't know where the smell was coming from; it was so strong that she almost expected to look around and find herself transported to an old-fashioned movie theater with the burgundy-colored velvet seats and the reel-to-reel projector that made a *click-click* sound as she crunched down on the popcorn and the butter coated her tongue, Richmond's hand squeezing her thigh. Imagined that it was Bow Peep's hand squeezing her thigh, covered her mouth then to keep herself from screaming at the thought. Told herself that she must be hungry, it was the popcorn, not Bow Peep that she desired. She fingered the change in her pocket. She turned and crossed Broad and headed in the direction away from where Bow Peep stood. She walked past Lord & Taylor, past what used to be a Woolworth's, now a spillover location for Society Hill furniture. Thought about Miss Goldie then, and that purple couch that Neena and Tish loved so that Miss Goldie bragged came from there, back when colored folk were hardly allowed to shop in such places.

She walked along Thirteenth Street. Passed the independent bookstore still surviving even with the big chain one right around the corner. Had come to this bookstore with Richmond often, the only place where Richmond could find *The Communist Manifesto*. Now she turned back onto Walnut Street. Looked at the address facing her. Realized that she was standing in front of the building that housed Cliff's law office. Realized too that the woman she'd just seen talking to Bow Peep was most likely an associate with the law firm; he'd said she checked up on Bow Peep when he, Cliff, couldn't get to him. He wasn't avoiding her, he was busy. She told herself that she shouldn't feel so floaty inside at that realization, though she did, discovered at that moment how it felt to swoon.

She went through the revolving door and inside the lobby lined with ficus trees in oversized brass pots. She took a seat on the backless bench and scanned the short line of people at the reception/guard desk waiting to sign in. Most looked like delivery people, two with food, one with flowers. She had a clear view to the elevator doors. Now she got up because she noticed a bowl of lollipops on the reception desk. She took three, smiled at the brawny receptionist almost busting out of his blazer. She sat back down and unwrapped and slowly sucked the lollipops one at a time. She was on the third one, lemon yellow, when Cliff walked through, walked quickly, and she almost missed him because he was wearing a hat today. Neena felt a heat that started in her toes and moved through her like a rush of light. Her heartbeat sped up suddenly, her breaths went shallow, she felt dizzy. She'd never been so affected by a man before, not even by Richmond who she'd loved. Realized that the sense of desire that rushed her out on the street and shocked her because she thought it was for Bow Peep, was actually for Cliff. The tinge of jealousy over the woman with the accomplished-sounding voice was not that she'd made Bow Peep blush, but that perhaps she made Cliff blush. She ran across the lobby, stomped on the thought that she might be considered a stalker as she tossed the lollipop sticks in the brass trash can, and slipped into the elevator just before the doors closed.

He was looking up waiting for the floor numbers to light. His face was set as if it had just been sculpted, as if her thumb against his face would leave a print that would mark his face from then on. She touched his hand. Now he looked at her and she could tell that it took a few seconds for her face to register. She let her face go serious, lowered her eyes without letting them leave his face. "I promised I'd be in touch," she said. "So I'm in touch."

He took her hand in both of his. He rubbed her hand. "God, Neena," he said. "How did you know? Huh? How did you know you're exactly what I need right now."

They were at his floor and he asked if she'd wait back down in the lobby. He had a couple of matters he needed to handle. "Ten minutes please," he said. "I promise, I won't be longer than that."

It was later, the middle of the night, and Neena lay awake in her bed at the Arch Street Hotel. She stared up at the pole of light pushing in from outside and making an equilateral triangle in the corner of the ceiling. She thought about all she'd have to do to pull it off with Cliff. For starters they'd need a consistent getting-together place. Couldn't dangle the line about an ex-boyfriend breaking in and hiding a camera and catching them on video without such a consistent place. This evening they'd gone right around the corner from Cliff's office to the Doubletree Hotel. He'd hoisted her up and they'd climbed to then crashed through that silvery place. And then Neena cried. She didn't know why she cried. Cliff befuddled as well that she cried. Concerned too. Thought he'd done something wrong the way he apologized. Then he took full responsibility and said they'd gotten together too soon. His better judgment had been to wait. It was his fault, he tried to convince Neena so that she'd stop crying.

She'd left the Doubletree Hotel in a hurry. Left Cliff there with his confused sadness, his complexity. Angry that he was so damned complex. She encountered Bow Peep on her walk back here. He blew into his flute and told her he'd just given her a double dose of the healing vibe. "Ah, little lamb, you're sad," he said. "Never fear, Bow Peep is here. Where are you going? Let me walk with you? Just call my name and I'll be there. Are you headed back to wherever your pillow is? Where is that? Smile, smile, just make a smile for me."

Neena smiled a mechanical smile.

"Ah, my lady love, I have been on point in the jungle, like I know the rhythms of the night, I know the rhythms of the human heart. All things have their nature. There's movement out this evening. I insist, I'll walk you home."

Neena waited while he packed his flute. She watched his long fingers take the flute apart. He handled the flute with such tenderness and she remembered the feel of his fingers against her shoulders the night she cried on the steps of the Hong Kong Restaurant.

She was quiet as they walked. Bow Peep talked though. Talked about the dinner he had at Delilah's at the train station, and how, when he returned, he'd had to compete with a shoe box preacher proclaiming the end of the world just steps from where he played.

When they reached the Arch Street Hotel Bow Peep said, "Here? Neena, you're staying here? This is the belly of the whale for sure. You only end up here if you're caught at sea when a storm rolls in, and just when you think this is it, I'm going down for the third time, a great white whale or maybe even a blue sperm opens its trap and swallows you alive. And you stay alive, 'cause it's warm in there. You warm, Neena? They got the best radiators in that place. Man, when those bad boys start hissing, you forget you on the down and out, you're like, thank you for the heat. Such a simple thing. Some heat in the winter. So easy to take for granted. But the hissing won't let you. The steam says, Yo, now don't this feel good, I don't care whatever ain't working in your life right now, I'm a radiator and I'm doing my thing on your behalf. Solid?"

Neena did smile for real then. She kissed his cheek and then headed in.

So now she stared at the pole of light and came to the realization that she couldn't do it again. Couldn't go through another tryst with a married man. In the best of times he'd provide her a furnished studio with a river view in a piano-lobby building; an allowance so that she could shop well, take all the courses she wanted, enjoy movies and music and books, surround herself with quality things, pay the people who specialized in locating the long-term missing. All she had to do in exchange was to keep herself pretty and inhabitable so that he could move into her like he would move into a house as the Patti LaBelle song goes. That's all she had to do. But she was tired. Tired of feigning desire, tired of lapping her sustenance like a lost dog from any man with the smell of meat on his hand. Wished she could get out of here right now, leave Philly for good. Didn't know why she'd come back here anyhow. Because some ticket agent at the bus station had eyebrows like Mr. Cook's?! She willed herself to sleep. Fell into a raggedy sleep. Then woke an hour later to a sound outside her window, her window open because once again, unbelievably, the temperature had turned unseasonably warm.

It was the sound of the flute. It was about five in the morning and the air outside her window was black as tar. She went to the window and looked out, though she couldn't see much since the room faced the brick building next store, a thin alley below. Still she heard the flute. He was playing "Shaker Song." Neena knew the words, said them out loud as he got to the part about the night hanging its head as the fool crawls in bed and his hungry heart is waiting to be fed. And then the chorus that he can't shake her, can't shake her. Now she wondered if that was even Bow Peep down there. It had to be, the way the notes hung in the air, his signature.

She got up then and pulled on her corduroy pants and peach sweater and went downstairs. It was him. His eyes were closed as he went into an extended riff. She lifted the case from where it was propped on the milk crate. She sat on the crate and put the case in her lap and then folded herself up so that her head rested against the case. She rocked herself as he played. Otherwise she was still. Her mind, so rarely still, came to a rest as he played. Wide awake and still. Felt now as if she was floating away from her body, looking down on herself, that poor woman folded over a street musician's flute case. All she ever wanted was her mother. "Be Still." He had stopped playing and was saying those words over and over. "Be still, be still, and after that just be," he said. And she wondered why she persisted in ascribing to him logic; he was a crazy man who played a mean flute. Levels off more on some days than others. Period. Get your stupid ass off of this crate and go back to bed, she told herself. She continued to sit there. The flute case was hard and cool against her face, not at all uncomfortable. "Just be," he said again. "Be, be, just be."

Now she was seeing her grandmother's face again, the face she'd seen as she'd drank and drank from the water fountain in the lower sanctuary of the church. That look of contained hope taking over her grandmother's face. No, now it was another look. It was fifteen years ago, 1989, Goldie's Sam had succumbed to cancer of the throat and Neena had rushed back to Philadelphia though she arrived too late for the funeral. Sam's brother opened the door and there was Goldie looking like a queen centered on the heart-shaped purple couch. Nan sat on the couch next to Goldie, their arms locked and Goldie patted the spot on the couch on the other side of her. "Sit, baby," she said. "Come sit with Goldie and your grandmommy." Neena did and Goldie locked her other arm around Neena's arm and they sat like that, without conversation, for the balance of the afternoon while Sam's brother lightly played the piano, a mix of jazz and the blues.

What was it about that afternoon that was rattling against her rib cage, disturbing her now almost fifteen years later? On the surface the peace of that afternoon was astounding as the brother journeyed around the piano taking Goldie to places that made her nod and smile when he hit on and then paused over one of Sam's favorite tunes. Everything about Goldie's demeanor that day, her poise, whispered acceptance. Nothing to do with Goldie agitating Neena now. Even Nan had been uncharacteristically quiet, no proselytizing about how important it was now for Goldie to put her hand in the Lord's hand, didn't even start in on Neena about her irregular phone calls, the color highlights in her hair, her lack of a church home wherever she was living these days. It was the memory of Nan's face that was bothering Neena now. How sad it was. Sad and resigned. Just sad and resigned. Where had all that contained hope gone? That's what was bothering Neena now.

Neena was quiet after Bow Peep's final note held and then melted into the predawn air. Bow Peep tried to draw her out. Threw around lines of poetry, about life not being no crystal staircase, and still you rise little lamb, and I too sing America and contain multitudes. He asked then what she thought of his playing? "Nice," she said, "very nice."

"And how's sis doing lately?"

"Fair, they say she's still doing fair."

"So you got big plans for tomorrow? What you planning to read?" Neena hunched her shoulders.

"It's almost breakfast time. You wanna go get some eggs and oyster crackers?"

"No thank you," she said.

"Neena, you're shattering my heart against my chest wall. What's wrong, please tell me, tell me, what's wrong?"

She didn't say, just unfolded herself from his flute case and asked if she could please use his phone.

She'd never called her in the middle of the night like this. She was surprised at how quickly she answered, how wide awake her voice. "Nan," she said. "Nan it's me, Neena."

"Neena? Are you still in Philadelphia, Neena? Or did your job take you away again?"

"When did you last speak to her, Nan?"

"What? Who? Oh sweet Jesus, Neena, I've told you, you got to pray about this obsession. The Lord will remove it but you got to ask."

"When, Nan, can you please tell me? Please."

"It's been some years."

"How many?"

"Many, Neena. It's been many, many years."

"Was nineteen eighty-nine the last time?"

Nan's voice fell to a shadow. "I do believe it was around then. Nineteen eighty-nine. The last time, yes it was, yes it was."

There was silence then as they listened to each other breathe. Bow Peep bowed his head as if he was praying. Neena broke first. "So how are you, Nan? I mean, I know you've got a lot going on with Tish and all. But how are you?"

"I'm doing, I'm doing, Neena. And I do believe, Tish's situation is gonna work out." Neena could hear that her grandmother's nose was draining, remembered that's how her grandmother cried. "How are you, Neena? Right now, that's what I want to know. How are *you*?"

Chapter 17

N HOUR LATER it was still dark as Neena kissed
Bow Peep's cheek and they parted ways at the Wawa
where he'd just bought her a large cup of coffee. She
pushed through a blossoming chill in the air headed to
Walnut Street to catch the 42 bus to get to Nan's. Wanted to get there
during Nan's sewing time when the hum of her sewing machine softened the air. Wanted to get there too before she lost her nerve to beg
her grandmother to tell her what she knew. She walked up Broad
Street that was yawning itself awake with the swishing sounds of
street-cleaning trucks shooting dense sprays of water that looked pink
in the loosening dark. She picked up her pace to try to out walk the
familiarity, the ways that this stretch of street felt suddenly like it did
when she was a child. She didn't see a bus coming, didn't want to keep
still and wait. Walked up Walnut until about Nineteenth, where a
small assemblage of people were gathered under the transom of the bus
stop, their quiet chatters commenting about the weather, the bus being
late, the price of gas.

Neena said good morning. Two black women who looked to Neena like Florida and Wilona from *Good Times,* both with green hospital scrubs hanging beneath their coats, said 'morning in return; a young brother said Yo, 'sup; union-looking white man in Eagles garb nodded; young white woman allowed a thin crack of a smile. "The 42 does stop here, right?" she asked of no one in particular.

"Better or SEPTA got some explaining to do," the Wilona-looking one said.

"You mean you got some explaining to do," this from Florida. "And you better pray that time clock you got to punch is in a good mood."

"Well," Wilona said, motioning toward Neena, "if I was still young and cute like this chile, I'd pat its head and put it in a good mood."

Neena focused through the dark gray air and looked directly at the woman in her faux brown shearling and hat and scarf and gloves in matching burnt orange chenille. She was accustomed to sarcasm from women. From a child she'd seemed to evoke the looking up and down that certain women did. Though Wilona's mouth painted in a brown as dark as her coat was pulled back in a half-moon, natural-looking smile. Neena smiled in return, blushed a little.

"Chile, hush," Florida said. "Was we ever that young? Or that cute?"

"And if we were, did we have sense enough to use it?"

"No, 'cause we was just about being hardworking, not smart-working."

"Girl, you ain't said a word. When I think back on the missed opportunities—"

"What you talking, watching people get promoted all over top of me—"

"People I trained—"

"And me getting indignant instead of putting on some false eye-lashes and batting them—"

"Get up on the down stroke."

They all laughed then. Neena too. Grateful suddenly for the feel of her laugh pulling from deep in her stomach. They backed up from the curb as the bus, not the 42 though, pulled in and all save Neena and Wilona and Florida got on.

Neena looked from one to the other. "You know what," she shouted over the sound of the bus pulling away, "I can look at y'all and see if you had it to do over you'd do it the same way, the right way, all over again."

"Go on and depress me 'cause you know you telling the truth," Wilona said.

"And you're still cute too," Neena said. "Both of you. Beyond cute, you're beautiful."

"You wanna be my daughter?" Wilona asked. "'Cause I need to hear what you saying 'bout fifty times a day. Your mama living? She willing to share you?"

"I lost my mother," Neena said as she rocked from side to side and sipped her coffee.

"Well, now you truly protected, nothing like having a mother doing her thing upstairs on your behalf."

"I guess," Neena said. "I mean, I just wish I knew, you know, one way or the other, you know, she's been missing."

"Oooh." Florida sounded as if she was about to sing as she held on to the word. Then Wilona asked Neena how long had it been.

"Years and years," Neena said, and then nodded. A firm nod. Felt the nod in her chest as if her insides were acknowledging something that hadn't yet chiseled its way to the surface. She finished her last swallow of coffee and then looked around for a trash can, saw one across the street at the entrance to the Rittenhouse Square Park. "Let me get rid of this," she said as she ran across the street to toss the cup. Then remained on that side of the street to allow the drizzles of traffic to pass. A car with its music sounds exploding zoomed up the street and screeched to a stop right in the turn-in for the bus. She recognized the song "Soul Man" by Sam and Dave. The driver's side door was half open, lighting the inside of the car and putting the man and woman inside—kissing with some fervor—on display. Neena almost chuckled as she looked across the street and watched Florida's and Wilona's faces frown and smirk as they talked. Imagined one was probably saying, Why don't they just get a room, the other saying, Or at least turn that music down, bad enough the young ones blast theirs, he's an old fool. The driver jumped out of the car to go open the passenger-side door just as Neena started to cross the street. She froze. Didn't know which registered first in her brain: the car: a burgundy Ford Tempo; or the man with the donkey-shaped head: Ramsey from the West Philly bar the first night she'd arrived, the one whose watch and ring had bought her a place to sleep. She edged away from the curb even as Flo and Wilona waved to her and called out, "This is the 42 bus coming." Neena coughed, pretending the cough as her reason for covering her face and turning away. She resisted the urge to run. Do nothing but call Ramsey's attention to her if she ran. Run to where anyhow. Through the park? An Episcopal church on another corner, closed stores up and down Walnut Street, gleaming high-rise doormen-protected condos otherwise. Told herself that he might recognize her. That night seemed so long ago, though really it had only been a couple of weeks. She leaned into the tubular trash can with her back to the street and pretended to vomit. Hoped a rat didn't jump up through the darkness and go for her nose. Had read that rats had been prolific around here, prompting the city to initiate swift containment efforts because this was a moneyed area, but environmentalists had begun to squawk because the squirrels started disappearing right along with the rats. She wished she'd kept up with the issue to know who won, to know what the odds were of getting mauled leaning over this trash can. Now she felt a hand on her arm and she was about to lift her foot and jab her heavy vinyl Salvation Army boot into his kneecap. About to holler rape. But then she saw the burnt orange chenille glove, felt the warmth from the glove pulsing all the way through her cashmere coat. "You okay, sugar?" the one who looked like Wilona asked. "You want us to hold the bus?"

Neena nodded. "I think that creamer in my coffee must have been bad," she said as she listened for the *whoosh* of the car door shutting, the music now muffled inside the closed-up car. She bent her knees to shorten her stance as the car zoomed away. Then stood all the way up. Wilona handed her a peppermint as they crossed the street. She tried not to look at the woman who'd just left Ramsey's car, but the woman was so prominent as she stood there blushing in a cheap wig and weathered complexion. Neena felt sorry for her that the likes of Ramsey made her blush. Relieved that the woman wasn't getting on the 42. Only Neena and Wilona and Florida got on the 42.

Once on the bus, Neena avoided the window seats, sat up close to the bus driver in the seats reserved for the handicapped. Slouched to lower herself and talked her breathing down. Florida and Wilona joked with her from where they sat further back, asking her if she'd craved pickles and ice cream lately, if the dry cleaners had started shrinking her clothes around the waistband. "Please don't wish that on me." Neena laughed.

"Last I heard, wishing ain't had too much to do with it," Wilona said.

"In my case it did," from Florida. "I got five kids and I can remember saying to myself before I got caught with each one, 'I *wish* this man would hurry up 'cause I gotta get up early for work,' and then to hurry him up, I'd let him come out of the raincoat I'd make him wear."

The several other people on the bus giggled, even the bus driver's shoulders moved up and down, and Neena wished they were going the distance on the 42, almost to the end of the line like she was. They weren't. They got up just as they neared Penn. Stood in front of Neena as they waited for the bus to stop. Wilona put her hand to Neena's forehead. "Well, it ain't the flu 'cause you not the least bit warm. You take care of yourself, you hear, sugar." Neena smiled and nodded.

"And just let him take his time," Florida said in her singsongy voice and they both laughed out loud as they disembarked.

Neena tried to hold the sound of their laughter in her head. Tried to use their laughter to keep her from looking into the bottom of the well and seeing the sludge there, the sludge being her behavior, the places her behavior had taken her, the justifications she'd use to obscure her behavior; the main justification, her mother, she had to find her mother, she had to eat and live while she tried to find her mother, live as well as she could while she tried, opulently if she could, a good-looking man to move against her late at night if she could. Tried to close her mind to the consideration that every man she'd been with had been Ramsey-like; they'd been smarter, more accomplished, they'd driven better cars, been younger, more handsome, taken her to hotels with turn-down service, she'd found them in places far and away from that ghetto bar with the lit apostrophe, but they'd all been Ramsey. Now her grandmother's voice was working its way into the fading swirl of the laughter, trying to say some insulting thing to Neena, asking her why she had so much hate in her heart. She thought about that the rest of the ride, thought really that was not an insulting thing to ask.

She was at her stop. Her hands were chunks of ice inside her gloves as she grabbed the silver pole so that she wouldn't fall when the bus jerked to a halt. The steps to get off the bus were like a mountain ridge and she looked back to smile and say thank-you to the bus driver before her descent. He was a young boy, a cutie pie she thought as her foot touched down and she got the sense that she was on dangerous ground, could feel the heat of the ground as she crossed the street, as if her footfalls now were stirring up some dormant gases and soon the ground would explode all around her. The row houses on Spruce Street seemed larger than she'd remembered, or was it that she felt shrunken, could even be because the trees were bare, more than bare, gone, saw stumps as she looked down Spruce Street. Crossed Spruce to walk up Fifty-eighth to Delancey. Overgrown hedges left a line of dew on her coat. And here she was, right back again where she'd landed her first morning here, at the corner in front of Mr. Cook's Hoagie and Variety Store. She stood in front of the door. Again, she could almost smell the cheese steaks, the Dixie Peach hair pomade that flew off the shelves on Saturday morning. Could almost hear the *ring-chime-ring* of the pinball machine. Though she couldn't hear it really. She sat on the steps and folded her head in her arms, put her arms against her knees. She tried to invoke Mr. Cook right now; surely his essence was here; surely he was sending her some message from that other plane where dead people were, saying something to return her to innocence the way he'd always done.

A sensation was coming to her now, nothing though to do with Mr. Cook. She was thinking of the way the sheets smelled that day when Nan and Tish had returned from the mother-daughter tea and Neena had cursed at Nan and Nan slapped her over and over again. She realized now that it wasn't day. It was the night before. Her sixteenth birthday. She was in bed and the air outside was introducing fall so Neena and Tish had removed the box fan from the bedroom window and put the sliding screen back in so that they could sleep under the natural breeze. Neena had just settled down between crisp cotton muslin sheets that smelled of the backyard clothesline, an airy smell that was comforting to fall asleep to. Neena fought sleep though. She fingered her new gold ring, a birthday gift from her Nan, an extravagance, but Nan said it was appropriate since Neena was sixteen now and on her way to young womanhood. Neena had an unsettled attachment to the ring though. She tried to shake the feeling by continually running her thumb around her ring finger. It really was a beautiful ring, graciously cut into the form of a cursive *N*, a diamond chip at the center. A sacrifice for Nan the ring was, Neena knew. Nan would probably be taking the next year paying the ring off to Mr. Knock, the sell-anything man who came through Delancey Street every Saturday taking orders for everything from window drapes with Travis rods to GE refrigerators to Singer sewing machines. He'd come through and collect twice a month, picking up as many hard-luck deferrals as cash but he'd take whatever they could pay; though if payment was continually deferred, Mr. Knock would just reprocess the unpaid-for item. Nan was obsessive about paying her bills on time, so Neena knew that she wouldn't lose the ring to forfeiture. Nor would the ring just fall off, she knew; Nan had confirmed that too by trying to pull it off and having to tug and twist the ring to ease it past Neena's knuckle.

Nan had also made chitterlings in honor of Neena's sixteenth birthday, something she did generally only once a year around New Year's because of how time-consuming they were to clean. Neena salivated as she tried to fall asleep at how wonderful that batch of chitterlings had been. Thought that night that perhaps Nan did have some feelings for her evidenced by the splurge of the ring, the chitterlings. She enjoyed a sense of contentment that night as she inhaled the airy aroma rising off the sheet and she listened to Tish whisper her prayers. Neena had stopped praying by then because she no longer believed that prayer changed things. And even though she no longer considered it an obligation to pray, she felt an unevenness about it, about religion in general, that she didn't believe because she was somehow incapable of believing, and that made her less of a person than her sister. Tish's nightly prayers just served to reinforce Neena's own feelings of diminishment. But the day had been so otherwise delightful that Neena wasn't even reacting to Tish's praying as she watched Tish's shadow on the other side of the room unkneel itself and go through the ritual of removing the dozen stuffed animals from the bed, lining them in size order on the bench under the window. Neena wanted to ask Tish how much did she think Nan had paid for the ring, but she knew Tish had old-woman ways to be only thirteen and didn't talk for a time after she said her prayers; instead she cleared her bed of the animals one at a time the way she was doing now, at the last animal now, finally, a palm-sized mink that she'd named Neena because she said that it had a beautiful dark coat just like Neena's hair.

She watched Tish kiss the mink on its snout and tell it happy birthday and Neena was partly agitated, partly embarrassed, partly overtaken with a wave of sisterly love. That's when Neena heard a pinging sound outside of the window and she would have assumed it was an alley cat scampering up and down the fire escape the way they sometimes did, but Tish let go a gasp as she stood there facing the window, the shadowed outline of her small face frozen in horror.

"What is it, Tish?" Neena called as she unshrouded the stiff muslin top sheet from around her and ran to where Tish was pointing wildly and letting go a series of uh, uh, uh's, trying to work herself up to a full-scale scream.

Neena pieced through the scraps of light that hung in this alley, left-over shimmers from the streetlamp on the corner. She didn't know how in the half-light of the alley the mouth was the first thing she recognized on the face that was pushed close in against the screen, squinting to see inside. But that's the first thing she saw, it was her own mouth, Tish's, Nan's, the one feature they all shared. She cupped her hand over Tish's mouth then so that Tish couldn't scream.

"Shh, shh," Neena pleaded, as Tish tried to pull Neena's hand off of her mouth. "Be quiet please, Tish, please don't bring Nan in here. Don't you know who that is? Shh. Don't you know Tish? That's Mommy out there. Uh! I can't believe it. That's Mommy."

The shock of it made Tish go limp against Neena and Neena used the opportunity to collapse the foldable screen and pull it out of the window so that her mother could navigate a couple more rungs on the fire escape ladder and then climb through the window into the bedroom. She tipped the bench under the window and tripped over several of Tish's stuffed animals and landed right against Tish's feet and that brought Tish back to life, who started shaking and jabbing her finger in the darkened air toward Freeda. "I'm telling," Tish said. "You can't come in here, you can't come around us. You're dead to us. I'm going to tell Nan."

Freeda was halfway to standing, but stopped right there on all fours. She almost looked like the grown-up on some children's show the way the stuffed animals were dispersed all around her. Almost looked comic except that her back was going up and down and Neena could see that she was crying. A rage moved through Neena then and she grabbed Tish by the collar of her pajama and got in her face. "I swear to God you say one word to Nan, you even raise your voice louder than a whisper right now, and I'll kick your ass. I'll kill you, Tish." Neena's own voice was shaking from crying herself. "You call yourself a Christian. You're a hard-hearted little bitch. I swear, you let Nan know she's in here—" Now Neena couldn't even talk. She was gagging on her sobs and she didn't even realize that Tish was gagging for real, that she had tightened the collar of the pajama completely around Tish's neck. Until she felt Freeda's hands pulling at her own hands. Freeda's hands so cold and thin, such a hungry needy feel about them.

"Let her go, baby," Freeda said in Neena's ear. "It's all right. Whether she yells for Nan or not, it's gonna be all right."

Neena gasped then and let go of Tish's neck and pulled Tish to her crying that she was sorry, she didn't mean to hurt her, honest to God she didn't. "But please don't tell Nan, Tish. She's our mother, our mother, our mother," Neena cried, struggling to keep her volume to a whisper.

Freeda pulled them both to her. She mashed their faces into the frailty of her chest and swayed. Her blouse was polyester and smelled like bug spray and yet Neena didn't want to move, just wanted to stand there all night with her head against her mother's chest. Not Tish though—she wrenched herself free and scooped up her largest stuffed animal, an oversized panda. She threw herself onto her bed and muffled her sobs with her pillow and clung to the panda with such force that had it been a living, breathing thing, she would have cut off its air.

Freeda pushed back from Neena and Neena could feel the longing moving through her mother's arms as Freeda just stood there watching this shadowed version of Tish cry. "I had a feeling it would be like this," Freeda said into the bedroom air so that it sounded as if she was talking only to herself. "I had a feeling she would hate me by now."

"But I don't," Neena said. "Honest to God I don't."

Freeda moved to the lamp closest to Neena's bed and fumbled with the switch. "I don't look so good under the light these days, but God knows I got to see you under the light before I leave. I thought it would be enough just to hug you, but darn it, I've got to see you too." She found the lamp switch and the dark bedroom air gave way to yellow. Her voice was staggered as she looked at Neena. "Lord Jesus, Neena, you pretty as you want to be. And you're sixteen today. That's so incredible. My firstborn sixteen. Whew." She sat down on the side of her bed and fanned herself. "This is overwhelming, you know, processing this. But it's gonna be all right. No matter what happens to me now, it's gonna be all right 'cause I'll always know I laid eyes on you the day you turned sixteen. Sweet sixteen."

Neena felt her eyes burning. They were burning now on the steps of Young's. She shook her head back and forth to shake her eyes dry. Fixed on a bright green van moving back and forth trying to be parallel parked across the street. Her mother's shirt had been shades of green in a psychedelic pattern. Neena was afraid to take her eyes off the shirt. Afraid to look at her mother's face. Hadn't even allowed her eyes to go much beyond her mouth. Such a pretty mouth. Now she did take in her mother's face. Not so bad, she thought. The way she would tell herself that her mother didn't look so bad even as her eyes were taking on that hollowed-out stare. Her eyes weren't hollowed out now though. There was a vibrancy to the dark intensity, Neena thought. A joy. It was hard for Neena to look at the joy. Freeda should be with them if she was holding on to joy. So Neena looked at Tish instead. Tish's sobbing had settled down to loud irregular breaths and now

Tish just rocked herself, still clutching the panda, face still burrowed in her pillow. "Come on Tish," Neena whispered, "sit up so Mommy can look at you. I'm sorry I choked you. Please sit up."

Freeda clicked the lamp off then, and Neena took that as a compassionate act of motherhood. It was as if Freeda sensed that the joy Neena saw was breaking her heart.

"Don't try to make Tish come to me," Freeda said. "Believe it or not, I know what she's going through. It's all gonna be all right in the long run. What were you getting ready to do? Were you in bed? I'm not gonna keep you up? I know Nan got y'all on a fixed schedule. She's good that way. Everybody can't fit their life to her schedule though, but let me tell you, if you can, shucks, what you talking? I'm talking, whew, you gonna be making your way in the world. Always try to stick to a routine, you hear me, Neena. A good routine'll save your life."

Neena was sitting on the bed next to Freeda now and Freeda took Neena's hand in her own. She rubbed her hand and squeezed it. "Like I said, I just had to be near you 'cause you turned sixteen today. I better get on back out of here the same way I came in before Nan comes in here and all hell breaks loose."

Freeda started to rise and Neena yanked her arm and tried to talk through the storm of sobs moving up her throat. "Don't go, Mommy," she begged in an irregular cracked and soupy voice. "Nan's asleep by now. Please don't go."

Neena guessed that it was the crying, the calling her Mommy that made Freeda sit back down. She did sit back down and Neena leaned her head against the polyester shirt and Freeda rocked her back and forth. Neena soothed now by the rocking, Freeda had always rocked her to a beat, a da da da da da da duh rhythm. The same rhythm Neena used on herself, the rhythm she used now sitting on the steps of Young's. Her mother rocked her and she nestled into the feel of her mother's heartbeat against the side of her face. And now her words bouncing from inside of her as she began talking, words pouring out of her as she asked Neena question after question and then didn't even give her a chance to answer. You got a lot of friends? Watch those girls 'cause you're cute and girls can get right petty. How are your grades? Keep them up, you hear me. Don't let those no-count boys get too close to you. I know Nan got y'all in church, you sing or usher? Ushering is nice, so humble, you not trying to be a star when you usher, you serving people, they say the secret to happiness is to serve others in need. Who is they, you ask? Probably the same person who told me to be thankful for what you got. Even if you don't have a pot to pee in, be thankful that you've got the ability to pee. Your pee back up on you and you're really gonna be dealing with something. You happy, Neena? It's probably better to put your energy into trying to be good than trying to be happy. If you're good sooner or later, happiness will find you. But I haven't been either in so long. I've been sick, Neena. I didn't quit on you and Tish. I didn't put y'all down. Your mother loves you, she's just sick. Just sick. My mind, Neena. My mind is sick. But you still got Nan. I want you to listen to Nan, you hear me. I know sometimes it probably feels like Nan's goal in life is to make your life miserable. But I know where she's coming from. She was a good mother for as long as I had her. Not long enough. No matter how long you have your mother, it's never long enough.

Neena nodded even as she hated Nan for not being a mother still to Freeda. Freeda continuing to talk, jumping subjects like lightning bugs until she heard faint rhythmic snores coming from Tish's bed. Freeda lifted Neena's head and stumbled in the dark over the stuffed animals muttering "Poor baby" as she unclutched Tish's hand from the panda and then put Tish under the sheet. She tucked the sheet gently under Tish's chin. She put her finger to her lips and touched Tish's forehead.

"Where'd she have these?" she asked Neena as she held the panda up in the dark and then bent over and started picking up the other stuffed animals.

"On the window bench," Neena said, getting up to help her. "She lines them up by size."

"How did I know that," Freeda said as she started with the panda and then Neena handed her each stuffed animal in order. She walked Neena back to her bed when they were finished. And before she could form her mouth to say that she was leaving, Neena was begging her all over again not to go, and even segued into asking Freeda to take her with her.

Freeda told Neena she'd make a deal with her then. "I'll lay down with you 'til you fall asleep and I'll think about whether I should stay, or whether I should take you with me or what. I am a little tired anyhow."

Neena agreed and Freeda put the screen back in the window so that the mosquitoes wouldn't suck their blood dry, she said. Then Neena nestled against Freeda and Freeda went back into her plethora of questions that she both asked and answered and her voice was like silk to Neena. But her chest, the arms she had around Neena were so frail and it occurred to Neena that her mother might need food. "You hungry, Mommy?" Neena asked her. And Freeda didn't answer at first, which Neena took to mean yes. She eased out of bed then. Moved like lightning through the dark quiet of the house and mixed up leftover chitterlings and rice and greens in a small pot and put fire under the pot, almost hopping up and down as if to hurry the heat along. Grabbed a fork and pulled the warmed-up pot from the stove and lightning again as she crept back into her room, her eyes closed at first because she wouldn't be able to bear it if Freeda was gone. The shadow of her mother was still there sitting up in the bed and Neena had to stop herself from squealing as she handed Freeda the pot and the fork and then squeezed in next to her. Freeda saying, "Mnh, oh my God," as she held the first forkful in her mouth as if she couldn't believe how good it was. Her hands started shaking then and Neena could see that she was crying so she grabbed the pot before Freeda dropped it. She told her mother that it would be okay and then she fed Freeda. A forkful at a time. Slowly, until she was scraping the bottom of the pot.

Freeda was quiet then so Neena talked. She told Freeda about school, didn't mention that she didn't have any friends, Tish was the one with the friends. Told Freeda that the guidance counselor said that she was college material, and that she would be eligible for grants. She talked nonstop as if her talking was holding her mother there. And then it did hold her because Freeda fell asleep and Neena snuggled against her mother and noticed that the polyester blouse that smelled of bug spray had now taken on the airy scent of the freshly laundered sheets. That was so reassuring to Neena.

The driver of the van had finally gotten the vehicle into the parking space and a train of people filed out. The Young family on their way to open their store. The four doors of the van closed in quick succession and Neena remembered that's how she felt that morning, as if a series of doors were banging shut when she woke to a banging silence that sounded like absence. Before she even looked at the window and saw the hastily tossed fold-up screen, Tish's animals in disarray again under the window, the empty pot on its side, she knew that Freeda was gone. Neena sat up then all at once and patted around the bed. The sheet was soaked down to the mattress. She hit against her pajama bottom; her own bottom was dry. Freeda had peed in her bed, peed in Neena's bed and then left her. "Mommy," she whined into the light of day. "Mommy. Why did you leave me? Why?"

She wrapped her thumb around her ring finger the way she'd been doing since yesterday afternoon. Her finger was bare. She held her hand up to the light of day. Her finger had a pulled-on redness and now it even throbbed. The ring was gone. The solid gold ring with the diamond chip centered in her initial that her grandmother would be paying on forever was gone. She pulled at her hair and clutched at her chest and tried to keep the hysteria from barreling down on her as it made its approach like a fast-moving train. Her mouth was wide open but she wouldn't let the scream out; the scream stayed locked in the back of her throat as if this was all she had left of Freeda, a scream that wouldn't come.

Then she felt Tish all over her, bouncing up and down all around her on the bed. "It's better, Neena. It's better that she left. She had to go. Please stop crying, Neena. It's better that she's gone."

Neena was choking. She couldn't get air in or out and her mouth was frozen in an outstretched O. Tish ran out of the room hollering for Nan. "Something's wrong with Neena," she yelled. "Mommy sneaked in here last night and now Neena's choking 'cause she left."

"What? Your mother did what?" Nan gasped as she bounded into the room on Tish's heels. "Lord have mercy, Neena! Neena!" Nan wrapped her arms around Neena with such force that she lifted her up and away from the bed. She pressed her fists into Neena's back and shook her, the whole while shouting for Neena to breathe. "Let it up, spit it out. What's caught? Lord have mercy, Neena, whatever it is, spit it up!"

Neena didn't spit up. She swallowed instead. The scream lodged in her throat and ricocheted through her with the force of a cannonball falling back to earth, caged and locked now. Internally bound.

She felt as if she was choking all over again sitting on the Youngs' steps. Surrounded now as they looked at her, pointing.

"We not open yet," the mother said. "You come back, come back after nine, we open then."

"Dude, is she like sick or something?" said the son. "She's like totally weirding out."

"She need tea." This from the grandmother who reached down to help Neena stand. The grandmother was half Neena's height and had to reach to pat her back. "Quick, open store," she said to her son. "Make her tea," to her daughter-in-law. "No charge. Okay, baby girl," she said to Neena. "Tea from me to you. No charge you for the tea."

Chapter 18

UST AS WELL that Neena spent the next hour sipping tea with the Youngs who owned Spruce Health and Beauty because Nan wasn't home anyhow. Nan was on her senior transport bus to visit her dearly departed Alfred. Alfred wasn't dead, but Nan sometimes thought of her trips to the Springside Nursing Home as a pilgrimage to a loved one's grave site where she'd place flowers and pull weeds and dust off the marble headstone. The nursing home was an hour outside of Philadelphia. She visited once a week like she'd been doing for the past twenty years after the sanitarium where Alfred had lived closed its doors because otherwise Alfred had no regular visitors. Neena came when she was in town for longer than a day, which had been rarely. Tish visited no more than once a year because the sight of Alfred in his paralyzed state cast her in a blue mood that lasted for days. And Nan had never insisted that they visit since they had no memory of their grandfather in the fullness of his life.

Nan made polite conversation with the young woman driving the senior transport van. Asked her if she had children, if she had a church home, because her church had a wonderful youth fellowship if she didn't. "I do, yes, ma'am," the young woman replied as she tapped her mile-long crystal-laden fingernails against the steering wheel and then shifted the van into neutral because she was stuck behind a newspaper delivery truck double-parked and taking up more than its own lane. The van rocked from side to side as it held there and the young woman, SHAKANNA, her name tag read, began whispering into her shirt and Nan realized she was speaking into a hands-free cell phone. Just as well, Nan thought, though she wondered if Shakanna was breaking a company policy using her cell phone while on the clock. And those nails, how'd they let her drive the van with those nails. That would have been Nan's next question after the one about the home church; she didn't intend to be so critical; knew that side of her sometimes pushed people away; couldn't help herself though when she saw something that needed correcting.

They started moving again and now they were on the expressway and Nan held herself from more talk. She thought instead about the layette she'd been working on to sell at the church's grand flea market scheduled for the first Saturday in March. The bonnet and booties were near perfect, cream-colored edged in pink and blue thread. The blanket, though, hadn't yielded that sense of contentment that she usually got from a finished piece of work. She'd taken apart the blanket several times, undone the footed portions and the pockets she'd designed that she'd thought at the time so clever. She pondered over the fix. Imagined the pockets at an angle, maybe a double top stitch around the pouch where the feet would go. And then she cleared her mind because the van had just entered the grounds of the nursing home. Lavish grounds with formal gardens and ponds and cobblestone walkways.

Counted her blessings every time she came here that a social worker had been worth her salt and been tenacious in getting Albert placed here for the price of what Medicare would pay plus his monthly disability check, though the accommodations, the level of care were worth much more.

She stopped at the desk to sign herself in. Said, "Tom, how do," to the desk clerk, a retired doorman from one of the apartment buildings in town.

"Nan, good as ever to see you," he replied, and the truly discerning would have captured the ripple in the air between them that carried the memory of their long conversations a decade ago where they talked about the Bible and hope and joy and their own dreams that been deferred. He was recently widowed at the time and Nan thought herself the same, given Alfred's condition.

She walked the marble corridor lined with pictures of silver-haired white men in glasses. Took the double-wide elevator to Alfred's floor and stepped into the lounge area filled with activity where the capable gathered in their wheelchairs, the truly fortunate on their own two legs, as a guitar player led them in the singing of "Frère Jacques." The air hung with the scent of muted urine and peppermint and Nan had the thought that all the money in the world couldn't stop a person's pee from smelling. Though Alfred's room didn't smell like pee, smelled like Old Spice aftershave and minty mouthwash and the Brylcreem that Nan supplied for the daily use on his hair.

Alfred was dressed in his black visiting suit and his white shirt. Nan checked the neckline to make sure that the shirt was fresh, checked Alfred's ears to see that they'd been cleaned, his cuticles to ensure that his nail beds were well oiled. Those little things told her all she needed to know about how he'd been cared for otherwise. Plus that preoccu-

pation delayed her looking at his face, at his eyes that were likely staring off in fascination at the painting of grapes and apples in a brass
bowl that hung on the wall over his dresser, or squinting at the high
hedge of holly and the Japanese cherry outside his window.

Nan puttered around his side of the room opening and closing his
drawers, taking inventory of his undershirts and boxer shorts. She
hummed "Lullabye of Birdland," one of his favorite songs. That usually brought his attention to her. It did now and she pulled a chair in
close to his and sat so that their knees practically touched. She lifted
both his hands and got a surge from the feel of them. They were large
and meaty and warm. "Magic hands," Freeda used to say. "My daddy's
inside goodness comes out through his hands."

"My, my, my, you sure are looking handsome today, Alfred," Nan
said as she squeezed his hands, told herself that he returned the squeeze.
Now she looked at his face, finally, at his eyes that moved slowly to
take her presence in. His eyes held on her face and she looked away and
laughed a nervous laugh. Felt so shaky on the inside with his eyes completely on her and she almost wished that his roommate was there now.
Alfred's latest roommate was an irritating man with Alzheimer's who'd
occasionally mistake Alfred for one of his employees at the string of
Speedy Printing shops he owned and he'd start congratulating himself
in a booming voice for not having a prejudiced bone in his body as he'd
point to Alfred and say, "Just look at how I've advanced the colored."
Nan had gotten in his ear once and told him to lower his voice and go
advance his momma and he'd scampered to get out of the room calling
for his mother as Nan felt both guilt and pleasure over what she'd just
done.

But the roommate wasn't here to distract her from the feel of Alfred's eyes completely on her and she detected that look in his eye that

she'd see from time to time when she visited. It was a look that whis-pered Please, please, not unlike the way he'd look at her when he still had reasonable physical health back when, after asking Alfred to leave, Nan had allowed him back to live in their Delancey Street row house, which meant her severing the discreet affair she'd begun with Mr. Edwards. She never knew if Alfred had knowledge of the relationship, but some-times when she'd return from a long evening of fitting the cast of the Christmas play for their costumes, spent and satisfied after engaging herself in work that she loved; or returning from an extended Sunday afternoon of visiting with people on the sick and shut-in list, her face lightly powdered, her hair pulled back in a soft bun, her pretty mouth pressed with the muted shade of red lipstick she wore; or even if she'd overstayed a run to Cook's corner store and got involved in a gossipy conversation with Cook's wife who knew the inner workings of most of the households up and down Delancey Street, a secret smile hanging from Nan's mouth when she pushed through the door home over the juicy tidbits she'd been served; she'd detect that look in Alfred's eyes, a longing mingled with a sad resignation as if he wanted to beg her please don't withhold the truth over where she'd been, even as he ac-cepted that he couldn't change the truth of the past.

After he'd been placed here at the Springside Nursing Home, she'd wonder if the look she was seeing now was the result of a yearning in Alfred for Nan to finish a conversation she'd started some fifteen years ago that she'd abandoned and never reclaimed. Since a series of strokes took away Alfred's ability to speak, she couldn't know for sure, though once many years ago when Alfred still had fine motor skills and could communicate through writing, he was printing in large block letters that Nan looked pretty, then he switched suddenly to an almost indecipherable script and wrote, *Please, Nan, say it, just say it once and for all*. Nan pretended to not know what he meant. Though she did know.

Right now she chattered on about the weather. "Hope you been spending time out in this bright sunshine we been having, Alfred," she said. "Though I told them to make sure they keep you in long johns 'til the crocuses start pushing through, I don't care how warm it gets. I don't care if it goes up to ninety outside. We got a different kind of blood from them; we'll catch the grippe for sure if we take off too many layers before the air changes for good."

She saw his lips come together tightly, saw his jaw shift, felt his hands slacken and she let his hands go. "Okay, so you don't want to hear about the weather," she said as she got up and walked to the window and looked out on the splendid scene of earth and trees and the deep blue of the daytime sky. "Well then, you want to hear about Tish? Still touch and go with her situation so of course I been spending a lotta time at her bedside." She walked to Alfred's back and stroked his thinning strands of hair. "You know Tish told me a story I never heard before. Told me that Neena ran away once when she was sixteen. Though she got no further than Sam and Goldie's. Isn't that something? I never had a clue because she was back before daybreak. Anyhow, Tish said Neena was struck that night by Sam and Goldie's love for each other. She called it a mighty love and told Tish to hold out for such a love. That was a large something for her to say to Tish, wasn't it, Alfred? I must admit. I never thought to instruct Tish so. Mnh." She leaned in then and kissed the top of Alfred's head. "Though I couldda told her how a mighty love feels. Couldn't I, Alfred? What you talking." She chuckled. "We had us a mighty love. My, my, my. Yes we did."

She looked down from where she stood and saw that his hands were balled into fists. She began massaging his back. "Okay," she said. "You irritated with me, I know. I can tell by how tightly you got your fists balled. You not satisfied unless I'm confessing like a Catholic school girl the morning after prom night. Right, Alfred? Let me see. What can I tell you about my recent soul-searching? Okay, so I will tell you about a mistake I made. This darm blanket I'm working on for the flea market. It just occurred to me as I'm standing here that the color border is too deep, too overwhelming. You know me, Alfred, I never see the mistakes in my design while I'm right there at the sewing machine; it's always hours, sometimes days later when my attention is elsewhere and my error taps me on my shoulder and introduces itself."

She walked over to his nightstand and fingered the leather Bible resting there. The red satin ribbon page marker had been moved, she could tell, because last week she'd read to Alfred from David; the ribbon had been moved to the New Testament to Luke and she figured it likely that one of the workers was a good Baptist and had taken it upon herself to read a few verses to Alfred. She made a note to find out who it was so that she could make sure to put a few dollars in a card to give them on the next holiday to come up. Easter that would be.

She was back in the chair facing him. His head was bent and she thought he may have fallen asleep the way he seemed to do more often after the lastest stroke. "Alfred," she said softly and he didn't raise his head. "She called me last night, Neena. She called in the middle of the night. Isn't that something? Called when she knew I'd be at home to pick up. Really me she wanted to talk to this time."

Alfred lifted his head. His eyes were blank for a time and Nan was patient until his eyes focused again on her face and she could see that he recognized her. "So the blanket, Alfred, the error I was telling you about, I think I can correct it by bordering it with a softer color. Now why your eyes going all downcast on me, Alfred? What do you want me to say anyhow? You want to hear more about Neena's call? Sure you do. I declare, I think Neena's your favorite, isn't she? Don't worry, I won't tell Tish. Mnh." She was quiet for a minute as she folded and refolded her hands in her lap. Then her nose started to run so she reached behind her to where she'd hung her purse on the back of her chair and pulled out her handkerchief. "I will say that that call touched me some place deep," she said as she dabbed at her nose, trying to avoid her red lipstick, though it smeared the handkerchief anyhow.

Alfred's fingers were curling against his thighs trying to go to fists and Nan lifted his right hand first and began pulling and massaging his fingers one at a time. "Yeah, let's loosen you up in your hands," she said. She looked at his face then and his eyes went big and soft, the way they had that first time when they stared at each other through the window of Sam's deli. "Oh Lord, Alfred. There you go with that those goo-goo eyes that I never could resist. All right all ready. I'll say it, Alfred. I was wrong for the way I treated her. Neena, I'm talking 'bout. You happy now, I'm saying it out loud. I was wrong. Lord knows I was wrong." She placed his hand atop his thigh and lifted his left hand and began pulling and massaging each of those fingers. "I put all my soft attention on Tish, I surely did. Then I gave Neena the mean shavings of myself. Mnh. Father forgive me, I guess I was doing the best I had in me to do at the time, but it was wrong. And the ironic thing is that Tish was likely gonna succeed in life regardless, Tish was just made up for success. A quick quiet study Tish always been. Faithful. Never bragged, always allowed her good works to do the talking on her behalf. Plus I must say that Tish adored me. You know when someone's looking up at you like, you're the bright morning sun rising in the sky; it's almost impossible to show them your harsher side." She finished the fingers on his left hand. She rubbed his wedding band and then lifted his hand to her lips and kissed it. She sighed, then she continued talking. "Tish used to ask me often if she could live with me forever whether or not Freeda returned. It would fill me up and empty me at the same time when she asked such a thing. On the one hand I loved the adoration we shared; on the other hand I knew that Freeda should of been the recipient.

"But now Neena made no secret of the torture she felt living with me. Face generally frowned up. Always whining, wanting to know how long before Freeda came to take them home. Neena's off-putting ways were like thick fingers poking around inside of my chest until they came up on that tender wound that was Freeda's absence; Neena would push and push right where the wound was open and raw."

She stopped talking to blow her nose. Her voice was soupy when she started talking again. "I guess it's small wonder that I would just as soon backhand Neena to the mouth as hug her. I shudder to think about the chastisements she suffered through. The night I was just telling you about when Neena ran away, well earlier that day I had gone to a lovely mother-daughter tea with Tish. It was a soft afternoon. And then when I walked back in the house I just exploded on Neena. Not that I didn't have some cause. Hettie around the corner had leaned over her bannister and whispered to me that she saw that boy from Richmond hanging around in my backyard with Neena and then a little while later she saw just their empty outline, and then after that saw the boy walking through the alley away from my yard. So I had some cause to extract an explanation from Neena. But I really beat her that day, Alfred. Went way beyond a chastisement for her sneaking a boy in the house when I wasn't home. I hit her over and over with my open hand hard as I could—" She stopped and swallowed and looked at her hands as if she was asking her hands how could they have done such a thing. "As I'm telling you about it, Alfred, I'm seeing it for what it was. Lord Jesus, Alfred. You know what had happened just the night prior? Freeda had crept into the girls' bedroom, yes she had. And I was on fire with emotion: relief that she was still among the living, but then, too, anger and hurt and grief and missing, oh the missing, Lord Jesus. The missing is what tears the heart wide open. All during the tea that afternoon, I listened to all the girls Tish's age saying Mom this, and Mother that, and Mommy come meet so and so. So I was missing Freeda for me, for my own longing, my own heartache, then I was missing her on Tish's behalf too. And then I got home to Neena's face looking at me like she hated me, and well I guess she compounded the hate I was feeling for myself. I hated myself that I wasn't able to cure my child. My beautiful cherub-cheeked daughter. I guess that's why Neena and I had such combative spirits toward each other. Guess we were both feeling in ourselves an essential failing that we'd not been able to make Freeda stay put."

She dabbed her nose again and then folded her hands in her lap. Alfred's hands were twitching now and she reached in and grabbed a hold of his hands. "I guess you just bursting you so glad I'm unshackling myself like this, huh, Alfred? Mnh. Guess I am too."

They sat like that with Nan holding on to Alfred's hands. His back was to the window and the day's brilliance spread out around him. Then she heard Alfred make a sound from deep in his throat and she realized that she must have gone into a semi-trance; she'd certainly lost track of time because she was aware suddenly how much the sun had moved while she sat there; now a dimmer light poked Alfred's back. He was staring at Nan, that pleading look in his eye again. This time she didn't distract herself from the look; this time she allowed the look to have its way with her, to rankle her, to shake loose the words that had been trapped and lodged for too long.

"It was the medical examiner's office that called me fifteen years ago, Alfred. Yes it was. Yes it was. Fifteen years ago this month it was." She squeezed his hands, then placed them palms-down on his thighs. She wrapped her arms around her chest and rocked herself. "I guess you knew. Guess it's been that long since she slipped in here and moved the chair close up to your bed and slept with her body in the chair and her head resting on your chest. I knew all about it. Gentleman who works on the front desk would tell me. Said the staff allowed it since otherwise she caused no disruption. Relieved my spirit to know it too, that she was finding her way periodically to you.

"That man had such a somber voice when he identified himself. I 'clare for God, Alfred, the walls and ceilings collapsed on me and I felt as if I was being buried alive because I knew that the medical examiner only called to inform you that a next of kin had died. This one was calling from Cleveland. Last I knew, Freeda was in Cleveland. But Neena was in Cleveland too. He said, 'I'm sorry to have to tell you this—' and I actually crawled along the floor with the phone receiver in my hand, pulling the phone base crashing down from the nightstand along with a crystal vase that contained a spray of baby's breaths left over from the rose bouquet Tish had sent me for Valentine's Day. But I had to get to the side of the bed where I kneeled every night to say my prayers. I needed to pray right then before the voice gave me the name that it was sorry to have to tell me about. Needed to pray that it not be Neena. Please don't let this devastation be about Neena, I prayed. Neena was still so young, Neena still had a chance at life. Please, I asked the Lord, not Neena. Let it be Freeda and not Neena. Freeda was tortured, Alfred, you know it. She was tired. She deserved to rest. Her poor, sweet sick mind, she was sick. Our beautiful dream of a daughter had just been so sick. I prayed so hard in the space of time that it took the M.E. to say a name. Please give my daughter a resting place in your arms, Sweet Jesus, I prayed. Please kiss her eyelids like I used to do, Lord. Give her peace. Take her, not Neena, please Lord, not Neena. I prayed for our daughter to have peace, and our granddaughter, life.

"And then the voice did say a name, said Freeda's name, and I was awash in gratitude that Neena had been spared. Until it settled in that I had lost my child. I learned in an instant that morning that the vessel that holds human suffering is boundless; it expands, Alfred. Yes it does. And not only that, it'll change shape on you so it won't spill over, so that all of the grief can be contained and not a drop go without you feeling the full boat of pain. The vessel that held my grief was shaped in the form of a C, the shape of Freeda when she'd fall asleep on the bed between us. Remember that, Alfred. Lord, Jesus. I stayed on my bedroom floor, flattened for the next day and night after the call. I was completely shrouded in grief. But it's like I heard your voice, Alfred. It's like I heard you saying, 'Nan, get on up from that floor.' I responded to the sound of your voice and got up. My grief sifted higher and higher, became more like a canopy than a coffin, became something that I could walk through.

"I went to Cleveland then. I don't know why I didn't say anything to anybody. Goldie was spending last days with Sam. Tish was settled away in college and I guess I just wanted to see it for myself before I told anybody. So I flew through the air, my first time on a plane, to claim her body. Except that there was no body to claim. No understandable explanations for the absence of a body. But I was summoned, I tried to explain. The medical examiner's office had contacted me by phone. I stayed in Cleveland for a week trying to sort things out and the best explanation I was able to get came from a low-totem-pole clerk who'd whispered to me that in the past the city-run crematorium had made grave, grave mistakes. So I returned to Philadelphia, and then Sam died, and then I didn't say anything to Neena and Tish because without having identified Freeda, what was there to say? The result was the same. Their mother absent still."

Alfred stared at Nan unblinking, his face so motionless that for a second Nan thought that he'd sat up there and died with his eyes wide open. His nose was draining now too and Nan reached in with her handkerchief and dabbed his nose. "They intimated that it was at her own hands," she said. "But I like to think that our girl saw Jesus standing there with his big old palms telling her to come on and climb on up in his hands. That's what I believe. Guess that's the beauty of belief. Like the vessel that holds your grief'll change shape, you can allow your belief to take whatever shape it needs to so you can get through whatever it is you got to go through. Like right now I believe you hearing and understanding every word I'm saying, Alfred. I don't care what portion of your brain they say is functioning or not. I know your heart's working, that's for sure. You hearing me with your heart, aren't you, baby."

She stood and lifted his arms from his thighs and put them on the arms of the chair. Then she sat in his lap and with some effort pulled his arm around her as if she was wrapping herself up in a shawl. She buried her head in his wide-as-ever chest. He smelled like the Pablum cereal she used to spoon-feed Freeda. Pablum and Old Spice and mint. "My, my, my, my," she said. "You always had the best arms, such love in these old arms of yours. Such a mighty love, even now, even now."

Chapter 19

ISH WAS DREAMING about Freeda when the contractions began. It was a Christmas morning in the dream and Freeda was sitting under the tree dressed in a pink furry robe. Tish was afraid to see her sitting there, meant that she was an inanimate thing if she was propped under the tree. But then Freeda started to talk and her voice was like butter as she called Tish to her. "It's for you, Tisha, just for you, come see what Mommy has for you," Freeda said. And Tish inched toward the tree as Freeda smiled. It was a magnificent smile and Tish wasn't even afraid the way Freeda's smiles sometimes terrified her because she never knew what would follow the smile. Tish sat under the tree next to Freeda; the smell of pine was strong and it felt as if they were in the middle of the forest.

Then Freeda unfolded the lap of her pink furry robe and there lay a newborn baby boy. He had a dark mat of hair and he was looking at Tish laughing such a happy laugh that Tish laughed too. She laughed and cried at the same time and said, "For me? Mommy, is this little boy really for me?"

"Really for you," Freeda said as she lifted the naked baby and placed him in Tish's lap and told her to cover him with her own robe to keep him warm because it would take time for his skin to grow.

Tish folded the baby in her robe. "Thank you, Mommy," she said. "Thank you so much, Mommy." She turned to give her mother a kiss on the cheek, thinking how she hardly ever kissed her mother. Freeda was always hugging her but Tish rarely initiated it on her own. And now when she did Freeda was gone, a pink light glowed softly in the spot where her mother had been. Then the first contraction hit, catapulting Tish from her dream. She felt as if her pelvis was a wishbone, Sumo wrestlers on either side fighting for the larger break. The alarm on the monitor strapped across her stomach began to cry and she squeezed the cord to call the nurse. "Thank you, Mommy," she said over and over as she felt hands on her, inside of her, voices rippling through her head calling out centimers dilated, pressure this, heart rate that. Don't push yet, Tish. Breathe, Tish, just breathe.

Then she felt her bed being moved, wheeled out of the room. "Thank you, Mommy, thank you, thank you so much," she continued to say. Then another contraction began to bloom, and she thought no way could it be worse than the first, and it was worse. "Thank you, Mommy," she said louder, trying to match the intensity of the pain with the gratitude she felt. After spending her life dreading her mother's return, over and over praying that she'd stay gone, then feeling guilty that she didn't return, thinking it all her fault, thinking too that should Freeda reappear, it would be just for Neena's sake, Freeda had come back after all. And this time when she came, it was just for Tish.

"Thank you, Mommy," she said. Louder and louder. "Thank you, thank you."

Nan had just climbed into bed when the phone rang. After her longer than usual stay with Alfred, she came home and called Mr. Thompson, the lawyer who'd drawn up her will. She told him she was ready to begin the process to have Freeda declared dead. Then one last time she took apart the blanket she'd made to sell at the grand flea market the next day. She gave the blanket a softer border, a more subtle top stitch. Finally it matched the vision she'd had when she'd started it, and her spirit over the blanket could at last settle down.

Then the phone rang and the next thing she knew Malik was crying in her ear.

"The baby's coming. Too soon, it's happening too soon," he cried. He was already in the car, halfway to her house, he said in a rush of words that she could barely decipher. Could she be ready in ten minutes or less? And then in five minutes he was on the porch, ringing the bell over and over again.

Nan snatched open the door. She grabbed Malik by the shoulders. "You go ahead and cry and shake and holler and do what you got to do while I finish throwing on my clothes. But when we get down there to the hospital, I want you to show your strength. I want you to put your hand in the Lord's hand because whatever the outcome, Tish gonna need to see your strength." He nodded then, seemed to find an instant surge of strength and told Nan he would be in the car, the car sitting in the middle of the street.

Nan ran around in circles herself after Malik was out of view. She cried herself and shouted Mercy, Lord, please have mercy as she took the stairs as quickly as she could and finished undressing from her nightclothes and threw her street clothes on. She started making her bed because she never ever left her house with her bed unmade, and then stopped suddenly with the making of the bed half-done. Neena. She needed to try to reach Neena. She pressed the menu on the new-fangled phone that she had yelled at Tish for buying. "I just want something that I pick up and hang up, not all the off-on buttons like I'm flying a plane instead of dialing the phone. Want something I can dial too." Tish and Malik had laughed at her, told her to come up to the new millennium, patiently taught how to work the phone, how to access her messages, how to store numbers that came up on the caller ID. She had stored the number where Neena called from last night. She scrolled to it now, a 267 exchange, then hit the ON button and listened to it ring.

Bow Peep was in Cliff and Lynne's family room. Thought it his duty to be here. Lynne had moved Babe and herself out several days ago and Bow Peep decided that his boy needed him. Cliff was in bed and Bow Peep was laughing through an episode of *The Many Loves of Dobie Gillis*. He'd always liked Dobie Gillis because one of the characters was named Maynard and that was his given name. Plus he thought Maynard was deep, like he thought himself deep.

The phone startled him when it rang and at first he thought it was Lynne, calling for perhaps a healing vibe through the phone. He wasn't sure he could help Lynne, too many layers for his notes to have to penetrate, he thought. "Yo," he said into the phone.

Silence. Then a thin line of a voice saying, "Please, I'm trying to reach my granddaughter, Neena. She called me from this number. Might she be there, please?"

Bow Peep jumped up when he heard Neena's name. She hadn't

stopped by his corner at all today. Though he hadn't performed his usual evening sets, left his corner earlier than usual to get here to be with Cliff. He worried that she'd gone all day without him hitting her with a healing vibe.

"No, ma'am, she's not, not here. Is this an emergency?" Bow Peep asked.

"It is, her sister's at the university, the hospital. She should get there. She should get there as soon as she can."

"Ma'am, I assure you, I will do everything within my power. I will call on power that's not even mine. I will reach Neena and let her know what you just said."

He ran upstairs and roused Cliff. Told him they had a mission to run, don't even think about telling him no. "Get up my ace boon, we got to roll."

Cliff shook himself awake. "Roll where, Bow Peep? What's going on?"

"University, my brother, on the ril."

"All right, hang on, man, it's cool," Cliff said as he began throwing on his clothes. He thought that Bow Peep needed to get to the hospital for himself, thought he was in the beginning stages of melting down. Cliff took it as a good sign that Bow Peep could recognize when he was close to the edge. "What? Are you feeling shaky?" he asked him.

"No. Are you feeling shaky?" Bow Peep replied. And Cliff thought this was going to be a long night.

"So why are we going down HUP?" he asked as they walked through the kitchen, then out into the garage.

"I've got to get a message to the little lamb," he said, clutching his flute case under his arm.

"So it's not for you? HUP, I mean. You're all right?"

"Uptight and outta sight. It's for the little lamb, I told you. The one who loves you so."

Cliff put the car in reverse and backed down the long driveway. He didn't even try to figure out what Bow Peep meant. Just followed Bow Peep's directions until he pulled in in front of the Arch Street Hotel. "Here?" Cliff asked. "Doesn't this place charge by the hour?"

"Ah, he scoffs at scars that never knew how much the shit hurt when it happened," Bow Peep said as he jumped out of the car, his flute already positioned between his lips.

"Oh yes I do know too," Cliff said as he sighed and leaned back against the headrest, angling his head so that he could keep an eye on Bow Peep. "I know how much the shit hurts." He hit the control to let the window all the way down. The air was heavy and warm and smelled sweet like overripened fruit. He started to turn on the radio but then didn't because the sound of Bow Peep's flute drifted into the car. He was playing "Let It Be" and Cliff allowed the melody to move through him, such a large sound, that flute had in the warm moist predawn air.

He saw the hair first moving in the direction of the sound of the flute. That soft bushy mound of hair going every which way. Remembered the feel of that hair as she'd moved against him and he'd known in an instant that what he was doing with her superseded an act of revenge against Lynne. What was revenge anyhow? An empty notion, like the notion of reverse discrimination that he encountered daily in his work. Discrimination, once experienced, could never be reversed, too ugly to be reversed. Ended, sure, compensated for the pain of, let's try, but reversed, no white boy, he'd want to shout, you don't know the scar or the wound.

Now the sound of the flute was replaced by the sound of her voice.

Her voice screeching, getting closer to the car. Bow Peep opened the passenger-side door and she got in. Her hand flew to her mouth when she saw who the driver was. "Somebody's got some tall explaining to do," he said. "Or did your aunt move?"

Bow Peep slid into the backseat. Cliff and Neena looked at each other and in an instant acted as if they were meeting for only the second time after a first introduction on a snowy street corner by the bus station that was not at all memorable.

Chapter 20

ISH LOOKED AT Neena rushing straight for her bed and at first she thought it was Freeda. She almost cried out, "Mommy." But then she saw it was Neena. "Neena," Tish said in a weak voice and then she started to cry for real.

Neena walked over to the bed. She was shaking with emotion and she hated for Tish to see her lose control. So she lost control anyhow. She didn't even try to rock herself to calm herself. She allowed herself to shake, allowed cracked sniffing sounds to come up from her nose, her mouth. She leaned her head down on Tish's chest. "Don't be trying to hug, girl," she said to Tish.

"Girl, please," Tish said through her sobs as she wrapped her arms around Neena and squeezed as hard as she could. "Nobody's trying to hug you. I'm just trying to like hide this mess of hair from view. I'mma have to pretend that you're no kin of mine."

And that's how they were when Nan came back in the room. Nan stepping back out in the hall then to allow them their time.

"They think he's viable, they're hopeful," Malik said as he walked Nan and Neena to the transitional nursery. "Twenty-six weeks you know is early, but they said he's strong, a real fighter. They think he's gonna pull through. You know, every minute he's alive, it's like there's more of a chance he'll stay alive."

They stopped at the entranceway to the critical care nursery. They washed their hands and put on gowns and gloves and masks. The back of Neena's gown had come untied and Nan reached up and then pulled her hand back as if she'd touched a burning stove. She reached up again, slower, pushed her hand through the heat of time. "Hold still, Neena, let me do your tie," she said. And afterward she let her hand rest at the base of Neena's neck. Then drew her hand down Neena's back. Making circles now on Neena's back, patting Neena's back like a soft snare drum as they walked to the incubator where their baby was.

Malik explained what he'd been told about the breathing machine, the bells and whistles and chimes going off constantly. Neena looked inside at her nephew. He was withered, misshapen, almost monstrous with the pads covering his eyes, the tubes going in and out of his mouth and nose. He'd been separated too soon from his mother. Was he cold? she wondered, shivering.

"Lord Jesus, bless him please." Nan breathed into the air. Nan still making circles on and then patting Neena's back.

Neena blinked, and then blinked again trying to blink away the tears. And then she couldn't and the tears came and she still looked at the baby through the tears. Now he was beautiful through the tears. He was alive, fighting to stay alive, and that was beautiful. He was perfect now through the tears. He was grotesque and beautiful and perfect and good. A human he was. A heart the size of a thimble beating soundly in his chest.

The sun had broken through the sky as Nan and Neena left the hospital. It was colder out too. Nan said she was going to go take her bath, then run the things over to the church that she'd made for the flea market. "I'm willing to fry you up some scrapple and eggs if you want to come past," Nan said. "You might want to come to the flea market even. You don't have to stay long. You could meet Charlene's twins. They're growing into fine boys with their devilish selves."

Neena thought about LaTeefah and her mother. She wondered if they'd show up. They started walking down the ramp toward the bus stop. She was about to tell Nan about them and the purse they might be bringing to sell, but now Nan was saying something about some man who'd come by early in the morning looking for Neena a couple of weeks ago. "Said his name was Nathan, and I don't know any Nathans."

"Nathan?" Neena said. "Nan, that's Richmond, you know the freckle-faced boy from Virginia."

"Richmond? Well, why didn't he say that's who he was?"

"I guess because Richmond isn't his name, so why would he say Richmond?" Neena said, feeling that familiar irritation building toward Nan.

"Because everybody knew him as Richmond, Neena. That's why."

"Nan, this looks like your 42 coming," Neena said as they approached the bus stop.

"Well another one will come just like that one's coming. First I want to know where you're staying."

Neena sighed and looked beyond Nan. The sky was shaking out puffs of gray and purple air. It felt like snow. And Neena had the thought that it was February, should feel like snow. "I'm staying in the belly of the whale," she said, and then she laughed.

"Belly of the whale? Sounds like you need to be staying with me," Nan said, as she pulled a cellophane pouch filled with tokens from her patent leather purse. Pressed a token in Neena's hand.

Neena folded her hand over the token, then stood there, considering what to do as they watched the 42 roll past. "Mnh, it's just, you know your house rules about church and all, Nan."

"Just church, or and all? I can relax on some things, like you going to church, but you know you never turn off the lights in my kitchen with a dirty dish in the sink."

"I can keep a kitchen clean."

"Well, then, sometime I'd like to hear about how you're replacing a God in your life. Just for my own understanding."

Neena thought about how she'd never be able to explain it to the likes of Nan. Like how the Mrs. Young woman replaced God in her life when she called her baby girl as she stood outside of what had been Mr. Cook's store. Or the eyebrows of the bus ticket agent in Chicago that prompted her to come back home. Or like right now as she saw Bow Peep walking toward them. He was smiling his long smile. And Neena thought, like that. God is alive in a smile like that.

Nan was telling Neena that she had something very important that she needed to say to her. Goldie could have visitors starting tomorrow and maybe they could go there together and the three of them could sit like they'd done when Sam died, and she could say it then. "Very important, Neena. Something I should have said years ago. I was wrong not to. I was so very wrong."

Then Bow Peep was right up on them talking fast. "My little lamb, you're overdue your healing vibe," he said. "And I trust from the looks of love in both your eyes that sis and the baby are well. Are they well?"

Nan was looking at Bow Peep with her mouth hanging open. What kind of people was Neena taking up with now? she thought.

"Oh, and little lamb, the tiger tiger burning bright says he surely hopes he might see you tonight." Then Bow Peep turned to Nan and extended his hand. "Maynard's the name, though they call me Bow Peep, and healing's my game. And I see I've still got quite a bit of work to do."